The Serene Republic of Venice does not, in the 16th century, live up to its name. The city is frequently at war with the Turks and with Rome, assassins roam the streets, and fear of torture, rumoured to be carried out under the Doge's palace, holds innocent men in an iron grip.

When former mercenary Sigismondo and his scruffy attendant Benno come to Venice, they are quickly enmeshed in the affairs of the Ermolins, one of the Republic's most distinguished families. Niccolo, Lord Ermolin, has been murdered, and Sigismondo is retained to find the killer. Isabella, the Lord's aloof young widow, claims his son Marco had the opportunity, while another son, born of the black housekeeper, has motive. Could the killer have been nurtured in the victim's own palace?

Surprisingly, it's Pasquale Scolar, the son of the Doge of Venice, who is arrested and, faced with a master torturer, confesses. Few would fail to confess in such circumstances, though, and Sigismondo won't let the case rest. But his persistence will bring him to clash with the most ruthless men in Venice, and all his courage and ingenuity may not be enough to save him from the worst the city has to offer...

Elizabeth Eyre is the pseudonym of Jill Staynes and Margaret Storey. They were pupils at the same school where they invented bizarre characters and exchanged serial episodes about them. Their first book together, at the age of fifteen, was called 'Bungho, or why we went to Aleppo'. It was not offered for publication. They have both written stories for children, and together created the highly praised Superintendent Bone modern detective novels ('S & S are by now as indispensable as Marks and Spencer, but far wittier' *The Sunday Times*) – A KNIFE AT THE OPERA, GRAVE RESPONSIBILITY, THE LATE LADY, BONE IDLE and DEAD SERIOUS are all available from Headline. DIRGE FOR A DOGE is the sixth in a series of Italian Renaissance whodunnits, following DEATH OF A DUCHESS, CURTAINS FOR THE CARDINAL, POISON FOR THE PRINCE, BRAVO FOR THE BRIDE and AXE FOR AN ABBOT (all Headline).

Dirge for a Doge

Elizabeth Eyre

HEADLINE

First published in 1996
by HEADLINE BOOK PUBLISHING

First published in paperback in 1996
by HEADLINE BOOK PUBLISHING

10 9 8 7 6 5 4 3 2 1

ISBN 0 7472 5500 8

Printed and bound in Great Britain by
Cox & Wyman Ltd, Reading, Berks

HEADLINE BOOK PUBLISHING
A division of Hodder Headline PLC
338 Euston Road
London NW1 3BH

CONTENTS

People in the Story

In Venice
Niccolo Ermolin, a wealthy aristocrat
Isabella, his recent bride
Marco ⎫ His children by his
Beatrice ⎭ first wife, Emilia
Rinaldo Ermolin, his brother and business partner
Zenobia, his slave, mistress and housekeeper
Cosmo, his son by Zenobia
Chiara, Isabella's maid
Vettor Darin, father of Niccolo's first wife
Claudia Darin, Vettor's wife
Doge Scolar
Pasquale Scolar, his son
Pico Gamboni, a ruined aristocrat
Attilio da Castagna, Captain-General of the Fleet
Andrea Barolo, ex-Captain-General of the Fleet
Miriam da Silva, widow of Joshua da Silva, a moneylender
Members of the Signoria, servants, jailers, gondoliers,
shopkeepers etc.

On the mainland
Guido, Duke of Montano
Il Lupo, his condottiere

Visitors to Venice
Ottavio and Nono Marsili, condottieri

The Master of Padua, a torturer
Brunelli, an architect and painter
Leone Leconti, an artist
Cardinal Pantera, Papal Legate
Master Valentino, a physician
Dion, an assassin
Sigismondo, a soldier of fortune
Benno, his servant
Biondello, a little dog

Chapter 1

The Secret Book

Gold discs floated on the ceiling, reflections from the water below the window. Gold discs glittered on the carpeted table. Niccolo Ermolin, in his study, was doing what, if he had been any less aristocratic, would have been called counting his money. The drifts of gold upon the table, which his fingers now rapidly stacked in tidy piles, were an infinitesimal fraction of the gold he could command. Some idea of how much that was might have been gained from the book in which he was writing, in an elegant cursive hand – a book nobody beside himself had, up to that moment, ever seen.

It was more a Florentine than a Venetian custom to keep such a book, a *libro segreto*, but Niccolo Ermolin kept secrets of weight in his. He came of one of the most distinguished families in Venice and, unlike some of these families, his had the wealth to do justice to its origins, wealth embodied in the person of Niccolo: a thick double chain of gold lay over the shoulders of the red velvet gown, gold framed the sapphires and rubies on his fingers, gold encircled the spectacles he had just fixed on his nose.

His sight was not what it had been. Money could buy spectacles. It could even buy his new, very young wife for that matter, although that morning had proved that it could not buy her good temper. Money, however, was tiresomely powerless to buy renewed youth. Ermolin was using the gratifying entries in his *libro segreto* to dispel melancholy thoughts.

1

His latest wife was recorded in the book, the date of the betrothal and wedding neatly inscribed in the margin beside a transaction he had made with Vettor Darin over some bales of silk from Constantinople. The ducats of her dowry had covered the price of the silk. The rest of her dowry, the embroidered linen, the jewelry, the respectable quantity of gowns of the best material – furred, sewn with pearls, worked with gold thread – was locked in the painted marriage chests he had caused to be made for his bride.

This memory made Ermolin frown. The fellow had decorated the chests with very pretty scenes of cupids leading the married pair by flowery garlands across a landscape of hills and trees, and had charged the most absurd amount merely because he'd last been employed by a duke. Ermolin briefly wondered if the fellow's charges had irritated the duke as well, and wrote the name, Leone Leconti, in his private blacklist. A word to a friend would ensure that the artist might have difficulty finding work anywhere else in Venice. Let him go and find another duke.

Ermolin put down his quill and stared at the gold discs dancing and merging on the ceiling. Had the marriage been worth it? She came of an excellent family, an alliance causing no regrets, though it was a pity her parents had died so suddenly as he did not get on well with Isabella's brother, who had inherited. The dowry, at least, had been promptly paid. Isabella was a great deal prettier than his last wife and of course, twenty years younger. She had certainly won the hearts of his immediate family: his brother Rinaldo was usually censorious, his father-in-law might not have cared to see someone in his daughter's place, and his son Marco could have resented a stepmother his own age.

No, the trouble was that he had perhaps expected to find his own youth again in Isabella's arms, but the unpleasant reality was that she made him feel old. She was so wilful, with that disdainful confidence only youth and beauty could provide. He had even felt obliged to show her she had made a good bargain herself: he had taken her, last week, on a tour of the palazzo, showing her every room in it, pointing out its worth in marble, in frescoes, in gold leaf, reminding her that he was employing the famous Brunelli on the alterations and additions which would make it even more valuable. He had shown her this study which normally he was the sole person to enter. He had solemnly unlocked his coffers, displayed the articles of gold shimmering within, the bags of coin; he had indicated the ledgers with their brass hinges and locks, that kept the record of possessions beyond this house.

What he had not shown her was his secret book. Not even his own son had seen it, though one day – long hence, he hoped – the key would be taken from around his neck and Marco would open this very book on which his fingers now rested, and would discover the things he showed no one. Marco would know then which families in Venice were bound to him for favours, which families were owed them, things which would influence the whole of his future dealings in the city and beyond, would give him clues how to treat each member of the Signoria, even how to approach the Ten. Marco would read of transactions with the East, those profitable links with the Infidel which had formed the basis of the Ermolin fortunes but which, at the present moment, were best kept quiet while war was being waged with the Turk. There were other entries, too, which might be safe to reveal one day but not yet.

Marco could also, if he wished, read the details of his own parents' marriage, some pages back . . . Niccolo turned to it. There was the betrothal date, the date of Marco's birth and that of his sister Beatrice, also those of his siblings (carefully bracketed with the years of their deaths, often the same). He could read the tribute his father had paid to his mother on her death by adding that she had always sought to please him.

How far would Isabella go to please him?

That was the interesting question, because so far – apart from their little tiff that morning when he had been forced to take a firm line with her – he had found himself trying to please *her*. He even seemed to remember trying to please

Marco's mother at first, when *she* had been a bride.

The cry of a gondolier rounding the corner of the Palazzo Ermolin broke into his thoughts and he closed the book, locked it, took off his spectacles and rubbed his left eye, which often gave him trouble these days.

Not for much longer, however, for it was shortly afterwards that through this eye the stiletto pierced his brain, wiping out thought, memory, life itself. In the study whose door he always locked, Niccolo Ermolin lay dead across his secret book.

Chapter 2

The Summons

Benno was confused.

To anyone looking at him, this state would simply tally with his appearance: the round eyes of an owl surprised by daylight, the mouth open to drink in situations the brain was not qualified to cope with. His mouth, in the short black beard, was open now, but he was extremely chary of drinking in Venice.

To start with, it was magic.

His master had explained to him that the city which he could see with his own eyes floating on the water was actually built on great piles – huge stakes driven into the bed of the lagoon and as safe as houses were anywhere else. Sigismondo had also remarked that Venice had stood here for a thousand years and would probably be here for a thousand more. Benno had picked up *probably*; *probably* was no guarantee.

Not that he doubted his master, for Sigismondo knew everything worth knowing – but even he accepted that you never knew what could happen next. So just as *probably*, Venice could suddenly sink . . . ahead of time. It was tempting Fate to come to such a place. Benno had to battle with a conviction that the solid stones beneath his feet must be undulating.

Why they had come here, his master had not told him, and Benno had not expected to be told. As far as he knew, Sigismondo had not been asked for his services by anyone in the city, but he thought it quite likely that, as soon as Sigismondo was known to be there, someone would make a claim on his services. When they entered the city, Sigismondo had given an account of himself to the official at the customs; nor was he hard to recognise, with his height, commanding presence and shaven head.

At the moment, though, the shaven head was covered. Benno's head too was covered, as a mark of respect. Inculcated with the habit of snatching off his cap if any respect needed showing, he found this a difficulty. He must wear it, however, it was what you did in a Jewish house where someone was dead. Benno stood at the back of the small room, breathing through his mouth, his hands uneasy with the instinct to pull off his cap, and stared at the lady sitting there. In spite of her black clothes she looked very stout, and the round face looked unaccustomed, even unsuited, to the grief it showed.

For Benno's master had been unlucky. He had come too late to see her husband, his friend. He was only in time to pay this last reverence. Benno, who knew nothing of his master's past but the most recent bits he had shared with him, listened with keen interest as Sigismondo and the widow talked. She had given him the warmest greeting, and now it was evident they had known each other in Spain, that Sigismondo had lodged with Joshua da Silva and his wife when he was studying at a university there, a place with a name whose syllables were too unfamiliar for Benno to make it out – not a vital point, as he had only the haziest idea where Spain itself might be.

'We owe you everything.' Miriam, as his master had called her, without title, like a sister, had hugged Sigismondo and wept for the husband who could not thank him in person. 'You brought us out in time. Had we stayed,' and she looked up into his face with brimming eyes, 'and I know if Joshua had listened to me we *would* have stayed, we would both have died before this. We heard last year that my brother was in prison and all his belongings confiscated by the Holy Office. Oh had he only listened to you!'

6

Sigismondo made her sit, and gently wiped her tears away. 'They treat you well here?'

She looked around her, at the small panelled room, richly hung with patterned silk; at the window with glass panes, open on a piazza where children played and shouted, and her smile was rueful. 'The Republic gives us more protection than most do. You were right to bring us here, Cristobal. There are regulations, of course, but we have a synagogue here and no one stops us from practising our religion and customs, or from trading. Venice needs our trade.'

From another room came a sudden burst of chanting: Benno had already found the Venetian dialect baffling but the chanting wasn't even in Latin, a language which he knew he didn't know.

Two young men had appeared in the room. The first one made Benno wonder why he went around in a gown of perfectly good cloth with a seam torn at the neck, but the second young man wore the same, so Benno guessed it was one of the customs which Venice didn't prevent. The widow was about to present these young men to Sigismondo when a sudden battering at the house door made all three heads turn and all three for a moment freeze. For that moment Benno had a glimpse of what it was like to be a Jew, always under threat. He'd heard of Jews shut up and cut off in their ghettoes, burnt alive like so many rats just because something – disease, defeat, disaster – had occurred in the city. Had something gone wrong in Venice?

Something, it appeared, *had* gone wrong but the Jews were not to be punished for it. The battering at the door, cautiously but immediately investigated, turned out to be nothing more threatening than a messenger enquiring for a Christian in the house. Sigismondo kissed the widow's hand and left, Benno following him out with a sense of relief.

'You're Signor Sigismondo, agent to the Duke of Rocca?' The messenger looked flustered, disturbed either by reason of his errand or by being in the Jews' quarter.

'I am Sigismondo, but I am no longer agent to the Duke. Who asks for me?'

The messenger glanced round as if his answer were not for the crowd of dark, pretty children that had gathered round the obvious strangers. 'You must come to—' He gestured to Sigismondo to bend his head, and whispered. Benno could only hear a sibilant sound but he was patient. After all, he'd soon find out where it was when they got there. His master liked a mystery.

When the gondola, a very smart one waiting for the messenger, with a gondolier in livery, drew up at the water-washed steps of the Palazzo Ermolin, Benno gazed at the fretted marble, the pilasters and the porphyry, and thought it looked a very expensive mystery indeed. It wasn't even spoilt by the workmen on the roof peering down at them like animated gargoyles.

The great main door did not open to them; heavy, forbidding, the iron-studded panels could expect to repel a siege. Instead, a small wicket in a lower panel gaped open as if by magic as they came up the steps, offering a dark oblong into which Sigismondo vanished without hesitation. Benno, having no wish to be left alone in a city that might collapse at any moment, scrambled after.

They were in a lobby screened off from a huge hall, with marble columns veined in purple and a marble floor of white and malachite green. Sigismondo was being greeted by a sturdy, gnome-like elderly man, richly dressed in a gown of dark red brocade.

'You don't know me, sir, though I know of you. I am Vettor Darin, father to the late wife of Niccolo Ermolin whose palace this is.' Here he paused, as if something he had said needed correction, but went on, 'I hope you will forgive us for disturbing you at a time when, as I understand, you have lost a friend; but we have heard in the Republic of your services to the Duke of Rocca, bound to us by treaties of peace, and to Gatta – I should say, the Lord Ridolfo Ridolfi – who has done Venice several favours in the past.'

As Darin accounted in this way for his knowledge of Sigismondo, Benno recollected one of those favours done by the condottiere Gatta: a severed head packed in the best

brocade and tied with ribbons, a present for which the Serene
Republic had expressed suitable thanks. He hoped the old
gentleman wasn't expecting something of the same now from
Sigismondo.

Sigismondo was his usual polite self, bowing
acknowledgement, studying the face before him with its
round pale eyes that fixed with disconcerting intensity and
then looked away as if in sudden distraction. This was a man
in the grip of some strong emotion but it was hard to say
what.

'Indeed I have served his Grace of Rocca and fought under
Ridolfi,' Sigismondo replied, 'but am in Venice, as you have
been informed, only to honour the ties of friendship.
However, it must be a very grave matter for Lord Darin to
send for me here.'

To this question framed as a statement, Vettor Darin
answered by leading Sigismondo by the sleeve, apart, to one
of the arched windows letting in a dapple of light from the
canal. There, like the messenger in the ghetto, he whispered
to him. Benno's curiosity almost hurt. What could be going
on in this gilded mausoleum that ordinary decent folk were
not to hear?

It was no use. Sigismondo, answering Darin in a low tone,
trod up the stairs' polished marble now without a backward
glance. Benno was therefore not to follow, and he resigned
himself to getting what he could out of the servants. If
anything terrible had happened, they'd be full of it, and
Venetians might be a cautious lot and have peculiar accents,
but there didn't exist a servant who wasn't ready to gossip
over disaster, let the gentry murmur never so discreetly. At
the jerk of the messenger's head, Benno trotted after in happy
anticipation. In the bosom of Benno's grimy doublet, his
small dog Biondello stirred. He was hungry too. Benno felt
there was bound to be some wench in the kitchens who'd
take pity on them both no matter what horrors lay upstairs.

Just as soon as he produced Biondello from his jerkin in
the kitchens, several voices broke into the fond exclamations
he had expected; only of course in Venetian accents.

Meanwhile Sigismondo was viewing the horror upstairs.

Niccolo Ermolin lay, more relaxed in death than he had ever permitted himself to be in life, supine on the daybed in his study, a piece of cloth, which he had used to put under his hand when he was writing, across his eyes. It made him seem to be indulging in some game, counting to a hundred before he rose and set about hunting down those who had hidden.

Crouched beside him was a beautiful girl, one of her braids only half-finished so that dark hair streamed across the face she turned towards the door as Vettor ushered in Sigismondo.

'This is the man I spoke of, my dear. If anyone is able to help us at this time, he will. Sigismondo: the Lady Isabella, wife to my son-in-law.'

'How soon am I called the widow?' By the smooth curve of cheek and long neck, Lady Isabella could be no more than seventeen at most, but she stood up with the self-possession of one much older. The large dark eyes that looked Sigismondo up and down were not swollen and there was no trace of tears on the pale cheeks. She let go the dead hand of her husband, laying it at his side, and stood tall and slender in her dress of figured bronze silk. 'And how is a stranger to help us at this time?'

'My dear,' Vettor bestowed on her a smile that patronised her youth and inexperience, 'we cannot keep this from the world for ever. Signor Sigismondo may be able to find the villain who killed Niccolo. A stranger may see what we do not.'

Isabella flung out a hand towards the desk before the window, with its ingenious compartments holding everything one might need: the heavy silver inkwells for red ink and black, an hourglass, rulers, a jar in violet glaze filled with mended quill pens ready to the hand that would never now use them. Spectacles lay on the desk, their gold wire frame crumpled but the glass intact, beside a book, bound in dark red leather and stained a darker red.

'Do we need a stranger to explain how Niccolo locked

himself in his study and yet died by an assassin's dagger? Isn't it obvious?'

The window gaped wide and Sigismondo, who had surveyed the desk, leant over the side of it to glance at the sill and down to the canal below. Vettor, without abating his kindly smile at Lady Isabella, explained.

'Certainly the assassin might have come by that way, sir. My grandson Marco, when we could get no answer from his father in this room, was forced to climb in by way of the balcony of the room next door. He found Niccolo dead here, at the desk, lying across this book.'

Sigismondo's deep voice spoke for the first time since he entered the study, and he turned not to Vettor Darin but to Lady Isabella. 'Why do you think the assassin came in this way, my lady?'

She tossed her head, loosening more of the dark hair. 'If Marco could do it once, why not twice?'

Chapter 3

Who Has The Keys?

'Who's this?'

The young man had burst into the room, and stared at Sigismondo with even more suspicion than had Lady Isabella. Vettor Darin came forward, a hand extended as if to soothe or control.

'Marco, be patient. I will explain. But did you find your uncle?'

The sudden appearance of an older man behind Marco answered this. He put Marco aside and came, without acknowledging anyone else, to lean over the still form on the daybed. He gently removed the piece of brocade covering Niccolo's eyes; and hissed like water on hot metal. 'Devils! Who did this?'

He turned and fixed Sigismondo with an intense frowning stare, as though the only man he did not recognise must in some way be guilty. Vettor put in smoothly, 'Rinaldo, this is Signor Sigismondo, whom I had heard of as one who is discreet and cunning to find out villains. He has worked for the Duke of Rocca and other princes, and is willing to help us find out who has murdered your brother.'

Sigismondo bent his head, though his arrival with Darin's messenger was the only sign he had given that he would accept such a commission. Rinaldo Ermolin did not look in the least impressed by Vettor's recommendation. Of the five people, therefore, crowded in the small room, three were inimical to the other two. On the daybed lay the only indifferent one.

'How do you propose to find this out?' Rinaldo had an uncompromising voice, not harsh but very even in tone. He was tall, probably in his late thirties, handsome, with a wide forehead, and eyes and mouth both long and narrow. His skin was sallow, his hair thick and brown under the tawny velvet cap. A chain of twisted gold links shone on the olive of his gown. Until now, Vettor had dominated the room.

Sigismondo answered this authority in his bow. 'By examining your brother's body. By questioning all who may throw light on this matter. By private enquiry in the city. With your permission.' He waited, relaxed and at his ease, leaning against the windowframe, a formidable shadow in his dark clothes, but that a reflection from the water sent a gold ripple over his face and the smoothness of his head.

'We must do something soon, Rinaldo. And the Signoria must be informed. Whoever did it cannot have gone far.'

A curious sound, more like a snort than anything, brought Rinaldo's attention to the young widow. She had gone to sit at the foot of the daybed, keeping the corpse company. He went to her side, raising her up.

'My poor sister. Never fear, the villains will be found and torn to pieces.' He regarded Sigismondo over the girl's head. 'Well, sir, do what you can, and quickly. You will be rewarded if you can bring the murderers to justice.'

Sigismondo, who in the past had received bags of gold pressed on him by grateful princes; and who could have produced a chain, given him by a duke, which would have made Rinaldo's chain look wholly inadequate, merely bent his head. Marco, kneeling by his father's body, now raised a face more petulant than angry.

'It's for me to say what is to be done in this house! I am my father's heir!'

He was a handsome boy, but his face was soft where his uncle's was hard. His hair was fashionably curled; in his short doublet of peacock blue he was the focus of light in the room. To Sigismondo, silently observing, Marco Ermolin was asserting himself because he knew people took little notice of him. His grandfather was quick to pat him on the shoulder, a gesture he shrugged off.

'Marco! What is being done is being done for the family. It is for your honour. For the honour of us all.'

'Aren't we wasting time?' It was the young widow, pointing at the still form on the daybed. 'If this Signor Sigismondo is indeed to find out who killed my husband, had he better not start at once? And are we not to send for a priest for the sake of my husband's soul?' Her tone, sarcastic in emphasis throughout, suggested that she thought her husband's soul beyond saving, and herself certainly beyond caring.

Marco was on his feet at once. 'I'll fetch Father Domenico—'

'Wait.' Rinaldo stopped him before he could reach the door. 'Say nothing to anyone – not even to your friends – of what has happened here. You told me the servants know only that their master is dead. Let them think he has suffered an apoplexy or an accident. Signor Sigismondo,' he moved the dark eyes sidelong to the man at the window, 'may find it more profitable to question their ignorance.'

Marco nodded impatiently and was gone. Sigismondo, as Rinaldo stepped aside and pointed, approached the daybed and bent over it, Niccolo Ermolin returning his gaze with one eye only. The widow watched with interest as Sigismondo unbuttoned the velvet gown, parted the fine linen shirt on the naked chest, and searched for other injuries. Finding none in front he put an arm behind the shoulders and sat the body up, preventing the head from rolling. As the blood-streaked face rose to survey the room, the widow for the first time shrank in her place at the foot of the bed.

A deep, thoughtful hum preceded Sigismondo's next words. 'Mm – m – m. Look at this.'

The widow made no move to join the men as they came to peer at the back of Niccolo's neck. She put her hand over her mouth as if further revelations might make her sick. Under the terrible regard of her husband she sat with eyes averted, hearing Sigismondo add, 'It could equally be this blow that killed him, I think.'

Vettor, astonished, was even peevish. 'Marco said nothing of this, yet he found him. See, there is blood all down his back.'

Sigismondo was laying Niccolo down again, carefully, and he replaced the brocade across the eyes, each accusing in its different way.

'He bled inside his gown. No doubt your grandson found him, head down on his desk, and went to lift him to see what was wrong.' There was a small silence as they pictured what Marco must have seen, and Sigismondo's deep voice continued, 'The wound through the eye would have seemed the obvious answer.'

'So the one who killed him,' Rinaldo had taken one of his brother's hands in his, as if the departed spirit needed reassurance that this cold talk of wounds did not preclude feeling, 'came up behind him—' He paused. The hard voice clogged. 'Stabbed him in the neck and then pulled him up to do this?' And he gestured with his free hand at the patient, covered face. 'In his eye.'

'Monstrous!' Vettor for the first time became agitated. 'They must be demons to do such a thing. And who could have come upon him without his knowing, in a locked room?'

The Lady Isabella rose, her bronze silk making a noise like leaves rustling. With her pale face and unbound hair she resembled a Fury, standing there.

'Why not ask the housekeeper,' she said, 'the person who has the keys?'

Chapter 4

The Key To The Door?

The housekeeper was black, beautiful and distressed. Rinaldo had been about to send for her to the study, when Sigismondo demurred. He said firmly but with a deference that clearly pleased Vettor, that he must be allowed some freedom in his investigation; the housekeeper might be in awe of them and might not speak her mind. The Lady Isabella again made the scornful sound he had already heard, but Rinaldo as well as Vettor agreed to let Sigismondo go by himself to Zenobia's room. A servant waiting outside the study was in fact delegated to take him there. As he left the study, Sigismondo stooped to examine the brass lock of the door.

Sigismondo dismissed the boy before he scratched on the housekeeper's door.

It was opened suddenly, as if Zenobia was more used to having it thrown open unceremoniously than scratched upon, and she stood there, staring.

She was tall and slender, her small head carried high on a long neck, a skin of brown satin set off by the white linen wrapped turban-wise round her head and the white apron over the grey dress. She had a straight nose, very large eyes, and a regal elegance. Tears glittered on her face.

'Zenobia, I have been asked to help in this matter of your master's death. My name is Sigismondo. Will you answer some questions for me?'

She opened the door wider, dipping in an automatic curtsey and backing before him. The room, on the ground

16

floor off the majestic hall, reflected the importance of Zenobia's role as housekeeper rather than her own importance. It had two long windows looking on to a side canal, was lined with shelves and cupboards, one open, revealing bolts of linen, and piles of sheets, pillowcases and towels, meticulously folded and stacked. A deal table with a ledger, an abacus, a bundle of lists, an inkwell and a jar of pens, had a stool drawn up to it. Zenobia, curtseying again, mutely offered it to Sigismondo. He sat, and glanced at the table.

'I'm interrupting your work?' The voice was gentle.

She shook her head in silence but, the movement making a tear run, she brought up the edge of her apron to dry her face in a few quick pats. Sigismondo looked at her gravely.

'You loved him?'

Tears ran again. She picked up her apron and half turned away. Sigismondo slowly nodded, taking the tears as her reply, and continued, 'How long did you serve him?'

She bent the elegant head, considering. 'Twenty years, sir. I was bought when I was reckoned to be fourteen.'

Sigismondo did not ask why a girl of fourteen had been bought by a man some ten years older. Fine bones and carriage do not need age to improve them; she would already have been beautiful. Young men not yet married need bedwarmers rather than housekeepers and slaves are powerless to make demands as a mistress might. Most likely Niccolo Ermolin had kept this exotic creature through two marriages under a useful disguise, though her beauty had surely given the game away.

'In your opinion, why was your master murdered?'

Her eyes opened, the apron fell; she turned, rigid, the very picture of horrified shock. 'Murdered – ' He regarded her attentively. 'They did not say he was murdered.'

'How did you think he had died?'

'I thought, his heart. He had complained lately of his heart. But who killed him?'

He answered her question with another, looking up at her. The shaven head emphasised the darkness of his eyes and brows. 'What did you think I meant when I said I was enquiring about the matter of your master's death? Why should I be asked to do this if the death were natural?'

Her long brown fingers interlaced tightly but she held her head high. 'I do not think, sir. That is not my function.'

Sigismondo smiled, lifted his hand from the desk and span a bead on the abacus; a slight gesture indicated the lists, the ledger. 'And I don't believe that you are not required to think.'

There was a flash of something not at all submissive. 'A slave is not permitted to think, sir. I look after the linen and the spices, I order and hand out supplies; but I do not have an opinion.'

Sigismondo had picked up a pen and was smoothing the piece of feather at its end. 'You are not allowed an opinion, but you have feelings, mm-m? Zenobia, your master was stabbed to death this morning in his study, which was locked as his custom was. Do you know where he kept the key?'

She gestured swiftly to her throat. 'It never left him. The master allowed nobody, not even his son, in his study unless he took them there. For instance, not long ago he took the Lady Isabella into every room in the house – even this one – and she must have seen it then; though not everything in it.'

'What would he not have shown her?'

'His secret book. He showed me the outside of it once; told me he'd written the date when I was bought and how much I cost. Everything to do with money,' she emphasised the word with a touch of bitterness, 'went into that book, but only his eyes might see it.'

Sigismondo could, at that moment, have reflected on the state of those eyes as *he* last saw them. 'What of your keys, then? Did no one have permission to clean the study, even if you supervised?'

For the first time, she smiled. 'He said dust would not spoil his treasures. The tapestries were wrapped away, the silver shielded from all light, the jewelry locked in cabinets. Nothing could suffer.'

Sigismondo came to his feet, and stepped to the window to look out over the water. A boat was being sculled by, with a man shouting his wares, lemons in a glowing heap before him, his voice echoing from the brick walls on either side. From where Sigismondo stood he could still observe, though without seeming to, Zenobia's face. 'Have you any thoughts on who could have hated him enough to kill him?'

Her face, her whole body, contracted fiercely. 'Hated? He had many enemies! He was hated for his wealth, his influence, in the Great Council and with the Ten. He had many secrets.'

She did not say why the secrets had to do with this hatred, and Sigismondo did not ask. He moved suddenly past her. He had seen something hanging on the inside of a cupboard door, and he unhooked it and held it out to her: a ring holding keys of all sizes, some big enough to unlock a cellar door, some small enough for a jewel box.

'Do you know what each of these is for?' There was a musical clashing as his fingers sorted through them, and she came to pick out this one and that.

'That, and those, are for store rooms. I have them at my belt too.' She pushed her apron aside to show another bunch of keys on a chain at her waist. 'If one were damaged or lost, there is a spare. For the others I am not sure. They were all given to me by the housekeeper here before me. She said some were for old rooms here, before the master's father had alterations made. She didn't like to throw them away and neither did I; but I sorted out for myself only the ones I use.'

'Is there no danger some servant will steal the bunch here?' He jangled it enquiringly.

'As you see, sir, it hangs inside the cupboard, which I lock, and I never leave this room unlocked. The keys I keep here.' She tapped the bunch on her thigh.

Sigismondo, feeling through the keys in his hand, stopped, and held one out, separated from the rest. 'You never leave this room unlocked or the cupboard open? Feel this.'

Looking at him doubtfully, she ran her fingers over the small brass key he offered.

'Wax, Zenobia. I think if you tried this key, it might fit the study door. Possibly someone thought it would.'

Chapter 5

Zenobia's Child

Benno was not at all disappointed in the servants' quarters of the Palazzo Ermolin. Biondello, the perfect passport, tilted his head fetchingly to one side and focused on the cook, who succumbed at once, plucked him from Benno's hands and, pressing kisses on his grubby topknot, clasped him to her heart. Benno understood her to exclaim, in her Venetian slur, 'The angel! What became of his ear?'

Benno shrugged and pushed out his underlip; the village where he had found Biondello was so impoverished that the missing ear was probably a sign of the dog's nimbleness in escaping the cooking-pot.

Their entrance had interrupted excited speculation about the master's death. The two kitchenmaids, who welcomed any stranger as alleviation of their toil, did not cavil at one even as vacant-looking as Benno, and put in his hands a bowl of excellent broth and some bread still hot from baking. One of them paused in her dramatic description of the young master, watched from all the available windows along that side of the house, climbing across from the balcony to the window of his father's room, to ask, 'What's *your* master doing here?'

Benno repeated his all-purpose shrug and they contemplated him for a moment, his beard dabbled with broth and his mouth agape, usefully for once, to receive sopping bread. By common consent they gave up the question and returned to their admiration of the young master. Benno noticed there was no time lost in more than perfunctory grief for the old one.

This he reported later to Sigismondo, as they sat drinking a pale soft yellow wine and eating grilled prawns and hard-boiled eggs in their lodging house on a narrow street. Benno was glad to have a street below their window, it made him feel they were perhaps on solid ground instead of the unchancy water. Shelling a prawn, he reported, 'There's no tears for the dead man in the Palazzo Ermolin kitchens.'

'Mm-m. I found some being shed, but not in his family – *they're* more concerned with the future. No man who leaves a fortune can be completely regretted when he dies.'

'Not his son nor his wife is sorry?' Benno, who had never had either, was shocked.

'His wife's somewhat annoyed to find herself a widow at – oh, I'd say she's seventeen. She's not long married.' Sigismondo poured more of the wine. They had put their table and bench on the balcony, with the dish of eggs and prawns and the big earthenware pitcher. 'The poor young woman's had little time to enjoy the status. She may feel he's cheated her by getting murdered.'

Benno waved a foraging pigeon off the balcony rail. He looked all round, at the room behind them empty except for a bed; down at the street where people passed and re-passed and shopkeepers called their goods for sale. He even looked upwards at the windows above, and dropped his voice to a murmur. 'How did he die? You didn't say.'

Sigismondo bit into a hard-boiled egg with his usual pleasure. 'Someone drove a stiletto through his spinal cord at the neck and then through his left eye. Or the other way round; it wouldn't have mattered.'

Benno found the cold resilience of the egg he had picked up made him think disagreeably of an eyeball. He put it down. 'Why'd they do that? It's disgusting.'

'"Why?" is my problem. The family wants it solved as quickly and as privately as may be. They have to report the death to the authorities but I'm not sure they will make the manner of it public until they know why or who. The lord who sent for me has ambitions, so I've heard; and no one is eager to have the family name stained by murder. Those in the Golden Book don't want trouble.'

Benno ate prawns to take his mind off eyeballs. 'What's the Golden Book?' It was the factual sort of question his master did not seem to mind answering, and he obliged now.

'Venice is a closed shop, Benno. If you're not in the Golden Book you don't exist.'

'You mean you're a peasant like me. Or them.' Benno pointed a prawn at the bustle down below, where two donkeys going opposite ways had come to a patient standstill, each with its load wedged against the other, while their owners argued the right of way and hit them to make them decide it with a lucky move, and people delayed on both sides shouted. Benno dropped prawn shells on the nearest donkey. 'I reckon *their* book'd be dung colour.'

Sigismondo laughed and drained his cup. 'You've got it. You have to be born to the right people to make it into the Golden Book, and marry the right people to stay in it.'

'And make a push not to get murdered, I suppose.'

'Mmm . . . though that can happen to the best of us. But to get murdered like that, in a locked room, your secret book in front of you . . .'

'*Secret* book?' To Benno all books were secret, and the idea of one that even those who *could* read couldn't read intrigued him.

'Some merchants keep a record for themselves that they don't want anyone to see. Venice has dealings with some unusual strangers.'

Benno had already been astonished by the number of swarthy faces he had seen here, the turbans, the evidence that there were people even more extraordinary and bizarre than those he'd met already since he first left his native town; and with accents more impenetrable. 'You mean Christians didn't ought to deal with Turks?'

'Hey, would I say that? When in Venice, do as the Venetians do: keep your mouth shut,' and Sigismondo reached out and closed Benno's lips over the mouthful of prawns and bread, making his cheeks bulge and his eyes widen. 'Where money talks, wise men are silent.' He let go, and patted Benno's face smartly.

When Benno had chewed and gulped, he ventured on. 'Reckon I was wise in the kitchen. Didn't say a word, let them do the talking.' He washed down his mouthful with a generous swig of wine, and closed one round brown eye. 'Would you be surprised to hear he left more than one son?'

Sigismondo raised an eyebrow. 'I only met one. There are others? Should I be surprised that there are more?'

Benno held up a stubby forefinger decorated with prawn whiskers. 'Only one. Problem is, he's black, he's the son of a slave and he's missing.'

Sigismondo blew softly between parted lips and looked out, unseeing, across the busy street at the plaster flaking off the bricks of the opposite building, where a small pied cat returned his stare between the iron rails of a balcony.

'So that's Zenobia's child. I thought she was too beautiful.'

Benno blinked. 'Zenobia . . . ? Oh, ah yes, she'd be the housekeeper they were on about. The slave. They have to jump when she tells them, though. And the cook has to keep on the right side of her if she wants the sugar and the costly spices. What they were saying was, she never got over Cosmo, that's her son, being sent away. This Lord Vettor lost his temper with him when he came to dine with his daughter.'

Sigismondo nodded. 'The first wife, Lady Emilia. Did you find out why he lost his temper?'

'I didn't do any asking and they didn't say. They were on about how it wasn't fair this Cosmo won't get a thing now his father's dead, and wondering if he'd ever turn up here again.'

Sigismondo raised his cup to the cat over the way; it stared at him unwinking, head between the bars. 'Hey, who knows? I think perhaps he may have.'

Chapter 6

The Key To The Book

Benno, when he had heard the tale of Zenobia and the keys, rubbed his head until his hair stood up in tufts. 'You think this Cosmo could of come back to get revenge on his father for sending him away? But then why didn't his mother *give* him the key?'

Sigismondo shrugged. 'It's possible she loved Niccolo as well as her son. She was the one I saw weeping.'

Benno took to ruffling the wool on Biondello's head, despairing of inspiration from his own. 'This key. If it was in a big bunch, how would Cosmo know which one it was, unless she told him?'

'Mm – m . . . She said she didn't, but one of the things to remember, Benno: people don't invariably tell the truth.'

'So she could of told him one time what the key was for, and just pretend to you she hadn't. But how'd he come back and none of the servants see him? You know servants. They see everything.'

'Suppose she visits the markets? She's a housekeeper. And people come selling stuff at the landing stage outside her window. The postern door is just at the side of her room. Besides, he might not be recognised. How old was this Cosmo when his father sent him away?'

'Just a little boy, s'far as I could gather. About seven, the cook said, she thought it was so sad. Beautiful, he was, and with a will of his own too. Led the little Lord Marco into mischief and told him what to do and all.'

'There,' said Sigismondo genially, 'you've hit on the reason why this lad Cosmo got suddenly to be elsewhere. It's conceivable Lord Vettor did not care to hear his grandson being ordered about by his son-in-law's bastard.'

'Not to mention he was black and a slave's son into the bargain.'

Sigismondo had risen and, leaning over the balcony, was chaffering with a man below who, held up by the still-stationary donkeys, took the opportunity to haggle with the sky. In a minute, Sigismondo had tossed a coin and caught a melon thrown up to him.

He sat down, cut the melon in two and gave half to Benno. Biondello had watched the transaction acutely, his head, like the cat's, between the balcony railings, and was plainly cast down at the results. He lay flat at Benno's feet.

'No, Cosmo wasn't born with luck on his side; though if he'd lived in his father's house until he was seven, allowed to play with his half-brother, we must assume that Marco's mother didn't object to him. He was sent away because her *father* Lord Vettor took exception to him; a man who struck me as having a high opinion of what's due to family.'

'That's why he sent for you, to keep things quiet for them, I suppose. How'd he know where you were when he sent for you?'

Sigismondo laid a finger alongside his Roman nose. 'The Venetians keep tabs on everyone, especially someone who has a reputation for coming in useful. And they've spies . . .' He was interrupted by Biondello, who, bored, evidently decided that the cat opposite was one of the spies, and launched into an unaccustomed bout of growling which the cat ignored.

Benno, putting down the melon rind and wiping his ears on his sleeves, still had Cosmo on his mind. 'If he did it, the black son, you'd never be able to find him in this city, would you? There's all sorts from all over, here. Just got to go to that Rialto and he vanishes, with all those other dark faces.'

'We don't know how dark he is, Benno. Mixed blood can show up any grade of colour. But although Lord Vettor would be glad to lay hands on the young man and have him flayed or broken on the wheel or whatever the Venetians like to do with parricides, I can't be sure I'd hand him over even if I could find him.'

'But I thought you fancied him for it, what with the key.' Benno pulled back Biondello, who had thrust a dangerous proportion of himself through the railings and was keeping observation, close but now silent, upon the cat. 'Who else is likely? What about the other son getting cross with Daddy?'

Sigismondo laughed, a sound deep in his chest. 'Yes. There's that. The widow, when I was there, gave her opinion: she said when Marco climbed in at the study window to investigate why his father didn't answer, it might not have been for the first time that morning.'

'Been in before with a stiletto . . . but wouldn't his father have thought it a bit off, Sonny climbing in at the window?'

'He wouldn't have much time to be surprised,' Sigismondo said. 'Hardly time to say, "Take those dirty feet off my table".'

Benno, swallowing wine, found this so funny that he half-choked. Tears came to his eyes. A light thump from Sigismondo between the shoulder-blades recovered him; he wiped his eyes and beard, and said, 'Suppose now Daddy's dead, this legit. son comes into all the money? Good reason to hurry Daddy off a bit. Particularly if he needs money.'

Sigismondo stretched, and shifted so that the sun, beaming down past a decorated chimney that had shadowed him until now, no longer struck his unprotected head. Across the way, the cat flung up a leg and insolently did its private laundry under Biondello's gaze. 'If he needs money! Mm – m! Is there any young man who doesn't? But young Marco isn't going to find coming into the family business as easy as he may have hoped.'

'But the old gentleman, his grandfather, he's a Vettor *Darin*, right, not an Ermolin, just related by marriage. He can't get in the way, can he?'

'Oh, the Lord Vettor isn't in question, though I'd not cross him in a hurry because of his influence with the Great Council.'

'Was that what his gondolier was boasting about when he took us there?'

'No. Marco's up against his uncle, his father's business partner and a very different proposition. When I'd talked to the housekeeper I went upstairs to have another look at the study door, with that key that had wax on it. Marco and his uncle were in there, quarrelling.'

'They should of been praying over the dead lord! All the servants were going up to pray over him in his bedroom when he was laid out. Gave me an invite but I said I had to be ready when you should call for me.'

'Marco and Rinaldo were arguing over who should have Niccolo's secret book with its records of all his dealings. My money's on Rinaldo; he was still cool while Marco was heated. Rinaldo had found Marco carrying it away and took it out of his hands. They were – ' Sigismondo smiled at the memory ' – ready to kill each other. Interesting. It was a locked book and apparently Niccolo wore the key always on a chain round his neck. It wasn't there when I examined his body for wounds.'

Benno, when he was thinking, looked at his most vacant. 'So if Marco had the book and was going to read it he must've taken the key when he climbed in and found Daddy dead.'

'Or made him dead, as his stepmother claims.'

'Looks fishy, doesn't it?'

'Even more than this.' Sigismondo held up the last prawn, and ate it.

Chapter 7

Liver And Onions With The Generals

The two men, so like and so unlike, had climbed the stairs, past curious faces raised to them from the inner courtyard. Now came another flight, leading a floor higher, achieved with growing annoyance by the second man, who was a dwarf, for whom stairs are never easy.

The antechamber at the head of the stairs did not hold them long, for they were bowed into a larger room where ambassadors to the Serene Republic normally waited. They stood there for a bit, looking round at frescoes and gilding as fine as frescoes and gilding meant to impress ambassadors usually are. They had seen it before, however. The dwarf, bored, stumped over to the window and looked out, frightening a pigeon that had been roosting on the sill outside. He was making faces at another when a servant flung open the doors at the far end and summoned them into the room where the Doge and his Council were sitting.

The interview with the Doge lasted perhaps an hour. Maps were produced and pored over. The tall, heavily built man smiled a lot. The dwarf grinned. They appeared to be in perfect accord and the Doge and Council heard them with approval. The Serene Republic was not in the habit of employing anyone without a very thorough investigation of their backgrounds and track records, and these two had proved they deserved their gaudy reputation.

Ottavio Marsili was the eighth son of village peasants. His mother would have earned the proud title of virago had anyone heard of her exploits in repelling bandits from the village, on one occasion braining the leader with a frying pan. Nono, the dwarf, was the ninth child; and these two were the only sons who had inherited her wits as well as her courage.

They had also inherited her knack of dealing with bandits, because they went on to lead a gang of them, eventually so well organised that others applied to join and the band grew to such proportions that they could hire themselves out on a grand scale as a *condotta*, robbing for states under-equipped to do it for themselves.

Now they were robbing for the Serenissima, though of course it was called war. Venice knew that her trade would suffer unforgivably if she did not at this juncture, with her trade affected by the war at sea with the Turks, annex cities on the mainland – admittedly belonging to the Duke of Montano – that were taking too much trade for themselves. That was the trouble with trade, it established a network and, as any spider can tell you, you've got to deal with the smallest twitches. And if you want to catch a really big fly, you send for Ottavio and Nono Marsili.

The interview with the Doge was over. Another and more important one was to come. They traversed the salon where ambassadors waited – there was one there now, more impressed by the presence of the two famous condottieri than by the frescoes – and were admitted by another door to another room.

It was a room feared by any who had done the Republic a disservice, a room dreaded by traitors. Here the Council of Ten met, in whose hands was the security of Venice. Here they gave their secret commands, here they questioned the accused.

Ottavio Marsili came out of the room smiling as he had entered; his brother's grin was fixed and he wiped sweat from his forehead – though he waited until the door had shut behind them before he did it. They exchanged no word until they had descended both the inner and courtyard staircases. Then, focus of fascinated eyes from all round the courtyard, Nono spoke.

'I'm famished. Let's eat.' Without waiting for his brother, he set off, through the archway and onto the crowded Piazzetta, where he stood looking round for a likely street vendor. In spite of his reputed appetite for grilled babies, Nono's real passion was the fried liver with onions for which Venice was so famous. He was quite prepared, though, to dull the edge of appetite with almost anything that came to hand, such as the squid he could see being turned on a skewer over a pan of fire not far off. He was busy trotting through an exploding crowd of pigeons towards this when his brother caught up with him, put a hand on his shoulder and pointed.

A tall man in black, his shaven head gleaming in the sun, was strolling through the crowd. The Marsili brothers exchanged glances, Ottavio raised his eyebrows and they started off, the squid temporarily on hold. They did not notice the ramshackle little man with a short black beard, carrying a small woolly dog, who followed their quarry, mainly because he was supremely unremarkable.

Ottavio, ranging alongside, said smoothly, 'Am I mistaking you for Sigismondo?'

If this was discretion, it was rewarded. Benno stopped short to avoid bumping into the embrace, cordial almost to violence. Emerging from it, widely smiling, Sigismondo looked round and down, and gave his hand to Nono who shook it with force. Benno knew that his master's evident pleasure did not guarantee that these were friends. It was entirely possible, Benno had found, to smile at people you were intending to kill, until the opportunity arose. No need to stop smiling then, either.

'Hey, I don't *need* to ask the Marsili brothers what brings them to Venice.' Sigismondo smiled at Nono's upturned face. 'Liver and onions, right?'

The dwarf, grinning, beat his hands together. 'Let's find some. I've an appetite such that I could eat one of these pigeons *with* the feathers on.'

Benno found that the three men in front of him, Nono in the middle, made a path through the crowd that drew him easily in their wake. Many in the crowd turned to look. Venice was, as he had remarked, full of outlandish people and contained plenty of dwarves, but this trio commanded respect.

What else the Marsili brothers commanded, he learnt as he waited on them in a tavern down a narrow side street which was where Nono led them, rubbing his hands in anticipation. Benno, posting Biondello into his jerkin, took the jug of wine from the inn servant and poured for his master and the two strangers. The large one, whose shoulders rivalled Sigismondo's, and who had a thick crop of iron-grey hair cut in the soldier's style, straight round above the ears to accommodate a helmet, had a large, handsome face; it gave the impression of having seen a fair number of bad sights not only without flinching but indeed with a certain enjoyment. Dipping a thumb in a wine puddle, he was drawing a map on the table top which Sigismondo leant to look at. Nono's interest in this was quite absent; he kept swivelling to look for his liver and onions.

'They've no chance at all.' Ottavio's smile extended to show yet more white teeth. 'They'll starve to death if they don't surrender soon. We have them sealed off.'

'Sent them an ass's head the other day,' put in Nono, 'by catapult. But they didn't get the message. Too busy eating it, I suppose, though it was putrid. Must have eaten all their rats by now, and they'd be fat rats. Always plenty for rats when you can't bury the dead.' His grin showed as many teeth as his brother's, with the exception of one that had been knocked out at the side, and although Nono's hair was thinning and black, the resemblance was very strong in a way that bypassed any actual similarity of feature, perhaps residing in the energy that drove them both.

Ottavio shook Sigismondo by the sleeve, still smiling. 'Come and join us. You've fought with us before.'

'*Against* you, if you remember.'

'If you'd been beside me I might have missed what you were doing. Pity your commander got cold feet and called it off – you nearly lost us that skirmish.'

Plates of fried liver and onions were dumped on the table.

31

Benno took his and leant on the wall, licking his fingers as he went. Nono, nearer his plate than the rest, lost no time. He spoke through the second mouthful. 'Come on. We want men like you.'

'There are no men like you. But if Duke Guido gets out of bed long enough to mount a horse, he might bring another army. Then you'd get a good fight. Won't you come? Rich pickings!'

Ottavio slid a note of gross wheedling into his voice, caricaturing his patent desire to win Sigismondo over, but in Benno's opinion it didn't disguise what a dangerous character they had met. Refuse this man something he wanted and you might not just need your hat to carry your teeth home in, you might not ever need a hat again.

'I'm bespoke, Marsili. My time's not my own.'

Nono, not a tidy eater, here stopped chewing, with his mouth open, and focused on Sigismondo with an exact echo of the curiosity in Ottavio's face. He pointed his wedge of bread. 'You've been to see the Ten!'

'I've not had that honour. No, I'm working privately for a family here.'

'Privately!' Nono snorted fried onion onto the table. 'Everything these Venetians do is private! Bet you they've got a spy under this table.' He ducked to peer and, coming up, caught sight of Biondello's small face regarding him from inside Benno's jerkin. 'You see? Everywhere we go we're watched!'

He bellowed with laughter, picked up a scrap of liver and fed it to Benno's jerkin.

'That's one spy satisfied.' The small shrewd eyes examined the owner of the jerkin. 'What's *he* doing with a lady's lapdog?' Before Sigismondo could answer the question thrown at him, Nono got a full view of Biondello's head, thrust further out in hope of more bounty. 'Ho, damaged goods!' He shouted with laughter again. 'Just escaped from a siege by the look of him, before someone moved on to the second course.'

'This siege,' Sigismondo's voice, serious, had their attention at once. 'How long do you think it will last?'

Ottavio jutted his chin, fingering it thoughtfully. 'Don't delay too long if you're thinking of joining us. They can't sit there much longer, it's come out and fight or starve.'

'We'll be fighting skeletons.' Nono was polishing his plate with a crust of bread, watched wistfully by Biondello. He pushed the crust into his mouth and chewed as he grinned. 'Lucky gold don't get thinner in a siege or it wouldn't be worth hanging about for.'

'War costs. We need the gold just to keep fighting.' Ottavio lowered his voice to a murmur Benno could barely hear. 'Venice is coughing blood to pay for supplies.'

'What of her patriotic citizens?' Sigismondo's voice matched Ottavio's, but Benno was used to interpreting the deep purr. 'Don't they contribute to the Republic's expenses?'

Nono leant forward, grimacing. 'When they don't get themselves killed. One of the richest, stabbed to death this morning, they said . . .'

Sigismondo shook his head gravely. 'The rich should stay out of brawls.'

'Brawls! This was in his own palazzo, in his own study. No one known to quarrel with him, although – ' he nearly tipped his stool over in getting the attention of the inn servant ' – there's plenty had cause to. You'd think a man would be safe in his study.' He turned to Sigismondo with a face full of malicious glee. 'Gone where his grand ancient high-stomached family and all his money won't do him a spot of good. Niccolo Ermolin loaned his soul to the Devil a great while ago.'

Chapter 8

Taking The Plunge

Pasquale Scolar, the Doge's son, dedicated his life to pleasure as single-mindedly as a priest with a burning vocation. He was young, he was handsome, he was incurably silly, the poisoned apple of his father's eye. Money dissolved in his hands. He listened to lectures on his extravagance with smiling good humour and at the end asked for more money. Everything he fancied, he expected to have – girl, horse or jewel – and the Scolar fortune, amassed over generations of careful trading, was rapidly dispersing. The Venetians, who elected a Doge for personal wealth besides family connections, were irritated. The election was for life and, if the young man kept up his present rate of spending, Venice might end up with a bankrupt Doge.

Advice and pressure had convinced the fond father that marriage might calm his son. The bride was of suitably important family, the dowry proportionate to the honour of the alliance though perhaps not proportionate to the spending capacity of the bridegroom. There had been three days' public holiday and as much brilliance and display as if the Doge's coffers were bottomless. A company of young men, two hundred strong, in crimson velvet and silver brocade, crossed the Grand Canal by a bridge of boats to fetch the bride. The wedding Mass was followed by a banquet and then the bridal pair, attended by a hundred and fifty ladies and a company of musicians, were rowed in the Bucintoro, the Doge's own galley, to the Scolar palace, where dancing began that did not end even at dawn. More feasts, jousting in the Piazzetta, regattas, were to follow. Marco Ermolin, with no bride to distract him, vowed to celebrate his best friend's wedding by not going to bed while festivities lasted.

Not only were all these festivities now months past, they had, in a sense, been wasted. The bride's exhaustion after the gaieties surprised no one. Her failure to pick up spirits alarmed all Venice. A fever supervened. Within ten days she was dead. Her power to calm the Doge's son could never be tested.

He found himself this morning at a loose end, with a desire to celebrate. His favourite companion, Marco Ermolin, was not available, and he was so full of suppressed high spirits that he must find some way to vent them. The gang of young men idled along the Riva; someone suggested a visit of condolence to their mourning friend, and Pasquale made a hurried excuse. The young men took it that he was not willing to undergo a tiresome, embarrassing interview merely because Niccolo Ermolin had had the bad luck – the bad taste – to get stabbed. Marco's father had after all been old, not as old as Pasquale's own unnaturally aged father but still near enough to death for it to surprise no one. They sensed that they must find something; they knew this effervescent mood though they could not see any cause for it.

Abruptly he sent for the horses and for wine. He surveyed the small company. Annoying that Marco was by far the best at creating amusements, schemes that amused partly by stirring up far more people than they amused. One of them tentatively suggested a race.

'Oh – too tame. A race!'

'Not so bad,' Pasquale said, seizing on it. 'A race, but keeping to the narrowest streets.'

'Full of things in the way . . .'

'Like people!'

They were not all willing but they were all instantly ready. Once mounted, and started, hallooing each other on, shrieking with the thrill of it, naturally letting Pasquale get ahead, aware of people scattering, of absurd faces of alarm and fright momentarily seen as they passed them, of the sound of hooves coming back at them from the walls – they jumped their horses over such obstacles as children playing, or an old man tumbled prostrate on the ground. Pasquale encountered two donkeys in peaceable single file, laden with goods. Shouting to their driver, he crammed his mount to the side, leant over and cut the nearest pack open, showering the ground with olives. He could now force his way past, and though the second pack was harder to hack open, it too poured its load on to the ground and, thus flattened, let him by. The donkeys, squealing and frenzied, held his friends up far more; the donkey man had to be all but ridden down; the horses baulked at the olives underfoot and the bucking, furious donkeys. Pasquale's flying figure turned a corner out of sight before they could spur and whip their way free. He looked back and yelled a challenge as the first appeared fifty yards behind. They were alongside a canal here and a dignified statesman fairly leapt into his gondola as Pasquale thundered down on him. Laughing and looking back, Pasquale never saw the child in his path, or the woman who ran out to save it. His horse reared, slipped, came down on its haunches and slung him into the canal.

Shock took his breath and he went down like a stone. Feebly floundering, he came to the surface, he choked and sank. This cannot possibly be happening, he thought – not to *me*. His arm hurt as something clamped round it, water gave way to air, to sky and towering walls. He was being carried by a man wading; he was being taken hold of and hauled on to the pathway. He tried to complain that they hurt him but instead he convulsed and threw up. Strong hands put him to the water's edge and he spewed into the canal.

He sat back, supported by the hands. Looking down on him were the Marsili brothers, dark against the bright sky. Beyond them, his alarmed friends, holding their horses and his. Beyond them again, a small crowd.

He became aware that the man he still leant on was, almost soundlessly, laughing.

'What noble young drowned rat have I fished out?' a deep amused voice said above his head.

Nono Marsili, hands on knees, brought his gargoyle face closer to peer. 'It's the Doge's son.'

'Drowned rats don't come nobler,' the deep voice said.

Chapter 9

The Republic's Methods

Sigismondo had no difficulty at all in reaching the Doge. Pasquale Scolar was as generous as he was silly, and would not let his rescuer stroll away, as this strange-looking man seemed inclined to do. The two Marsili, he was pleased to find, had business elsewhere as he had absolutely no desire to see more of them. They had witnessed his humiliation. However, he did want his father to reward the man who had jumped into the canal after him.

So Doge Scolar was called out of Council to find his beloved son dripping water on the marble floor, ignoring attendants fussing round him and grasping the sleeve of another who stood sleek with wet, while the sun laid gold through the windows across the swimming floor.

'Pasquale! What's happened?'

'My horse threw me in the canal. He fished me out.' A tug on Sigismondo's sleeve in exposition produced an elegant bow and the Doge, hurrying forward to embrace his son, spared the rescuer a glance.

This was not one of his son's boon companions, not a man to encourage senseless exploits. He'd expect to see this face on a condottiere or in the Grand Council, come to that, a face that had seen and coped with danger. The Doge, having satisfied himself that his son had no injuries but a small bruise, turned to survey the man. Dark, deep-set eyes, a Roman nose, a mouth both full and secretive, and the bare brown head – this was, he suspected, a man he had heard of.

'You are Signor Sigismondo? Agent of the Duke of Rocca?'

'Your Grace. Duke Ludovico is one of the princes for whom I have worked.'

In this disclaimer, the blunt 'for whom I have worked' struck the Doge, whose ear had half-expected 'whom I have had the honour to serve'.

What also struck him was the damp on his brocade gown where he had pressed his son to him. 'Before I can fully thank you, sir, you and my son must be dried and have a change—'

'Father, I must have a wash! A rat nearly swam into my mouth! I shan't feel clean until I've had a pint of wine to take the canal taste away. Come, Sigismondo . . .'

The Doge watched them go, ushered by pages and servants, Pasquale already laughing at his misadventure, the stranger turning at the door to bow. He himself would go and make his excuses to the Council; they would not smile, he knew, until he had left the room. The prodigal son made a habit of returning safely and some of the Council could well have borne it if he never came back at all. Pasquale needed friends who were neither silly nor subservient. If it took only money, this man might be enlisted on his side but there was a subtlety about Sigismondo's face that argued money might never be his main concern. This was a fish to need careful playing.

Sigismondo, washed, dried, and dressed in dry linen and a loose gown of the Doge's of indigo silk, studied, in his turn, the man who once more came forward to take his hand and thank him. Doge Scolar was old indeed to have such a young son. At a guess, he was in his late seventies but still held himself upright without that stoop which makes some old men appear to be looking about for a grave to plunge into. His son's good looks were clearly inherited but the father wore his with dignity, the deep lines only emphasising austerity and strength. He clasped Sigismondo's hand in both his, and then drew him to a window seat, the same from which Nono had glared at a pigeon only hours ago. Perhaps it was the same pigeon that came now to croon and strut on the sill.

'We heard you were in the city, sir.'

Sigismondo smiled as he bent his head. 'I know, your Grace, that nothing escapes the eyes of the Republic, even something as trivial as my presence on its waters.'

'*In*, my dear sir, *in* its waters!' The Doge too could smile; it gave great charm to the lined face. 'And how fortunate for me, when my son was thrown. Neither he nor any of his friends, I believe, can swim. Many, alas, have drowned in our canals or indeed, as he suggested, have choked to death on floating rubbish. I trust you are recovered?'

'Entirely, your Grace; your son bade me tell you he will be delayed.' Sigismondo did not say that Pasquale had been tipping most of a flagon of wine down his throat at the time and showed little haste to get out of the bath of steaming scented water. The Doge's fleeting smile showed he understood perfectly.

'All the better, Signor Sigismondo. There are things I wish to ask you.'

A silence followed, while the Doge examined his rings and Sigismondo sat quite still, a silence broken only by the foolish noise of the pigeon, which had inflated its chest to impress the female who sat at the end of the sill, looking over the city. He strutted up and down, his spread tail rustling on the stone, crooning with passion and optimism.

The Doge looked up, his eyes pale in their nest of wrinkles. 'Are you here to work for Duke Ludovico?'

Sigismondo shrugged and turned his hands palm upward. 'As I have explained, your Grace—'

'Are you working for anyone here in Venice?'

'I am employed privately at the moment.'

'You are investigating the Ermolin murder.'

This might be either a guess or a statement. Sigismondo said nothing, and the Doge laughed. 'Vettor Darin told me this morning when he came to report his son-in-law's death. A dreadful affair, but I cannot be as surprised as it would seem to warrant. Niccolo Ermolin was not given to sparing the feelings of others – some men come to eminence by treading on the faces of those they deal with. Have you formed an idea of how the assassin reached him?'

'At the moment, your Grace, it is in doubt. Someone may have climbed up from below, or from the canal. There is a landing stage below, from which someone might ascend without too much difficulty to the balcony next to the window of Lord Ermolin's study. His son climbed across from there when Lord Darin could get no answer at the study door. As for being seen, the side canal seems little frequented and there is only a convent opposite, with few windows.'

The Doge was shaking his head, as though Sigismondo's words implied more than they seemed to. 'That boy Marco – a friend of my son's, to my son's disadvantage.' He paused, and fixed Sigismondo with the pale eyes. 'You don't, I hope, suspect Marco.' He might well feel that a conviction for murder would efficiently subtract Marco from Pasquale's side.

Sigismondo sustained the Doge's gaze with gravity. 'Does your Grace know of a reason for Lord Marco to wish for his father's death?'

The Doge returned to examining his rings. 'Oh – rumours. Rumours. My son tells me Marco is always short of money; but what young man is not?' He waved the matter away, perhaps taking for granted that Sigismondo would have heard of Pasquale's sensational skill in squandering his own father's money. 'But I am sure you will not have to look far. Niccolo Ermolin's enemies have scarcely concealed their hatred.'

'Your Grace knows of many?'

The Doge had intended to question rather than to be questioned. He raised his eyebrows and held up the gnarled ringed hands helplessly. 'All Venice knows of one at least: Pico Gamboni has not ceased to abuse Ermolin since his own fortune failed. You'll find many who'll tell you about it.'

Doge Scolar rose, and Sigismondo stood to face him, tall in the glowing dark blue. He had no chain or rings, unlike the man opposite, with his gold-worked brocade, hat of office bordered with gold thread, and his laden hands, yet he had a presence the Doge seemed to find intimidating for he

41

stepped back. He gave his hand, with the Doge's ring, and as Sigismondo bent to kiss it the Doge said, suddenly as if the words were forced from him, 'Remember, the Republic does not permit its citizens to bring it into disrepute.'

Benno, with this casually reported to him, exclaimed, 'What's he mean by that, then? He can't have been warning you not to do anything dodgy. You're not a citizen, you're a visitor. Why'd he say that?'

'It's likely,' said Sigismondo, strange to Benno's eyes in the indigo silk, and incongruous against the hired boat's dingy cushions, 'it's possible he was hinting that the Republic itself might have got rid of Ermolin.'

Benno had learnt to row only a year or so ago. His next stroke missed the water completely and he fell backwards on to the wet bundle of Sigismondo's own clothes. Biondello gave a solitary bark.

Chapter 10

No Secrets?

'You don't mean the Doge had it done?'

Sigismondo watched Benno scramble back to his place and reassemble the oars. A long hum preceded his reply.

'. . . mmm! You don't know about the Doge. He wears a very pretty cap and he marries the sea with a great big ring but he has not much to do with what the Serene Republic decides. He has a vote, of course, and influence.'

Benno, aware of the echo from the tall houses close on either side of this dark canal, dropped his voice to a murmur and timed his question to go with his forward swing. 'Would they,' he had an idea of shadowy people behind the Doge, working him like a puppet, 'would they kill anyone like that? I mean,' he gestured towards his left eye and nearly lost the oar, 'like *that*? Wouldn't he just be executed the usual way?'

'In this city, justice doesn't always have to be seen, only known. If the Ten want to make a splash, you'd notice.'

'The Ten?' Benno's picture of the Doge's puppeteers multiplied out of control.

Sigismondo put a finger to his lips, but he was smiling. 'That's not a question you ask here, Benno, but I'll pass on to you a Venetian saying: "The Ten send you to the torture chamber; the Three, to your grave". Hey, steer to the right!'

Benno looked over his shoulder and struggled valiantly, assailed by shouting from the boat he scraped past, that was unloading at a small landing stage. The boatman and the house servants were free with speculations about Benno's parentage, a matter on which he happened to be as ignorant as they were but far more optimistic; happily the full power of their aspersions was lost on him because of the Venetian accent. They knew him immediately as a foreigner and an idiot, which made his handling of the boat, though not excusable, natural. The torrent of coarse jokes checked suddenly when they took in Benno's passenger. Impossible to tell what kind of man this was, rowed by a halfwit in a boat without pretensions to smartness, but there was that about his calm look, not to mention his build in the gown of indigo silk, that silenced the words on their lips. Sigismondo's question as to their livery received a respectful answer. Benno rowed on, sweating, until he managed to turn the corner, reasonably neatly, out of the little side canal.

The front of the house whose side door they had passed presented a very different show. Marble engaged pillars supported an arch with a stone shield held aloft by a pair of grim gryphons. On the shield flew some kind of bird looking as though he'd had a close escape from their claws. The huge oak doors beneath the arch stood open, and liveried servants on the landing stage were helping two women from the bright-painted gondola that lay there. Sigismondo signalled to Benno to hold place where they were, and Benno, idling oars, looked over his shoulder and saw the women; one not young, tall and commanding, rich in burgundy brocade, her grey hair braided under gold-edged gauze. The other, disdaining a helping hand, skipping up the steps with little care for her embroidered slippers, was only a girl, flinging back her travelling veil. Her hair was red, a colour Benno was beginning to associate with Venetian women, and it was in the latest style, many slender plaits twisted with silver threads into a coronet, and long crimped waves over her shoulders.

Both of them disappeared through the doors without looking round, and Benno was sorry, for he thought the girl well worth a stare. The servants unloading luggage at the side door had said that this was the Ca' Darin, home to the lord who had commissioned Sigismondo. Sigismondo, with that eerie sense of the geography of a place that seemed natural to him, had known where he was directing Benno to go.

The gondola moved, Benno took its place and Sigismondo, gown reefed, stepped on to the marble and strode forward.

'Is my lord Darin at home?'

'Who is it who asks?'

Sigismondo was once more presenting a problem. He had arrived in a very ordinary boat, powered by a gaping halfwit and with a very small and dirty one-eared dog peering over the side; at the same time he was unmistakably not someone you could dismiss, and wore a gown fine enough for the Doge himself. The servant altered his question. 'In what way can I help you, sir? My master is not at home.'

'Enquire if your mistress will receive me.'

The man held the door for a moment, nonplussed by this unorthodox proposal from a stranger, but before he could refuse or question further, a voice from indoors, gaining resonance from the size of the hall, called out and the man turned. Sigismondo, stepping past him, made his bow.

'Sigismondo, at your service, my lady. I am here to report to the Lord Vettor.'

'Report? On what?' Dark eyes, lively under dark brows, surveyed him with both interest and surprise. Perhaps those who came to report to her husband came by the backstairs, failed to wear gowns of indigo silk of a quality Lord Vettor himself would wear, and had heads with orthodox covering.

'My lady, may we speak in private?'

'Grandmama!' The girl with the cloud of red hair was leaning over the stairs' elaborate ironwork and studying the unexpected stranger. Benno had been right; she was worth looking at. The older woman was handsome, the girl startlingly pretty. That hair was not wasted as a frame for the pale, pointed face, faintly strewn with freckles even rice powder could not conceal. The huge dark eyes still examined Sigismondo. Girls of good family did not see many men not related to them and she was making the most of this chance.

Her grandmother made an imperious gesture that said: Get out of sight. However, she turned to Sigismondo with quite an amiable look.

'Very well. We will take wine upstairs. First, I shall change the clothes I have travelled in. We come from my sister's villa over the lagoon, a tedious journey, sir, threading channels in the mud.'

Sigismondo, who had experienced this, bowed again, and watched her sweep up the stairs. Two maids detached themselves eagerly from the bustle of welcoming servants and followed her, saying in urgent undertones, 'My lady – my lady . . .' A man in livery approached Sigismondo to escort him up the stairs and leave him in the great reception room on the first floor. He stood there in one of the window alcoves, looking down at Benno who had made fast to one of the striped poles topped with a gryphon. Next to the magnificently painted gondola the boat looked like Biondello next to a wolfhound. Benno, unconscious of his master's gaze, was listening to one of the liveried servants who was pointing along the canal. Sigismondo smiled. Benno would be making out quite enough from the Venetian dialect spoken, as Sigismondo could just hear, very loudly and slowly to this obvious lackwit. Biondello, a minute object at this distance, sighted Sigismondo and his single bark, magnified by the house walls, made the servant jump and all but lose his footing.

The doors' opening made Sigismondo turn.

'If you are the bearer of bad news, sir,' the mistress of the house was regal; now in black damask, but with sadness in face and voice, 'you are too late. Servants are like rats that run from house to house and feed on what they can pick up. My husband will have heard your news; he went to the Palazzo Ermolin this morning, so I am told, to call on our son-in-law.'

A servant entered with wine and small cakes, and addressed her. 'Donna Claudia, Lady Beatrice is in great distress.'

'I know.' Donna Claudia dismissed the servant with an

impatient flick of the hand. 'Of course I will come as soon as I can. Look after the poor child.'

The servant went out, the maid poured wine, offered the cakes, and withdrew to stand by the door.

Donna Claudia sat, and beckoned Sigismondo closer. 'What's your news, sir? My husband has no secrets from me.'

A sudden unfocusing of her eyes suggested this might be more wish than fact, but Sigismondo showed nothing but willing belief. 'My lady, I come from the Palazzo Ermolin on hearing that Lord Vettor is not there. He has commissioned me to enquire into the murder of Lord Ermolin this morning. I am here to tell him what I have found so far.'

'You were there! Did you see—' She hesitated, probably over the picture that presented itself. 'I hear he was – mutilated.' Her hand sketched a movement. 'The eye?'

'I fear so, my lady. And in the neck.'

'Dreadful!' She rose and swung away, pacing down the room, her silks sighing along the marble. 'Dreadful! Who could have hated him so?' She turned and came back, the tips of her fingers to her temples as if she tried to conjure such enemies to mind. 'Of course he was ruthless in his dealings – what successful man is not? But . . . enemies?' She halted, and stared into the distance, then shook her head. 'Oh no. No, that's not possible.'

'May I ask, my lady? What is it you find impossible?'

'That a madman should have killed Niccolo. Yet,' she touched her eyelid, 'it was surely the act of a madman.'

'It would need a determined madman to climb up from below and attack one who had done him no harm. Easier to stab someone in the street, surely.'

'But what if he thought Niccolo *had* done him harm?'

'Tell me who this madman is, my lady.'

She was pacing away from him again, shaking her head so that the gilt-edged gauze shimmered on the grey braids, while he stood still, not a movement betraying impatience. As she passed one of the windows, her attention was distracted by shouts below, and she paused to look.

'My husband is here. You will be able to ask him anything you want to know.'

Sigismondo bowed. He had been within an inch of hearing what Lord Vettor might not choose to tell him.

Chapter 11

A Glut Of Suspects

Lord Vettor came in with his arm round his granddaughter's shoulders; he had evidently not been told there was a stranger waiting to see him and that Donna Claudia had therefore banished Beatrice to the private rooms. The girl was tearstained, very pale, and looking paler for the black dress she had put on. Lord Vettor released her, giving her a little push towards his wife, and turned to Sigismondo. His balding dome and round greenish eyes gave an impression of a series of circles; he spoke without much opening his mouth, as if he were wary of allowing words to escape.

'Have you news for me, sir?'

'I came to ask, my lord, for further help in the matter. Donna Claudia was about to tell me of one who might have wished Lord Ermolin dead.'

Vettor turned to his wife enquiringly. She might have read reproof in his look, for she said with raised eyebrows, 'Indeed, I was thinking only of Pico Gamboni.'

Vettor laughed, and seemed almost pleased. 'Gamboni? Yes. He has been telling the world for years that he wanted Niccolo dead. What brainstorm might have caused him to make his wish come true?'

'But,' Donna Claudia had taken her chair again and Beatrice leant against the arm of it. The shimmer of her hair showed that she was trembling, and her grandmother captured one of her hands, 'Pico would know people would at once think of him.'

'My lady, the most likely suspect is sometimes the right one. What cause had Pico Gamboni for hatred?'

Husband and wife exchanged glances, but it was Lady Beatrice who burst out with, 'He said my father had put a curse on him! He blamed everything that happened to him, everything that went wrong with him, on my father!'

Donna Claudia rose, took her granddaughter's pale, tearstained face between her hands and kissed it tenderly.

'Go, my child. These matters are not for you. Go to the chapel. Pray for your father.'

The girl submitted to the kiss pressed again on her forehead, but then broke from her grandmother's hands, darted to Sigismondo and looked up into his face.

'Find who killed my father and *kill* him. Show no mercy. *Kill him!*'

Donna Claudia hurried over and reached for her hand, but she whirled round and rushed past and out of the room.

Vettor clicked his tongue. 'You must excuse her, sir. She is young, and loved her father as dearly as he loved her.'

Impossible not to think she seemed to be one of the few who did. Her brother Marco had not shown any amazing grief that morning. Perhaps, where a son may be disciplined, it is the happy fortune of a daughter – in particular a pretty one – to be petted. Sigismondo bowed in answer but took up his question.

'This Pico Gamboni, my lord. He is in the city? He would have had opportunity to commit the murder?'

'Certainly. We would have been informed if he had left.'

This was a chilling reminder of the continual watch the Republic kept on its citizens, a circumstance which made it all the more remarkable that an outside agent such as Sigismondo had been called in, even by a member of the victim's family. Lord Vettor went on, 'I cannot tell you where he lives but he can be seen daily in the Piazza, begging.'

'Begging?'

Donna Claudia flung up expressive hands. 'Begging! He claims he is ruined, that Niccolo ruined him. It is senseless! What happened to him could happen to anyone. His son goes abroad on business, leaves heavy gambling debts for his father to discover—'

'So that when Gamboni's ships come in, they are sold to pay these debts.' Vettor overrode his wife's voice, shaking his head. He took his wife's hand and patted it as she began to speak. 'The son dies of plague at a distant city, then Gamboni's wife dies – of grief, he proclaims, though she had been ill already – and to cap it all, Gamboni's house burns down.'

Sigismondo looked from one to the other, from the little bald man to his tall, dignified wife.

'And he said this was all the fault of Lord Ermolin? A comprehensive curse indeed.'

'You see how mad he is?' The black silk sleeves gleamed as Donna Claudia flung her hands wide. 'He wanders the streets, telling anyone he meets how Niccolo ruined him.'

'Most of them know by now,' interrupted Vettor drily. 'He even accused Niccolo to the Ten.'

From Donna Claudia's sharp glance at him, she had not heard this before, and her husband went on, 'Of course, no notice was taken. He was not even called on to answer for a false accusation; one does not treat a man crazed by grief as one would any other.' He took a step towards Sigismondo; the round eyes were still inexpressive but the voice had hardened. 'Perhaps notice should be taken.'

Sigismondo bowed. Vettor waited as if he thought more acknowledgement would be made, but then nodded and turned to his wife. 'My dear, I meant to tell you – Isabella will not be coming here as I had hoped. She wishes to stay where she is, certainly until after the funeral, but she is quite happy for Beatrice to remain with us.'

'I shall go and see her. Poor child! So recently married.' It was to be wondered how this strong-minded woman got on with the seventeen-year-old who had taken her own dead daughter's place.

Vettor spoke now to Sigismondo in the quick tones of one who has much to do. 'I must leave soon. Attilio da Castagna comes this afternoon to be given command of the Fleet against the Turk. I have to be in the Basilica for the service. Continue your efforts, sir, to find the murderer. Justice, justice must be done! If you go abroad in the city you'll find plenty who can help you. And even, I hear,' the mouth twitched into a smile that left the greenish eyes cold, 'those *you* can help. The Doge himself owes you a favour, I believe.'

'I was fortunate in being at hand.'

'Pasquale Scolar,' Vettor addressed his wife, who had shown alert interest at a possible story, 'is thrown into a canal – by a horse, my dear, merely by his horse . . .'

'Ridden as he usually rides, I suppose.'

'I've no doubt. And he is pulled out by this man here. Spared to plague his father yet more. Well, sir,' the smile finally reached the eyes, 'our good deeds cannot bring luck to all. Perhaps you were meant to bring death rather than life to someone else. I will see you later today.'

'My lord, I shall report to you anything worth your hearing. Then you will see me.' The deep voice was firm and Vettor blinked in surprise at being informed what was to happen rather than ordering it himself. After a moment's pause he kissed his wife's cheek and, with a nod to Sigismondo's bow, left the room.

Donna Claudia stood tapping her lips with a finger consideringly. As Sigismondo approached to take his leave, she gave him her hand and said, 'Attilio da Castagna is not the only one to come to the city to receive command. The maids tell me the Marsili brothers have been visiting the Great Council. Do you know them?'

Sigismondo did not say that he had undoubtedly been reported, as eating with them in a tavern, to those who kept tabs on strangers in the city. He merely smiled and nodded, so she went on, 'I do not know if you are a friend of theirs or not, but I should tell you that Nono Marsili had reason to dislike my son-in-law.'

'Indeed, my lady? Why was that?'

'It's too absurd, really it is, as absurd in its way as Pico Gamboni. You may not know, sir, that the boy you rescued, Pasquale Scolar, was married a few months ago and his poor bride – now, alas, dead – was attended, in procession and so on, by the usual number of ladies of good birth, my granddaughter among them. Well . . .' she made a careless gesture as if disclaiming her obvious pride in the girl, 'you've seen her yourself. Shortly after this, Niccolo was paid a visit.'

She almost laughed. 'Nono Marsili came to offer for Beatrice's hand. Of course, he had no idea, not being a Venetian. The man's a famous condottiere, it's true, and rich on all the loot he has acquired, but his family! Peasants, every last one, and Nono himself what he is. I'm afraid Niccolo told him.'

She bit her lip, smiling, and Sigismondo raised his eyebrows. 'Told him . . .'

'Niccolo informed us that he had felt enraged by this insult to the family. He told Nono Marsili flatly that the Ermolin did not marry peasants and did not marry dwarves, nor did he wish for deformed grandchildren . . . I think perhaps he was unnecessarily harsh. Nono stormed out, apparently, vowing that Niccolo would live to regret his words.'

There was silence for a minute, while both probably contemplated the bizarre image of Nono clambering up to the study window to plant the lethal blow in what must have been a very surprised eye. Then at a signal from Donna Claudia, the maid opened the door. Sigismondo bent over the ringed hand and left her.

Benno unshipped his oars at the sight of his master being bowed out of the great oak door under the stone gryphons. Sigismondo stepped into the boat and sat, looking thoughtful, and Biondello jumped into his lap with no deference for indigo silk.

The thoughtful look did not invite questions and so Benno put out into the canal without any idea of how many more suspects had joined the list.

Chapter 12

Head Of The Family

When the man chosen by the Republic to lead her fleets goes to the Basilica for investment with his staff of office, Venice has, and does not miss, an opportunity for display.

There was the canopy of scarlet and gold, wavering somewhat in the grasp of four priests in vestments dazzling with gold thread. There were gowns of brocade, velvet, satin, gold-embroidered, jewelled, furred; hats of silk, fur and brocade, turbans, hats with dagged scarves, wide-brimmed, brimless; brooches, chains, rings, armlets, glittering belts. Overhead, banners shimmered in the hot air. The drums and fifes sounded.

The audience for all this, on its passage round the Piazza, was international. Word would go back home as far as the snows of Scotland and of Muscovy, to the Most Christian King of France, the Emperor in Germany, the Sultan of Turkey and, nearer but vitally important, the Pope in Rome, that the Serenissima could not be matched for magnificence. Every Venetian knew the importance of ceremonies that looked as if fortunes had been spent on them whether the fortunes were there or not. This particular procession had all the confidence that only thousands of ducats could confer.

On their way back to the Palazzo Ermolin, which Benno found to his relief, for his arms were aching, not to be far, he and Sigismondo had caught glimpses, tantalising at the end of canals, and on bridges and in passing gondolas, of crowds on their way to view the procession. Benno was resigned to missing the fun and waiting outside the palazzo, helped by the thought that if the grand folk had first to march round the Piazza, as Sigismondo said, and then attend a Mass, it would take some time and they might catch the procession on its way back. He was keen to see the Doge. So far all he had seen was one of his gowns, capably filled by Sigismondo.

As it happened, when the Ermolin servant, a depressed but dignified old man in livery, tied up the boat, Benno could catch a side-angled view of the Piazzetta in the distance, filled with people, and he heard the sound of fife and drum on the breeze. He held up Biondello to have a look while Sigismondo, imposing in indigo still, was admitted indoors.

A servant ushered him into a room decorated with frescoes of nymphs and satyrs at play, and, asking him to wait there, said he would inform Lord Rinaldo of his arrival. The long windows were open and the tattoo of the drum and shrill of the fife was carried to Sigismondo's ears too as the procession got under way. The servant crossed the room and tapped at a door leading off it, emerging after a moment to say that the Lord Rinaldo would shortly be at liberty; then he went about his business, but the sound of a raised, angry voice beyond told that he had neglected to close the door completely. Sigismondo silently crossed the marble floor to stand close to the door and, by the lightest of pressures, open it a fraction more.

'Let me tell you,' and as usual with this introduction the second speaker did not wait for the permission he seemed to request, 'that you are incapable of taking over from your father.' This voice was incisive, not raised. 'You to stand in his place! You have no grasp whatever of the business.'

'Whose fault is that, I'd like to know? If Father—'

'*Your* fault, without question. Your father did his best to inform and instruct you, with more patience than I would give to the matter, but he was wasting his time, for you never listened.'

The curt disdain made the other voice become more shrill.

'Of course I listened! The whole thing was complicated and deadly boring—'

'Then why trouble with it? Leave it in my hands where it belongs. As your father's partner I knew all his dealings—'

'Even those in his secret book?'

'I assure you it is unlikely, to a degree, that he would keep anything of importance from me.'

'Then why hadn't you a key to it?' Marco's voice taunted. 'Father didn't trust you any more than—'

There was a scuffle, a yelp, and a thud as someone stumbled backwards and landed against the door, closing it with an unmistakable click.

Sigismondo was at the window, craning out of it to catch a sight of the activity on the Piazzetta, when after a moment the door abruptly opened and Rinaldo Ermolin surveyed the room. He had to call twice before he could attract Sigismondo's attention.

'Your pardon, my lord. I came to ask if I might be allowed a further look at the room where Lord Niccolo was found. I should like to get a better idea of how close the workmen's rope is to the window, from the inside.'

This was, as they both knew, the room from which Rinaldo had just come. Rinaldo hesitated, perhaps seeking any reason why Sigismondo should not examine the room. His expression showed that he would like to think of one, but then with a sudden half-smile he flung open the study door and gestured to Sigismondo to enter.

Marco had not expected this. He was bent over the table, tinkering with something there, and as the door opened he swung round, eyes wide and mouth compressed.

In his hand was a small gold key on a thin green cord and, on the table, a book bound in red leather. This was all seen in one moment before Rinaldo thrust past Sigismondo and snatched the key from Marco's hand. They glared at one another, for that second oblivious of the stranger's presence.

Through the open window which had that morning perhaps admitted an assassin, came distant shouts and cheering and the bray of trumpets as the Doge made his appearance; as though brought to their senses by this, uncle and nephew turned to stare at Sigismondo.

Anything they might have said was forestalled by a tapping that made both start and wheel to look at what Sigismondo, a second before, had been observing with interest. A man in a dirty red cap was swinging gently to and fro outside the window, sitting comfortably like a gargantuan baby in a shield-sized basket slung from the rope above. Steadying himself with a foot to the sill he smiled cheerfully and, now that he had their attention, he took off his cap, releasing a shock of tousled black hair.

'Begging your pardon, sirs, but the tiles is done. Was you wanting that parapet stonework seen to, or is it to wait another day? If it was, me and my mates'd be in time to see his Grace and the Captain-General come out of church.'

He grinned hopefully, the dirty red cap crushed to his chest, the other hand grasping the rope. Sigismondo, by the door, was smiling. The other two were not amused.

'Be off with you.' Rinaldo made a thrusting gesture which, had it been near enough to connect, would have swung the workman perilously out over the canal. 'Ask the major-domo! Don't come interrupting your betters.'

'Right you are, m'lord.' The man's smile had not dimmed. The cap went back on his head with a flourish, he looked up and whistled piercingly between two fingers and descended out of sight, still smiling as if grand folk never ceased to entertain.

'With your permission, my lord.' Sigismondo's voice, not yet free from amusement, drew Rinaldo's gaze. 'I'd like to question that man before he goes. If he was on the roof this morning . . .'

'Do what you will.' Lord Rinaldo's face was flushed, as with repressed anger. 'Lord Darin wished you to make enquiries, but now I am head of the family—'

'*I* am the one who gives orders now in my father's house!' Marco's hair had fallen over his brow, making him look absurdly young and at a disadvantage.

Rinaldo asked scornfully, 'And what *orders* do you give?'

Marco hesitated and then, pressing the red book to him as if for inspiration, he said in a rush, 'Find my father's murderer. You should not have to look far.'

Chapter 13

They Don't Like Failures

Luckily for Sigismondo, the workman had been delayed by the grudging major-domo. Biondello, standing at the boat's prow like a mascot, the strengthening breeze blowing his one ear back like a tiny banner, drew the man at once to pat him, scratch his head and ask questions of Benno, even though his mates had packed tools and left in a hurry to watch the procession. If Sigismondo was pleased to see the workman, Benno was pleased to see Sigismondo. The slurring Venetian dialect was still giving him some difficulty in understanding the man, though Biondello was having no trouble at all.

The workman in his turn was pleased, with the coin Sigismondo gave him. He had little information – had heard about the murder, of course, who hadn't – and was only anxious to ensure that he and his mates were not suspected.

'You were working on the roof this morning? In the front here? Had you a view of the canal and the craft on it?'

The man removed his cap to scratch his head, tilting it to look at the roof. 'This side we was working, not the other, over that window where you just saw me. And Zeno, he went up to look at the parapet where a bit of the stonework's crumbled.'

'Did he get to it through the house?'

'Nah, that major-domo thinks you make the house dusty by looking at it. Zeno went be the rope same's the rest of us.'

A prolonged bray of trumpets here made Biondello yelp and the man turn to look longingly towards the Piazza.

'Row us there?' Sigismondo held up another coin. In no time they were being swept at a surprising rate, along between the houses and out on the Grand Canal. The procession had made its circuit of only half the Piazza by the time they arrived. The workman leapt ashore and was lost in the crowd.

'Come on or you'll miss the Doge,' Sigismondo adjured Benno as he tied the boat up. 'I can't promise to rescue his son every day.' Benno saw Sigismondo's noticeable head moving forwards in the throng and followed, oblivious of shoves, shielding Biondello's place in his bosom with one arm. He came up with Sigismondo near the front of the crowd.

Benno's curiosity was wholly satisfied by his sight of the Doge, dignified, covered in gold. He was sorry for the old man having to trail around under his canopy with trumpets going off in his ears. The man who had just been made Captain-General of the Venetian Fleet looked, conversely, as if it would take a very great deal to tire him. As he passed, acknowledging the shouts of the crowd, Attilio da Castagna, as if he felt one gaze more than the rest, turned his head to look back. Benno knew quite well he was invisible to most people, but this time he had the disconcerting sense that the dark, keen gaze, sweeping over him before it came to rest on Sigismondo, had taken him in as well. The face was stern, not without humour if the lines round the mouth and at the eye's corner were anything to go by, and the general look suggested a man of vitality, of great resources, tough mentally as he was physically. Benno reckoned that the Turks had a nasty shock coming to them.

One thing that made the face, so briefly turned to them, sinister besides tough, was a black eyepatch. If this man had lost an eye to a Turk, thought Benno, they'd do well to look out. As he was thinking this, the man's good eye closed in an unmistakable wink and the gilded baton that proclaimed the holder Captain-General of the Venetian Fleet was raised in a salute, to Sigismondo.

'You know him then?' Benno at his master's shoulder spoke upwards as the procession moved slowly past, dignified men in red silk with grave expressions, the shrieks and clamour of the crowd plainly beneath their power to hear, in a superior domain where little dogs did not stare at them out of peasants' jerkins.

What Sigismondo might have replied was lost in another blare of trumpets, but he nodded. Benno supposed that Attilio da Castagna was like others who had met, and fought beside, or against, Sigismondo at some time. It didn't seem to matter which; respect and a kindly feeling seemed to result from either. Benno had also got used to a number of aliases by which these men had known Sigismondo, and it had made him wonder what his master's real name might be. And if Sigismondo had stuck to fighting instead of amusing himself finding out who murdered people, he might well by now have been chosen like this Attilio to lead a fleet for the Venetians.

He found out later that this might not be quite the good idea it seemed. In their lodgings, Benno was handing Sigismondo a clean shirt and, taking the gown of indigo silk to wrap it carefully away, happened to remark, 'What with the Doge grateful to you and all, reckon *you* could've had that baton if you'd wanted.'

Sigismondo's laugh was muffled in the folds of the shirt he was pulling on, but he was still smiling when Benno handed him his plain black doublet from the pack lying open on the bed.

'You have to do rather more than pull a highborn youth out of a canal to earn that. More like winning a few battles for a start. Or at least helping to win them.'

'I thought Venice lost the last battle with the Turks?'

'Oh, she did, she did.' Sigismondo stood while Benno tied the black cord drawstring at the shirt's neck and started lacing the doublet. 'I advise you as you go around to avoid mention of the fact. Attilio da Castagna – and that's not the name *I* knew him by – didn't lose that battle or he would not have been honoured with that delightful procession.'

61

'Somebody did lose it, though?' Benno chivied Biondello out of the pack, which he was excavating as a possible bed. 'Somebody was in charge, right?'

'In charge, then. In prison, now.'

'In prison? The Turks got him? I thought they cut up their captives, like. In pieces, someone said. Or – isn't it called impaling?' Benno felt suddenly sick at the thought. Even animals put on a spit were dead first. Sigismondo gave a long, thoughtful hum.

'No. He's in prison here. He won't be impaled if he's found guilty, the Serene Republic is too civilised for that, and he *was* a Captain-General after all. I'd put my money on a simple beheading.'

'Beheading? What for? Did he betray them to the Turks?'

Sigismondo was threading his fine leather belt through the loops on his falchion's hanger. He looked up with a smile.

'Hey, he lost the battle, Benno. He was a *failure*. The Venetians don't like failures. That's a good reason why we'd better find out who killed Niccolo Ermolin quite fast, before they start thinking of me as one.'

Chapter 14

Family Council

'But should we have a family council without my grandfather?'

Marco's question was directed rather at his uncle than at his stepmother, and Rinaldo answered more pleasantly than he would have done if Isabella had not been sitting there, her ivory face framed by black gauze over black braids twisted with pearls.

'Vettor is busy with the reception for the Captain-General, while we have urgent matters to discuss. We can let him know of our decision later.'

Isabella held a cat on her lap, white and tortoiseshell against her black silk, and she was stroking it, but she spared a glance for Rinaldo and the remark, 'He's not an Ermolin. Do we have to wait for his approval?'

'His daughter became an Ermolin, as you did.' Rinaldo held her eyes for a moment. 'He's allied to our interests. Were your parents alive, they would have the same place in our councils but, alas!' He looked down at his hands, cutting off the glance, and she was silent, her hand still smoothing the cat's head. Her parents had succumbed, shortly before her marriage, to food-poisoning, which had carried off her old nurse as well, who had eaten of the left-overs. Her father had never been able to resist shellfish, even from the lagoon where it was well known they fed off the bodies of those the Republic sent there to be strangled, or left tied to stakes to drown. She had only a brother to protect her interests as a widow, a brother who had never liked her and who had already sent his excuses, for the official reception required his presence. An aristocrat might get murdered but the Republic expected those not of his immediate family to fulfil their duties regardless.

Her brother was quite likely to feel his duty to her fulfilled by getting her into a convent. A young widow without children might not be welcome in her husband's family and would not easily find a second husband when so many highborn Venetians chose to remain bachelors.

'Never fear.' Marco had leant forward and was smiling up into her face. 'We shall look after you. You'll want for nothing.'

His attempt to put his hand on the hand stroking the cat was not taken well: the cat hissed at him. Rinaldo regarded them as if this reassurance were too warm to be diplomatic. Widows are usually forced to want for quite a few things.

'What is necessary to consider is your father's wishes.' Rinaldo's tone was repressive and it reminded Marco that all their speculation and any encouragement of Isabella was wasted until they knew what was in Niccolo's will. To Marco's fury, when he had returned that morning from arranging Masses for his father's soul with Father Domenico, and inspected the laying-out of his father's body, he had been unable to look for this will. The door of the study had been ajar. It had given him a strange feeling: here was a room he had hardly entered in his life, which contained his father's treasures, now as unprotected as the body he had just left.

He forgot this feeling when he went in, for there was his uncle, turning that austere face on him. His uncle had evidently found the will, too, for here it was, under that long hand decorated only with the family signet ring.

'I should be the one to read that! Give it me!'

To his surprise, Rinaldo, smiling slightly, did. Marco wrestled with the seal, finally breaking the wax off with his dagger. He was conscious that his father had pressed his big seal ring on that wax – a ring he had taken care to remove straight away that morning; some things, at least, no one would dispute with him.

The parchment crackled as he unfolded it, and Isabella's cat rose to peer at the cause of this sound. For a moment, Marco could hardly read the notary's beautiful script because his eyes refused to clear. This could be the end to his problems, the beginning of his freedom, of his proper adulthood. He began to read. His uncle's sardonic voice interrupted.

'Out loud, please, Marco. We all wish to hear.'

Marco began again, impatiently, hurrying through the commendations to the Virgin, the solemn assurances of his father's desire to look after his dependants, to stand justified before the throne of God. What had he left to those dependants?

'. . . To my beloved wife Isabella, if she should have no issue by me . . .' Absurd, for if she had, this will would have been the first thing to have been altered . . . 'her widow's portion of my estate and the jewelry and clothes she brought with her as her dowry'. Neat, that, but mean. Now, *here* we are: 'To my dear son Marco, a hundred thousand ducats—'

A hundred thousand? Only a hundred thousand? Marco faltered and then, his eyes reading on, his voice stopped altogether.

'What then, Nephew?'

Marco sat, staring at the table, while Rinaldo twitched the document out of his hands, found the place, and continued smoothly. 'To my brother Rinaldo, partner with me in my enterprises, the family business to control as he sees fit, for the purpose of the preservation of the name and fortunes of the Ermolin for my children and my children's children—'

'It's not fair!' Marco gripped his head between his hands as if to hold in thoughts that made his brain seem ready to explode. 'I'm his son! *I* should control the family business!'

Isabella had not ceased to stroke the cat, even when her own clothes and jewelry were kindly allotted to her, and now she turned her gaze from Marco to Rinaldo as if expecting the next move in a play; something about her mouth suggesting that it was a comedy, at that.

Rinaldo had assumed a kindly smile. 'You must bring to mind, nephew, our city's customs. For your father's sake, for your sake, I renounced marriage and the hope of children in order to devote myself to furthering the prosperity and the reputation of the Ermolins. Your grandfather's brother did the same. Is it not fair, then, that I should continue to serve the family as your father and I long ago agreed that I should?'

Both Rinaldo and Isabella watched Marco snatch his hands out of his hair and shake his head. The rage in the childishly handsome face had given way to despair, the large dark eyes filled with tears he tried to hold back, to ignore.

'Your portion's larger than mine.' No sympathy came from Isabella. His uncle, however, appeared concerned.

'Surely a hundred thousand ducats is generous. You must consider how much you will have at interest. I will not offer to advise you on it, since it is yours to control, but the interest will bring an income not to be despised. And don't forget you will have more.' He tapped the document under his hand. 'Your father told me, and it will be recorded here, that he arranged for an additional and liberal allowance when you are married.' He picked up the will and was beginning to read when Marco leapt up, crashing both fists on the table. The cat fled.

'No! No! I will *not* marry Maria Gondi. You, Uncle, since you are in charge of our fortunes,' the sneer was too obvious to be effective, 'I authorise you to break off the negotiations forthwith.'

Rinaldo looked at him a moment in silence. Isabella, her hands now folded in her lap, did the same.

'And, Nephew, your reasons? They will have to be good ones. The Gondi are in the Golden Book, they are rich, she will have an excellent dowry—'

'She's twice my size and as ugly as a monkey. Why should I – how *can* I – marry what no one could desire?' His eyes as if without intention were directed towards Isabella's pale, cool face. 'To live without love?'

'Marco.' The hard voice now had a smooth sweetness. 'Marriage is not where one looks for love. Your pardon, sister,' he said across the table. 'It may lead to love, in due course, but young men can and do pursue their desires elsewhere. You know that.'

After a short silence, 'There is another marriage to be thought of.' Rinaldo glanced down at the will again. 'Niccolo left very detailed instructions about Beatrice's dowry.' The narrow, watchful eyes regarded both faces. 'What we shall soon find out is how the world regards us after this murder. We may hope no one fears to be linked with the Ermolins because of some feud or evil luck.'

Isabella asked, in a tone of polite curiosity, as if the victim had not been the husband whom she had seen only that morning, 'Who do you think did it?'

'That madman Gamboni?'

'Why wait all these years?' Marco demanded. He had turned away from them and spoke to the floor. 'This can't be the first day my father left the study window open.'

'It may be the first day that there was a rope hanging by the window.'

'The answer,' said Isabella coolly, 'lies in Zenobia's keys, as I told that bravo whom Vettor hired.' A sound between indignation and contempt came from Rinaldo. She went on, 'Niccolo may perfectly well have been mistaken in thinking only he could unlock his study door.'

Marco swung round suddenly, shock on his face. 'You don't think – you can't think of Zenobia?'

'Of Zenobia,' observed Rinaldo, 'I would repeat what you said of Gamboni: why, after all these years? Has she spent these years planning revenge on my brother for sending away their son?'

Isabella raised her eyebrows. 'Isn't revenge worth waiting for?'

Rinaldo thoughtfully flattened the parchment under his hands. 'It's true,' he said, scanning it and placing a finger on a name, 'he left her son some money. Not a great deal, but some. Zenobia too.'

'You know everything in my father's will before you even read it. As you know his affairs so intimately, why do you need *this*?' Marco pushed forward the book he had been leaning his arm on, red-leather-bound, Niccolo's *libro segreto*. Rinaldo's smile was virtually a showing of his teeth.

'Have I not explained? Indeed I thought I had. If I am to do as your father wished and handle all the affairs of the family, I must have his record of every deal, every action, his private record. Any person familiar with business methods would know that.' The tone was that of a man drawing on a vast store of patience.

Marco suddenly picked up the book and threw it with force on the table.

'Well then, take it. I've no use for it.'

It would appear, though, that he had tried quite hard to find one. Rinaldo still had the key, but the book's lock had been forced and it fell open as it was thrown. This made clear to all why Marco had surrendered it.

The book was in cipher.

Chapter 15

Reward For A Job Well Done

The night before the Ermolin murder, Giulio da Tolentino's wife found that he had sent a friend to tell her of his imminent return. He was coming home earlier than expected and, as it happened, she was glad to know this. Not that she at all wanted to see her husband again but she was glad to have warning not to be entertaining her lover when, in a few days' time and weather permitting, his ship would dock at Venice.

Giulio's friend was a stranger to her but, when the maid had brought wine and then left them alone in the little dark room over a side canal, she was pleased as she looked at him. Candlelight showed her a tall, wiry man with a handsome, lined face, a wide mouth and an intriguing mole near the left eye. She looked at his mouth. She was a woman who looked at mouths and wondered what they would be like to kiss. This one looked well worth a try. Besides, he seemed politely indifferent to her charms as he sat there, though she fingered the curls before her ear coquettishly, contrived to wriggle her bodice down under pretence of rearranging her skirt after her little dog had jumped down, and leant forward invitingly as she poured him wine.

He had little to tell her about her husband, no more than the letter he brought from Giulio told her – not that she wanted to know but she was obliged to ask. Indeed he had little to say about anything. She did not mind. It was not conversation she wanted. However, he did not respond to any of the usual signals and she began to think she was wasting her time. With Giulio coming back next week she was certainly entitled to a little fun. This man was a challenge.

She was no challenge to the stranger, who had seen early on that he need make no effort. This little peach was ready to fall into his hands and he was ready to eat when it did. He drank his wine and idly watched her, waiting for the moment when she would offer to show him something in her room. He'd go, of course. He'd rarely had an easier job, though it was not turning out quite as his employer had envisaged.

Maria da Tolentino's maid was used to sitting up late to see out those who left her mistress's bed before dawn, and was always well rewarded for it. She too had been struck by the stranger's good looks, and hoped for a kiss when she saw him to the door and unbolted it for him. She got the kiss but not the tip which, the stranger considered, would have been wasted on her.

Easing her body out of the way with his foot, he closed the door gently and set off down the side alley. Mother-of-pearl gleams of the dawn sky were reflected into his face from the canal water alongside. He raised his head and sniffed the air. Another pleasant day! Just time to get some rest and break his fast before setting about his next job, which he did not expect to be as easy as the last. He set fire to Giulio da Tolentino's letter at an expiring lantern by a house door and crumbled the ashes under his foot.

The maid was discovered before the mistress; the cook, irritated that no one arrived to collect the wine and cakebread always taken up to the mistress's bedroom at the start of day, came looking. People who have been strangled are rarely attractive to view and the cook's hysterics fetched a crowd of domestics anxious lest their mistress should hear. They debated among themselves how to break the news to her that some fellow – the door was neither locked nor bolted – had choked her maid to death after some sordid assignation.

There was, after all, no problem. When they came to tell her, Maria proved incapable of listening. They got the shutters open and still she had not roused; they urged each other to wake her and found her lying on her side in the great bed for which her husband had paid such a sum only last year. Very likely at that time he had not foreseen paying an equally large sum for the sight that met their eyes as they turned her over.

Under her curls the embroidered pillow was soaked with blood. Maria da Tolentino's pretty throat had been cut from one charming ear to the other.

If that job had been easy, the next piece of work the stranger had undertaken turned out, in spite of his conjectures, to be easier still. An hour or two later, after a brief sleep, he was sitting in a cookshop eating an excellent stew of beans and chopped pork when he gathered, from the general chat at the table, that the job had been done for him.

It was typical of Dion (like Sigismondo he had no other name, in his case because no town cared to lay claim to him) that he showed no surprise, but continued to eat. Someone had beaten him to it but that was no reason to alter the whole of his plans. From what was being said round about, no one knew who was responsible; therefore his employer might not know either. He had not promised any particular method – some of his clients were amazingly fussy about this – and he had no objection to this business of a stiletto through the eye being attributed to him by the client, though he'd never used the method so far. Whoever had in fact done it had been within kissing distance, perhaps a relative or an angry wife. The detail that amazed the gossips at the table, about the locked room, Dion silently dismissed as absurd. Never was there a key, as he well knew, that couldn't be copied; or a servant who wouldn't, for the right money, get one for you. Besides, as he'd already found out, there'd have been no difficulty getting into any room – there were workmen on the roof with ropes and pulleys.

That reminded him. He'd done the preliminary work on this job already and of course received the down payment. No reason not to collect the final fee. Was anyone going to dispute with him for it? And if they found the murderer,

71

they'd string that one up. His client was hardly going to shout they'd got the wrong man.

He finished his plate, paid the reckoning, and left. Half an hour later he had the money in his hands – it had been waiting for him, and he was given to understand that his client was well satisfied. So was Dion himself, quietly strolling among the crowds on the Rialto, glancing at the shops, turning over in his mind whether to allow himself some treat to commemorate a day which had turned out to be as delightful as any he'd known.

Then he saw his treat strolling, as he was, through the crowd.

He had the description from a former client who had hoped to employ this man and got Dion instead. There was no professional challenge, for evidently this man was into the profession of tracking down those who were to be the victims of justice rather than those who were vexatious to some client. It was almost certainly the right man. Nearly a year had gone by since he had heard the news, but various commissions had made it impossible to devote time to a serious search. This was his day indeed. The target had chosen to come to Venice of all places, now, when Dion was here.

Normally, Dion's face showed little emotion but, as he watched the shaven head in the distance, a smile creased the lines round his eyes and made the mole under the left one ride up. He began to hum the refrain of a song very popular in Venice at the moment – every gondolier was singing it – about the sad fate of a lover who had killed himself for his girl. Dion was not touched by the lover's fate, for his own natural impulse would be to get rid of the girl, but like his brother Pyrrho whom Sigismondo had killed in Altamura, Dion had a sentimental feeling for a good tune. He was still humming it when, going with the tide of the crowd and at the pace of the man he followed, he left him, and a scrubby-bearded fellow with him, turning into a doorway off a side alley while Dion continued to drift on his way. No need to hurry. This was going to be something planned to the last detail. Pyrrho deserved no less.

Chapter 16

The Evil Eye

The new Captain-General of the Fleet had got his baton and his standard from the Doge; the procession had reached its destination at the Doge's Palace. There was to be a great banquet there that night, with fireworks over the lagoon.

Crowds in the Piazza had dwindled. Idlers remained, to evaluate the show that had been put up so far and to speculate on Attilio da Castagna's chances of winning the sea victory so much needed. Would he return in triumph, or in chains like his predecessor now awaiting, in the Doge's dungeons, the announcement of his fate? And if in triumph, it might be like the Captain-General the older gossips could remember from twenty years ago – in no state to enjoy all the ceremony but only to inhabit the very best tomb the Republic could buy.

Sigismondo and Benno did not concern themselves with any of this. They were on their way once more to the Palazzo Ermolin. Now Sigismondo rowed and Benno sat admiring the ease with which they surged through the water. Biondello went from side to side, still puzzled and luckily also a little daunted by being within a few inches of such an expanse of water. Sigismondo seemed able to see behind with only a slight turn of the head and they got in no one's way; he even understood the weird cries of the gondoliers, veering accordingly. Benno was wondering why they needed to visit the palazzo again. He felt that Sigismondo was working in unusually difficult conditions: no Duke had given him a warrant to question anyone he wished, and indeed the family of the dead man were by no means keen to co-operate, looking on his master as an intruder officiously called in by a father-in-law.

They were moving down the narrow canal at the side of the Palazzo Ermolin, in the echo of water noises and a lugubrious smell. Benno leant forward and ventured one question. 'This Lord Vettor you saw just now – did he have any idea who it was that . . .' He pointed to his left eye.

'He and his wife were discussing one idea, of a man they say is mad, one Pico Gamboni whom I want to find. You and I know that being mad doesn't stop one from murdering people.'

'Why are we coming here? Does he live round here?'

'I think you'll soon see.'

What Benno did first was to hear. Before Sigismondo's powerful strokes brought them to the corner and the broad canal on which the palace fronted, a burst of shouting sounded, as of one gondolier rating another. Sigismondo nodded in satisfaction and swung the boat round the corner.

A gondola, brilliant in red and white, was being rowed past the Palazzo Ermolin by a tall, handsome black gondolier in red and white striped hose and a gaily plumed hat. His passenger, in ragged red silk, his long hair streaked with grey and hanging over his eyes, was sitting forward of the little roofed cabin and doing the shouting. He was shouting up at the grand façade, and Benno craned to see if anyone stood on the balcony or looked from a window. No one was to be seen, but the man in the gondola still shouted and now shook his fist in a frenzy that seemed quite likely to project him overboard. To Benno, a little of his message was still obscured in the Venetian pronunciation but what he made out was clear enough.

'Rot in hell, Ermolin! Burn as my house burnt! Suffer as my son suffered! Scream . . . my wife! Die for eternity . . . as you cursed me! May the Devil . . . your eyes on a spit and . . . on a slow fire for ever and ever!'

It was a novel way to offer condolence. What could anyone

inside the place think of this madman? It was then, so to speak, that the ducat dropped.

'That's—'

'Pico Gamboni, Benno? Yes, I think we'll find it is.'

Nothing proved easier than to make the madman's acquaintance. Past the palazzo he stopped his tirade and Sigismondo hailed him. He paid off the gondolier at the next landing stage, gripping his arm like an old friend, and then he was perfectly willing to be rowed to Sigismondo's lodgings. He did not show any reluctance to share the meal that Sigismondo had sent up, but attacked the sausage dumplings and onion sauce with as much enthusiasm as he had shown in predicting Ermolin's fate in the next world. Benno had thought when he first saw him that he was a young man prematurely greying but, close to, the lines round eyes and mouth, the disappointed sag of skin, showed he was more likely in his forties than his twenties. Hollow cheeks and bony wrists argued that a meal of the sort he was now engaged with was a rarity.

Sigismondo filled his cup with the straw-coloured wine and asked no questions, but sat, and ate enough to keep him company – though in Benno's opinion Gamboni would not have noticed if nobody else had any, so completely was he absorbed in his own eating. It was Biondello, putting a paw on his shoe, who made him glance down away from his plate, at the devoted grubby face. He woke to the fact that he was not alone, and he threw his hair back, smiled, and offered a scrap of sausage left on his plate. Then, he looked at Sigismondo.

'Is this the hanged man's last meal?'

'Why should you say that?' Sigismondo, smiling too, topped up Gamboni's cup, grasped in the gaunt hand and watched greedily as it was filled. Gamboni drank before he answered.

'Obvious choice, aren't I? I've been threatening Ermolin daily for years. It's no secret I wanted him dead. If you're the man Darin has got looking for the murderer, here I am.'

He threw back the greying hair again and held out his bony wrists as if offering them to be bound.

Benno thought he must have been good-looking once. He had regular features and there was charm and energy still; but the eyes fixed on Sigismondo were manic, showing white all round. Sigismondo, setting down his own wine cup, gave a long, cynical hum.

'Then why did you wait so long?'

Gamboni was surprised. He shrugged and spread the offered hands wide. 'The time had come. I had waited long enough.'

Sigismondo leant back against the wall, elbows out and hands on thighs. 'How did you do it?'

Gamboni grinned, shut one eye, and tapped the lid.

'All Venice knows. I stopped the curse at its source.'

'The curse?'

Gamboni opened his eyes wide once more and, leaning forward, hissed, 'The Evil Eye, man! He had the Evil Eye, as the world knew. Why else, do you think, my son died?' He kept his voice low and darted a glance to left and right although they were alone in the room. 'Ermolin said to me, "You have all the luck, a fine son hard at work while mine spends his life playing the fool." And he looked at me *so* . . .' Gamboni narrowed his eyes into an intense glare. Then he sat back, triumphant. 'You see? And it followed. Caterina died after my son's death. She was ill already and after that she no longer wanted to live.' His voice dwindled and stopped. He looked down at his empty plate. 'It did not finish there. My son had incurred debts abroad of which I knew nothing until my ships came in and were seized by his creditors. Another ship which might have saved me was wrecked in the autumn storms off Cyprus. My palazzo burnt down . . .'

He began now to laugh, as though his account was too appalling to be taken seriously, but the sound was as painful as weeping.

'Yet I'm still in the Golden Book! Nothing changes that.' He raised his arms in their ragged red sleeves. 'And I must dress like this still. Aristocrats, if brought down to begging, must beg in red silk.'

Sigismondo, thoughtful, leant his elbows on the table, drawing his forefinger slowly over his upper lip. A burst of shouting from the alley below attracted Biondello's attention and he wandered to the balcony to look down. The altercation in the street reminded Benno of Gamboni's vituperative shrieks at the impassive front of the Palazzo Ermolin. The noise died, and Biondello transferred his attention to the little pied cat on the balcony opposite, a permanent observer of the street, its eyes glinting in the glowing dusk. At last, Sigismondo spoke.

'You stabbed him simply through the eye? No other blow?'

'Of course, the eye. I told you, the eye. Where else?'

'How did you get into his room?'

For a moment Gamboni glanced vaguely round, then he rallied. 'I climbed. There was the rope. The palazzo has workmen. It was easy.'

Benno envisaged Gamboni swarming up the rope, his scarlet tatters flapping.

'What did Ermolin do when he saw you?'

Gamboni fisted his hands at either temple, screwing his eyes up violently. 'He tried to kill me with his eyes,' and spreading his hands out with a wild giggle, 'it didn't work. He'd damaged me all he could already. He was at my mercy.'

'Mmm . . . and you hadn't any.' Sigismondo nodded. He added, offhand, 'Which eye was it?'

'This.'

Pico Gamboni brought up his finger to his right eye, smiling happily.

Benno bunched up his doublet as a pillow on his mattress and twisted his head to watch Sigismondo as he leant on the balcony rail surveying the street, himself the object of the cat's scrutiny.

'You don't think he did it, do you?'

Sigismondo turned, leaning back on the rail. His head

showed pale above his dark clothes, and then was framed in sudden red light from the distant fireworks over the lagoon. A far roar of applause followed each explosion, thunder after the lightning.

'Mmm . . . hey, you tell me.'

Flattered, Benno began: 'Well, he got the wrong eye for a start. Only he could've forgotten, or maybe, like looking in a mirror, he got it back to front, right? But he didn't know about the back of the neck, did he? Could've gone a bit funny and not known what he was doing. I mean, he doesn't have it all upstairs.' Benno twirled a finger at his temple. 'And all that about the Evil Eye.' He hesitated. 'I mean, there are people that do have it, right? But if your Ermolin did, why aren't more people around him getting bad luck?'

'He was a rich man; so perhaps other rivals of his did.'

'And what about climbing up a rope? Lord Gamboni doesn't look strong enough. And how could anyone not notice him, in that red silk?'

'Good point, Benno. Either he went out not wearing it, and he might be recognised as one supposed to be wearing it; or he took it off – hired a gondola and took the robe off under the canopy. And yes, that would mean a gondolier must be in on it. Pay a man enough money and he lets you get away with murder, hey?'

'Only he hasn't any money.'

'So the gondolier must keep quiet from love; or hate. Did you notice the gondolier Gamboni paid off was black and seemed to be an old friend?'

'There's lots of black people here . . . But you mean *Zenobia's* son? The one Ermolin sent away?'

'I mean he may not be far to seek. But all that can wait until tomorrow.'

A hiss like a giant viper and a green light heralded another firework, turning Sigismondo temporarily into a demon lounging there. Benno, not for the first time, wished they could have gone to the Piazza and seen the show. Venice was doing its new Captain-General proud. Pico Gamboni had gone away to the Piazza without an apparent care in the world since he realised he was not going to be hauled off to prison.

'The thing I don't understand,' Benno picked the first of many that came to mind, 'is why he thought you were asking him all those questions. He couldn't know about Lord Darin, could he? The family want to hush it all up, don't they?' Benno abandoned his mattress and came to see what could be glimpsed of the fireworks from the balcony. Biondello at first came with him, but at another screech from an ascending rocket and the roar of the crowd's greeting of it, he went back to the mattress and dug himself into Benno's doublet there.

Under the sound of the crowd's applause for the last rain of sparks, Benno heard Sigismondo's deep voice saying, 'He thought I was sent by the Ten.'

Benno gripped the rail. Numbers had always puzzled him, but this shadowy sum of his two hands had assumed a special and actual horror for him since Sigismondo had explained it.

'He thought you'd bring him in to be tortured?'

'That, or—' Sigismondo wrapped both his hands round his own throat, rolling up his eyes in a way that turned Benno's stomach. 'The Republic doesn't always bother with bringing people in. There are times when the Ten like their justice to be seen to be done; and others when it is merely done and no one the wiser except the one they bury. Remember what I said: Ermolin himself may have been despatched by an agent of the Ten.'

Benno found his appetite for fireworks distinctly lessened. Had they once given the defeated, imprisoned Captain-General a display like this, too? Not for the first time since their arrival, he wished they could be leaving Venice. He'd been quite right in his first impressions. The whole place was deeply unreliable if not downright dangerous.

On the balcony opposite, the little pied cat yawned, stretched and went inside to make the acquaintance of the new lodger who had just arrived, a tall man with a mole near his eye, who made quite a fuss of her. She curled up on his bed while he took over what she had been doing all day: observing the street and the room over the way – only, unlike the cat, he chose to do his observing from the darkness behind the open shutter.

Chapter 17

Lions In The Night

Barely an hour after he had fallen asleep, Benno was woken by a muffled thumping at their door. He rolled off the mattress and was on his feet, his heart taking up the thumping, to see Sigismondo already opening the door, sword in hand.

Their landlady, wrapped in a quilt and carrying a pottery lamp, her hair in a tousled grey braid, was offended at the sight of the sword. 'Why, sir, what are you expecting in this house? We have no thieves here, I assure you – but you are sent for, this very minute, by Lord Darin. His man,' she pointed to the servant waiting on the stairs, 'will take you there now. I wasn't going to let him wake you himself.'

She furled the quilt more tightly, accepted the coin Sigismondo inserted into her hand and, having protected her guest and her modesty, took the lamp away to her room. Sigismondo and Benno put on their doublets, Biondello was stowed in Benno's, and they set out. Darin's servant was impatient and led them fast down the alley, by the lights of the householders' lanterns, to a gondola rocking at rest, the gryphon of the Darins rising and falling as it gazed from the prow over the dark waters. A torch flared, lighting up the face of the gondolier in Darin livery, and turning to a pallid green the moss clothing the wall of the house across the way.

As they tied up to the striped posts outside the Ca' Darin, in a city now almost silent except for the slap and *schloop* of the water, a strange noise made Benno's skin prickle and brought Sigismondo's head round sharply. It sounded at first something like a dog growling, then swelled to match a dog on a scale to which Biondello would be a flea, gathering and vibrating in their ears, a roar magnified by the echo. Biondello quivered against Benno's chest.

The servant, jumping to the landing stage, said with pride, 'My lord's lions. He keeps them in his garden there.' He gestured towards a wall beyond them, hung with creepers whose long trails shadowed the bricks and flickered in the torchlight. 'Venice has lions all over, you'll have noticed. Lord Darin likes to have them not only in stone but live.'

As he followed his master up the marble steps and through the great carved doors and past the bowing, yawning doorkeeper, Benno thought: that's one garden where I'm not picking flowers! He had never seen an actual lion and was happy in his ignorance, glad he hadn't known about them last time he came here. The stone and marble lions all over Venice, small though most of them were, conveyed an unpleasant idea of their ferocity. True, some of them were smiling, but then you asked yourself *why*? And they had wings. Sigismondo said the lion of St Mark had wings while real lions didn't, but Benno, glad when the doors shut, had a nasty vision of the creature who made that noise in the garden soaring over the wall on a hunt for its dinner. He wondered how big an actual lion was. He watched his master going up the stairs to see the man who kept creatures like that for fun.

Vettor Darin, when Sigismondo was ushered into the room where he was pacing up and down, had not the bearing of a man intent on fun. Yet he looked excited; for a small, balding man with no imposing physical characteristics, he conveyed a surprising effect of power and authority. The round eyes that turned now to settle on Sigismondo seemed to have their own pale light.

'I would not wait until morning to speak to you. I have reason to believe I know who killed my son-in-law.'

'Indeed, my lord?' Sigismondo stood still, waiting while

the little man roamed up and down, the red silk of his gown, damasked and gold-bordered, unlike Gamboni's tattered robe, rustled like autumn leaves across the green marble floor.

'I have only now returned from the reception for da Castagna . . . My wife spoke to me. She had found our granddaughter in tears – oh, not just with grief at her father's death. She was disturbed at something – something you should hear at once.' He clasped his hands together almost violently and gazed at Sigismondo. 'You may not be able to believe what you hear.'

The calm, intelligent face before him might have given him the idea that its owner's credulity could safely be put to the test, and he went on, holding his clasped hands under his chin as if he had captured a thing that was trying to escape.

'My granddaughter had remembered what she had found one day last week. A letter, Signor Sigismondo, a letter to Lady Isabella Ermolin, wife to my son-in-law.'

He paused, and Sigismondo, perhaps finding this less than astounding, made a polite contribution. 'A letter, my lord?'

'Oh, I know, I know.' Lord Vettor released the invisible object, to flap a hand dismissively. 'She ought not to have read it, letters are private, it was wrong of her. But girls are inquisitive, and in this case I am glad she gave way to her curiosity. She was there, sir, to borrow a jewel from her stepmother. She has few of her own though, of course, she will have some in dowry and doubtless more from her husband when she marries – I say this to explain how she came to see this letter. Lady Isabella promised her a jewel – a pin, a pendant – and had opened her coffer . . . her best jewelry her husband keeps – *kept* – in his study properly locked up, and then was called away by a visitor.'

Lord Vettor came close to Sigismondo and tapped him on the chest, looking up into his face with the pale eyes.

'Beatrice saw a letter under the chains and trinkets in the box and took a chance,' he gave a sudden smile, 'while her stepmother was out of the room, to read . . . girls, girls are made of curiosity, my dear sir, or Eve would not have eaten the apple. But,' the pale eyes grew rounder, 'it was a *love* letter! A love letter to a recent bride and not from her husband!'

Sigismondo not appearing unduly astonished yet, Lord Vettor gave the black-clad chest an admonitory tap.

'Think, sir, think what this means. My son-in-law is murdered. Who stands to profit from his death? Why, his wife's lover, am I not right?'

'It is sometimes harder, my lord,' Sigismondo spoke as one with possible experience, 'to visit the widow than the wife. A love letter is not a death warrant.'

The eyes were affronted.

'Signor Sigismondo, jealousy will stop at nothing. A lover, and this is well known and attested, cannot bear to think of his mistress in the arms of another. Men have killed for far less.'

This, Sigismondo could not deny. Lord Vettor's eyes glittered. He was working up, with a strange excitement, to the final revelation.

'And who do you think, sir, was the one who wrote the letter?'

'It was indiscreet of him to sign his name, my lord.'

The little plump hand had waved away the indiscretion. 'There was no signature as such. No, no, merely the first letter of his name. But in the letter, *in* the letter, sir, he spoke of his father and what he was to do one day in the following week. He spoke of the chance of seeing my son-in-law's wife at the Basilica. That day was today, sir. His father was to give baton and standard to the Captain-General before us all in the Basilica.'

There was triumph in the pale eyes and in the voice.

'His father, Signor Sigismondo, is the Doge. The lover of Lady Isabella – the murderer of my son-in-law – is Doge Scolar's son, Pasquale!'

Through a long window, open to the warm night breeze, came the roar of the lion again, a sound both brutal and threatening, as savage as the smile Lord Vettor wore.

Chapter 18

Present From A Dead Man

The journey back to their lodgings was made in silence, Benno venturing no word as he watched Sigismondo sitting relaxed and thoughtful in the torchlight, shadowed one minute, boldly lit in the next as the gondola glided on its way. The Darin gondolier gave more than one jaw-cracking yawn as he swung on the oar, making Benno's face ache in sympathy. Nothing could be more desirable than to get back to their safe refuge, away from importunate lords and hungry lions, and to get some sleep at last. Benno, though longing to put his head down and drift away, was still anxious about what could have happened that his master was sent for in the middle of the night. Had someone taken a stiletto to another Ermolin? But why should Lord Darin, whose only connection with the Ermolins was through his dead daughter, mind at all? Family was responsible for a lot of odd behaviour, to be sure, but this seemed too much.

They arrived at the landing stage. The gondolier came out of his half-dream to accept the tip, and was rapidly away. Sigismondo, his arm across Benno's shoulders, led him into a side alley awash with moonlight.

'We can talk better here. Landladies have especially sharp ears for lodgers who are sent for by members of the Signoria. In Venice even the humblest can earn money by informing.'

Benno had an uneasy feeling, centring in the back of his neck, that a city so full of informers might run to a tidy number of assassins, any of them likely to favour just this sort of alley. Still, he was eager to hear something at last. They strolled towards the street where they lodged, under balconies that patched them with shadow, in the strange, stagnant smell, half-sewer, half-canal, hearing the patient lapping of water not far away, eating the walls; and quite near, what was probably a rat ate something pulpy with audible gusto. Not trusting Biondello against the rats of Venice, Benno suppressed the little dog's efforts to get down and investigate.

Sigismondo's voice was only a murmur. 'It seems I must turn thief to please my employer.'

'What's he want you to steal?' Benno was sure that theft in Venice was an even dicier business than in most cities.

'A letter belonging to his son-in-law's widow. I believe he hopes it will incriminate a person whom he'd like to see in trouble.'

Benno, working things out, breathed, 'Someone wanted to get rid of her husband?'

'Possibly. I don't see that the letter will prove anything but he is determined to have it.'

'Do you have to get it?'

After a slight pause, Sigismondo gave a rueful hum. 'We're in Venice, Benno. If I want to survive, I must accommodate powerful men if I can.'

'Who wrote the letter? He must hate him a lot to want to get him for murder.'

'You saw the writer earlier today. Fished from a canal.'

'Not the D—' The words were lost in a grunt as Sigismondo's hand caught him on the back of the head.

'Never trust the shadows.'

'Why's he want to get – that person – into trouble? Your employer, I mean.'

'Mm – m . . . You remember that noise we heard? From his pets?' The deep voice held a bubble of laughter. 'Those pets show his ambition, Benno. They stand for this city and its power. I have a feeling he'd like the job of our wet young man's father.'

'The D—' Benno slapped a hand over his mouth, feeling

the wind of Sigismondo's clout pass him harmlessly by. "Course, it wouldn't look good, would it? The,' he hesitated, 'the Number wouldn't care for it, I sh'd think. But did he do it?'

They had reached the door of their lodging now and Sigismondo put a finger to his lips. The next moment he had jumped and caught the edge of the balcony overhead; the minute after, he was reaching between the bars to take Biondello from Benno's upstretched arms. Then, with a powerful haul, he hoisted Benno until he could seize hold of the rail and get purchase for his feet. Easy to see why Sigismondo did not care to advertise his return by rousing the landlady, but now, about to go in between the long shutters, he stopped abruptly, sniffing the air. Then he had drawn his sword in a brief glitter, pressed Benno into a corner of the balcony and gone silently in. The moon by now was brilliant, steady light falling in a silver bar across Benno, the shutters, and into the room beyond. Benno, down on all fours, clamped hands round Biondello who was poised, nose forward and quivering, to follow Sigismondo. Whatever terror awaited there, he was not the size to tackle it.

The next thing Benno knew was Sigismondo's hand on the back of his collar, dragging him swiftly inside while the shutter was kicked to. Above the shutters, moonlight flooded the opposite wall and the thing on it.

Biondello was at once at the foot of the wall, paws up on it, sniffing as though he were all nose.

Skewered there at head-height was a dead rat, one that had fed well when it was alive and yielded plenty of blood in death for the message scrawled on the wall alongside it.

'What's it *say*?'

Benno, still crouching, went rigid in horror as Sigismondo read it out.

'*From Pyrrho*. Mm-m. It's a kind thought, but not one I expected.'

'He's *dead*. You killed him. He couldn't come back?'

In Venice, this city of magic, was there black magic?

87

Chapter 19

The Architect, The Thief And The Housekeeper

'So, we've had the warning and it works both ways. He wants me to feel under threat, but hey, now we know to look out for him. He won't come back tonight,' Sigismondo had paused and suddenly smiled, 'unless he *thinks* we'll think that.'

'You think he's just a friend of Pyrrho's?' Benno would have liked to be rid of the picture in his head: of the man he had seen lying dead in his lifeblood, rising up from Hell – to which he had surely gone – with permission to haunt Sigismondo to his death.

'Mm – m . . . perhaps a friend, perhaps family. Pyrrho killed for a living. Either way I believe we're up against a professional. From now on, Benno, it's not just the Venetians watching us.'

It was not the easiest night Benno could remember. Though instructed to sleep, and though he had looked forward to sinking into unconsciousness as swiftly as he usually did, he could not relax in that room now. Sigismondo, not in the least perturbed, lay on the bed in the shadows, sword at hand, while the moonlight shifted serenely across the room through the window their visitor had most likely used.

Benno knew he should feel safe with Sigismondo on guard but he did not at all fancy waking suddenly with a fight going on over his head. He lay on his mattress, dozing fitfully, aware of city sounds, jolting awake every so often to monitor the window where Sigismondo had left the shutter invitingly open . . . Finally Benno opened his eyes on the pearly mist of dawn suffusing the room as though it had seeped in from the lagoon. Sigismondo had rolled his pack up, ready to leave, and he was feeding Biondello scraps of a sausage he was slicing, which he now handed to Benno together with their leather bottle of wine.

'We'll eat more on the streets. Time to find another place to live but, if we can help it, not while our friend may be watching. Kind messages from the grave are nice but I think what he's really offering *is* the grave.'

The dead rat had found its grave already in the street where some of its own kind had given it a swift and noisy burial.

Sigismondo produced coins that cut short the landlady's protest at their sudden departure, enough to compensate for the unpleasant decoration of the wall. The message was now indecipherable after Benno had wiped it over with a splash or two of wine. He wondered what she'd think when she saw it, but it would give her a tale to tell her cronies, or to the authorities if she were indeed an informant. Benno, hurrying after his master down the alley, felt even more uncomfortable out in the open, imagining another's eyes upon them assessing the moment to let fly an arrow or to throw a knife.

At the Palazzo Ermolin, someone had arrived ahead of them, someone who was proving almost as disruptive to the peace of the house as the murder of the previous morning.

The renovations and improvements to the palace involved more than repairs to roof and balcony. Niccolo Ermolin had entertained, in the head so terminally invaded, visions that would dazzle the city. The mosaic floor of the hall and its intricate designs was already finished, the antique porphyry columns set up weeks ago, but major alterations to the *piano nobile* had still to be carried out and were in the hands of the architect Ermolin had hired to make the palace the cynosure of an envious city.

The present problem lay not in the plans but in the architect.

Brunelli had a reputation which preceded him from city to city. He was the best, but you paid for what you got and you paid not only in money; though plenty of Ermolin ducats had been contracted for this particular job.

Brunelli only, ever, noticed the task in hand, which had to be performed to his complete satisfaction. As workmen are human, this led usually to a lot of shouting, a walk-out, and a spot of physical violence. People were afraid of Brunelli; in another part of Venice at this moment Leone Leconti was working at a fresco in a church. Brunelli had been asked to leave this particular fresco after felling two apprentices who had not applied the base as he liked it. Leone Leconti, called in to finish the job, had seen fit to remove a part of the fresco Brunelli had completed and, someone having reported to him Brunelli's opinion of this act, Leconti now worked in a breastplate, sword as near to hand as his brushes.

Brunelli had been away from the Palazzo Ermolin the day before, from the combined effects of over-eating, carousing, and getting involved in a florid tavern brawl. He had missed the excitement of the murder but he was here today, with a black eye to match his mood, determined to make up lost time. It did not cross his mind that anything could change simply because his employer was dead. It was while he was bawling out the workmen on the roof for taking a half-day's holiday in his absence to see the Captain-General's procession, that Sigismondo and Benno arrived by boat.

The shouting, audible from afar, made Benno suppose Pico Gamboni to be making his customary call but, as they swung round the corner, there was Brunelli's unmistakable burly form, head back, roaring towards the roof where the workmen naturally preferred to remain. Benno noticed that they had drawn up the rope. Benno himself had managed to offend Brunelli when they first met some time ago. It had been the result of a misunderstanding and Benno was glad that Brunelli, once he had delivered a hefty kick to Benno's backside, had considered the matter closed. Another such kick in this neighbourhood might land you in a smelly canal.

Recognition came swiftly. Brunelli stepped back while shaking his fist with vigour, and was rapidly saved from the canal himself by Sigismondo springing onto the landing stage. He embraced his rescuer with the energy he gave to everything.

'I owe you a drink, Sigismondo! Let's find a tavern when I've finished here.'

'If you're seeking to do me a favour . . .' Sigismondo genially led Brunelli along the landing stage, itself a little raft that quivered under their feet. The workmen returned to their toil, making a loud noise of it to demonstrate their devotion to duty. Benno paid the gondolier from the purse entrusted to him, and stood monitoring Biondello's exercise and watching Sigismondo talking to Brunelli.

Their conversation ended with Brunelli, unresponsive to the vigorous sounds from above, striding up the steps, assaulting the great carved doors with his fist and pushing past the servant who opened them. Sigismondo followed, Benno close behind, while the servant was still protesting as Brunelli strode up the grand staircase. Benno stood in the hall, holding Biondello and hearing the servant's grumbles, and wondering why the new plaster on the staircase walls had been carefully pitted all over. He thought it was an ugly fashion. Brunelli, mounting, noticed that his assistant had keyed the wall for the frescoes almost as well as he could have done himself at half the lad's age.

As it happened, the master of the house (acknowledged by the servants at least, to be Lord Rinaldo and not young Lord Marco) was absent, confirming arrangements for his brother's funeral. Where Lord Marco was, no one knew, but it was assumed he was out amusing himself somewhere in spite of his father's murder. It is very hard to break the habit of even a short lifetime.

No one of authority, therefore, was on the spot to confront Brunelli. The major-domo who had emerged to find out who had demanded admittance in so unmannerly a fashion, had already had dealings with the architect; judging it politic to suppose that whatever Brunelli was about to do had been sanctioned by either the late master or Lord Rinaldo, he retired. The man with the shaven head at least must be here on the same invitation of Lord Darin.

Isabella, sitting in her room reading a French romance with ironic enjoyment, had heard the commotion below and supposed it to be some servants' dispute in which she had no intention of becoming involved. She had been putting up with an interminable procession of condoling female visitors, and she was very bored with Pathetic Widowed Bride. A French romance was precisely the kind of absurdity to take her mind off the realities of life, and a very nice change from the Book of Hours she had been holding on her lap to make a suitable impression on her visitors; though she doubted if it had deceived the sharp eyes of Donna Claudia, no more overcome by grief for her late son-in-law than his widow was.

She was therefore not in the mood for interruption, but Brunelli consulted his own moods alone. She looked up in astonishment as the door to her room was abruptly pushed wide and the stocky, scowling architect strode in.

'You'll have to move, m'lady. I must measure your room.'

Isabella did not immediately see why his measuring should require her to vacate the room, but it became clear to her as he, not waiting for an answer, pulled out a rule from his belt, flipped out the hinged lengths to their full extension and began to measure the window by which she sat. He blocked out the light and whistled loudly through his teeth. He smelt of plaster and of drink.

She considered. She could call the major-domo and have the man thrown out, but there was that about him which argued he would not give up anything he had in hand without battle. She was as tired of the wretched alterations, the hammering, the singing of the workmen, as she was of her doleful visitors. Without a word, Isabella got up and took her book out of the room.

A moment later, Sigismondo, who had been waiting behind one of the newly established porphyry columns in the upper hall, slipped in. He found Brunelli absorbed in measurements. He took no notice as Sigismondo swiftly scanned the room and crossed it to lift down a small coffer bound in iron from a high shelf. The lock presented no difficulty, more a deterrent to the inquisitive than a serious handicap to a knowledgeable man with a small piece of wire. Sigismondo, lifting up the trinkets on top, extracted the letter and bestowed it in an inner pocket, and relocked the coffer. Then he touched Brunelli on the shoulder and lifted a hand in salute.

Brunelli, busy writing figures on his tablets, nodded absently, incurious as to the nature of the favour he had just rendered, already forgetting that there had been a favour. Sooner or later the room would have had to be measured and he would have been unlikely to consider its occupant then either. Buildings were a great deal more important than anyone who was going to use them.

Isabella, therefore, in a loggia of the Palazzo Ermolin overlooking the courtyard garden, stroking her cat which had found her, and reading her romance, had no thought that anyone but an uncouth architect had come to disturb her peace.

Zenobia, in the housekeeper's room, had *her* peace disturbed by the visitor her mistress had not seen. Once again, she opened her door to Sigismondo's scratching on it, and stepped back to let him come in. She bobbed her curtsey but there was no pleasure in the proud, fine face.

'I have told you all I can, sir. I don't know why you are here again.'

Sigismondo strolled to the window overlooking the side canal and stood gazing out, his face gilded with shimmering reflections.

'I believe you do. Your son's in Venice.'

He was aware of a stillness behind him, then she spoke.

'Cosmo is not an exile. He has a right to be in Venice. His father sent him away, Venice did not.'

Sigismondo turned to look at her. 'He comes to see you.' He indicated the narrow door in the shadows that led to the small landing-steps visible from the window. 'Did he copy that key?'

She stood there, hands at her sides, still slender as a girl, returning his look indomitably. 'He would never harm his father. I know it.'

'Did he copy the key?' The deep voice repeated the question calmly. She flung up her hands as if to ward off attack.

'I did not see him do it. You cannot say he did it, nor do I believe he would. Why not enquire of the other son? He had more chance than Cosmo did to copy that key.'

Chapter 20

Your Brother's Murderer

Benno, directed to the kitchen by a major-domo reluctant to have his hall further polluted, found a warm welcome from the cook, who tweaked Biondello from his bosom, covered the little dog in kisses (which he accepted with enthusiasm because he knew what they heralded) and gave him a knuckle of veal to battle with on the flagstones. The kitchenmaids were too busy chopping meat for fritters, and discussing the handsomest workman, to spare attention for this vacant, grubby creature with a short dishevelled beard. The cook, however, stretching beauty from dog to owner, had some fresh-baked bread and another bowl of broth to offer him, and while he enjoyed this she chatted sociably. In the course of her talk, unceasing as a mountain stream, Benno heard something he thought his master ought to know.

'She had a terrible quarrel with him, that morning.' Benno stopped, anxious that no one should hear this but Sigismondo. With vacuous face he checked – nobody at the windows, no one else on the landing stage where they waited for the hailed gondola to make its leisurely way over to them. Yet, conscious of the city itself listening, Benno dropped his voice further still. 'Lady Isabella. Her maid, who's called Chiara, told the cook the lady'd shrieked and slammed the door of her room and the master went and locked himself in his study. The maid didn't know what it was about – as her mistress isn't the kind to tell her anything.'

'Mm-m. That rings true. Interesting. Now,' Sigismondo raised his voice as the gondola came smoothly in and was checked, 'we are for the Ca' Darin.'

Benno never thought to ask if his master had the letter he had come to steal, for if the letter existed Sigismondo would have got it. What worried Benno now was not if they were being overheard but if they were being watched by hostile eyes. Someone who left a dead rat as a present was not going to call again with flowers unless in a wreath for Sigismondo's grave. He hated feeling that his master was a target from any windows in the walls that towered closely above. Common sense might say that Pyrrho's friend or relative would have to know their route, and that it wasn't necessarily easy to commandeer a window in any house, particularly if you didn't want to be identified. Pyrrho had been a professional; his friend wasn't likely to be an amateur.

Nor was Sigismondo. After all, that he was here alive now proved that he'd always been quicker than his enemies, and that he was not contemptuous of precautions. Benno gave up scanning the peeling plaster, the dank bricks, the mossy stone and the dark blanks of windows, and tried to let go. With any luck this skulking attacker would show his hand before long and get it chopped off. Pyrrho had tried to kill Sigismondo several times before death persuaded him to stop.

At the Ca' Darin, a resigned Benno was outside the action again. In a ducal court he had often slipped in after Sigismondo as an attendant, carrying cloak, letters or a sword. Here in these small magnificent palaces he was relegated to the entrance hall or the kitchen. He had not even seen some of the people Sigismondo was dealing with, and had no idea if Lady Isabella, to whom the Doge's son had written this important letter, was the sort of person you'd be willing to murder for. The Ermolin servants weren't devoted to her but then the young man was likely to have fallen for her looks, not her character. He was in for a nasty shock if he found himself saddled with the Ermolin murder just because Lord Darin wanted to discredit his father and get to be Doge instead.

The maestro di casa at the Ca' Darin had perhaps unfortunately been instructed to admit the shaven-headed man in black to his master's presence at any time, such was Lord Darin's impatience for news of the commissioned burglary. As a result, Sigismondo was shown into a room where Vettor was already talking to a visitor. Rinaldo Ermolin had come in courtesy to tell him the arrangements for Niccolo's funeral. The two men turned as Sigismondo was announced, with very different expressions, Vettor's of acute eagerness, Rinaldo's of cold dislike.

'You have the letter?'

Sigismondo produced it from the inner pocket of his doublet and silently held it out. Vettor all but snatched it in his desire to know its wording but then, obviously conscious that an explanation was due, he showed it briefly to Rinaldo.

'A letter Beatrice said she had seen, written by Pasquale Scolar to your sister-in-law. We have him, Rinaldo! Look here!' His eyes travelled swiftly to and fro over the page and now he struck it with the small plump fist. 'He says it! He speaks here of wishing to kill the man in whose arms she lies! What of that? Is that not enough to hang him?'

Rinaldo glanced from the letter to Sigismondo and back to Vettor, without moving his head, lips drawn tight over his teeth, the flare of nostril indicative more of rage than elation.

'How did you obtain this letter? Did Lady Isabella give it to you?'

Sigismondo silently waited for Vettor to reply.

'I told him to get it by whatever means he could.'

'He stole it.'

Vettor tapped the letter impatiently. 'What does it matter how he came by it? We have it now. We have our murderer – we have Scolar by the throat.'

'Let me see.' Rinaldo took the letter from Vettor's unwilling hand and held it to the light streaming in from the window, scanning it with narrowed eyes. Vettor could not let him read alone, but followed him to the window.

'He gives himself away!' He leant close and traced a line with his finger. '"If Fate had but given you to a Scolar sooner than to a wretched ermine not worthy to touch your divine limbs . . ." and see here, "I shall not rest until the ermine is dead who dares to defile you . . ." – what about that?'

Rinaldo suddenly folded the letter as if finished with it, ignoring Vettor's hand waiting to take it back. He moved away, saying, 'Why was I not consulted about this?'

Vettor's face was quite comical in surprise. 'My dear fellow—'

'I am the head of the Ermolin family now that my brother is dead. Why did Beatrice not come to me about this letter?'

'She was here in this house, Rinaldo. She naturally told her grandmother.' Vettor was amazed to find himself criticised.

'And you did not send to tell *me*. Why employ *him*,' Rinaldo with a slight jerk of the head indicated Sigismondo, unmoving in the shadows, 'to rifle my house in my absence, when I could have approached Isabella myself and simply asked her for the letter.'

Vettor's surprise was succeeded by amusement. 'Oh no. Forgive me but I think you might not have found the lady ready to hand this over. Should a devoted wife keep a letter from a lover? Is it wise, when her husband has been murdered?'

'Precisely my point.' The paper, as Vettor watched in disbelief, was finding its lodging inside Rinaldo's doublet. 'If this becomes public, as you seem to wish, what do you suppose the world would say about the Ermolin? Our name would be soiled for ever.'

Vettor fell silent, his protesting hands falling to his sides, as this aspect became clear to him. Rinaldo waited for his answer with a sardonic sidelong regard. From the shadows came a deep voice.

'May I suggest, my lords, that the Lady Isabella might be persuaded to offer the letter to you of her own accord? Then Venice can only admire the virtue of a lady who, having received a letter from an admirer – and no harm in that – put it by to laugh over at her leisure, even to show her husband. Perhaps she forgets it, as unimportant to her, but then, after her husband's murder, she brings to mind something which might have a bearing upon the crime. Then she at once submits the letter to the head of the family, to do with as he thinks fit.'

Vettor had wheeled to look at Sigismondo, the talking burglar. After a second, he struck his hands together. About to speak to Rinaldo, he closed his mouth and waited, as if in deference, for the younger man to break the silence first.

'And if she does not consent?'

It was already a concession, that Rinaldo spoke directly to Sigismondo; who in reply was respectful, presuming on nothing. 'No doubt, my lord, she must be aware of her position, or may be helped to see what it is: that it would be better for her to discover the letter to you, in duty, than to have it discovered. If Lord Pasquale is your brother's murderer—'

'As is evident!' Vettor could not help himself.

'—then surely he must be brought to justice.'

Rinaldo stirred, about to speak, when the tall double doors were flung open by a flustered servant and Donna Claudia sailed in, resplendent in black damask, a net of silver and emeralds on her grey hair. As Vettor went to give her a morning greeting and kiss her hand and cheek, the dark eyes turned their disconcerting gaze on Rinaldo by the window, then Sigismondo half-lost in the obscurity of the room.

'What's happening? Has the wretched letter been found?'

'My dear—'

If Vettor was about to explain, he lost the chance as Rinaldo strode forward and made his excuses to Donna Claudia. There was business he must attend to, she would forgive him; and with a brusque farewell to her husband and not even a glance at Sigismondo, he was gone.

'I have a feeling,' said Donna Claudia, raising her eyebrows at the two men left behind, 'that no matter what business he may have to attend to, he isn't pleased with either of you. Now tell me about the letter.'

Chapter 21

An Eye For An Eye

'So you see, we have time to spare. My employer is at a standstill until he can get news of what is done about the letter.'

Sigismondo, joining the crowds who strolled in the sunshine at the Rialto, made Benno want to beg him to cover that conspicuous bare scalp, to give at the knees to make himself less tall, to transform himself in one way or another into someone not recognisable for who he was. Crowds were no comfort. What could be easier than to slip away unseen after lodging a knife in a man's spine? For a moment Benno was separated from his master by a portly foreigner in green silk robes and a snow-white turban and, so nervous was he, he almost expected to find Sigismondo gone when the obstacle had paraded by. Yet there was Sigismondo a few steps away, asking the price of something in one of the shops along the arcade. Benno edged towards him, turning to see if anyone in the crowd, in all that cheerful bustle and shouting and the constant movement of people this way and that, was watching his master.

He was so busy doing this that when a man stepped suddenly into the arcade and put a hand on Sigismondo's shoulder, Benno gave a yelp that would not have disgraced Biondello.

'Ercole! Found you at last. I thought, where do I look for one man in a thousand and I decided: the Rialto! And here you are among the thousand.'

The voice was strong, thickened on the sibilants; the man, Benno recognised with relief, was the one who had raised his gilded baton in private salute to Sigismondo. This was Venice's new Captain-General of the Fleet, mingling with the crowd on the Rialto like any private citizen. He had a face full of humour, the net of lines round eyes and mouth witness to it, but the thrust of jaw and the dark intensity of the one eye visible, argued it would be better to amuse than annoy him. Sigismondo, laughing, embraced him.

'Brother, it's been a *long* time since I was called Ercole. And you too, Bestia? I must name you, I find, Attilio da Castagna and you know me as Sigismondo now, at least in this city.' He held Attilio at arms' length, looking him up and down, Attilio showing excellent white teeth in a short dark beard frosted with silver. He stood tall, in velvet doublet and silk hose all plain-coloured grey, only the fine leather of boots and swordbelt, and a silver chain round his neck, hinting at anything more than a man of ordinary rank. The black eyepatch was an incongruous touch, a reminder of battle. 'You've come some distance since I saw you last.' Sigismondo gave the broad chest a friendly punch. 'You'd have been hard put to it then to hire a boat, let alone command a fleet.'

The shopkeeper behind Sigismondo wore a disappointed look; he had evidently failed to hear the exchange. Benno had not yet found out that the Venetians, inquisitive to a fault, could also be infinitely discreet. If their Captain-General chose to pretend he was nobody, they would go along with it. What the shopkeeper regretted was not being able to hear anything as to who the man with the shaven head was. Anyone who was clearly old friends with someone in power could have connections with his past that the Ten would pay to know.

'A drink, then, *Sigismondo*. I need to launch a few boats.' Attilio had a comradely arm across Sigismondo's shoulders, steering him out of the arcade, Benno at their heels and Biondello at his. Seeing a companion like this, the unknown assailant might well think twice about attacking Sigismondo.

In the tavern the drink came, with an order from Attilio of fried dumplings stuffed with spinach and cheese. It reminded Benno of the dwarf condottiere Nono Marsili and his passion for liver and onions. The fighters Venice put in charge of its forces tended to have vigorous appetites.

'You've not said what you are doing here.' Attilio speared a steaming dumpling on his knife. Benno, at the end of the bench beside his master, swallowed saliva. 'If you're not busy, come to sea with me. You and I fought anything that moved in the past. A few Turks won't bother you.'

It was the Marsili brothers over again. It wasn't at all surprising that people wanted his master to fight for them, it was simply sensible, if they'd fought with or against him before, whatever his name was at the time. Someone who'd never known him at all, under any name whatsoever, would also want him on their side as soon as they set eyes on him, as a matter of course. And Sigismondo was, after all, a mercenary. Benno pictured his past as a kind of patchwork of battles in foreign lands, a patchwork in which blood-red must often have figured. He knew of the long scar round Sigismondo's ribs where someone had made a miscalculation – probably fatal – in locating Sigismondo's heart; and in the time since Benno had met him, his master had acquired other tokens of people's regard for him, including a memento from the dead Pyrrho.

Wounds were the subject of their talk, as it happened. Attilio had progressed from the dumplings to a stew of spare ribs, sausage, bacon, cabbage, carrots and onions, which he insisted on sharing with them both, ladling part of his generous helping onto pewter plates he took off a stack being carried by. Sigismondo asked him about a cicatrice on his wrist, a mixture of silver and blue, so ugly that Benno turned queasy thinking what could have done it and how it must have looked fresh, so to speak. Attilio examined it as if it was so much part of him that he had long ago forgotten about it.

'Didn't that nearly lose you a hand?' Sigismondo spooned up stew, looking across at it.

'You know how it is. You only notice when you *do* lose

something. And then you sometimes only find out after.'

Sigismondo broke a piece off the loaf to dip in his stew. 'And when did you first realise you weren't seeing straight?'

Benno froze on a mouthful of hot stew. You don't – surely? – talk about missing eyes to a person regarding you with only one. Attilio flung up his head on a bark of laughter.

'You think you can come up on my left side and surprise me?' He tapped the eyepatch. 'I've got used to turning my head fast, and I promise you there's nothing wrong with my hearing. No, Sigismondo,' and the thick sibilants almost made another alias out of the familiar name, 'my enemies'll have to gouge out the other one before they can hope to dance on my grave.'

'Tell me, who was lucky enough to get the first? I imagine he's not alive to be congratulated.'

Attilio's black brows drew down, and the lisp seemed to worsen, underscoring the fierceness of his reply.

'Not now. Not since yesterday morning. Niccolo Ermolin lost me this eye.'

Chapter 22

The Likely Candidate

'Niccolo Ermolin? How did *he* come to lose you your eye?'

Sigismondo's tone was cool but Benno knew that particular calm glance with the head tilted back. If they were really sitting at table with Ermolin's murderer, now was not the moment to start clapping the hands with joy.

'In a fight, how else?' Attilio had gone from genial to brusque. He swept a crust of bread round his plate and stuffed it into his mouth as if he dismissed the subject. Sigismondo drank his wine and, cup in hand, spoke casually.

'I don't see Ermolin getting the better of you in a fight.'

Attilio's one dark eye focused on him suddenly. 'You knew Ermolin?'

Sigismondo shrugged, finished his wine and put the cup down. 'I've seen him. No competition for you.'

Not in the state you saw him in, thought Benno. There aren't many people can provide competition when they're dead. Attilio still studied Sigismondo and there was the beginning of a smile round his eyes.

'Shall we call it luck – the Devil's luck? He'd plenty of that.'

'*Forgive* me for asking,' Sigismondo echoed the smile, 'but how did you come to be on opposing sides? Ermolin was no soldier, surely?'

Attilio filled the cups all round and leant his arms on the wine-stained boards. 'No soldier; and this was no real fight. Twenty years ago, brother, after you and I had been boys in

104

Paris, when we set the philosophy schools in a roar . . .'

Benno gaped to drink this in. Rare was the chance to catch up on Sigismondo's past. He failed to picture these two men, laughing at their memories, so experienced, so much in command of themselves and of others, as boys. Take away some of the strength of shoulder, and the silver in Attilio's beard, give back his other eye and cover Sigismondo's head with thick black hair . . .

'Twenty years ago, I was in Venice at a time of great celebration—'

'As yesterday, when you got your baton?'

'Ho, even more fuss than that, I assure you. Someone was getting married, someone in the Golden Book – enough money to throw around. There were regattas, feasts – and jousts . . .'

'You lost your eye in a *joust*.' Sigismondo sat back as if he had seen the culmination of all surprise.

'In the Piazza no less, with enough young fools competing so it was worth the City's while. Enough beautiful young ladies to make it worth the fools' while. Emilia Darin among them.'

'Emilia Darin.'

Attilio's eye gazed over their heads into the past. 'A beautiful girl, with hair like flames and the neck of a swan . . . Dead now, may God have mercy on her sweet soul. As He may, for her purgatory in this world.'

'How was that?'

The dark eye saw Sigismondo again. Attilio spoke slowly. 'Fifteen years of marriage to Ermolin. Purgatory enough.'

They were interrupted by a serving girl with another flagon of wine Sigismondo had signalled for. Benno took it and filled Attilio's cup and Sigismondo's, regarded intelligently by Biondello who had jumped on the bench and was visible from the eyes up, his single ear pricked towards the hopeful sounds of eating. Attilio glanced at him and demanded, with a deepening of the lines around his mouth, 'Have I set a fashion for one of everything? What does your dog joust with – mice?'

Sigismondo took Biondello on his knee and fed him scraps of meat and sausage. 'Jousts aren't meant to maim. What happened?'

'As *you* would say – mm – mm . . . Ermolin should have aimed his lance at my shield but somehow,' Attilio's hand made a glancing thrust towards the eyepatch and Benno nearly spilt the wine, imagining the howling cheers in the Piazza, the gallop of hooves, the hot sun, and the searing pain, 'somehow, he made a mistake. Girls are apt to prefer a man with both eyes.'

'Had you offered for Emilia Darin?'

'There were plenty of suitors for Vettor to choose among; Ermolin and I were two among many. But he spoilt Emilia and it was rumoured the final choice would be hers. She chose Ermolin; I left Venice. And now,' he looked up at the sky where the sun beamed into the courtyard as into a well, 'to judge by the light I am expected at the Arsenal. We sail tomorrow and I want to check everything in the galleys I'm collecting.'

They took a gondola a little past the Rialto Bridge and were carried, it appeared, almost straight across the city. Benno had been wondering what Sigismondo would disclose about his doings, his services to dukes and princes, but the talk was of wars in France and the Low Countries, of journeys to the East and the African coast. Benno sat in the sun outside the little canopy and watched the glittering, rocking water, while the deep voice described things he could not visualise and Biondello played at being mascot, his one ear lifted by the wind.

At the gateway to the Arsenal they disembarked and Attilio saluted Sigismondo again, this time with an invisible baton. 'Call on me at any time, brother. I name it a happy day when I lose an old enemy and find an old friend.'

'I'll be there to see you off tomorrow and cheer for victory.' Sigismondo wagged his head. 'You must believe me that if I were not privately engaged, nothing would please me better than to kill Turks at your side.'

'I'll kill some for you. Then you'll owe me again.'

Attilio sat forward to wave as he was borne away. They set off walking and came past the great carved arch with the lion of St Mark in its winged glory, paw on a book as it stood everywhere in Venice. Benno had asked what the words said on the open pages of the stone book, and was told: *Peace be with you, Mark, my evangelist.* Now he stopped dead, and tugged at Sigismondo's sleeve, pointing.

'The book the lion's got. It's shut, there's no words.'

'Hey, *Benno*, inside those walls they make stuff to go to war with, cannon, weapons, some of the best galleys in the world. Look at those walls, it's a fortress for secrets. Inside there, they can lay the keel of a galley in the morning and have it ready to sail by evening. Can you think of any way you could have the evangelist's lion promising peace as it comes out?'

Benno had seen a war galley in the past. He was silent, thinking of the man who had just gone in there. After a bit, as they strolled along the canal side, he ventured, 'D'you think he did it? Here he was in Venice and it was Ermolin's left eye you said he was stabbed in, and your friend had got a grudge, extra, on account of Ermolin getting the girl he fancied.'

Sigismondo stopped to shade his eyes and stare out at the sea, dazzling in the noonday sun.

'Who's to know? I don't see him shinning up that rope and climbing in at the window to even up old scores. A man like Attilio isn't of a nature for hole-and-corner stuff. Yet who is to know what could have gone on in his mind? A sore, festering for twenty years . . . It's possible. Yet one thing I'm sure of.'

Benno's mud-brown eyes looked up hopefully. 'Yes?'

'I do know that Lord Darin has only one assassin in mind and it's not the Captain-General. Even Vettor Darin would hesitate to tell the Senate it had just wasted so much time and money. No, if there is to be a Doge Darin, then Doge Scolar must be shown to have a murderer for a son.'

Chapter 23

Niccolo's Child

The servant informed Rinaldo that Lady Isabella was walking in the garden. Any physician might order a little air and exercise for a girl of seventeen, recently bereaved in so horrible a fashion, but Rinaldo, making for the inner courtyard, intended to provide some mental exertion which would prove salutary for her future.

Niccolo Ermolin had been fortunate in having room in his palace for one of the secret gardens of Venice, not to be suspected by anyone passing outside, and he had not been tempted to encroach on the space in any of the alterations he had put in hand – a decision with which his architect Brunelli concurred, fortunately, or the disappearance of the courtyard and of Brunelli might have been successive.

Arcades round the courtyard gave shelter from the sun, but Isabella was sitting in the shade of the big stone fountain in the centre, on the seat that surrounded its basin. This pleased Rinaldo. The gentle plashing of the fountain, lightly echoing round the walls, would prevent anyone from overhearing their conversation, a circumstance not to be guaranteed indoors.

She looked up at his approach but made no attempt either to smile, or to draw her skirts aside to allow him to sit near her; and not for the first time he thought how beautiful she was and how curiously uninviting. Another woman might try to ingratiate herself with the head of the family, on whose favour her position must now depend, but Isabella remained as coolly aloof as she had been when his brother was alive.

He bent to salute her on the cheek, smooth and unexpectedly warm. 'I am glad to find you at leisure, sister. We have matters to discuss.'

'You have made the funeral arrangements quite clear already.'

It was a statement, not a reproach, but it irritated him. With one hand putting aside the folds of black damask lying on the warm stone, he sat down, and felt cool spray from the fountain lightly bless his hair and face in the heat.

'Are you enough out of the sun, sister? It can burn at noon.'

For answer, she put back the dark gauze from her head, as if repudiating his suggestion, and turned herself to face him. 'What is it you want to say?'

'Perhaps you may recognise this.'

She looked at the paper. The water softly splashed behind them and a bird swooped overhead and, landing on one of the bay trees in their terracotta tubs, warned any rival off his territory with a liquid brilliance that sparkled like the water.

'How did you get it?'

There were to be no silly denials, Rinaldo saw with approval. The last thing he required was a hysterical display that would attract the eyes of servants, always anxious to monitor the private doings of the family. Isabella's maid Chiara, though evidently dismissed from accompanying her, would not be far off.

He pointed to the name Scolar. 'That is what matters, not how I came by it. Foolish enough to put his name in it and, more foolish still, to write of his father in such a way that leaves no doubt of his identity.'

She said nothing to that. Indeed, she turned her head as if she listened to the bird and not to him. He rolled the letter up and tapped his thigh with it. 'Far more foolish, sister, than the one who wrote this, is the one who receives it. Receives it *and keeps it*.'

The large hazel eyes turned to him. 'You can prove it was

in my possession? I suppose some servant stole it and you have their word for it?'

'Why did you keep it?'

She flung up her hands, which had laid idle in her lap, startling the bird into a flurry away to perch on the roof tiles. 'I've little enough to amuse me here. Perhaps I kept it to take out and laugh at from time to time.'

'He is not your lover?'

Isabella did laugh. 'Whoever stole it can't have read it properly. He longs to do all the things he *couldn't* do. All dreams. What chance would he have had?'

'These matters can be arranged.' Rinaldo spoke from experience, and she smiled.

'Well, nothing was. Give me back the letter and I will burn it. You shall see me do it.'

She held out her hand, its slender wrist clasped by a bracelet of pearls Rinaldo was aware Niccolo must have spent thousands on. He slipped the letter back inside his gown. 'It's too valuable to burn, Isabella. This will convince the Ten who it was that had my brother killed.'

She stared, lips parted. 'You think *he* had it done? That idiot?'

'He threatens Niccolo; he speaks of rejoicing in his death. What more proof will they want?'

'And what will they say about me? Don't you care about dishonouring the Ermolin name, or are you going to throw me to Lord Vettor's lions?'

The girl was more acute than he had thought. One forgot that these creatures, designed to be passive, could also be observant. He summoned a smile.

'You know well that the family is more important to me than anything. Why else would I have foregone marriage and children to devote myself to it, although it is the Venetian manner?'

'If you've done all that and got Marco as the future hope of the Ermolins, you must think you've made a poor bargain.'

This coincided so exactly with his feelings that for a moment he was unable to speak. She was watching him, however, and he rallied. 'We are straying from the point, sister. We have a murderer to bring to justice, and it lies in your hands whether it is done with credit to the family and yourself, or whether there is rumour in the city as to your virtue.'

The slender hands were at rest in her lap again, and she contemplated them, pale against the black damask, the pearl bracelet gleaming.

'And how may I avoid these rumours?'

'You have only to declare that the letter was delivered to you the day before Niccolo's death; that you put it aside for some reason or other without opening it; and then when you read it and realised, after the murder, what significance it had, you came straight to me, the head of the family, and gave it to me as was your duty. In that way all will be well. You will be praised, not blamed.'

'And if I don't do that?'

Rinaldo struck the edge of the stone basin so hard that it hurt his hand. 'What possible reason could you have for not doing it? Do you long for your name to be smeared with slander? To be thought the adulterous mistress of a murderer, perhaps accessory in her husband's death?' For all his intentions, his voice had risen above the gentle sound of the water. He made himself speak in measured tones, setting out her future. 'You would have to spend the rest of your life in a convent – and do not think I would not find one to take you – that will overlook much in return for a substantial dowry. Your brother, with no knowledge of this latest circumstance, has already one in mind.'

Her hands flew to her mouth and she looked at him over them. 'Oh! A convent! I am threatened with a convent!'

If she were laughing at him, she ought to know the threat was real. He had ascertained from her sole kinsman, the brother, that no support would come from him. She was only a widow, without children, an Ermolin dependent entirely on his mercy. He took hold of one slender wrist and jerked her hand from her face. As he had thought, she was smiling.

'You do not seem to realise, sister—'

'Oh no, *brother*. It's you who don't realise. I am carrying Niccolo's child.'

Chapter 24

The Arrest

The servants at the Palazzo Ermolin assumed, with the natural cynicism of their kind, that young Lord Marco, so conspicuously not the head of the family now that his uncle had assumed control of affairs, was off enjoying himself out of habit. They were wrong.

Marco Ermolin was out hunting, certainly, but not in his usual style, starting off for the Veneto with dogs and yelling companions, annoying people and chasing animals. He was alone, and chasing money.

As soon as the news of his father's death got about, creditors from all over the city who had hitherto shown an obliging patience, were at once eager to share in the shower of gold that must be his. Polite but pressing notes had arrived. When he went out he had been approached with suggestive condolences. Worse, when he spoke politely to these creditors about postponement, there were hints, gentle but terrible, that matters might be referred to his uncle. This intimation, that everyone knew Rinaldo was handling the Ermolin fortunes, exacerbated Marco's feelings; to be driven to admit to Rinaldo that he had incurred debts his inheritance would not cover – he was enough his father's son to know, unlike Pasquale Scolar, what his debts amounted to – drove Marco frantic.

It also drove him to a gondola, paying money because for this purpose he could not take one of those with the Ermolin badge moored at his door. He got himself rowed across the

Grand Canal to the Giudecca. There, in a small but richly decorated house off one of the side canals, Sigismondo saw him trying to muffle his face in his cloak as he was ushered, by a servant accustomed to these shy visitors, to the back of the house.

'That was—' Benno stopped himself in time and Sigismondo hummed as if the world had gone no other way than he had always thought.

'So it was.'

'D'you think he saw you?'

'Oho, I doubt it. He was too busy not being seen. If he saw me, he'll think his grandfather is having him followed, and that will do wonders for his temper.'

'What's he doing here?'

But Benno had exceeded his ration of questions. Besides, Miriam da Silva was now at liberty to receive Sigismondo. Difficult to believe that so short a time had passed since they were last here and had found that Sigismondo's friend was dead. Another death had at once called them away; the death of a man not mourned like this one even though Niccolo Ermolin was in the Golden Book and Joshua da Silva was only a Jew who'd left Spain in a hurry and had come to a city where anyone who made money was welcome.

As Benno's thoughts reached this point, he slapped himself on the forehead, provoking an astonished grunt from Biondello but no surprise at all from the waiting servant, as used to despair as to excessive shyness in the house's visitors. Of course Marco Ermolin was here to borrow money. Most Gentiles who came to a Jew's house came on business, unlike Sigismondo, and their business was mostly to do with lending money because Christians weren't supposed to.

Benno, looking round at the gilded leather panelling, the lamp hanging on its bronze chain, the branched candlesticks of beaten silver, reflected that perhaps Marco was here to pay back money. After all, he must have come into a tidy bit of a sudden; no lender can be always dishing out money and never getting it back. Really it was nice of young Ermolin to be in such a hurry to pay it back; probably he wanted the widow to know she needn't dun him for debts.

The widow was under no such apprehension. Miriam was sitting in the company of female relatives, while the sons and male mourners took boats across to the graveyard with the coffin. She came out into the anteroom to Sigismondo, gravely pleased to see him, and stood holding his hand while she listened to his news and a servant brought him pale, delicate wine that shone in that dark room as if sun had been poured into it.

'My husband gave me these glasses not a week ago. They're Murano, of course . . . but the Ermolin murder! A strange thing! When I saw the Darin badge on the caller yesterday, I wondered, before I knew it was you he was after, if Lord Vettor were not the rich man they say he is. Many men put up a fine show on the ducats they get from here . . .' Miriam's face was more at home with dimples than with the sadness that haunted it. 'Did he want you to find his son-in-law's murderer?'

Faced with such frankness, Sigismondo laughed and patted her hand. 'Mm-mm! You may be sure he wants the *right* murderer. He's not a man fond of having his time wasted. Wasn't that his grandson I saw just now?'

Miriam, dimpling once more, put a finger to her lips. 'We're all blind here, Cristobal. But it was a surprise, I confess, to find he came not to give but to receive. I had to send him away – I can't conduct business today. In any case I'll lend no more until Joshua's affairs are settled . . . unless to a friend?' She pressed the hand holding hers. 'You need anything I can give you, Cristobal? Joshua would want you to lack for nothing. That I know.'

Sigismondo raised the hand to kiss it, humming deep in his chest. ' – Mm. There is something, Miriam.' He bent to murmur in her ear, while she listened with black eyes sparkling like pieces of jet.

'No difficulty at all, Cristobal. If you want a rat-hole, come to a rat.'

Shortly afterwards, Benno was following Sigismondo down some twisting stairs into a cellar, led by a hunch-backed old man with a lantern, who opened a door, hardly visible behind stacks of casks, and showed them into a tunnel very like a run for human rats. In the wavering light as the old man hobbled ahead of them, the tunnel's bricks, bleached from their natural rose, sweated as if the lack of moving air and sun had afflicted them. The strong smell of mushrooms had also a stronger and nastier smell running like an oily thread through it. Benno picked up Biondello who had been pattering at his heels, and carried him under his arm. Now the old man, his shadow looming huge as he put the lantern down, took out a heavy key and unlocked a door in the tunnel wall. More steps went up into the dark and they followed him.

After two more passageways, one so narrow that Sigismondo had to go with one shoulder forward, they reached a room of reasonable proportions; a wooden bed stood on a low platform in front of a plain wall hanging; there was a window, to Benno's relief, and the old man opened the shutter an inch or so, and then handed over three keys, pointing to another door across the room. There was a painted cupboard, an x-shaped stool and a bench under the window on which an unlit lantern stood. The old man hobbled towards the way they had come and Sigismondo stopped him to put a coin in his hand. The door shut, becoming almost invisible in the wooden wall; and Sigismondo locked it.

The lack of dappled light on the ceiling already told Benno they were not on a canal. Sigismondo opened one shutter and, standing back behind it, looked out. He hummed in a satisfied tone.

'D'you know where we are?' Benno had great faith in his master's ability to find his bearings in any place, even if it was new to him.

'The point is, Benno, whether our friend from the grave knows where we are. A live rat is one up on a dead one.'

Marco Ermolin, still muffled in his cloak, hired another gondola to take him back over the canal to the Piazzetta.

His gondolier, supposing his passenger to be returning from an assignation, concluded it had been an unsuccessful one. Marco, hunched and depressed, was debating the wisdom of what he was about to do. He had half a mind to tell the gondolier to veer and head for the elaborate façade of the Ca' Darin, where his grandfather might just be persuaded into another loan; but then he would be forced to explain why his inheritance had not covered debts he had not confessed to when he asked for the first loan. The confusion made his head ache. Besides, his grandfather might not be at home, and his grandmother would be sarcastic about any excuse for such a sudden visit; she would not be likely to accept that he had come to see her or his sister. No, Pasquale would be a safer bet.

The problem here, as with his grandfather, was that he had borrowed before. Pasquale, as generous with his father's money as if it were his own, had scarcely seemed to notice the loan, but it would be difficult if the mention of money led him to think Marco was coming to repay rather than to ask more.

Once at the Doge's palace, Marco could throw off his disguise if not his cares. The odds were that Pasquale was wandering abroad looking for expensive amusements, but Marco was lucky. Pasquale was not only at home but delighted to receive him.

'In good time, Marco. I was dying of boredom and Isepe has no ideas.' Pasquale, in mid-embrace, caught sight of Isepe Tafur, who was making strange faces and gestures at him from the window seat. There was something he was forgetting, doing wrong, that Isepe was trying to warn him about. The mischief was that he had usually plenty to choose from, and he was successful at forgetting because he preferred to forget. He frowned.

Isepe, from long practice, came to the rescue. 'We wanted to see you, Marco' – he bravely used the plural – 'to tell you how sorry we were to hear about what happened to your father. It's terrible.'

Pasquale's face suffered a complete and swift change of

expression. His welcoming smile vanished, he stood back, holding Marco by the arms and looking at him with sympathetic gloom. Then he clasped him again.

'Terrible indeed. I would have called to condole yesterday, only,' a look of strain relaxed as he remembered his perfectly valid excuse, 'my horse threw me in the canal and I struck my head. The physicians made me stay in bed most of the day.'

Isepe was still anxious to help out. 'Is it known who did it? I hear there's a master torturer from Padua in the city, that the Ten have sent for. If the villain's found he'll soon confess.'

'He'll never be found!' Pasquale was cheerfully confident. 'Someone from under the piles who'll disappear back there. It's some private revenge, you can bet. Don't be so glum, Marco, it's in the law of Nature to lose a parent and you always said how you couldn't get on with yours.' He ignored a recurrence of Isepe's warning grimaces behind Marco. 'You must take courage and think of the fortune you'll be master of.'

'Well, it's about that—'

Marco got no further because Pasquale put a hand over his mouth and said, 'Don't talk about money,' and with a look of sentimental tenderness asked, 'The widow, Marco, the beautiful widow. How is she taking it?'

Marco had no wish to discuss how she was taking it, but any attempts to return to the banned subject of money were prevented by the sudden opening of the double doors at the end of the long chamber.

First came two grave-faced men in long gowns of red silk whom Marco knew for two of the Ten he had seen at the Ca' Darin. Then came the Doge himself, the gold-embroidered cap of his office on his head, anguish in his eyes. Two guards stopped by the doors as if ready for action.

'Pasquale Scolar. We are charged to arrest you for questioning on the murder of Niccolo Ermolin.'

The master torturer from Padua was not to be wasted after all.

Chapter 25

The Zonta

With the scrupulosity typical of the Serene Republic, all the rules had been observed. As soon as Rinaldo Ermolin submitted the letter from Pasquale Scolar to the Ten in private, various operations were initiated. The Ten instantly requested a *zonta*, the supplementary Council called in moments of emergency. Messengers were sent all over the city until twenty-eight people were assembled in the Council Chamber and the letter lay before them on the Levantine silk table-carpet, a piece of paper on which several fates depended. There should have been twenty-nine people in the *zonta*, for it would normally have included the Doge but, with a certain delicacy which struck terror to his heart, Doge Scolar was first informed of the business in hand then compassionately excused attendance. This was done in such a way that he dared not insist, as he would be thought anxious to exercise undue influence on behalf of his son.

As a precaution against his warning Pasquale, who might attempt to escape justice, the Doge was asked to wait – was virtually immured – in the room next to the Council Chamber, guards at the door to ensure he did not wander in search of his son. There Doge Scolar sat, hands tightly clasped, head bowed, ears straining to make words of the murmur of voices next door. He had for years sadly known his son was a fool, but never before had Pasquale approached complete disaster. He felt ill. His age weighed upon him. He tried to pray, while his eyes followed the squares of black marble alternating with white on the floor to the window, and he counted them under his breath, starting again with the next line as if he recited a charm against the fate relentlessly moving towards him.

The wait seemed long to him, but the members of the *zonta* were also well acquainted with the reputation of Pasquale Scolar and they found it quite easy to believe that he had finally gone beyond the limit. While young men might even be expected to do wild things, having a member of the Signoria murdered because of a lover's jealousy was to invite the rigour of the law.

Some members of the *zonta* argued that the letter, although patently written by Pasquale, with its references to his father's office, and certainly intended for Ermolin's wife, might conceivably not be the death warrant for him that it seemed. The threat implied in the letter might not have been carried out, might have been mere bombast, some unknown person might have forestalled Pasquale and he was innocent in deed if not in intent.

The only way to find that out was to question him, and that was where the torturer from Padua came in.

In due course, he *had* only to come in, looking intelligently prepared to do anything, however complicated and horrible, for Pasquale to confess. The shock of being arrested, the gloom of the cell to which he was led, the appalling discovery that his father was powerless to extricate him this time, all this preyed on Pasquale's soul; but not till he saw the master torturer, followed by his assistants carrying a brazier and various instruments suitable for wrenching, tearing and burning the shrinking skin, did Pasquale realise he was a coward.

The *zonta* gravely considered the confession. Pasquale admitted to hiring an assassin, name unknown, description inadequate to nail him among so many known to be in the city, to kill Niccolo Ermolin for a specified sum of money duly paid on completion. Yes, his motive had been jealousy. Yes, he adored Ermolin's wife. No, she had not encouraged him in any way, she had not lain with him, she had no knowledge of any of his designs. The letter was the first and only one he had written her . . . Pasquale was a gentleman as well as a coward.

What was to be his punishment? In the ordinary way, execution would have been the sentence for such a crime. Many of the *zonta* were in favour of this, led by Vettor Darin and the victim's brother Rinaldo Ermolin, but some put forward other factors: the boy was young, was in the grip of the disease called love, he had not committed that worst of all crimes, treason to the State. Besides, his father was Doge, had been a good one, serving the Republic generously with no hint of corruption. Something was owed to his dignity, in which theirs also was involved.

When the vote was taken, twelve voted for death and sixteen for exile. It was to be exile under the strictest of conditions, as far away as Cyprus. Never was he to return, even were his father dying. It was to be a parting for life from home, from friends, from family, and he was to think himself lucky to get it.

To Lord Darin's poorly-concealed rage, there had been no suggestions, other than his own and Rinaldo's, that the murder contaminated not only the murderer but also the murderer's father. The *zonta* could not be got to take seriously the idea that Doge Scolar should be asked to resign and an election be put under way. On the contrary, there was sympathy for the old man in this supreme folly of his son's, and relief that they did not have to announce a sentence of execution to him. Lord Darin, outwardly consenting to this compassionate view, went home to his lions that night in a mood to add his roars to theirs.

The Doge was permitted to see his son in the cell where he was to be confined until he was put aboard ship. Weeping, he embraced Pasquale. Yet it was better never to see his son again than to view his remains for weeks chained between the columns of the Piazzetta as a reminder to all foolish young men never to put anything in writing.

Pasquale, whose thoughts had dwelt on nothing but physical agony since he was arrested, could not easily adjust to his future. He had worked up to at least a romantic end watched by an admiring crowd which included the tearful, remorseful Isabella Ermolin; now he heard he was to be hustled away from all society, from all the city's accustomed pleasures, from his friends, his pastimes, to an island which, however reputedly charming, would be his dismal prison. His father broke it to him that there were strict limitations placed on the amount of money he could take with him and on all remittances. Venice had no desire that her Doge's ducats should leave the city along with his son.

Pasquale, spared torture, spared execution, was not truly grateful for the Republic's mercy.

Meanwhile, Isabella Ermolin, obscured by black gauze, had been escorted by her brother-in-law to the Council Chamber where the *zonta* wished to question her about her husband's murder. Pasquale Scolar had been defiantly firm about his sole responsibility, but they were not eager to take the word of a murderer. Young women were at least as capable of folly as were young men. Indeed, quite a proportion of the Signoria remained unmarried and, deprived of the moderating influence of a wife, believed that *all* women were intrinsically foolish. Isabella Ermolin might well have instigated her husband's murder although there seemed no good reason why she should – the position of widow could hardly be thought an improvement on that of a wife – but reason was not to be expected. Eve had been notoriously ill-advised when she handed Adam the apple.

Yet when, standing in the centre of the room lined with the councillors' carved stalls, Lady Isabella put back the black gauze to frame the beautiful pale oval of her face, opinions throughout the *zonta* underwent a brisk change. The young woman had clearly suffered. She was worthy of sympathy. How could she be blamed? She ought rather to be praised for having gone, so dutifully, so swiftly, to her brother-in-law once she realised the purport of the letter she had received. So lovely a girl, with her modest glance, her low clear voice, could never be blamed for attracting admiration, for driving a young man to desperate lengths. One of the councillors left his place to go to her, take her hand and pat it.

When she let it be known, and with such delicacy, that she was expecting a child, the whole business was settled. The shrewdest minds in Venice questioned no further. The elderly signor now raised her hand and kissed it, and Rinaldo Ermolin was given leave to escort her back to her house. When she had left, trailing soft perfume and veils, not a soul was so crass as to suggest that the child she carried might be not Niccolo's but Pasquale's.

Chapter 26

Gesture From The Grave

In the room Miriam da Silva had provided for them,
Sigismondo completed their unpacking. Since it was likely
that they had been watched leaving their previous lodging,
they had not wanted to be seen carrying their belongings
away. It could be useful if, for a short while, they could be
thought to be braving it out in their former lodgings.

Under their everyday clothes, Benno and his master had
all day worn their spare garments, which they now shed on
the large bed in the corner. Benno had sweated inside his
two shirts and extra jerkin, but he noticed that Sigismondo,
discarding his good black velvet jerkin and his leather one,
looked as cool as if he had never strolled in all of it under
the noonday sun.

Exactly what they needed, however, was to hand. A
scratching at the door, and one of the da Silva servants was
there with a can of water, wrapped in a towel and still hot
even after quite a journey. The man brought with him, too,
a message from Signora da Silva: a servant had come from
Lord Darin seeking Sigismondo. It was the same man who
had found him a day ago and knew therefore that he might
once more find a Christian among the Jews. She had told
him she had no idea where Sigismondo might be, but that
she would pass the message among those who might see
him about the city.

'How did he find us here before?' Benno asked. 'I mean,
it's a big city, isn't it?'

'When we arrived, remember I was required to tell the official why I had come. I told them Joshua da Silva, my old friend, had written that he was ill. In Venice, that's enough.'

'Why would he want to see you now?' Benno felt once more the oppressive sense of the Signoria overlooking all that was done. He sat on the bed watching Sigismondo strip and wash. Benno had poured the hot water into a big majolica basin he had found propped in the painted cupboard. The message was a worry. He had no desire to return to the danger which for him comprised the whole of Venice. Here they were in a refuge, out of the sinister reach of Pyrrho's friend. How much safer it had been before, when his master worked for dukes and princes. Whatever the risks, he had the backing of the State, and people knew it wouldn't pay to meddle with him. Working for a private family was like trying to get comfortable in a hornets' nest. You were disturbing what was bound to be resented by someone and there was no authority to protect you.

'Hey, do I know?' Sigismondo swept water off his bare scalp and reached for the towel Benno had ready. 'We don't know what good the letter I stole has done him. He may want to kiss me or kick me. Or he may want never to see me again.'

'Aren't you sorry for the Doge's son? I mean, if he didn't do it.'

'I'll be sorry when I know that for certain, and when I see his head cut off on the Piazzetta.'

Benno considered this. 'And the Doge? Will they get rid of him like Lord Vettor wants?'

Sigismondo took his shirt from Benno and pulled it on. Emerging from its folds, he said, 'Unless it looks as if the Doge had a hand in Ermolin's murder, which I think would be very hard to prove, then I doubt it. The Venetians are fair. You can usually count on that.'

Benno was not sure he wanted to count on that. Venetian justice seemed to include rather too much spying and beheading to feel entirely safe. Sigismondo stood still for him to lace up the velvet doublet; Benno arranged the gold laces with misgivings. You couldn't trust this old Lord Vettor round the next corner. It wasn't his son-in-law's murderer he was really after, he just wanted to get the poor old Doge into trouble so he could take over and justify his beastly lions of St Mark. Benno looked up from spreading out the bow knot and Sigismondo tapped him on the head.

'Don't *fret*, Benno. He could be going to pay me, not eat me.'

They did not leave by the passages and tunnel. Sigismondo sorted out the keys he had been given and turned one of them in the door in the corner. This led to more passages and more doors, and to stone steps with a door at the foot of them that let them out into a dark little street, narrow and made narrower still with rubbish – broken pots, rotten wood, bones – where the late-afternoon sun saw only the tops of the houses, and where shuttered windows kept their secrets. Benno was beginning to understand something about the lives Jews were forced to lead even in a tolerant city like Venice. He had long ago given up wondering why the Jews were supposed to be so wicked, when Sigismondo trusted them.

The alley led to a sunlit little square where a few scrubby trees threw long evening shadows across the beaten earth. A distant noise of cheering came suddenly. Sigismondo shaded his eyes and Benno saw, at the end of a street some way off, a forest of tall masts and taut sails gliding slowly away.

'The Captain-General's putting to sea. If he's our murderer it's up to the Turks now to do something about it. Lord Vettor is most likely there with all the other scarlet robes, so we'll go to the Ca' Darin and wait for him there; I'm too late to do as I said and wave Attilio goodbye.'

The canals were almost deserted as their gondola moved along what should by now have been a familiar way, but yet was confusing with its side canals off the wide ones, as much like rat-runs as were the dark passages of their new lodgings. Indeed, a large rat more than half the size of Biondello was sitting in a nook above the water as they passed, grooming his whiskers and regarding all that passed with sharp eyes.

Benno grimaced. The dead rat pinned to their wall last night – where was the man who had planted it there?

Before they reached the Ca' Darin, the crowds that had seen off the Captain-General were dispersing. Boats and gondolas made the water rock more violently, and the small wooden bridges over the side canals looked more than usually risky with no parapet to keep the strolling, chattering crowds from the water. Benno, happier not to see anybody since the episode of the dead rat, watched the increase in numbers along the side paths and the bridges with an anxious eye. How easy it would be to throw a knife, say, from one of those bridges, and then vanish in the throng.

What was thrown turned out not to be a knife.

They were approaching one of the wooden tarred bridges when Sigismondo suddenly flung himself sideways, making the gondolier yell as the boat tilted. Benno had seen in that moment a dark thing coming at them from the bridge, low like a swooping bird; lacking Sigismondo's reflexes he sat where he was, gaping, gripped by nightmare, till the thing landed.

The nightmare was not over. The object arrived with a soft thump in Benno's lap and he stared down at it, refusing to know what he saw. It was a hand. It had been severed at the wrist, quite neatly, and lay in Benno's lap, stiff fingers curled slightly as if looking for work to do.

A man on the bridge, dark against the low sun, waved to them as he walked away.

Sigismondo leant over to pick up the hand, and examined it, humming speculatively. 'Another gesture from the grave, I think. Our friend's playing with us, Benno. Time we joined the game.'

Chapter 27

Orders To March

Guido, Duke of Montano, had two hobbies which he found difficult to pursue simultaneously: military strategy, about which he knew a great deal in theory from study of the campaigns of Julius Caesar and Alexander; and his health. He had been a sickly child, cosseted by an anxious mother and an even more anxious father whose sole heir he was. Accustomed to being the focus of concerned attention, he had every wish granted, every whim indulged. Doctors had surrounded him, arguing as to the best way to preserve his life. Now that his life had been preserved into his early thirties by a series of miracles, he felt it essential to employ more than one physician to ensure his continued survival. Besides, he then had a choice of advice to follow, since they rarely agreed.

This did mean that his fighting days were curtailed. It is very difficult to undergo purges, to rest in bed, to follow meticulous and strange diets, and to visit medicinal springs, when you are in a military camp. Riding out to war with leeches attached is inconvenient to a degree. So the Duke spent his time listening to his doctors quarrelling, reading Livy and *The Gallic Wars*, studying maps, and sending commands to Il Lupo, his captain in the field. Any time now, when he felt better, he intended to visit the sphere of war and stir up the action.

It was a war, which, like his poor health, he had been used to from earliest times. His father's domains, now his, bordered territory on which Venice kept a rapacious regard. The Serene Republic, with amazing power that extended over the trade routes from Constantinople and even the snowy wastes of Muscovy to the shores of England and beyond, found that power gives an absolute requirement for more power. Secure in her islanded lagoon, she needed control of the land as well as the sea.

This was not beneficial for the Duke of Montano who owned several cities which could be of use to Venice on her overland trade routes. In his father's lifetime Guido had sat through audiences given to diplomatic envoys of the Republic offering financial interests for concessions, but the old Duke had been ferociously opposed to ceding an inch of influence, let alone concessions which amounted to parting with a single one of his cities, however well compensated he might be; and Guido had inherited the sentiments along with the cities.

A year ago, Venice abandoned diplomacy and plumped for war, possibly because the Marsili brothers had just finished a successful campaign for the Pope. Condottiere like these were a serious challenge and Guido, his head full of plans for attack and counter-attack, looked forward to meeting it – one of these days. He meanwhile sent directions to Il Lupo based on information that was necessarily out of date by the time the directions arrived.

Whether as a result of this or no, the war was not going very well for the Duke. The Marsili brothers had surrounded Piombo, one of those cities coveted by Venice, and were slowly starving it out. Il Lupo was waiting for reinforcements, without which, he had told the Duke, he felt unable for any push to raise the siege.

The Duke was negotiating with the Holy Father for an alliance against Venice. He had hopes of this because Venice was irritating His Holiness both by trading with the Infidel – though that was nothing new – and notoriously continuing to create her own bishops instead of submitting their names for Papal permission. Once Montano had the Pope's backing, he hoped to raise money enough to buy another condotta that would rout the Marsili brothers and relieve poor Piombo before it was too late.

Things had reached uneasy stalemate, when the Duke acquired a new physician. Master Valentino came to him with a recommendation from the Pope, whom he had started to cure of a mysterious illness even before he acquired the triple tiara, when he was only an insignificant and invalid cardinal. The cure had proceeded so well that the Holy Father felt confident enough of his health to allow Master Valentino to leave his side. In fact, it was very hard to keep Master Valentino anywhere for very long as he was nomadic by nature. He liked to travel in various countries – not in search of patients, for they presented themselves wherever he went – but from natural curiosity.

The Duke of Montano submitted to this new physician's examination in high hopes of a fresh regime. His rests had made him feel very poorly of late. He was not disappointed.

'Everything must be changed.' Master Valentino raised his head from the Duke's chest where he had been listening attentively. 'The humours are gravely out of balance.'

The Duke sat up, surprised but not perturbed. He had been expecting to die next week for many years now. Besides, the man who had saved the Pope was fairly sure to be able to save him. His other physicians, gathered to watch the examination, hear the verdict and defend their own opinions, looked carefully at Master Valentino's sardonic, lined face, framed by wings of grey hair under his furred cap, the eyes made more emphatic by thick black brows, and decided that thoughtful nods of reserved agreement would best meet the case.

'Should I rest more? Purge more?'

The doctor finished taking his patient's pulse and restored the ducal wrist to the ducal knee. 'On the contrary. No more purges for the moment. A strengthening diet. And exercise. Much, much more exercise.'

So it came about that the Duke of Montano, believed by Ottavio and Nono to be welded to his bed, found himself on a horse at the head of a troop of his household cavalry, making for Piombo and war. Master Valentino rode nearby, for the trip. He was very interested in the treatment of wounds and in experimenting with a new salve said to prevent gangrene.

Sigismondo, as impelled by natural curiosity as was his old friend Master Valentino, was finding satisfaction of it at the Ca' Darin. Donna Claudia Darin, hearing Sigismondo had arrived to await her husband, sent immediately for him to be brought to her. Dressed today in purple silk embroidered in silver, she swept towards him as he entered, a look of lively interest in her dark eyes.

'Is he to die?'

Sigismondo bowed, smiling. 'All men are to die, my lady. Which one do you want?'

She was near enough now to prod him in the chest, with a glance definitely flirtatious. 'One would think you were a hired assassin, sir. No, I mean Pasquale Scolar, of course.' She paused and the dark eyes scanned him in hope. 'You mean you've not heard of the boy's arrest?'

'I know enough of the matter to guess that it would come. If he's already on trial, the Ten have lost no time.'

'They seldom do. Sooner heads than time. My husband left this morning to sit with the *zonta* in interrogation and judgement. I begged him to send with the result but he was too busy, no doubt, going straight on to the leave-taking of the Captain-General . . . So you have heard nothing?'

'I'm just come from the Giudecca and no news has reached me.' If Sigismondo reflected that a dead hand had reached him, that was news on a personal level only. No one had thrown Pasquale's head as yet.

'Poor young man! What could have possessed him to do something so terrible? My grand-daughter is very distressed, for she discovered the letter and very properly let us know of it – poor child! Since her mother's death she has spent much of her time here, with me, and Niccolo was not a lovable man yet she felt his death deeply. To think that boy could have a man brutally killed who was the father of his friend Marco.'

131

Her grandson's name was spoken in the same instant that a servant flung wide the gilded doors and announced him. Marco, striding in, pulled off his grey velvet cap and sent Sigismondo a look of quite ludicrous surprise and annoyance. He kissed his grandmother's hand and cheek, hardly taking his eyes from her visitor.

'When will my grandfather be here? I must speak to him. Do you expect him, madam?'

'Soon, soon. Marco, do you know the verdict yet?'

'What verdict can there be but guilty? He may rot in hell for all I care.' Marco's handsome face contorted violently. 'Pretending to be my friend and plotting my father's death! The Judas! I hope the torturers tear him to pieces!' He jerked his head at Sigismondo. 'What is he doing here? Is he to haunt our family for ever?'

Donna Claudia frowned, with a brief headshake, a reproof of his manners that only made him scowl. 'You will have to ask your grandfather that, Marco.'

He would not have long to wait; there came shouting and bustle below the windows as Lord Vettor's gondola arrived and he was helped ashore and welcomed back by the servants and, in a muttering grumble just audible beneath the commotion, by his lions.

He appeared shortly, magnificent in scarlet brocade for the farewell to the Fleet, and he greeted his wife, embraced his grandson and nodded to Sigismondo, all without the least appearance of pleasure.

He had hoped to return that evening with news of a Doge forced into resigning – and news of a possible Doge Darin to succeed him. He was in a mood already so bad that it would only be exacerbated by a request for money, but his grandson was too young, too inexperienced and too self-absorbed to see that, and asked to speak in private with him.

He was met with a stare from the round pale eyes that ought to have warned him. Donna Claudia knew her husband, and put a hand on Marco's arm in an attempt to draw him away. Lord Vettor's attention, however, had already left Marco. The eyes focused on Sigismondo with no increase in pleasure.

'You, sir. Come with me.'

Marco's 'Sir . . . !' was cut off by Donna Claudia's sweeping him round with her in a walk up the length of the room. Without a glance at them, Vettor led Sigismondo into a room at the side. It was a smaller room, but equipped as a study far more lavishly than the study where his son-in-law had been found; that was a room as private as a casket for Niccolo's treasures. Here Lord Vettor showed the scale of his ambitions in the size even of the cupboards; one, large enough to be windowed, harboured a table and a revolving reading-stand with books propped open on all its sides. Across the room was a gilded, near life-size statue of Christ. Shelves all along one wall held ledgers bound in coloured leathers stamped in gold. A structure in cedarwood incorporated a chair with a red cushion, a sloping desk, more cupboards still and compartments in which were an hourglass, a bronze candlestick, an astrolabe, a silver hand-bell, a conch shell, and a majolica bowl in which grew a small myrtle bush. Were Lord Vettor to become Doge Darin, his study could be nothing but a credit to him.

'I owe you for your services, sir. I have not forgot that you brought me the letter . . .' he paused a moment, perhaps remembering that the letter had passed so rapidly into Rinaldo's hands '. . . which revealed the guilt of that murderer Pasquale Scolar which led to the pronouncement of his exile.'

'His exile.'

Something in Sigismondo's voice made the round eyes fix on him intently. 'His exile, sir. The *zonta* was merciful beyond the villain's deserts. He is to go under escort to Cyprus and stay there for life.' Lord Vettor went up the steps to the desk platform and busily unlocked one of the cupboards under the sloping desk. 'Naturally I voted for the death penalty. Should one who procured my son-in-law's death have the right to live? But the Signoria had regard to the dignity of the Doge,' and now there was no disguise of his sour tone, 'and so the boy lives.'

A small coffer made its appearance. Lord Vettor, his back
to Sigismondo, bent rather awkwardly to unlock it; evidently
Venetian aristocrats liked to keep special keys on a chain
round the neck. A clinking followed, the coffer and then the
cupboard were locked again and Lord Vettor turned with a
leather bag, drawstring pulled tight, in his hand. He held it
down towards Sigismondo standing below.

'Here, sir. I hope that this will recompense you not only
for what you have done for us,' the plump hand made an
expansive gesture as if to include the family of the Ermolin
as well as his own, 'but also what I trust you will continue to
do.' The little man in his rich robes, bald head shining, drew
himself up and clasped his hands in his sleeves. He assumed
an air of authority, not without menace. 'Let no word pass
your lips of what you have seen or heard in our houses, and
you will leave this city in peace.'

Any indiscretion on Sigismondo's part, it was clear, and
so far from leaving the city in peace, he might never leave it.

On the way back to the Giudecca, Benno got very
indignant when Sigismondo told him of this.

'You've worked for dukes and princes and people far
grander than him and not said one solitary word of what
you've seen or heard or done. And they knew you wouldn't.
Who does he think he is? Hasn't even managed to be Doge.'

'That may be the problem.'

Benno heard a tone in Sigismondo's voice and, looking at
his master's face in the dusk, caught an expression there
that he hardly knew. It occurred to him that Sigismondo,
too, was angry.

Chapter 28

Save Him Again

The dimples were lost in anxiety, the heavily ringed hands twisted together on the black satin.

'The Doge has sent for you, Cristobal. He knew you might be here but I told the messenger I'd had no word of you. Did I do right?'

Sigismondo unclasped the hands and kissed them. 'Perfectly right, Miriam. I am only sorry you are pestered by people seeking me.'

'Will you go to him? Is it about his son?'

'One doesn't refuse the Doge, I think. What have you heard about his son?'

Miriam spread her hands. 'The whole city's talking of nothing else. They say he had Lord Ermolin murdered for love of his wife, and is to be exiled for it. Is it true?'

Sigismondo hummed. 'Truth, Miriam? It looks possible that he did, certainly.'

She put a hand pleadingly on his arm. 'You'll not run into danger, will you, Cristobal, if you go? I know nothing, but Lord Darin has twice sent for you; you may have had a hand in what's happened to that boy whose father he'd like to see at the bottom of the lagoon. Doge Scolar may want revenge.'

Sigismondo leant to take a sweetmeat from the silver dish between them. 'Have you met Doge Scolar, Miriam?'

She dimpled delightfully. 'I've met many of the Signoria, but the Doge's ducats have so far kept him from my door. If his son had stayed in Venice I might have seen him yet. Even the Scolar fortune couldn't withstand that boy's spending. His exile will at least save the Doge's purse . . . Why do you ask?'

'Because, unless I'm very mistaken, he's not the man to take revenge. If he is,' and Sigismondo raised his finger against Miriam's protest, 'if he is, I must take that risk. Believe me,' and he smiled broadly, 'it's only one among many.'

Benno, with too vivid a memory of the dead hand nestling in his lap, only just prevented himself from agreeing out loud, but he nodded vehemently. Miriam, seeing him move, picked a sweetmeat from the dish and tossed it to him. Benno, sucking away at a sugared violet, was glad to see his master at ease and properly appreciated for once in this uneasy city. Here, in the little dark-panelled room crammed with rich things, he was able to hear for himself what was going on instead of waiting to see if Sigismondo was going to tell him about it. Benno had hoped that, now his master had been paid and dismissed by Lord Vettor, they could get away from the nasty families Ermolin and Darin – even, with luck, away from Venice altogether, and the stranger who kept giving them horrible presents.

And now, after all, they were on their way to the Doge's palace to see the Doge, whose son Sigismondo had been instrumental in getting exiled. Benno, hunched in the gondola and looking gloomily at the remains of the sunset in purple and gold over the north-west sky, wished himself back in that rat-hole Miriam da Silva had so kindly provided for them in the Giudecca. Biondello slumbered in his bosom, immune to care. He was a dog philosophical about people throwing things from bridges, though he would prefer something more succulent than a dead hand.

Benno was allowed up the great stone stairs in the torchlit inner courtyard to the palace but, as he expected, Sigismondo alone was escorted by a page in the Scolar livery, to the Doge's apartments. Benno was left, as a great concession considering his grubby appearance, in an antechamber all frescoes and gilt, where a guard kept a wary eye on him. Benno sat on a marble bench and wondered how far down in the layers of the building poor Pasquale had landed; prison walls were always going to be a nasty change from frescoes of people dancing in a wood.

Pasquale's fate was all that Doge Scolar could think of. When Sigismondo was announced, the old man turned a face which anguish had lined more deeply than ever. His back was still straight, though, and dignity had not left him. After Sigismondo's bow, the Doge regarded him for a moment without speaking, then wheeled to look out of the window again as if help might come from the darkening sky.

'You have heard about my son.'

'Your Grace.'

The Doge gave up his search for angels and turned again, the eyes, hooded in wrinkles, searching Sigismondo's face.

'You worked for Lord Vettor; do you still work for him?'

'He has paid me off, your Grace, today.'

The Doge gave a faint, bleak smile. 'After all, it was not you who discovered the murderer. It is thanks to Lady Isabella Ermolin that my son is to be exiled. No doubt you have heard of his letter to her.'

Sigismondo bowed in assent. The Doge now began walking up and down, a few paces, a turn, and back, as if he unconsciously measured the limits of a cell. When he spoke, it was as if he were speaking to himself, disconnected and low. 'She must have done it . . . I have seen the girl. There is a will there, the Devil drives her . . . the Devil drives her . . .' He stopped his pacing and said, 'My son is innocent.'

Sigismondo remained attentive, with no shadow of incredulity and the Doge, watching him, went on. 'He confessed, but to protect her. *She* has done it. She killed her husband to be free to marry Pasquale. Then the moment she fears suspicion may fall on her, she uses his letter of love. She was prepared to see him die.' The old voice broke, but anger, not sorrow, overcame him. 'It's *she* who deserves exile – deserves death.'

'What makes your Grace so certain of her?'

'She knew my son desired her. Do you not think that such a girl would prefer to be wife to a handsome young man ready to spend money on her? Niccolo Ermolin never let a ducat leave his fingers if there was a way to keep it.'

'Was an offer made for her hand on behalf of your son before she married Lord Ermolin?'

The Doge sat down on the embroidered cushions of the window seat, suddenly, as if his legs would no longer support him. Beyond, the sky was a dark blue as the dusk deepened, the glow of day succeeded by the glow of torches in the courtyard. He raised a fragile hand to shield his eyes, but not from their light; from his own regrets.

'I should have listened to him. Would I had listened to him . . . I told him it was only a fancy, that he would have a thousand such fancies; that one does not marry for love, that he would get over this.' He sighed, and raised his head to look towards Sigismondo. 'I did not like her parents or her brother. I did not wish to be allied to them although the family was a good one and she was known to have a fair dowry. I mistrusted . . . but how was I to know what would come of it?'

A page entered, murmuring apologies for his interruption, with a lighted taper for the great candles. He went round the walls, reaching up to the bronze torchères, and gracefully withdrew. He passed Benno who sat in the gloom of the anteroom debating whether he would be stopped from eating a raw onion and a nice piece of bread he had stashed inside his shirt; Biondello, meditating between shirt and jerkin, had long ago learnt not to try to dig through to any food. Benno caught the eye of Apollo toying with a nymph on the wall opposite and decided against the raw onion. When the page came out with his taper, Benno could just catch the deep tones of his master's voice before the door shut.

'What does your Grace wish me to do?'

The old man beckoned him nearer, nearer until Sigismondo all but stood over him, and then he caught hold of the velvet sleeve with a hand that, for the first time, trembled.

'Prove that he is innocent. Prove it. You saved him once. Save him again.'

Chapter 29

The Fate Of Piombo

The Duke of Montano achieved a good deal of the exercise recommended by his physician, on the way to join his army encamped not far from Piombo. He had flown his hawks, which of course he had brought with him, at quite a few birds along the way; a pleasure his poor health had limited until now. When he arrived, it was a different story. The chance of exercise in battle seemed unlikely indeed.

This was because his captains were uncertain of success.

Battle, unless the outcome was a pushover, was altogether too dangerous an activity for a condottiere. They might, from time to time, be forced into it if taken by surprise or browbeaten by tyrannical employers, but not one would voluntarily take the chance of depleting his precious stock of men, his bargaining power. War was a business, like any other, a matter of chaffering, market forces and strategies and insider dealings. The Duke's captains expected to effect a bargain with the enemy at some point and, when he arrived in their midst, they could be forgiven for supposing he had come to initiate such bargaining.

But the enemy was Venice, which had hired the Marsili brothers. Unless the Duke had brought a respectable amount of money with him, enough to tempt Ottavio and Nono to the risky act of doublecrossing the Serene Republic, the odds were that, before many days were out, Piombo would be forced to surrender and the Duke would have lost one of his favourite towns. Such an event would not merely make the old Duke revolve in his grave, it would probably fetch him out of it to haunt his incompetent son.

The Duke, however, besides the household cavalry who were good only for parades, seemed to have brought only his physician. His captains, led by Il Lupo, must persuade him that to advance on the Marsili condotta encamped round starving Piombo would simply add one disaster to another. Gold, not blood, would solve their problem.

Feeling fitter, and therefore more impatient, than he had done for several years, Guido discovered that his captains had no idea of strategy, such as he had studied so diligently in Caesar and in accounts of other military geniuses. Il Lupo and the rest had an exclusively pragmatic approach to glory. Useless to have a statue erected to your renown if you were not alive to enjoy it. Now, if his Grace were to bribe the Marsili brothers – had he ever seen them in battle? – then the siege of Piombo might be raised in time for everyone to go home for the winter.

The Duke, after a pause, pointed out that this was the month of July. They reminded him that they could not be expected to fight much beyond September – the beginning of September at that. He asked sarcastically if the Marsili brothers would also disband in September, and they replied with a lot of shrugging that the Marsili brothers made their own rules; they were monsters, capable of anything.

This idea, however, held more promise than the Duke had realised. Il Lupo, who had earned himself the name without having to carry off any children in his jaws, leant forward on the trestle table – spread with maps, scarred with knives and stained with wine and grease – and thrust his cadaverous face towards the Duke.

'Hold out your hand long enough and the apple falls into it.'

Not all the amount of learning Guido's tutors had endeavoured to put between his ears could help him now with this gnomic utterance. Il Lupo shifted impatiently and gave him a hint. 'Of course you understand the hand can't be *empty*.'

Now the Duke saw. It was a message he had received before: the Marsili brothers, like any other condottieri, were bribable. He had made complicated efforts in that direction already, with all the subterfuges and precautions necessary, and it was still possible that they might succeed. His agents told him that the Marsili were not wholly happy with their employer but that was hardly news. Very few non-Venetians working for the Serene Republic were wholly happy. Although Venice was prepared to reward success, and very handsomely, failure had catastrophically unwelcome results. The really enormous difficulty of the matter was that if they did accept his bribes and raise the siege of Piombo, it must be done in such a way that Venice could forgive it, think it an unavoidable accident and continue to pay up with a smile.

The Duke did not expect any of this to happen.

Il Lupo nevertheless was sanguine. He glanced round the other captains, with a shrug. 'Piombo, now; you may have to give up Piombo, it's true.'

The Duke seemed to see his father's face of incredulous fury. He thought of the inhabitants of Piombo, with their Duke's forces within sight, having eaten their cats, their dogs, their rats – a crowd of skeletons with outstretched hands, his name on lipless mouths.

'I can't give up Piombo.'

Il Lupo's fist jolted the table. 'Your Grace, this is war! Piombo is lost already. The Marsili have to give Piombo to Venice if they are to do us any good in the future.'

The Duke quite abruptly found he regretted his former regime of frequent rests. It would be so consoling, at this moment, not to have to listen to this unpleasant man who was looking more like a wolf at every moment, and to be forced by some stern physician to take a rest. He could not understand why the Marsili brothers were expected to do their enemies any good . . . Why had he brought Master Valentino, who believed in exercise and not rest? All his recently recovered energy was deserting him under the cynical gaze of Il Lupo.

'After Piombo has fallen, your Grace, we can start talking.'

Great minds think alike; professionals in particular can come to similar conclusions. Outside Piombo, Ottavio and Nono had called a council of their captains and decided the time had come to put the people of Piombo out of their misery.

Only a few hours after the council of captains had broken up, the Piombese were astonished to see wagons – oxcarts – trundling laboriously over the rutted ground between their walls and the besieging army, carts loaded with sacks. These sacks, so plump, so many, were enough to make the mouth water, especially the mouths of those who had kept going on rat soup for weeks.

One sack had a slight slit in it, leaking a thin trickle of wheat. No one on the walls of Piombo, seeing that, could prevent himself from smelling hot bread straight from the oven.

But why? Who could be sending them food at such a point, through an army dedicated to their destruction by starvation? Some sanguine souls believed their Duke had come to their rescue and, as the Marsili army had clearly not removed itself, he had managed to come to peace terms with them, resulting in these blessed sacks of corn. Others feared the worst: it was Venetians they were dealing with, famous for their trickery. The carts were a ruse, designed to get the gates open, the sacks stuffed with rubbish.

They called down to the old man driving the first oxcart, and his answer bore out the hopes of the most optimistic Piombese. The wheat was from their Duke. The Marsili had accepted a truce while terms were being arranged, and one of the conditions their Duke had insisted upon was that his starving subjects should be fed. To show that all was above board, each wagon would enter the gates alone to be searched, before it was unloaded and the next one brought in.

Hunger opened the gates. Slowly – with what cruel slowness! – the first wagon creaked and rumbled over the drawbridge that crossed the deep ditch. The gatehouse echoed to its thunder. Piombese with pikes they were not

142

too weak to use were there to unload and search, while the other wagons lurched forward, waiting their turn.

Suddenly there was confusion, shouting and cracking of a whip. The second cart's oxen had come on, not stopping on the bridge, and their driver only got them halted in the gateway, his wagon slewed into one of the great doors, making the gates impossible to shut. The driver of the first wagon made an alarming recovery from old age and produced a sword, leaping down among the wretched Piombese and their pikes. The sack that had trickled wheat now split entirely and discharged a gargoyle of a man who, in a shower of corn, swung another sword, large for him but dreadfully suited to his capabilities. Ottavio and Nono could boast that they were the first inside Piombo, a definite plus to their credit with the Serene Republic. The following wagons had already proved full of soldiers, under the sacks, and there were plenty more now, racing to kill, burn and loot – to carry off anything left in the city that had not been edible.

Those who had been most mistrustful among the Piombese did not live long enough to have the sour pleasure of saying 'I told you so' to the rest, who could not anyway have heard.

Chapter 30

Different Sons, Different Problems

While Ottavio and Nono were solving the Piombo question for their Venetian employers, other losses and gains were occurring in Venice itself.

On a minor scale, the servants at the Palazzo Ermolin were fascinated to observe the speed with which the Lady Isabella had gained the respect and protection of Lord Rinaldo now that she was known to be carrying his brother's child. He visited her in her apartments every day, they dined together as a matter of course now, and it was noticed with astonishment that he consulted her wishes as to the alterations and extensions Brunelli was supervising in the palace; her late husband, who had commissioned these, would as soon have dreamt of consulting her pet cat's opinions as hers. It was also seen that Marco, formerly devoted to his young stepmother, had lost all interest in her and avoided her, though that might be because he was avoiding his uncle, so often in her company.

Marco had reason to avoid Rinaldo. He had been unable to raise money from the Jews once word passed round that Miriam da Silva had refused him. His best friend Pasquale, source of infinite largesse in days gone by, was convicted of having procured his father's murder, and the source of Pasquale's money, the Doge, was not really likely to part with any ducats to Marco. Lord Vettor, Marco's last chance and sometimes a kindly grandfather, was in so foul a mood over failure to involve Doge Scolar in Pasquale's disgrace that Marco had decided after all not to approach him, and Donna Claudia flatly refused to make any intervention on Marco's behalf. His sister Beatrice had no money and they had never been on such terms that he could beg her to give him her jewelry to sell, even if such little trinkets as a young girl was allowed would bring in anything worthwhile; yet he looked at her filigree earrings and wished he had bothered to be affectionate towards her. Matters were more urgent hourly, because creditors who had joyfully expected full settlement on his father's death, became aware of his reluctance or, worse, his inability to pay; and they began by common consent to present their bills to the man in charge of the Ermolin purse, Lord Rinaldo.

Sooner or later, Marco was bitterly aware, heads would roll. Not Pasquale's, for a wonder, however richly he deserved it, but his own – truly innocent, he felt, of all but a natural presumption on what should have been his fortune. He had taken it that his father's death would solve all problems; he had never thought that Niccolo's fortune would not devolve upon him. Now it looked as if only his Uncle Rinaldo's death would be of use, and the latter's way of life offered no hope of an early natural death. Rinaldo was not reckless or dissipated, would not easily be caught unawares, and was the man to throw caution to the winds only if it were fully insured.

It crossed Marco's mind that if Pasquale had, as he claimed, been able to find an assassin without too much difficulty – though the whole business of the assassin was a puzzle to Marco – then it would not be impossible, if of course he could bring himself to do such a frightful thing, to find one on his own account. The problem was, whom to ask for word-of-mouth recommendation, as it were. Hardly possible to nip down to the prisons and ask Pasquale for a tip.

Marco sighed deeply at the pure unfairness of everything.

There was such a particular poignancy in his father's lack of trust in him, handing affairs to Rinaldo, leaving his only son such a paltry amount . . . Now he had to skulk in corners, waiting for the moment when his uncle would descend on him with accusations of wasting Ermolin money, when all the money should have been his by natural right. Well, if he had to skulk away from his usual haunts, perhaps he could strike up acquaintance with someone who had a professional, perhaps useful, reason for avoiding the public eye.

One such was visiting his uncle just as the idea crossed Marco's mind. Rinaldo, as his nephew knew, was not one to draw a bow at a venture: the man who stood calmly before him, listening to instructions, was there because Rinaldo had received the very word-of-mouth recommendation Marco could see no way to get. Giulio da Tolentino, recently and so mysteriously bereaved – no one had yet found who could have cut his wife's throat in so horrible a manner – was a trusty acquaintance (Rinaldo did not have friends) and had confided in him, with the help of a good deal of wine taken to drown his happiness at his wife's funeral, that people inconvenient in life need not be suffered if one were willing to disburse a quite reasonable sum of money to remove them, and that he, Giulio, knew of a removal man. The Ermolin trade connections were quite sufficient to exert pressure on Giulio. He produced a name and a place where enquiry might be made.

The result lounged before Rinaldo now. He looked unbothered, a man to whom death was probably familiar, and Rinaldo, though naturally suspicious, felt confident in this man's discretion. He began to put forward his wishes in detail.

Another man of whom the same could be said was also in the palace at this time, his presence unknown to its owner or indeed to anyone but the housekeeper.

Sigismondo and Benno had arrived by hired boat this time, at the small landing stage on the side canal that was close to Zenobia's store room. As Benno rowed up, his arms reminding him that he'd done a lot of rowing lately, there were two people at the landing stage, one with a basket of lemons he was handing over in exchange for some coins and a charming smile, and the one who smiled, Zenobia herself, graceful in her gown of charcoal grey, a plain white cap framing her face. As she turned towards the new arrivals, her smile vanished.

'Why are you here? I've no more to tell you. The affair is closed.'

Benno, scrambling on to the steps after his master, thought it was certainly closed for Pasquale and that poor old gentleman his father. No wonder Zenobia was annoyed that Sigismondo came visiting now. The Ermolin family had not given a welcome to Sigismondo poking about in their secrets to start with. Benno understood from his master that Lord Rinaldo, right at the beginning, had had it broken to him that Sigismondo had been hired over his head by an interfering Lord Vettor and had further distinguished himself by burgling a compromising letter from Lady Isabella – a letter whose contents he knew all about. Lord Rinaldo for sure wasn't going to come rushing down to kiss them hallo.

Neither was this Zenobia by the look of it.

'I have things to tell you, all the same, which you may prefer to hear in private.'

Benno had known this ploy of Sigismondo's to work before; his master said there were few people who didn't have secrets that might be discovered, and they always preferred to limit the damage as Sigismondo was suggesting now.

The ploy worked again. Zenobia, after a swift glance round, indicated the open door of her room with a peremptory jerk of the head as if to an inferior servant, and went in. Benno, following Sigismondo closely in the hope that for once he would not be left out of the action, stumbled on the threshold when he saw the person who was already in the room.

A tall, handsome young man, in a scarlet doublet and hose brilliantly striped in scarlet and white, had started warily to his feet when Sigismondo came after Zenobia. For all their bright colours, his clothes were not of silk or velvet but of good cloth such as a respectable working man might wear. What was interesting about him, however, was his face.

It was not just its glowing deep brown, like Zenobia's, but also the proud aquiline nose, the large eyes and high cheekbones. This was clearly her son Cosmo, son also to the murdered man.

Chapter 31

The Evil Eye Will Be Shut For Ever

'What do you have to tell me? Lady Isabella wishes to see me soon and I have little time to spend.'

She certainly had spent no time on introductions. Cosmo sat down once more on the stool at Zenobia's desk and she made no effort to invite Sigismondo to be seated. Benno lurked behind him in the doorway and wondered what he would come up with now he was challenged to produce a secret Zenobia needed to hear.

'The matter is perhaps not closed, as you fancy.'

Sigismondo's tone was sombre, and Zenobia, not skilled in intrigue, glanced involuntarily at Cosmo. 'Lord Pasquale's in prison. We heard he is to be exiled for the murder.'

'You must have heard why he is supposed to have had your master killed.'

A hint of contempt curled Zenobia's lip. 'He loves my mistress. So they say.' Perhaps it wasn't so much contempt as disbelief, thought Benno. Pasquale, vanquished by the lady's beauty, wouldn't know half as much about her character as Zenobia must have learnt. Without ever having seen the lady, Benno had an unattractive picture of her: a young witch, who didn't mind coming up with a letter that must lose an admirer his head. Of course, if she really thought he'd had her husband killed . . .

'Do you believe your mistress loves another man?'

Zenobia raised her head a little as she regarded Sigismondo. 'On whose authority do you ask?'

Disconcertingly, Sigismondo laughed, a laugh that simmered deep in his chest. 'Hm – mmh! Do you need to ask that? Do you really?'

After a moment of bewilderment, Zenobia was alarmed. Behind her, Cosmo sat forward, his look a mirror of hers. At her sides, her hands clenched, a small movement Sigismondo certainly saw. 'You mean—'

Sigismondo was silent.

It came to Benno why Zenobia was so much afraid. If Lord Vettor, as she must guess, no longer had need for Sigismondo's services, the old lord was after all acquainted with the Ten themselves; who therefore might very well be using this man who had worked for so many noble people. Sigismondo, not denying what had not been said, had put these two deep in anxiety. The Republic, Benno reflected, might be serene but its subjects frequently weren't.

Zenobia brusquely gestured Cosmo to his feet, and offered Sigismondo the stool. He took it, with judicial gravity. Hands spread on thighs, he regarded Zenobia under his brows.

'Do you know of any time when your mistress might have met Lord Pasquale Scolar?'

Zenobia thought, then shook her head. 'I am not her maid, nor does Chiara tell me anything. I do not encourage gossip. She might have met him at weddings, dances . . . there's always an occasion to waste your time if you're in the Golden Book.'

'Was she on good terms with your master?'

'She pleased him well enough.' There was open bitterness now. This woman had pleased Niccolo Ermolin once, had caught his eye when she was younger even than Lady Isabella, when he was not yet married at all. 'They had one of their arguments that morning, it's true. I don't think she can have told him she was with child. If he had known that, he would have been very different to her. He would have been happy indeed.'

Benno's vacant gaze was on Cosmo, and he saw the grimace at this. A hard difference, to be born of a slave; yet surely Niccolo Ermolin must have rejoiced when this eldest son was born. He had let him grow up here, part of the family till that interfering old Lord Vettor decided he wasn't fit company for the legitimate children. Had Sigismondo quite given up the idea that if Pasquale was innocent, a resentful son might have done the murder?

Apparently he had not. He swung towards the young man. 'And you, Cosmo. Where were you, the morning your father was killed?'

Zenobia instinctively spread her arms to protect Cosmo but her son put her aside and faced Sigismondo, head up, contained. 'You know who I am, that's plain, sir, but you don't know *what* I am – no murderer. Nor would I kill my father, no matter what he had done.'

Sigismondo smiled, a wide, bland, not at all reassuring smile. 'Then you won't mind telling me where you were when he was killed.'

'I can tell you where I was that morning, but I can't tell you where I was when he was murdered.'

'Naturally, if you had nothing to do with the murder.'

Zenobia, pressed against the wall by the window, light from the water below flickering over her face, turned her eyes from one to the other as they spoke. It came to Benno suddenly that she was not at all sure of her son's innocence.

'I was at work. I'm a gondolier and I can't be sure now where I was employed that morning or what passengers I carried – except,' he paused and glanced out at the water, frowning, 'except that one of them might have been Lord Gamboni.'

'Pico Gamboni? Your father's enemy?'

'Crazed by misfortune, sir. Fate itself was Lord Gamboni's enemy.'

'He was often your passenger?'

'He knew who I was, so it amused him to hire me when he wanted to be carried past this house. He thought I, too, was a victim of the Evil Eye and he believed I shared his feelings towards my father.'

'You did not tell him otherwise.'

Cosmo smiled. 'I'm a gondolier, as I said. I must work to

live. I cannot offend my passengers.'

'Even the mad ones.' Sigismondo was smiling too, and Benno saw Zenobia's fists relax. 'How did Lord Gamboni pay you, reduced to beggary as he is?'

Cosmo had no immediate answer. Benno thought: doesn't look so good if he's been ferrying the madman for free, so he can shout curses at Lord Ermolin – even shin up a rope so conveniently left by the workmen, and stick a dagger in that Evil Eye. That's carrying not offending your passengers a little far. Far as a scaffold, shouldn't wonder.

'Lord Gamboni has friends, those who are sorry for him. They give him money. He would sooner pay me to bring him past here to rail at my father than pay for food.'

'So you had him as a passenger that morning?'

'I'm not sure now that I did . . .' Cosmo shook his head decisively. 'It was the day before that I brought him by here.'

'The day *before*.'

'I remember now quite clearly. He hailed me at the Piazzetta, told me he had great news for me and I must take him by the usual route, past the Palazzo Ermolin. He was in a happy mood, singing and clapping his hands as we went out along the Grand Canal.'

'What was his great news?'

'He said to me: "Lord Ermolin will die soon, and the Evil Eye will be shut for ever".'

Chapter 32

He'll Catch You First

Benno steadied the boat for Sigismondo to step in. Biondello, a hardened Venetian by now, had taken up his position in the prow, in miniature competition with a large black dog standing forward in another boat being rowed by, that passed without even deigning to bark. As Sigismondo sat and cast off, and gave Benno directions where to head for, on the other side of the palace someone else was being ushered out with just as little ceremony, and minding as little. Assassins never expect red carpets, unless they're in charge of the dyeing.

Dion lounged at the door, wondering whether to walk up the alley or to hail the gorgeously dressed black gondolier rowing slowly along the water.

He had plenty to celebrate, so he hailed the gondola. Relaxing on the cushions he stretched out long legs and listened to the gondolier, who was singing in a good baritone the very tune that had caught his ear on first coming to Venice.

> Do you remember once we swore
> Only death could part us?
> Now on a foreign shore
> Whose arms are around you,
> Whose arms?

He hummed the refrain. Fate had been very entertaining

recently, paying up for things he hadn't done and, now, offering him a job he'd been going to do anyway, more of a pleasure than a commission – not something he was going to rush, though. If he were to get his fun out of it, he must see the target sweat a bit first.

In the heat of noon, the target was in fact sweating a bit, but that was because he had taken over the oars from Benno. They were in search of Pico Gamboni but, even given the comparative rarity of impoverished members of the Signoria, or at least those reduced to actual begging, Benno had little hope of spotting the one they wanted. It was even harder now that he no longer needed to be rowed past the Palazzo Ermolin shouting curses and making a spectacle of himself.

The real problem before them was that too many people were ready to admit that they wanted Niccolo Ermolin dead. Benno counted them up on his fingers. The dwarf condottiere they'd had liver and onions with had been delighted at the thought. Attilio da Castagna the Captain-General gone to fight the Turks had a really good reason for skewering Ermolin through the eye to pay for his own patch. Pasquale Scolar had actually said he'd hired it done and this Gamboni madman had been promising it for years.

What Sigismondo wanted to know was why Gamboni thought the time had come for Ermolin to die, just before it did.

Pico Gamboni proved to be not totally elusive. When they brought the boat back to the Piazzetta and moored there, they found a shifting crowd centred round the two tall columns. Sigismondo could see over the heads of many, but Benno had to jump up and down before he could find out what everyone was looking at. Then he wished he hadn't.

Someone, in chains, was kneeling between the two columns, the chains holding him up. This was entirely necessary because he hadn't got a head. Or he had, but it was on the ground in front of him.

Benno, landing on his feet again after discovering this, stumbled and was held upright by a firm grasp on his collar. He got his voice going and croaked, 'Who is he?'

'He *was* Andrea Barolo. He was also Captain-General of the Fleet when they lost the most recent battle against the Turks. I told you it was a mistake to lose if you worked for Venice.'

Sigismondo's information had been given in a bass murmur which, as the gazing crowd was inclined to whisper rather than comment aloud, Benno heard perfectly. Someone else who heard it had come up close behind them and now seized them each by an elbow.

'Justice, justice, sirs. Here in this city we have the best justice in the world. This is the public kind – but I prefer the private.'

Pico Gamboni, his tattered red silk shining in the sun, his greying hair blown round his face by the breeze from the lagoon, smiled cheerfully up at Sigismondo.

'We need to talk about that private justice, my lord.'

Pico laughed with manic enjoyment, rubbing his hands. 'Oh, we'll talk about anything, if you like. Put a cup of wine in my hand and I'll recite the whole of the *Divina Commedia*. Two cups and we'll have a debate on Epicureanism. Give me a barrel of wine to empty and I'll be Diogenes and crawl inside it and then heaven help the man who stands in my sunlight.'

Benno had the impression that this made sense of a sort to Sigismondo, however much it was gibberish to him. At any rate his master was smiling and pointing to a stall across the way where a number of those who had come to see the Republic's justice had found themselves compelled to take a little heavy refreshment, possibly to keep their stomachs down. Pico's eyes lit up and he made his way through the crowd towards the stall, followed by Sigismondo and Benno, who could not resist a glance back at the unfortunate ex-Captain-General, on his knees as suppliant to a Fate that had showed him no mercy.

Gamboni was as good as his word. When he had drained his first cup of wine he looked expectantly at Sigismondo and held his arms wide. 'What do you want to know? Now that Pasquale Scolar is to suffer for it, you're surely not still looking for Ermolin's murderer.'

They moved away from the stall a little, and Sigismondo held out the fried chitterlings on their cabbage-leaf wrapper. Gamboni eagerly seized one and started to chew, while Sigismondo, a hand on his shoulder, guided him on further to a small space near the water. Behind them the crowd slowly moved, constantly replenished with those who had yet to see what remained of the man who had lost his head for losing his head in battle with the Turks. Here, between the soft lapping of water and the subdued sounds from the crowd, Pico gnawed at his chitterling and Sigismondo put his question.

'How did you know when Ermolin was about to die? You spoke of it the day before his murder.'

Pico flapped greasy fingers. 'I spoke of it every day this last year. Sooner or later the Devil would claim him.'

Sigismondo held out the flagon he had bought, and Pico held out his cup, but Sigismondo did not pour. 'You can do better than that, my lord,' he said genially. 'You know far more than you're saying. Why did the Devil foreclose on that day?'

Pico laughed, holding back his blowing hair with greasy fingers and waggling the cup under the flagon as if coaxing it to pour. 'Ah, if it's a drinking matter I'll tell, though I'd not bring harm on anyone who does the world a favour by sending Ermolin out of it. Still, you'll not catch the man.'

'The man?'

A few feet away, an impressionable lad who had once received a pat on *his* head from Andrea Barolo was losing his breakfast into the lagoon. Pico turned his face up to the sun and smiled, while the dazzle off the water turned his ragged gown to flame.

Sigismondo poured the wine and Pico lowered his face to the cup and drank. Then, lifting the cup as if in a toast, he said, 'A man with courage to face the curse Ermolin put on all who were against him.'

'How do you know this man did it?'

The whites showed all round the brown eyes that stared

at Sigismondo. 'Are you mad, man? Or is Ermolin still walking the earth?'

Sigismondo held the cup steady, as a turbaned man of ferocious expression pushed past to view Venice's justice. Benno thought that anyone but his master would have lost patience and started throttling the madman. Did he really not understand what Sigismondo was getting at?

'Did you see the man who killed him?'

Pico's Adam's apple bobbed as he drank, and Benno noticed how dirty were his hands on the cup. If his house had burnt down, where had he been sleeping this past year?

As it turned out, this was entirely relevant to the question.

'I saw him. For a minute. There's a bench,' Pico gestured vaguely towards the whole of the city, 'where I sleep sometimes in summer. The night before last, there was a cold mist at dawn; quite usual. I'd wrapped my head,' the thin hand sketched a brief encirclement of the flying hair, 'and I suppose I must have looked like a corpse, nothing of note in this city, and two men stopped not far off to talk. The tall man was given money and was promised more on completion.'

Sigismondo waited and, as Pico held out his cup again, said, 'Is that all? There are several hundred, perhaps several thousand, assassins in the city. There are murders every day. What told you who the victim was to be?'

'The man paying the money told him.' Pico flourished his cup, spattering his wrist, which he paused to lick. 'He told him, "His study window is over the side canal and he works there from daybreak until noon." Have I earned another flagon?'

Sigismondo handed the empty one and some money to Benno, who took it off for a refill at the stall. Pico had found a scrap of chitterling stuck to his red silk, prised it off with a fingernail and, about to eat it, saw Biondello's face turned up to him and sacrificed the fragment with a smile.

Benno, hurrying back with the full flagon, found Sigismondo, still trying to get Pico's memory moving, offering the cabbage leaf; and Pico helped himself once more.

Benno thought it showed he was a gentleman in that he took only one. A lowlife like himself would have taken more while they were going.

'If you saw him for a minute, in the dawn light and with your head wrapped up, can you say what he looked like?'

Some hopes! The madman didn't strike him as the observant type in any conditions; on the lookout for free food, maybe, but not faces.

Benno was wrong. Pico Gamboni had been keenly interested in the face of the man hired to kill his soul's enemy. Under the fold of cloth round his head he had screwed up his eyes – he showed them how – in order to focus his gaze.

'Oh, make no mistake, I saw him clearly. Handsome, a thin pale face, dark hair, a mole by his eye. If you want to see him, I could show him to you. He's been watching you for some time.' Pico extended an arm in its perished red silk, pointing.

Through the crowd, a tall man in olive drab, cap pulled down over his dark hair, lounged by one of the stalls, cup in hand like Pico. Seeing them look at him, he smiled, raised the cup and with a little bow to Sigismondo, poured the wine out on the ground where it lay like a splash of blood.

A gang of young men, pushing each other boisterously, came running to feast their eyes on the execution, and when they had gone by, the place at the stall was empty.

'You'll not catch him in a hurry,' Gamboni remarked. 'He'd catch you first.'

Chapter 33

If Faith Moves Mountains . . .

Attilio da Castagna had set sail with so much panoply and splendour, trumpets blowing, the Doge himself waving goodbye, the Patriarch of Venice busy with blessings, that he would be excused for thinking that the Serene Republic put its trust in him. However, he was a Venetian. He did not make that mistake. In his train were several people there to keep an eye on him and on whom in turn his one, singular eye was kept. One was his confessor, who came with the blessing – the insistence – of the Patriarch, a benevolent old despot whose wishes must be respected if he were to remain benevolent. This priest reminded Attilio of a snake, for he slipped in and out of sight soundlessly and, whenever Attilio looked up, he might find eyes of reptilian brightness fixed upon him.

Attilio promised himself that when battle eventually came, he would find a way of ensuring that the priest kept an eye on him then too. Perhaps tying him to the mast would answer. Then afterwards he'd give him some Turks to convert; Attilio knew Turks.

His confessor was not the only one. A man of his own, a good fighter whom he had reason to trust, asked him for a private audience not long after they sailed. Attilio imagined it was to ask for some favour, probably a loan; sailors notoriously bankrupt themselves in port and Venetian courtesans were the world's most expensive. He beckoned the man into the cabin and handed him wine to make the asking easier.

What he was asked for was not money. Rather, as the creak of rigging and the slow beat of the drum as they moved down the straits made a background, he listened and realised that he was being *offered* money. He was being sounded out to see if his loyalty to Venice was as unwavering as the Republic hoped. It came into Attilio's mind as he regarded the man twirling his winecup and seeking for the right, the most discreet words in which to put the invitation to become a traitor, that perhaps Andrea Barolo had lost that battle against the Turks for reasons other than incompetence or bad luck.

This might be a Venetian feint or it might be a genuine offer. Attilio was not a man to commit himself, particularly with a confessor trying to listen at the door. Once it was hinted to him who it was who might be interested in providing him with a fortune to betray Venice, he cordially clasped the man's hands and, alleging that a matter on deck would at this moment need his attention, he cut the interview short.

He gave his answer an hour later when he had the man hanged at the masthead, and had it proclaimed that he was punishing one in the pay of the enemy. He had instructed his confessor to shrive the traitor, and it provided the Captain-General with the satisfactory thought that if the whole thing were a put-up job to test his loyalty, then the confessor was the right man to offer consolation.

While the Captain-General was giving his galleys something to look at as he led the way down the coast, and the former Captain-General was supplying his own spectacle for the crowds in the Piazzetta, Sigismondo and Benno made their way back to the bolt-hole given them by Miriam da Silva. As they'd had pointed out to them the man who'd probably killed Niccolo Ermolin and who evidently meant to kill Sigismondo, Benno would, if left to himself, have got out of Venice as fast as legs, oars and terror could take him. However, his master did not function like that. He would take the threat seriously but he would enjoy the challenge.

He noticed all the same that Sigismondo was careful to

leave the crowds behind as rapidly as he could, and take to narrow alleys and deserted side streets where not even a dog wandered today when there were rich pickings to be gleaned elsewhere. If the sinister stranger were following them, he'd have to be doing it by the rooftops. Benno remembered Sigismondo's own dreadful agility on rooftops in the past, and glanced up nervously at the thought but saw only pigeons, some wheeling overhead, some looking down from parapets and tiles. On the corner of one house a small carving of the Lion of St Mark stared dourly down at them.

It wasn't possible to cross to the Giudecca without taking a boat, and Benno felt they were a sitting target on the water. He too well remembered the dead hand that had jumped so confidingly into his lap and he did not feel comfortable until they had landed and no boat seemed to have followed them among the crowded shipping. In fact, he did not feel comfortable until they had negotiated the dark passages, unlocked all the doors – and locked them again – and arrived in their snug rat-hole. It was all the more snug for a covered dish of vegetables and cheese left for them by friendly hands. Benno had sincerely thought his appetite was gone after the chitterlings and the glimpse of the tall man watching them, but when he took the cover off and smelt the cheese, he found it had not.

Sigismondo nodded permission, and it was with his mouth full that Benno asked, 'Have you seen that man before?'

'Mm . . . m.' Sigismondo behind the shutter looked down at the dark alley below, his face in shadow. 'In a sense, I think I have.'

'Looked just like Pyrrho, didn't he?' Pyrrho, when Benno last saw him, had been as dead as anyone can get with a sword in his throat, asprawl in his own blood as if glad of the rest. 'You think he's his brother, maybe?'

'Probably. And probably a professional assassin too. These trades can run in families. So Pico Gamboni is very likely right and the man was hired to kill Ermolin. The question still remains, was it Pasquale Scolar who hired him?'

'Likely he did, though, right?' Benno was scrupulously

leaving half the grapes, baby onions and soft Venetian rice for Sigismondo even though he showed little interest. 'I mean, he confessed and everything.'

Sigismondo hummed, *basso profundo*. 'And if you saw the master torturer from Padua perhaps you too would confess you'd hired someone to kill Ermolin. Pain does marvels for the memory – and even for the imagination.'

Benno, considering this, slowed down over licking his fingers. Again, the food lost its relish. Biondello, completely untroubled by imagination, helped himself under Benno's arm to a stuffed buckwheat polenta roll.

'What're you going to tell the Doge, then? I mean, it's hopeless to prove his son's innocent if he says himself he's guilty. And if it's Lady Isabella that really did it, and he's shielding her, how do you get to make her say so? She isn't just going to, is she?'

'Hey *Benno*! When I want logic I turn to you rather than Aristotle.' Sigismondo had strolled over and was sampling his share from the big dish. 'We're in a cleft stick and it's holding us steady for someone to shoot at. Doge Scolar put his trust in me, although I warned him of the poor odds, and in our turn we have to trust Fate to send something. At present we've little to go on, but that is the moment when faith moves the mountain.'

'Does it really? I wouldn't want to be on the mountain if it did. And if you were underneath where it moved to you'd have to have a lot of faith it wouldn't kill you.'

'An interesting theosophical point.'

'Do you think she did it? Lady Isabella?'

Sigismondo did not reject the question. 'It's possible. Even if there was a convenient rope hanging near Ermolin's window, the men who left the rope were never far away on the roof. There's the building opposite, and though it's a convent with shuttered windows, the shutters are louvred; someone might see. It takes some nerve, which of course professional bravos must have or they're out of business, to climb that rope, appear at Ermolin's window without his giving the alarm, kill him, and leave by the same route with the same chance of discovery on the way down. It was always more likely to be an inside job.'

'You mean whoever copied the key to the study.'

'Or someone Niccolo let in.'

'The housekeeper said he never let anyone in.'

'No rule's never broken. One thing, though. The key to his study was on a chain round his neck, along with the key to his secret book; Marco took it when he climbed in? Unless he took it after killing his father, and let himself out with it and locked the door.'

'Or he could've had a copied key and not had to climb in to kill his father. Or *she* could have.' Benno saw a maze of possibilities. 'Why stab him in the eye, though? Or if Marco or the lady thought he had the Evil Eye too.'

'I rather believe she thought her evil luck lay in marrying him. If she fancied Pasquale Scolar, though she struck me as far too shrewd to *love* him, she may have been very angry indeed when her parents insisted on Ermolin as a safe bet. Too late to ask her parents about her. Donna Claudia told me they both died quite suddenly, shortly before their daughter's wedding. Something they ate.'

Benno turned, agape, and Sigismondo laughed.

'Have no fear. I'm not likely to be asked to dinner by the lovely widow. Now she's carrying the hope of the Ermolin clan she'll have other things to think about; nor would she have any reason unless she thinks it was I who stole the letter.'

In this Sigismondo was perhaps correct, but he had possibly forgotten about the knowledge of the man who was now her protector.

Chapter 34

An End To Troubles

The taking of Piombo was celebrated with a thanksgiving Mass in St Mark's. The red robes of the Signoria flamed and gleamed in the candlelight in the incense-laden gloom. Above, light flickered and glinted on the gilded mosaics and below on the gold *cornu*, the embroidered horned cap of the Doge; the light caught the tears on the lined old face. Some might interpret these as tears of joy for the victory; most knew better. The wind had been favourable that morning, and the ship ready, to carry Pasquale Scolar to Cyprus and exile; and the Doge knew he had embraced his son for the last time.

There were those among the Signoria who were truly sympathetic to the old man's grief, and there were other carping souls who thought the Head of the State, figurehead though he might be, should not show himself distracted by a private loss from his proper function. Lord Vettor Darin scanned the Doge's face with outward indifference and inner eagerness: how badly was the old man affected? The great age of Doge Scolar had until now been matched by an iron constitution, but there was still hope.

The victors of Piombo, the Marsili brothers, who had so signally justified their employment by the Republic, had asked to return as soon as their campaign allowed, to receive all that was due to them from the Senate and the people. There was the future to consider. The Duke of Montano had, so unexpectedly, arrived at the battlefield after so long and, if he were spoiling for action, then he should have it. Ottavio and Nono should bring back, if not a noble head to add to the Senate's collection, at least grovelling terms of surrender, but the prime reason for their return must be to collect a suitable reward and let the world see what Venice had achieved.

Besides Lord Vettor Darin, Marco and Rinaldo Ermolin were, as members of the Signoria, present at the thanksgiving. The two first were in a different mood: Vettor consumed by impatience, Marco by despair. The grandfather's ambition had still to be realised, the grandson saw his future extinguished by debt. By chance he stood near Pico Gamboni, and was deeply irritated by his cheerfulness. Only that morning, as the ship bearing Marco's once best friend cleared the harbour, another ship had limped in with terrible news. It was the sole survivor of the argosy on which all his final hopes rested. His uncle had refrained from investing money in the enterprise, guided no doubt by that sure instinct which had made him the successful organiser of the family fortunes until now. Marco was as wrecked as any of his ships.

Time to employ his charm. There was one who might put in a good word for him with his uncle, who seemed to have earned his uncle's respect, seemed on better terms with him than she had ever been with her husband. Marco decided it would be prudent to renew his attentions to his stepmother, and ask for her help.

She was surprisingly gracious. He had come to see her straight away on returning from the Basilica, and found her as usual reading and playing with her cat, which kept dabbing its paw on her book. Marco disliked cats and was plagued by the quantity of them in Venice, peering down at him from balconies and sills, lying in wait for him round corners and assaulting his ankles with their repulsive fur. He managed to repress a grimace as Isabella gave him the cat to hold when she stood up to fetch him a glass of wine. As she bent over the painted tray on the window seat, with its glasses and flagon, he thought again how independent she was, how apt to do things for herself sooner than call her maid. He had little time to appreciate the graceful curve of her figure – not by any means yet showing her pregnancy – as she busied herself with the silver-gilt flagon and, her back to him, with something else at her gold chain belt. The cat, disliking him as much as he disliked it, jumped down, kicking his chest and scratching his hand in the process.

'Poor Marco, you have no luck.' Had Isabella any idea how right she was? Marco, sucking his scratch, sipping his wine, wondered how to begin. This reference to luck should give him an introduction to the subject, but he was unsure how to use it and as always, he felt furiously, let it go.

'Is my uncle at home? I lost sight of him coming out of St Mark's.'

Isabella shrugged and clicked her fingers at the offended cat, washing itself to be rid of the touch of Marco. 'No, I don't expect that he is. This is the day he usually visits La Imperia.'

Marco experienced shock. Of course women, respectable women, knew of the existence of courtesans, but that Isabella should refer to one by name and allude to his uncle's visits to her . . . Imperia was one of the most beautiful and certainly among the most expensive in the city. Marco had never been able to afford her himself though he knew Pasquale had. It was peculiarly bitter that his uncle could not only afford her but made it a practice to do so, while he, Marco, was forced to crawl to him for what was rightfully his own.

'Who told you that? That he goes to – her?'

Isabella opened her large hazel eyes wide. 'All the servants know. Am I supposed not to?'

He could not say she should have shown a greater modesty. After all, he was trying to get on her right side. He muttered indistinctly, and she went on, 'Did you want to ask him something? He'll be in a good mood when he returns.'

Another thing she shouldn't have referred to. He threw back the rest of his wine and watched her pour out more. It was wine with an unusual taste, something to do with the herbs, no doubt. Although a little bitter, it was refreshing in this heat. 'You're not having any?'

'It's not good for me to drink too much.'

His face felt hot at this indirect reference to her condition. It was as if she was determined to embarrass him. He drank hastily, wondering how to ask for her intercession without appearing a fool, a loser whom she would despise.

As it happened he need not have worried. Even as he finished the second glass, a powerful nausea and cramp overcame him and, dropping the glass and clutching at his stomach, he fell to the floor. Isabella watched him with interest.

However, when five minutes had gone her shrieks brought the servants running. She was discovered kneeling by her stepson, trying in vain to revive him, crying his name and begging him for his father's sake not to die.

Doctors were sent for, as much to attend a woman in a delicate condition who should not be distressed, as to help a young man for whom it was obviously too late. The doctors did what they were best at – they shook their heads wisely and pronounced one of their patients dead; as to the cause of death they were divided. It was a hot day, the young man had been ill-advised to drink wine that, the maid informed them, had been chilled; such imprudence had been known to cause death, there were documented cases. Had he taken violent exercise before drinking? The doctor who voiced this question had the sudden thought that he might be taken as suggesting some impropriety between the lady and her stepson, and turned his attentions towards calming her hysterics.

By the time Lord Rinaldo returned home, in the good mood Isabella had predicted, having consoled himself for the idiocies of the world in the arms of La Imperia – so much more fascinating than any woman he might have married – he found plenty to change that mood.

The major-domo wore a face of doom as the great doors were opened by weeping servants, and Rinaldo found that in his absence another Ermolin had died, the last male of the name save for himself and possibly the child Isabella carried.

With that thought he went straight to her bedside, where two crows of doctors argued in fierce whispers as to the best sedative while a third, more pragmatic, was already mixing a concoction from the phials in his medical chest. Isabella opened her eyes as Rinaldo possessed himself of her hand and asked, 'How did it happen? I can get no sense from anyone.'

This marked a change in their relationship: now he expected sense from her.

'He was poisoned.'

'*Poisoned?*'

'I am sure of it.' She spoke weakly but with conviction. The doctors stared at one another in angry astonishment. This had not been their diagnosis. In fact, not one of them had examined the cup from which Marco had drunk, and it had now been taken away.

'Who could have done it?'

Isabella raised herself on one slender arm and pointed to the window. 'I saw him arrive. He was eating something given to him by his gondolier. I saw him take it and eat it. Then he came up here and collapsed. He had been poisoned, he told me.'

Rinaldo was crushing her hand in his. 'Who? By whom?'

She sank back, her eyes closing again. 'The gondolier. His half-brother, you know the one. Marco said, he hadn't known he hated him.'

'Cosmo . . .'

The doctors, satisfied that they could not possibly have deduced this from what they had found, now united their authority to persuade Lord Rinaldo that the health of a future Ermolin depended on his leaving the lady to their ministrations. They were also privately satisfied that they would be much in demand after this, as witnesses to a tragedy all the city would be discussing; nor would their reputations suffer from their failure to save the young man, dead before they came. First the father, now the son! Really quite a pity

Pasquale Scolar was on the seas already or he might have been blamed for both deaths. The weight of such a scandal would certainly have submerged the Doge at last.

In another room Marco, already washed and laid out, Father Domenico gabbling frantic prayers over him, had gone to pay all his debts in another world where he had better hopes of mercy.

Chapter 35

Beyond The Door

Benno slept, like a log with no memory of being sawn up and no fear of a future fire. In the refuge Miriam da Silva had provided there was a comfortable gloom most of the day, thanks to the tall houses across the narrow alley. Sunlight penetrated for only a brief time, when it lay like the finger of God pointing to a niche in the wall where, ordinarily, Benno would have expected a little shrine to the Virgin; and he was disconcerted, every time he glanced at it, to find it empty.

When he woke, however, the sunlight was picking out the strong features of Sigismondo standing with his back to the niche, arms folded, silent and brooding. Benno knew without having to ask that his master did not care to lurk in corners and wait for things to happen. In the past he had deliberately gone out as bait to catch someone, but here he did not seem to think it appropriate.

As he had already said, there seemed no way he could satisfy the poor old Doge's desire to clear his son's name; and there wasn't much point anyway, Benno thought, now that Pasquale had sailed off into exile. Somehow he couldn't see those horrible Ten saying they were frightfully sorry they'd made a mistake and would Pasquale come back and give them all a big hug.

Benno sat up, yawning and scrubbing his head and beard with both hands to freshen himself, and Biondello looked alertly from him to Sigismondo, wondering which of them was going to conjure fun or food out of the air. There came

suddenly a scratching on the door like a rat asking to be let
in. Sigismondo was there in an instant, head bent for the
murmured password the other side, which brought out one
of the keys at his belt.

The little old man who had first led them there was
standing at the threshold, his lantern throwing a cloudy light
up through the thin white beard that hung to his chest. He
was breathing hard as if he had been hurrying, and the
lantern shook in his bony hand.

'You're wanted. Madam says they're asking for you . . .'
He tried to gather a little more breath and Benno wondered
why Madam didn't send someone with younger lungs;
perhaps this man was the most trusted.

'Do you know who wants me?'

'He said he was from the Ca' Darin. I didn't see him
myself.'

'Lord Vettor has dismissed me from his service.'

The old man puffed and appeared to gain a little energy,
his shadow dipping and swelling on the wall behind him as
he put the lantern down at his feet.

'No, no, not from Lord Vettor. They said he was quite
particular that it was Donna Claudia who wants to see you.
Her grandson is dead.'

'*Marco Ermolin*? How?'

The old man wagged his head, beard brushing to and fro
across the braid on his chest with a susurrant sound.
'Poisoned, I heard. All Venice is talking of it. And they've
found the poisoner.'

'Who?'

'Some black fellow or other, a gondolier. They say he's a
by-blow of the dead boy's father.' He stepped in and collected
the empty platter; and carrying it out, he bent to pick up
the lantern and spoke, his voice constrained by stooping.
'Family! When you can't trust your own family . . . Are you
coming, then?'

Sigismondo turned to pick up his cloak and falchion. The
sunlight had left the room and the lantern gave out more
light than came from the street. Falchion was buckled on,

171

Biondello posted into Benno's jerkin, the door locked, and they were on their way behind the old man, who hobbled along at a surprising rate, the lantern making alternate dwarves and giants of their shadows on the passage walls.

When finally they reached her house, Miriam da Silva came to meet them, small and plump as a partridge in mourning, concerned. 'I told the messenger again that you were not here, and sent him off. Was that right?'

Sigismondo bent to clasp her hands in his and raise them to his lips. 'It was right, of course. You must not be linked with me and what I do.'

Miriam irresistibly dimpled. 'Is it not honest, then?'

'You ask that in Venice? I'm as honest as you, Miriam, and yet you too must have places to hide.'

'Will you go to Donna Claudia?'

'Out of curiosity, if nothing else.'

'That curiosity of yours . . .' but her expressive face had saddened. 'The poor boy. So young to be in such trouble. With his father dead he might have expected money, and in plenty.' She was accompanying them to the door, her hand in Sigismondo's arm, and she stopped now, looking up at him. 'Oh, it's not possible! He and Pasquale Scolar – they could not have arranged it between them? His own father?'

Sigismondo took her face, this time, between his hands and stooped to kiss her forehead. 'I've known sons who'd do that for less than a fortune. But gossip says his stepmother was the cause of Pasquale's crime.'

Miriam's generously-sized mouth pursed up. 'They could all have been in it together.'

'I'll whisper that in the ears of the Ten.'

'They'll have thought of it already. Go with God, Cristobal, and may He guide you safely through danger.'

That's what we need all right, thought Benno, as the grey oak door, small, but strong enough for a siege, swung shut behind them. Going anywhere near the Ca' Darin with that evil old Lord Vettor and his pack of lions seemed no less than daft. Everyone connected with that family was bound to be trouble.

It was dark by the time they got there and the moon, nearly full, was behind cloud. They arrived at the small door on the canal, at the side of the palace, and at Sigismondo's knock the judas slid back and a servant peered out. Sigismondo let the hood of his cloak slide back, and the lantern beside the door showed the servant that this was a man known to him. As Lord Vettor had not thought to inform his household that he no longer employed Sigismondo, his quiet announcement that Donna Claudia had sent for him was not questioned.

The wicket was unbolted and opened. As Benno lifted his foot over the threshold he heard again that sound which made the hairs stand up on the back of his neck – a lion's roar. It sounded horribly near, as though the creature were roaming within a few paces; pausing, he glanced along and saw the wall, plaster pitted with damp and patched darkly with moss, down which ivy, black in the shadowy light, dripped nearly to the water. Thank God only the lions of St Mark had wings!

Donna Claudia's maid, informed of their arrival, came hurrying to usher them up a spiral back stair, in her hurry including Benno as one of the party. She had certainly no idea that a small dog was being jostled upstairs in her wake. Sigismondo now handed Benno his cloak and it turned out to be a passport to Donna Claudia's presence, a function as a clothes peg excusing his vacant look. Benno pressed himself against the panelling and did a swift cancellation in case Donna Claudia's eyes should light on him.

Donna Claudia's eyes, though, were too full of tears to see anything clearly. She came towards Sigismondo with the stride of a tall woman and gripped him by the arms before he could bow.

'You've come! They told me you were not to be found – have you heard the news?'

Sigismondo bent his head, his grave look her answer. She turned on her heel and paced away, dashing tears from her eyes with her fingers and then the back of her hand.

'Poisoned! God knows he was a fool but he did not deserve

that. And I know who did it too, the she-devil.'

'My lady? They told me, a gondolier—'

'*She* told them a gondolier. Very convenient.'

'You suspect Lady Isabella?'

Donna Claudia turned again, so close to Benno at the wall that her skirts brushed his boots and he was overpowered by the scent of musk and cinnamon as she swept away from him towards Sigismondo; Biondello's nose worked hard at the edge of his jerkin. This was some lady. How did Lord Vettor cope with her? She was a match for the lions outside – she was even growling like one of them.

'Suspect? I don't *suspect* – I'm sure! Now that she's going to have a child – and we've no proof that it's Niccolo's, mind – who stood in her way but poor Marco? Now he's dead, her child will be sole heir if it's a boy, to the Ermolin fortune. Of course she did it.'

'And Cosmo the gondolier?'

Donna Claudia's eyes, wiped of tears, were black and flashing.

'What a happy chance for her that she saw Marco step from Cosmo's gondola. And what more likely? They saw much of each other. Since Cosmo came back and took up the trade he never charged Marco, no matter how far he took him.' Donna Claudia paused and frowned. 'Marco took advantage of him. I dare say he even borrowed money from Cosmo, whatever he had to give. They loved each other as children, you know. My husband did not care for it, but—'

The maid eased the door open beside Benno and carried in a tray with a flagon of gilded crystal and cups to match. She put it down on a table near her mistress and went out; before the door shut, another opened somewhere in the house and a wail, infinitely pathetic like that of a wounded animal, escaped before both doors shut. Donna Claudia had paused again. She looked towards the sound and spoke more softly.

'That child has lost father and brother in these last weeks. I'll not let her go home while that young fiend rules the Palazzo Ermolin. Let Rinaldo look out for himself,' her voice strengthened, 'for if she learns to mind the money as astutely as he does, his life won't last a moment longer.'

Sigismondo spoke just as she turned to resume her pacing, the deep, calm voice making her check her stride and glance back.

'These are grave accusations, my lady. Why have you called me here? Your husband is satisfied Pasquale Scolar is guilty of your son-in-law's death, and has paid the price for it. It would be difficult to make anyone believe that Lady Isabella both stabbed her husband and poisoned her stepson when there are others arrested or even punished for these crimes.'

Donna Claudia pressed her hands to her temples.

'Something must be done! Beatrice is not safe while that fiend is alive.'

'Surely here, under your care . . .'

At the far end of the room, Donna Claudia flung up her hands in despair. 'And how can I keep her from visiting her home and her stepmother, or prevent Isabella from visiting her here? She needs only one chance, the she-devil.'

'A warning to Lady Beatrice is out of the question?' His measured tones, contrasting with Donna Claudia's quick speech, made her stop to consider.

'Poison her mind against her stepmother?'

'My lady, if you believe her stepmother killed her father and brother, would a warning not be better than the risk? Better poison the mind than the body.'

Donna Claudia had come close to Sigismondo and stood regarding him. Plainly she was unaccustomed to accepting opinions not her own, but she listened. 'You're right, of course. I have no choice. I shall warn her and swear her to secrecy . . . but she is a child! She is in no state to keep secrets. She had no great feeling for her brother, but she was her father's pet – and to lose both within a week!'

'Lord Rinaldo will surely make it his business to care for her, and she is here with you. Is she not soon to be married?'

The dark eyes flashed. 'Rinaldo cares for Ermolin money and the Ermolin name. My granddaughter will marry where the greatest fortune is offered, provided that the name is in the Golden Book. Niccolo kept his negotiations over her marriage secret from all of us, though he hinted at great things. I thought he might have been considering a marriage with Pasquale when his bride died. Imagine if she had married him and been involved in his fall!'

And in particular, thought Benno, if the poor girl was married to the young man who killed her father for love of her stepmother. Things don't come much more messy than that.

Somewhere in the house another door was opened and a commanding voice was heard. Donna Claudia, suddenly anxious, said, 'My husband is at liberty – he has been closeted with some person till now. He would not be pleased to know you are here . . .'

Sigismondo kissed the extended hand which then took hold of his sleeve and led him towards the panelled wall. She swiftly opened a door, invisible till now, and gestured abruptly at the darkness it revealed.

Benno, hurrying after Sigismondo, was glad to find that they were at least not shut in a cupboard but, more dangerous if less suffocating, were on another flight of twisting stairs that had to be followed down by experiment in the blackness towards a faint smell of fresh air. Benno had an idea. He fished Biondello from his jerkin, put him down and heard him sniff loudly as if to get his bearings. Then he started off down the stairs past Sigismondo with a skitter of small claws on wood. The next thing Benno knew was a friendly cuff on the head from Sigismondo, who had turned to deliver it after listening to Biondello's rapid descent.

'Mmm . . . so now we know the stairs take a sharp turn to the right and don't go far. What shall we do next – set Biondello to fight the lions?'

Sigismondo was already descending with a speed that Benno, his hands on the wall either side, envied. People talked of having eyes in the back of your head, which Benno found horrifying, but his master had a cat's eyes for the dark. At the foot of the stairs, Benno, expecting another tread, put his foot down with force, stumbled, and hit Sigismondo between the shoulder blades with his head.

'Hey, you won't get out of here by using me as a battering ram. Take the dog.' Biondello was scooped up and presented to Benno's chest, where he clasped him while Sigismondo examined the door.

'Is it locked?'

'Do you expect to find a door unlocked that can lead to the heart of a palace?'

Benno tried to think that they were not likely to be left in the dark here until Donna Claudia sent to let them out. *If* she remembered . . .

There was a sharp click, a soft groan, and a wedge of – not light, but paler dark – widened. Benno, relieved, silently scolded himself for supposing his master could be defeated by a lock. Had he not, in the past, broken out of prison?

Sigismondo's arm across the doorway blocked it, and his voice came in a murmur once more.

'Never rush out of a place, especially at night. Have you forgotten the dead hand?'

Benno froze. He had in fact forgotten that the tall man who had saluted them in the Piazzetta, the look-alike to the dead Pyrrho, could perhaps be on their tail even at this hour.

As it happened, he was not, but all the same as Sigismondo stepped cautiously out, looking round him in the dim light of the cloud-covered moon, it was Dion whom he first saw.

Chapter 36

Thrown To The Lions

Sigismondo moved instantly. Just as the moon slid from clouds, his falchion slid from its sheath, the light swimming on the blade confronting Dion – who was no slower, but who held a sword, outreaching the other weapon. They crouched, silent, unmoving as in some tableau. Benno, frozen, his back at the shut door, thought he heard a drum beating loudly and realised it was his heart pounding in his ears.

A sound all three did hear at that instant was unmistakable. Beyond the wall of the alley they were in, a wall ivy-draped like the one facing the canal, rumbled a sudden throbbing growl.

It broke the spell. Dion moved fast, perhaps hoping to use the distraction, and slashed at Sigismondo's head. Benno heard someone's choked cry – his own – as he saw Sigismondo strike upwards, fending off the blow. Dion countered with a slash at Sigismondo's legs. Benno did not like the thought that the man was a professional; he didn't look a match to Sigismondo in strength but he might have as much skill and cunning. Clasping his hands round Biondello, Benno whispered prayers, incoherent, heartfelt, as he watched the two circling each other. All the rest of his life he was to have this scene imprinted, living, on his memory: the wall with its drape of ivy, shadowy under the moon, the intent figures moving, the oily gleam of the canal at the alley's end; the sound of feet, of breathing, the deep grating growl inside the wall; the smell of canal water, damp stone, and rank animal.

But the lions were not the only ones to growl that night. Biondello, disturbed at Benno's disturbance, frightened by his fear, suddenly erupted from his arms, hit the ground lightly and scurried into the charmed circle. Dion, never taking his eyes off Sigismondo, acquired a small woolly fetter on his ankle.

Benno, who would have leapt forward to sweep Biondello to safety, was paralysed by Sigismondo's rule: don't enter my fights unless I tell you. He looked to his master, but Dion acted. He leapt backward, wrenched the dog free, and tossed him high over the wall. There was a yelp, the crackle of twigs and foliage, and a surprised, short, interested roar.

In this moment Sigismondo had pounced. The next thing that frantic Benno saw was a sword flashing, spinning over the wall in a high arc, followed by the falchion's glittering parabola. Then the ivy jounced and swung as Sigismondo climbed. He stood on the coping in the moonlight, hands on hips, smiling.

Dion understood the silent language of challenge. He chose a spot further along the wall and started to climb. The bulk of a cypress over the wall between them protected him from Sigismondo who, however, did not wait but descended on the inside. Benno, distraught, almost choked by his heartbeat, climbed where his master had gone up, finding handholds, footholds by inspiration until he was hanging over the top and looking down into a place of inexplicable shadows and a smell of broken vegetation and, overpoweringly, of animals. He could not see his master, but Dion's sword lay on the gravel, nosed at by a sinister shape.

The lion was larger than most of the statues had led Benno to expect, but its mane was shorter. It was making dissatisfied noises in its throat.

A whimper made the lion raise its head. It and Benno saw Biondello simultaneously, caught in the upper branches of a shrub beneath the wall, and struggling. Benno got a leg over the coping and began to calculate how to reach him. The lion moved to investigate and at once Sigismondo crossed the gravel, picking up something as he went. The lion's head swung, but it seemed to see nothing. Under the far wall in the shadow came a glint of steel.

The lion paced about, looking up at Benno and the dog but unable to work out how to reach either. It reared against the wall by the shrub and snarled; its breath was worse than anything Benno had ever met, and he gagged. Biondello, on his back in the twigs and leaves, looked at the lion upside down and kept still. Dion's sword lay on the gravel all this time, and at this moment the tall wiry figure of Dion appeared, making for it. He trod quietly, but from under the far wall something was thrown, skittering on the gravel, and the lion flopped its forefeet down from the wall and whirled.

Dion had retrieved his sword and faced the lion, treading softly backwards; something moved beyond him, not Sigismondo but a low shape, silver-furred as it came into the moonlight. Benno had not seen a lion like this in all Venice, swag-bellied, sway-backed, but its sudden roar made Dion leap, twisting like a cat, and back away from both of them. As if they were trained hunting dogs, they split apart and circled.

At this moment Biondello struggled again, and Benno took a deep breath, set his teeth and began cautiously to climb down towards the little dog, to pick him up before his struggles made him drop further. With one eye on the lions (and how many *did* Lord Vettor keep? Was there another watching him from the shadows?) Benno reached for Biondello, touched him, and just as his joyful response freed him from the supporting broken twigs, Benno nipped him by the scruff.

Dion had retreated to the house wall and was moving towards the fragile aid of an orange tree in a terracotta tub. The lions were closing in. They seemed neither hungry nor annoyed, but nor were they ready to tolerate this intruder. The younger one's deep snarling broke into short coughing roars; the old one seemed silent until one heard the subterranean threatening growl. Dion reached the orange tree and put one foot on the rim of the tub. As the older lion came within reach he kicked the tree down over it with violent force and swung to slash at the younger lion's head. He cut its face across, and it reared back and came at him. This time he thrust upwards through its open mouth, let go his sword and made another twisting leap, caught the underside of jutting window bars in the house wall and pulled himself up.

The young lion's jaws snapped shut as it fell. The old one, furious, orange leaves in its tattered mane, sprang at Dion and raked his side before he had climbed out of reach. He pulled himself further up before it could spring again; and indeed it did not try but paced below him, snarling. Dion hung on the window grille. His side poured blood.

No one in the house seemed to pay any attention to the disturbance. No torches appeared, no one leant from the high balcony to see. Benno on the wall, cradling Biondello, thought he saw a pale face behind one grating.

Sigismondo appeared suddenly, climbing along the house wall like a great spider. He reached the grating where Dion hung and spoke to him. Benno thought that Dion shook his head; but he was now seized by a shudder. Benno had seen this before in a wounded man, it was not fear, but a strange force that took hold of one after an injury. Sigismondo reached for Dion's wrist and closed his hand round it, so that when, a moment later, Dion's feet slipped from the grille, he still held him.

After a long moment, they began a curious, crablike progress across the house front, by way of its rustication and the top of another window grille, to the garden wall. Below, the old lion divided its attention between them and the drops of blood Dion was shedding. They reached the garden wall.

As Dion sat astride it, still in the grip of waves of shivering, Benno saw his wounds clearly by the white moonlight, and wished he hadn't. Part of him had rebelled furiously when Sigismondo had snatched Dion from the lion's jaws – why save a man who wants to kill you, when Fate kindly takes him off your hands? But it's one thing to kill your enemy, face to face in combat, quite another to leave him to be chewed up alive for dinner.

Sigismondo was speaking. Benno couldn't immediately make sense of what he was saying, a question he was putting to Dion. As Dion too did not seem to hear it, Sigismondo repeated: 'Monks or nuns?'

Dion gasped some reply, so he must have understood. The lion was now sniffing loudly, almost snuffling, at the base of the wall where Dion was straddled. In Benno's jerkin, safely gripped there by his hands as well, Biondello also trembled violently, like a heart that would burst free. A sudden roar just below made Benno flinch and he had to take a hand from his jerkin to grab the ivy stems on the coping to save himself.

Sigismondo had now put an arm round Dion's chest from behind, and swung him round to face the alley just as the lion leapt. It missed Dion's leg by almost a yard but its impact on the bricks, the scrape of its claws and the fetid smell of its breath made Benno scramble his own legs over to the alley side, ivy stems doing terrible things to him as he went. He was in time to see Sigismondo do what an acrobat might have envied, descend the wall into the alley, supporting Dion down as well.

Benno started his own undignified clamber down, his burden lightened by Biondello dropping from his bosom like a stone and uttering a small *woof* as the breath was knocked out of him.

In the moonlight, the blood oozed blackly down Dion's side, soaking his torn clothes, as he stood swaying in Sigismondo's embrace, eyes closed as if near to unconsciousness. Don't trust him, Benno pleaded silently. The blood's convincing all right, but he could be pretending to be that bad. He could have a dagger to slip into you . . .

'Nuns it is, then,' said Sigismondo jovially. 'The campiello isn't far to carry you.'

Dion's eyes opened wide, their gaze set on the dark face

next to his. His voice was low, harsh, distinct. 'This isn't the end. I shall kill you.'

Sigismondo, with Dion's blood seeping over his hands as he held him from collapse, replied gravely, 'If God wills. And if His will is otherwise, *I* shall kill *you*. Meanwhile, the nuns will decide your future.'

Beyond the wall, the lion who might have decided Dion's future already, should his wounds fail to heal, gave a dissatisfied roar.

Chapter 37

A Child With The Face
Of A Gargoyle

The dead lion was discovered by the keeper next morning, when he went with his assistant to cage them for the day with the routine feed inside the barred enclosure. It was no mystery how the lion had died – there was the sword transfixing it. Whose the sword was, and why its owner was in the garden was the mystery. The track of dried blood showed that he had escaped over the wall; an immediate search outside found nothing but a patch of blood from which, strangely, no tracks led. The lionkiller had vanished like the morning mist.

The news was conveyed to Lord Vettor at once and he, temporarily disturbed by such a bad omen – since the lions were a covert sign of his ambitions – was somewhat consoled to hear that one lion survived. He was inclined to interpret the business in a wider sense: as the lions represented the Republic, should men perhaps fear for the life of the Doge? Harassed by grief at his son's departure into exile, what more likely than that poor old Scolar should be so struck down, as the lion had been? As the sword had been found in the lion's mouth, piercing through to its spine, Lord Vettor had the attractive theory that the Doge might be seized by a sudden apoplexy which would choke him.

When her husband had left the room, all but rubbing his hands with satisfaction, Donna Claudia turned to Beatrice, a pallid hearer of the news, and demanded, 'Did you hear anything? I thought they made no more noise than usual.'

'They woke me up. I went to the window to look.'

She hesitated. Donna Claudia, thinking of the armed man she had hurried from the room the night before, urged, 'What did you see?'

'I couldn't see clearly . . . the moon wasn't out all the time. But there seemed to be two men in the garden. I thought it was strange. Everyone knows Grandfather keeps lions there. And they *smell*. No one in their sense would go in.'

'Two men? Were they attacking the lions?'

Beatrice put a hand to her mouth and laughed. When one is fifteen even bereavement does not remove one's sense of the incongruous. 'Oh no. The lions were attacking *them*! I thought they must be trying to rob us or something, so I didn't call the servants. After all, the lions were doing what they are there for. Grandfather says they're to protect us.'

'Yes, he would say that.' Donna Claudia had Beatrice by the arm. 'What happened? Did you see them kill the lion? Did you see them get away?'

'It was too dark to see much, down on the ground anyway. I only saw them properly when they got on the wall. At least, I saw one of them.' Beatrice gestured at her head, where the crimped auburn hair was piled up, ringleted, and twisted with black gauze and ribbons. 'You know, that man with the shaven head who came to see Grandfather the other day. I'm sure it was him.'

Donna Claudia betrayed agitation, and paced away down the room. 'What was *he* doing there?' she muttered, and Beatrice, overhearing, giggled again.

'Killing our lion, I should think. Grandfather'll have him flayed for it if he gets caught. Is he the one who left all the blood behind?'

'Listen, child.' Donna Claudia had returned, and stood over her granddaughter. 'Was the other man a scrubby little fellow with a beard? Could you see? His servant?'

'Little fellow with a beard? I should think not! This other man on the wall wasn't bearded. The moon shone straight on his face. He wasn't little, either. *He* was the one who seemed hurt, come to think of it. Grandfather's man was helping him. But the moon kept coming and going.' She played with the pearls at her wrist, reflecting. 'There *was* a scrubby little man further along. He could have had a beard. I didn't really notice him.'

Donna Claudia was not to know how exactly this last remark identified Benno, but it was the final identification for Sigismondo. That extraordinary man had evidently left her the night before and at once descended into their garden and with the aid of some accomplice, killed one of their lions. She might think, from what she had heard of him – from that quality he possessed that had made her summon him when she was in trouble – that he had been attempting to save the lions from attack . . . but in that case, why was Sigismondo apparently helping the attacker to escape? She frowned and bit her knuckle.

Beatrice looked at her with curiosity. 'What does it matter, Grandmamma? Grandfather's sure to get another lion. They're from Africa, aren't they? At least it's something to talk about, after not going anywhere or seeing anything for so long. I can tell Isabella when she comes this afternoon.'

'Oh no.' Donna Claudia put the back of her hand to Beatrice's forehead, then took her chin and turned her face to the light. Surprised, Beatrice heard her say firmly, 'You're not seeing Isabella. Have you forgotten what I said to you? You have a fever. Isabella,' she added in a moment of inspiration, 'Isabella must not risk the child. Now off to bed with you.'

If Beatrice Ermolin was reluctant to be sent to her bed, even for her own protection, the Duke of Montano would have been touchingly grateful for anyone to send him to his. He marvelled at his own naivety in imagining that directing a campaign would be fascinating. If he had really been in charge, it would have been an exercise for mind and body, but certainly it was nothing of the sort, sitting in a tent listening to Il Lupo telling him what *he* meant to do. It was no consolation to tell himself that as he was paying this unpleasant man – had he by any chance got his name from being an actual *were*-wolf? – to win the war for him; their interests must be identical.

But Il Lupo showed no tendency to fight at all. The Duke had been made to feel it was childish of him to expect his captains to ride out and avenge the fall and pillage of Piombo. He was reminded, as if he had never studied the strategies of war, that Piombo had been the bait; now was the time to negotiate, secretly of course, while to fight would spoil everything. The Duke had also studied humanist philosophies, as was the fashion, and he felt uncomfortable about the sufferings of his Piombese.

He knew too that Master Valentino, who had wrought such beneficial changes in his patron's health, was for his own reasons disappointed; there was not only no fitting exercise for the Duke but also no interesting wounds. The army provided run-of-the-mill cases of the flux, swamp foot, ague, and luxations from manoeuvring carts and trebuchets in sodden ground, but these were beneath the attention of a learned physician, one who had saved the life of the Pope.

The Duke, swathed in a cloak but still shivering in the penetrating night air, despite brazier and the double-lined tent, waiting for the visit Il Lupo had arranged from the enemy, wished for the forty-third time that he had been content with inferior medical attention. That way, he'd be home still, warm in his great bed, under a brocade, fur-lined coverlet, under orders not to exert himself in any activity more strenuous than a game of chess.

He reflected on this. His head nodded.

A sudden scuffling in the tent roused him from a doze. For a moment he thought his pleasant dream had become a nightmare. A small figure, as swathed in a dark cloak as he was, confronted him. It threw back the hood from its head. A child with the face of a gargoyle smiled.

'Good morning, your Grace,' said Nono Marsili, the conqueror of Piombo.

Chapter 38

The Message Of The Sword

'Is it bad?' Unlike Master Valentino, Benno was no expert on wounds. Sigismondo, he knew, was – so for once this seemed a legitimate question to ask. The slash that showed dark with dried blood on Sigismondo's ribs might be more serious than it looked and he pressed the wet cloth on it cautiously. Their room was supplied continually with a flagon of wine, fruit, bread, and a ewer of water, but so far they had only once seen the purveyor of all this.

'Hey, that depends. If he uses poison, it's bad.' Sigismondo, seeing Benno's look of horror, relented and smiled. 'Mm – m! If it had been poison, I'd have known by now. Poisons are irritants, Benno. Besides, that man has too much pride to use them. He'd expect a wound he gave to be effective without that help. He's the one now to fear being poisoned.'

Benno gaped, water dripping from the cloth to the floor. He knew Sigismondo didn't use poison – surely? His master laughed, looking down at his ribs and placing his herb poultice on the angry red cut.

'The lions, Benno. A mauling by animals like that can do more damage than a poisoned blade unless the nuns know how to deal with it. Let's hope they do. In this city they should be acquainted with such things.'

Benno found in himself the fierce hope that the nuns were totally incompetent as regards lion-inflicted wounds – that the best they could come up with were prayers to St Mark and that the saint would be feeling deaf for quite a while. Knowing that the man who had been dogging them, who had skewered the rat to the wall, had thrown the dead hand into the boat, had tossed Biondello to the lions, was out of action gave him a sense of relief so profound that he thought the saints would forgive him the hope that it would be for ever. If Dion died, staying on in Venice would not be so scary.

'The nuns looked properly startled, didn' they? You bringing someone in, middle of the night, dripping blood all over everything. Sister Portress was cross as two sticks.'

'Their business must be to ignore their feelings and get on with the job. Their pleasure's in nursing him back to health.'

Silently wishing for the nuns' disappointment, Benno wrung out the cloth into the stained water and emptied the bowl into the soil-bucket in the corner. He said cheerfully, 'They didn't seem to think it funny he'd had a hunting accident at night. I reckon Venetians get up to all sorts you wouldn't expect.'

'We can hope,' Sigismondo said, holding the cloth while Benno applied the bandage round his ribs and round one muscular shoulder to keep it in place, 'that if, and when, he's fit to hunt again, the quarry will have moved on.'

Benno was quick to pick this up. 'Not much to stay for, is there? I mean, you can't bring the poor Doge his son back, not when the son's dumped himself in it. If it's the Lady Isabella, you're not going to be allowed near her and she's not going to come over all weepy of her own accord . . . "Sorry I had to stab my husband in the eye that morning, don't know what came over me, would you mind waiting while I have this baby"' – Benno heaved his jerkin into a pregnancy more visible than Isabella's – '"before you garrotte me?" . . . Though, I suppose if they sent the Doge's son into exile, they might go all romantic and send her to join him in Cyprus.'

'Certainly. It's the isle of Venus, after all. No, I can't prove Lady Isabella guilty of anything at the moment, but I can talk to those who may know something useful about her.'

'Like her maid, you mean? How will—'

'I mean Zenobia. There's not much in that household that she misses. Besides,' Sigismondo swung his feet on to the bed and blew out the candle, 'have you thought what may happen to her at the Palazzo Ermolin once her son is in prison awaiting trial for poisoning the Ermolin heir?'

'With Lady Isabella in charge?'

The deep voice said in the dark, 'We can't do anything now, not until dawn – which will be soon. And I need to sleep.'

Benno curled up on his pallet, cuddling Biondello who lovingly licked his beard. Since his escape from the lions the little dog had been particularly affectionate; perhaps he was aware it was his nearest approach to being a meal since he left the starving village in which he had lost his puppy ear.

Benno's last vision before he slept was a happy one: a group of nuns posting the dead Dion into a handy canal.

Later that day, Dion's fate was being considered by others than Benno, Sigismondo and the nursing nuns who were tending his wounds. Lord Vettor and Rinaldo Ermolin were both examining a sword. It had been in an unpleasant condition when first it had been dislodged from the lion's body and shown to Lord Vettor but now when he had brought it to show Rinaldo, it had been cleaned and looked, as it lay on the cloudy pink of the marble table, almost ordinary. Nevertheless, they both recognised it.

'The binding.' Rinaldo pointed but did not touch. The binding was the grip, where scarlet and black cord had been twisted to ensure a firm hold. The effect was practical rather than ornamental, the colours disagreeably suggestive of blood and death.

'Yes.' Lord Vettor was frowning. It looked as if he had lost not only one of his lions, which would be thought a bad omen by everyone in the city, but also and more importantly, he might have lost someone on whom he was relying. 'I am sure I remember that.'

'What was he doing in your garden?'

Lord Vettor turned his round childlike eyes up to the

painted ceiling, where a nymph reclining on a cloud returned his gaze seductively. 'You do not suppose I told him to go and kill one of my lions, do you?'

Rinaldo said nothing; the sidelong glance under his eyelids intimated that Vettor was devious enough to have given any instructions at all, whose purpose might be discovered only later. Men can judge only by themselves.

Lord Vettor picked up the sword and weighed it in his hand, wistfully. 'It is possible he is dead. There was a good deal of blood, both in the garden and outside.'

Rinaldo was still silent. His disappointment could not find expression. In the distance, a church-bell began to toll for some Venetian whose fate was definitely known. Overlying the sound of the bell, a harsh shout from a gondolier averting a collision came up to the long windows of the Palazzo Ermolin. It distracted Lord Vettor, who put the sword down.

'That boy. Cosmo. He's safely in prison?'

'I am urging his immediate trial, but it can end only one way.'

The word of a widow of one of the Signoria, and that she was a lovely widow was not irrelevant, against the word of a gondolier, son of a slave, would naturally prevail, and the strangler's cord made no distinction between black neck and white. Something else struck Lord Vettor. 'The housekeeper – Zenobia, isn't it? Was she in the plot with him? Have you questioned her?'

Rinaldo unexpectedly gave vent to his feelings, striking the table with the flat of his hand, making the sword ring and slither an inch along the glassy surface as if an unseen touch had moved it.

'Too late. The servants report that she has gone. The door of her workroom gives onto the canal.'

The round eyes looked accusing now. 'You let her escape? She should have been imprisoned when he was.'

Rinaldo did not waste time being indignant, but his smile was not pleased. 'She's of no account. We must concentrate on those who do matter.'

No argument there. The sword in front of them had a

message neither of them could afford to ignore. Plans must now be changed. Neither man knew what the other's original plans had been nor what changes had now to be made.

'I must see that poor child Isabella before I go. Is all well with her?'

'She is in excellent health, although grieved at Marco's death. And shaken, of course, at having witnessed it.'

'Did she! What does the physician say?'

Rinaldo rang a silver bell on the console table. 'She refuses a physician.'

Lord Vettor raised his eyebrows into the ridged dome of his forehead. The idea of a young woman rejecting anything suggested by the head of her household was little short of anarchy.

'Is that wise?'

Rinaldo shrugged. 'I think she knows what she is doing. She asks for what she needs.'

The corollary being that her brother-in-law then supplied it. Lord Vettor became thoughtful.

He had regretted his grandson's death. Marco had been a complete fool with money, but there was no real harm in him. He might have grown more sensible with age, and marriage. As a little boy he had been adorable, so coaxing in his ways. Now there was to be another Ermolin heir, perhaps not even male, yet it seemed that Rinaldo of all people was prepared to do what its mother wanted. Marco had been a liability because his father had spoilt him – the sole survivor of Niccolo's sons. Rinaldo must believe that Isabella's child, trained by him, would be very different.

Yet, if it should be a girl?

In that case, Vettor thought, Rinaldo would probably adopt an heir, a procedure not unknown among those who had sacrificed marriage for the family's sake, when the future of the line was in hazard. He might even marry. Looking at Rinaldo's cold, clever face, the gaze not giving anything away, Vettor could not like the man; yet, if he needed his vote and his interest, in future times, Rinaldo would have to be courted.

'I am sure you know how to manage her,' Lord Vettor said, and he smiled.

Rinaldo, escorting Vettor courteously to his gondola, was thinking that, if his own plans were to succeed, the old fox would have to be humoured.

He passed once more through the room where they had been talking on his way to the study. Though he paid no attention to it, the assassin's sword still lay there on the table's polished pink marble, measure of how far both men were prepared to go.

Chapter 39

The Blow Falls

In the Doge's palace soon after this, rapid preparations for a Great Council involved everyone. Members of the Signoria were arriving on foot, on horse and by gondola, ascending the vast stair in the inner courtyard, assembling in their red silk in the Council Chamber. There was a good deal of whispering, soft as the rustle of their robes, as to why they had been summoned. Pico Gamboni had already collected, in his grimy hands, alms amounting to several ducats from acquaintances he saw only at such times. He was heard cheerfully guessing that the Turks, unable to bear the appearance of Attilio da Castagna's one eye, had sent a message of surrender; their Captain-General's luck was, after all, now bound to prevail as he was free of the Evil Eye since Niccolo Ermolin's death.

The Council's business turned out to be connected with the Republic's enemies indeed, but not the Turks.

In view of grave news just now received, the Council of Ten was requesting another *zonta*. Everybody knew at once that, unless they belonged to the Ten or were chosen to make up the numbers for the *zonta*, they would not get to hear what the grave news was until after the fun was over. The first move of almost every *zonta* was to decree the death penalty for anyone who divulged a single word of the subject under discussion.

The *zonta* granted, the extra members selected joined the Ten in their own Council Chamber. The Doge was already ensconced in his Chair of State, lines of grief now etched on his face, and his pallor shown up by the white linen of the cap worn under the *cornu*. He had uttered barely a word in the proceedings up to now, and it was rumoured among the Signoria that he had lately refused to attend a ceremony requiring his presence. Of what use is a Doge, as Lord Vettor had murmured to an influential few, who cannot bother even to be a figurehead?

Each member of the *zonta* solemnly swore, on relics produced in a jewelled box by one of the Three, never to reveal what was to be said. The news was then laid before them by another of the Three; that function belonged properly to the Doge, and Lord Vettor looked significantly round at this, but the members of the *zonta* were too disturbed by what they were hearing to pay much attention to the manner of its delivery.

When they had finished deciding on what action to take, business was not quite over. Lord Rinaldo Ermolin had a matter to lay before them, one which surprised them all not on its own account but because it brought a spontaneous protest from the Doge. Lord Vettor might have been disappointed that the old man took part at all, but he was quick to show, with all the tact in the world, that the Doge's protest was based, not of course on sympathy with an enemy of the Republic – for who could credit that of Doge Scolar? – but on a misunderstanding, natural in one who had lost touch with events in the city.

By the time the *zonta* had left the building, certain things had been decided upon. The Marsili brothers, Ottavio and Nono, had requested to return to Venice, to receive the congratulations of the Senate and to discuss further strategy in the war against Montano; this was granted at once. The Chief Secretary of the Council was to carry the invitation to them, his manner and speeches being detailed in his brief. Also, instructions were to be carried to all Venetian governors in cities between Piombo and Venice that they should provide, in courtesy, armed escorts for the condottieri.

The web was woven, the spider waiting.

While this was going on at the Ducal Palace, Sigismondo and Benno were feasting on a large dish of wheat polenta, topped with chicken livers, leeks and bacon, grilled. They ate at a long trestle table outside a tavern not far from the Rialto. A linen awning overhead kept the sun from beating down on them, and gave a mellow glow to the food and the diners' faces. A plate of fresh apricots scented the air beside them and Sigismondo poured generously from the flagon of Lombardy wine. Benno ate and drank with all the strength of his appetite, increased now by a sense of relief. The last time he had eaten in the streets of this frightening city, his fears of their being watched had proved horribly true, when that man pointed out by Pico Gamboni had spilt his wine on the ground and smiled at them as if to say, 'Your blood next time.'

Well, ha ha! Thanks to those excellent lions it had turned out to be *his* blood instead, a tidy pool of it outside Lord Vettor's moonlit garden. Benno guzzled down the last of the polenta and reached out for an apricot. Safe to bet that one who'd been mauled by lions wouldn't be up to a meal like this, if indeed he ever ate again. Biondello lay with his chin across Benno's boot, so replete with chicken liver that he had given up begging for more. Sigismondo, elbows on the table, was telling of an ambush laid for him once in the Low Countries which had had entertaining consequences, though not for those who had laid it.

Then the blow fell; or rather, a hand, and it fell on Sigismondo's shoulder.

Sigismondo, his own hand to his sword, looked round and up, Benno gagged on his apricot, Biondello lifted his head and barked sharply.

'You are under arrest, sir. If you resist we have orders to kill you.'

The men were quietly spoken, drably dressed, but there was no mistaking their authority. Sigismondo, with hardly a glance at Benno, stood up at once. Other diners, a minute ago eating, drinking, talking with gusto, now were silent, staring, the nearest drawing back as if Sigismondo carried the plague.

'Where are you taking me?'

'To the Palace prisons. The Ten wish to interrogate you.'

Benno sat frozen; a movement of his arm had knocked his cup over and the wine ran unheeded across the table to drip on the ground. He watched, dumbfounded, as Sigismondo, his arms gripped by two of the men, moved away. What was he to do? Whom could he tell? Who could help?

Sigismondo's words came back to him: The Ten send you to the torture chamber, the Three, to your grave.

Chapter 40

The Man From Padua

Although for geographic reasons they were not underground, the prisons of the Doge's palace were very dark. Light filtered through a grating high in the wall, a light so dim that it served only to make the darkness below more gloomy and impenetrable. Sigismondo ran his hand over the walls and found nothing but rugged sweating stone blocks, the cracks between them filled with mortar that seemed recent. A stone bench in the corner presented itself with extreme suddenness to his knee and he sat on it, relaxing the muscles in his neck and shoulders, and thinking.

What would Benno do? He knew no one in Venice. There was no one to whom he could turn for help. He scarcely knew his way about the city. There was some danger to Miriam if he returned to her house to get to the bolt-hole in the Giudecca, for which Benno had not his own keys. It was possible that as Sigismondo's servant he would be followed to see if he set a trail to anyone else. Would Benno realise that? And if he did, where else could he go?

There was a strong smell of mouldering straw. Sigismondo, who knew how much worse a place like this might smell, stirred the straw with his foot. An immediate rustle told him he was not alone and, now that his eyes had adjusted to what little light there was, he picked out the glint from another pair of eyes, too close together to be human, regarding him with alert interest from near the door. Prisoners, alive or dead, could be a source of food, and this rat was prepared to show friendliness.

Friends were the point. In so many cities Sigismondo had them. If his plight were known in Rocca, Duke Ludovico would send the strongest representations to Venice – would use all his influence to free a man to whom he owed much. Duke Ippolyto of Altamura would do what he could, for the sake of his Duchess. There were others as powerful who were his friends, but they were just as far away and ignorant even of what city he was in. By the time any news reached them – and who would send news? – it was likely to be of his death. He had not been joking when he told Benno the saying about the Ten and the Three. After the Ten had interrogated him, there was no reason for the Three to keep him alive. In a very short time he could be one of those tied to stakes in the lagoon, officially strangled and ready to feed shellfish rather than rats.

If Sigismondo had Benno in mind, Benno thought of nothing but Sigismondo. It had taken him time to collect his wits, pick up Biondello and leave the tavern, watched covertly or openly by the other diners, who were now whispering where they had been talking. The meal had been paid for, so he had no cause to linger. He left the apricots, he left the wine. To eat or drink now would be as impossible as forcing down molten lead.

As he stood forlornly among the shifting crowds passing up and down to the wooden Rialto Bridge, Biondello squirming under his arm, it was things like molten lead from which his mind shrank. Interrogation didn't mean polite questions, it meant red-hot pincer and thumbscrew questions. The thought of Sigismondo being tortured nearly made Benno throw up on the spot. The braver and stronger you were, it stood to reason the worse you got tortured.

Unless you confessed. But what on earth was it they wanted him to confess? He hadn't killed anyone in Venice. All he'd done was to try to find out who'd killed someone else. Benno, wandering with the crowd, not seeing anyone, stopped suddenly. You didn't have to be guilty for people to think you were. Lord Vettor could have heard from his wife of Sigismondo's presence in the house the night his lion got killed and thought he'd done it. Benno had a wild picture of bursting into the convent where they'd left Dion and holding a knife to his throat until he confessed. But you didn't get into convents that easily, and, if he did get in, it would be just his luck to find the man dead. He'd been wishing him dead, wishing it really hard, and God might just take him up on it.

After he had been jostled once or twice, and pushed aside, pestered by beggars and ordered to move out of the way of customers at a stall he hadn't noticed he was in front of, Benno stayed where he had been pushed, leaning against a pillar of an arcade, blind to all around him and seeing only the terrible pictures in his mind.

The only people in the city who seemed to be on his master's side were Miriam da Silva and the Doge. Could a Jew, or particularly a Jewess, influence what the Ten decided? And from all he'd heard from Sigismondo and all he'd observed about the fate of Pasquale, the Doge was not likely, poor old gentleman, to be much use. He had about as much influence as the stone lions.

Benno's mind seized up. His instinct was to make for their bolt-hole and hide up until he thought of something he could do.

But Sigismondo had all the keys to the doors that had to be unlocked before he could get to that room. He supposed he could ask Miriam. She would be very sorry to hear about Sigismondo and she might think of some way of helping.

Suppose they were torturing Sigismondo this very minute.

He had a few coins, perhaps enough for a gondola, perhaps not. He would have to cross to the Giudecca for a start.

It was his turn to push through the crowd, panic driving him. He earned a few kicks and blows which he barely noticed. When his jerkin was grasped from behind, though, he stopped and his heart stopped with him. Was he arrested too?

'Where's my friend with the free drink?'

Benno's heart, unclogged, began to beat again. He knew the voice. Looking down at his arm, to which the hand had shifted its grasp, he knew too the broken nails, the grimy elegance, and turned with relief to Pico Gamboni.

'Oh, I'm glad to see you, my lord!' Benno greeted him aloud but dropped his voice for the corollary: 'He's gone. He's been taken.'

'*Taken*.' Even with wild grey hair blowing round it, Pico's face had the look of one who, however accustomed he was to misfortune, had not so far been misfortunate enough to cope with the baffling remarks of halfwit servants. 'What took him? Lightning? The plague?'

Benno came closer. Of all people, he would be the last to notice, far less complain of, the state of Pico's clothes and person. 'Arrested. They *arrested* him,' he breathed. 'Just now. They've taken him to the Palace prison. I don't know what to do.'

Pico inexplicably clapped his hands and whirled about. Benno thought with misgiving: of course, he's mad. He can't help.

His arm was seized again by the grimy hand. 'No one seems to be watching you. But you can keep walking, that's what you can do. You can't improve on your expression – it's perfect. But keep walking.' Then, as Biondello thrust his face out of Benno's jerkin and worked his nose at this new companion, he said, 'Let me have the little dog. He could make you a bit conspicuous.'

Benno was too alarmed to refuse, though jealous to see how willingly Biondello transferred to the tattered silk sleeve. They were now making their way quite briskly through the crowd, Pico acknowledging with a wave acquaintances of every colour, from stall-holders to dignified men in long white robes and turbans of rainbow brocades; he accepted offerings pressed into his hand benignly, as though he were doing the bestower of alms a favour. They were moving away from the Rialto, and Benno shelved his plan of getting to Miriam da Silva until he had found what advice Pico could come up with. He did feel misgiving. Could the man who had been living in the world of fantasy for so long produce any useful ideas?

He was wrong in this. Pico Gamboni had been living in a very real world, where only the continual exercise of one's wits kept one fed at all. He had lived as a rich man and survived as a poor one. Above all, he was a Venetian and understood the Venetian mind, which Sigismondo had once told Benno was like a maze.

Here he was, providing a clue. They stopped in a filthy alley some way from the Rialto, where washing hung in huge dingy banners high above the scavenging pigs, where women, arms on sills, gossiped across the way and the stagnant smell of the canal at the end was almost visible. Pico had been given a length of sausage; he stuffed a piece up his sleeve for Biondello, offered Benno the rest and, on his refusal, ate it while he talked.

'Why was he arrested?'

Benno shook his head, afraid he was going to start weeping. Pico did not seem daunted. 'He was trying to find out who killed that son of Satan, Ermolin,' he said. 'Did he get across anyone while he was doing it?'

'I don't think anyone liked him very much,' said Benno desolately. 'I mean, nobody enjoys being suspected of killing someone, do they? In particular if they have killed them.'

'Well, it can't be Pasquale Scolar. He's on the ocean wave on his way to Cyprus. But if it's not personal, it's to do with the State.'

'They said the Ten wanted to interrogate him,' faltered Benno. Pico's face cleared and he brought his hand down smartly on Benno's shoulder, forgetting Biondello who slid half out of his sleeve and had to be fielded from falling on a hen in the gutter.

'Why didn't you say so at the start? It must be to do with the war.'

'The *war*?'

'That's right. Either with Montano or the Turks. My guess is Montano. I've just come from a council and though I wasn't elected for the *zonta* it doesn't take a soothsayer's crystal to see that "grave news" which we didn't get to hear is connected with the war.'

Benno, bewildered, flung out his arms. 'My master hasn't had a thing, not a single *thing* to do with the war. He's been here in Venice all the time.'

'If the Ten believe he has something to do with this "grave news", whether he has or not, they'll pull him in to question him.' Pico shook his head. 'And I've just remembered . . .'

After a moment, Benno said, 'What?' Perhaps Pico had thought of someone powerful who could put in a word for Sigismondo.

'The master torturer from Padua. He hasn't left yet. I dare say the Ten won't waste his journey money.'

Chapter 41

The Visit

Cardinal Pantera had not been looking forward to his visit to Venice. The city was not the problem. He could solace his eyes by gazing at the fine palaces, some new since he last was here. There were some splendid pictures he would be glad to see again, and always Cardinal Bessarion's magnificent library, donated to the Republic.

These were consolations for the task before him. The Cardinal's peaceable nature, and the fine tact born of real consideration for the feelings of others, made him a perfect choice for what he had to do here. True, there were those in the Curia who argued that he lacked the deviousness needed in negotiations with the Serenissima, but nevertheless the Holy Father had appointed him and it was conceivable that, in the mind of Pope Felix, a certain innocence about Cardinal Pantera's approach to diplomacy might prove more baffling to the Venetians than the cynical one they would expect.

The Cardinal, as an ambassador, was travelling with a good deal of the proper pomp. His retinue was suitably large and he had far more secretaries than he could employ. There had to be a mule train for presents sent by the Pope to the Republic as the customary tokens of goodwill. These gestures had particular importance on account of some choleric exchanges between Venice and the previous Pope, who had taken great exception to the Republic's habit of appointing its own bishops without proper referral to Rome. That was one of the things Cardinal Pantera was here to discuss.

The mule train also carried the trunks containing the Cardinal's various robes and vestments, embroidered in gold and silks and sewn with a coruscating array of jewels, thought necessary to make the right impression on the Republic. It was never going to be easy to impress a city that had for centuries dealt in the very materials and even the gems that adorned these garments, but the nuns of two convents at Rome had ruined their eyesight making sure that the embroidery, at least, could not be matched by any Eastern show.

But it was in the full scarlet of a Cardinal's robes and wearing his hat weighed down with tassels that Cardinal Pantera came to Venice and was greeted by the Doge in the ducal barge and brought to the Piazzetta. There, the crowds waited. The Venetians had not bothered to clear away the dismaying remains of their recent Captain-General, kneeling chained between the columns and contemplated by his head. Rome must note how important it was to play fair with the Signoria.

In his cell in the ducal palace, Sigismondo heard the braying of the trumpets as the Cardinal set foot on the stones of Venice, but there was no one to tell him what occasioned the fanfares. His jailer, a morose swarthy man with the build of a wrestler, had not spoken a word to him since first turning the key of his cell. Bread, cheese, and a jug of what was more vinegar than wine, had been dumped inside the door, but Sigismondo's essays at conversation had been countered by grim silence. What might be going to happen was not about to be spoken of beforehand. Once or twice an eye had appeared at the grille, barely visible in the gloom, and had studied him. Perhaps to facilitate this, a lantern had been left in the cell along with the food and drink.

Aware once of this eye, Sigismondo picked up the lantern and held it to illuminate his face. He put his head on one side and smiled engagingly. The eye blinked and vanished.

Not long after this, he had a visitor.

The jailor ushered him in with an obsequious bow, received a coin and backed out, jangling his keys. The visitor looked around with distaste. Sigismondo had risen and, with a courtly sweep of his arm, offered his stone bench to Rinaldo Ermolin.

'You know why I am here?'

'Ah, my lord, I was just going to ask you that very question about myself.'

Rinaldo spoke hurriedly, glancing sidelong at the door as if he feared the coin would not guarantee the jailer's absence for long. 'You are accused of treason.'

'I am not a subject of Venice. How can I be a traitor to her?'

Rinaldo, in the poor light of the lantern, stood rigid, and glittered as if he were sweating. His voice grated with impatience. 'Don't play with words, man; this is a flaying matter. The Ten mean to tear you to pieces for this – you'd do well to listen to what I have to say.'

Sigismondo folded his arms and leant back on the wall. His head was inclined towards Rinaldo and he gave his full attention. 'I'm all ears, my lord, until you choose to cut them off.'

Rinaldo, mindful of the jailer, lowered his voice to a hiss, increasing his resemblance to an aristocratic snake. 'I can prevent you from being tortured.'

Sigismondo raised his eyebrows. 'What kindness must I do in return?'

'Your service for Lord Vettor must remain secret.'

'Mm'hm. If it's known that Lady Isabella didn't present Pasquale Scolar's incriminating letter to you in dutiful haste, but that I stole it at Lord Vettor's instigation, her role as innocent widow is suspect.' Sigismondo smiled widely. 'Why, thank you, my lord.'

'For what?'

'For showing me the cards in my hand.'

Rinaldo shot his head forward, a striking snake. 'Play those cards and you die. I've warned you.'

'No, my lord. You came to do something quite different.' Sigismondo still smiled, more at his ease in the cell than was the free man visiting him. 'You came to offer a favour and to ask one in return. But now I have to ask you the one question that matters. If I grant your favour, if I say nothing of what I did at Lord Vettor's command, and in return I am spared the torture, what happens then?'

'That depends on the decision of the Ten.'

'Mm – m . . . It also depends on what I am accused of. If you know so much, can you tell me what "treason" I am supposed to have committed? And who accuses me?'

Rinaldo Ermolin's eyes under the heavy lids flickered. 'That is a thing I may not speak about.' A distant jangling of keys made him glance at the door. 'Already I run considerable risk coming here.'

'But no more than mine in staying here, my lord. Can I count on Lord Vettor's support as well as yours?'

The irony in Sigismondo's voice was not lost on Rinaldo, and he had started to reply when the jangling grew suddenly louder, the key was rammed into the lock and turned, and the huge jailer appeared. Rinaldo said swiftly, 'You will remember what I have said,' and furled his cloak round him as if suddenly conscious of the air's dungeon chill.

'Could I forget, my lord?' Sigismondo sat down on the stone bench, long legs out before him as if warming himself at a fire. He raised his voice just before the door clanged shut. 'Give my duty, pray, to the Lady Isabella.'

Left alone, he had time to reflect. Ermolin was offering him protection from torture – though how far he would be able to withstand any wishes of the Ten was in doubt – but he had still not told Sigismondo why he was imprisoned.

However obscure that mystery, there was none at all about what happened to those who played the Republic false. Oh, there'd be no interesting display of dismemberment on the Piazzetta. For those such as Sigismondo, punishment was private, carried out in the prison with a cord for the neck. Benno would probably never get to hear about it.

Chapter 42

Someone To Share

Cardinal Pantera might not be charmed to arrive in Venice, but there was one in the city who genuinely welcomed his arrival.

Brunelli had tired of his work extending and improving the Palazzo Ermolin. He had also got across Rinaldo Ermolin, his new employer, over the decoration of the upper floor. It was a feature of Brunelli's commissions that, at one point or other in their execution, his opinions ran counter to those of his employer; with the result that he had often walked or in some cases was thrown out, and with some violence, leaving his work unfinished. Leone Leconti, who loathed his fellow artist to roughly the same degree as Brunelli despised him, said that as sculptors went, Brunelli had left as many statues with missing limbs as were ever dug up from the days of ancient Rome – though, of course, readily distinguishable as inferior work.

Nobody reported this to Brunelli because nobody wanted to be pushed into a canal. Nor had Lord Rinaldo reached the point of dismissing him since, for one thing, Brunelli's designs were excellent and the Palazzo was already attracting envious attention in the city exactly as its late owner had desired when he engaged Brunelli.

The year before, in Rome, Brunelli had been commissioned by Cardinal Pantera to do a bronze bust of him; but thanks to the death of the Pope and all the business contingent on that, including the enforced absence of

Cardinal Pantera in the Conclave shut up in the Vatican to elect the next Pope, it had not been done. Brunelli had made several very striking sketches, but by the time that the Cardinal was at leisure – he was now adviser to Pope Felix – Brunelli had quarrelled with another patron in Rome and was on his travels again.

Now was his chance to make the bronze after all.

In his exuberance at the prospect of doing something which he really wanted to do – Cardinal Pantera had a genuinely interesting face – Brunelli decided to do another thing he had contemplated for some time with enjoyment. He borrowed a longbow from a friend he had made in the Ducal Guard and took a gondola to a church near the Campo San Polo.

Leone Leconti was singularly satisfied with his painting of the wooden panels of the triptych over the high altar in this church. So many representations of St Sebastian had the martyr simpering as he gazed heavenwards, his body a porcupine of arrows and streaming decoratively with blood. Leconti flattered himself that he had given *his* St Sebastian a look of manly endurance rather than effeminate rapture. On this delightful morning, Leconti smiled to himself as, after assessing the effect with half-closed eyes, he stepped forward to add the last touch, a highlight on the blood issuing where an arrow pierced the saint's chest.

A sudden noise like a rushing wind made him for a split second wonder if he had been chosen as the object of a miracle, perhaps an angel come to show heavenly approval of his work.

A violent thud succeeding the wind made him flinch in fright.

An arrow, a real arrow, quite superfluous to those already painted, was quivering with its impact, touching Leconti's shoulder as it vibrated, its point buried in St Sebastian's ivory breast, exactly cleaving the image of one Leconti had supplied.

As Leconti whirled round, tense with rage and fear, he saw against the light blazing at the west door, a burly figure turn and, bow in hand, stump off out of sight. No need to ask who had committed this outrage on the best piece of work he had ever done. Leconti had been working in a breastplate for weeks, fearing just such an attack, but there was no putting armour on a naked martyr.

Outside the church, Brunelli walked straight into two other people who recognised him.

'Off to the war, Brunelli? No, no, we can't risk a genius like you.'

Pico Gamboni had not thought it beneath his dignity to sit to Brunelli for sketches and, in reverse of the usual procedure for an aristocrat, to accept payment rather than give it. Brunelli had in mind a fresco of Dives and Lazarus, Pico to be poor Lazarus begging at the rich man's door, assured, in the midst of poverty and humiliation, of his place in Heaven, while Dives' purple splendour was to be transformed to scarlet in the flames of Hell – he saw this also as a sly moral comment considering it was to be in the house of the Ermolins. Therefore, because he had drawn him, Brunelli recognised Pico. Benno he'd had the pleasure of kicking in the past so for once he too was noticed.

Brunelli scowled pleasantly at them. 'War? No, I'm off to see Cardinal Pantera. You coming?'

To Pico Gamboni, cardinals could be fountains of generosity, so he followed Brunelli into a gondola without hesitation. Benno scrambled in after. To his sad heart all roads were alike, but a little hope sprang up. Cardinal Pantera had liked Sigismondo, as had Pope Felix. Perhaps something could be done?

While Benno was grasping his thread of hope, Sigismondo had another visitor. Once more the clash of keys, once more the door groaned open and someone, almost invisible in the shadows, was propelled in at a run colliding with Sigismondo who had got swiftly to his feet – it was unlikely that the Ten should send a dagger rather than a cord, but he was alive now because of being ready for anything. This might even be Rinaldo Ermolin's humane method of sparing him the torture.

As executioner the man was inefficient. Sigismondo fended off the collision, seizing the man's hands in case of a dagger. This produced, shockingly, a scream of agony.

Sigismondo, as the man reeled away from him and landed, sobbing, against the wall, picked up the lantern, rescued its weltering wick, and held it high. The light showed long legs in scarlet and white striped hose, now dirt-smeared; broad shoulders; tightly curled hair and, as the man turned his head, the tear-streaked face of Cosmo. Sigismondo at once put down the lantern and was by his side, leading him to the stone bench without touching those awkwardly held hands.

'What have they done?'

Cosmo mutely held out his hands. It was hard to see the swelling on dark skin in that wretched light, but Sigismondo could feel their heat, and he hummed thoughtfully.

'When was this?'

'I don't suppose it took as long as it seemed.' Cosmo spoke as if picking his words carefully could spare him pain. 'Just now. Then they brought me here.'

'Just now. Mmm. We're in time.' Sigismondo was reaching inside his doublet. 'Here, put your hands on the stone a moment. Cool them all you can.'

Cosmo flinched and stifled a brief gasp as he touched the hard chill of the bench on either side. Something beside pain was beginning to penetrate his mind and he watched Sigismondo spread a narrow roll of cloth on the bench beside the lantern and pick out this or that sprig or leaf, and a garlic clove.

'How did you get here?' Cosmo asked. 'Do they think you killed someone too?'

'Hey, they're not telling me. Let's see your hands.' Sigismondo pulled out his shirt, tore the hem with his teeth and ripped a strip away. He laid it on the bench, dripped some of the vinegary wine on it, crushed a garlic clove onto it with his thumbnail, added bruised thyme leaves, comfrey and valerian and, making a poultice of all these, wrapped it gently round Cosmo's right hand, binding it securely with a thong from his doublet. As Cosmo hissed involuntarily at the sensation, Sigismondo repeated the process with the left hand.

'Mmm. That may prevent any permanent damage. Lucky I saw you so soon.'

'Lucky you carry the herbs.' Cosmo regarded his bandages, luminous in the dim light, then turned his eyes, luminous too, on Sigismondo. 'Will they torture you as well?'

'I shall have to wait to see. Did they tell you what is to happen?'

The question of course was: Have they told you when you are to die? Men in prison for poisoning members of the Signoria very rarely leave alive. Cosmo shrugged, and winced. 'Nothing. They told me nothing. They asked what I had given Marco, to kill him. I said I hadn't, and they did this.' He raised the bandaged hands.

'Did you admit it, then?' The question was impersonal, without judgement. Still Cosmo did not meet Sigismondo's eyes.

'I don't know what I said. I think I'd have said anything to get him to stop.'

'Him?'

'By his accent he's from Padua. He said: "We'll start with these. People need to use their hands, whatever they do." And there was someone, a clerk, in the corner, writing everything that was said.'

Sigismondo was silent for a while. There was no need to mention that those who talk of starting at the hands have as a rule plans for going on to other parts. A lot depended on what Cosmo did not know that he had said, what had been written down by the clerk in the corner.

He picked up the earthenware pitcher, still half full of wine and icy from the damp flags, and motioned Cosmo to hold it in his hands. As he did so, he leant to speak in Cosmo's ear in a bass murmur no louder than the buzz of a fly, 'Did anyone see you in the gondola with Marco?'

When Cosmo opened his mouth to reply, Sigismondo laid a finger on his lips and jerked his head at the door. Cosmo had not been put into his cell to bring him presents.

Cosmo widened his eyes and dropped his voice to a murmur that matched Sigismondo's for vibrancy and depth.

'I only took him because Marco told me to. He was there all the way.'

'Who?'

'Lord Gamboni. He hires me whenever he can, or I take him if he has no money and I have no other fare. And Marco hailed *me* because he sometimes can't pay either.'

Sigismondo's laugh rumbled softly. 'Are you a gondolier or are you running a charity? So Pico was there all along. He could say whether you offered Marco food or drink. Did you?'

'*No*! They kept asking me that. Marco was eating already when he got in, something from a street stall. He offered me some but I wouldn't.'

'Did he offer Pico some?'

'Oh yes. I'd say Lord Gamboni ate at least half.'

'Mmm . . . and he's still alive. Which,' as an eye appeared at the grille again, but with no preceding jangle of keys, studying them, 'may be more than we shall be, if we can't get someone to believe this.'

Chapter 43

The Cardinal Is Consulted

Cardinal Pantera's slight fatigue after his journey had not been lessened by his grand reception. His secretary, a formidable priest who resembled a vulture dressed in black, would have liked to protect his superior from anyone who sought to break in on what leisure and rest could be got before the exhausting succession of entertainments, audiences and meetings set in. However, although both of those wishing to see his Eminence were clearly afflicted by God, the foremost, with his wild grey hair and tattered red silk was, incredibly, a member of the Signoria and could not be simply dismissed; that he had, in the first place, been admitted to the Patriarch's residence showed as much.

And, as luck would have it, the Cardinal himself put his head out of his room at this moment and recognised one of the two, the unkempt halfwit, who knelt with great alacrity at the sight of him. The Cardinal's tired face lightened, and the secretary was obliged, after the Cardinal had blessed them, to usher both into the room. He had then to endure being dismissed before he could find out how the Cardinal came to know this frowsty gutter-rat. Saints could come in all disguises, of course, and if this were one he would deceive all but the most perceptive eye – which he knew his Eminence to possess.

When Pico Gamboni and Benno emerged, therefore, from a surprisingly long interview with the Cardinal, his secretary managed to bow and smile at both, to Benno's astonishment. Benno had hardly recovered from being recognised by so eminent a person as the Cardinal: the long-practised anonymity, which had saved him from much damage all his life, must be slipping, and now this priest was treating him as if he counted!

Not that Benno was ready to complain. Cardinal Pantera's recognition had got them the interview, and Benno had been able to explain that Sigismondo was in prison and needed help. Cardinal Pantera had looked thoughtful. His eyebrows had always a plaintive slant and, though he was troubled at the news, he had not much that was hopeful to say. If the Ten had imprisoned Sigismondo for a reason not divulged, his Eminence believed he could not ask for his release without first finding out how Sigismondo had come under suspicion.

'I must tell you,' he had said, his sad, kind, dark eyes resting on each in turn, 'that I myself am not in the best position for asking favours. The last Papal Legate here came to bring word of an interdict on the city.' He paused, and with the faintest smile went on, 'There has, of course, been a new Pope since then, but the Venetians cannot be supposed to have forgotten.' He raised the scarlet glove in a farewell blessing. 'Luckily for Sigismondo, neither will Pope Felix have forgotten. He knows of services done at a shrine of the Virgin's by Sigismondo last year.' He sighed, and stood up with a great rustle of heavy watered silk. 'We must hope that my representations will be accepted and that they do not come too late.'

The Patriarch of Venice having lodged the Papal Legate in his own palace on the Grand Canal, Cardinal Pantera did not have far to go to his next meeting. It was a personal call of courtesy on the Doge, but even Benno could have told the Cardinal that, if he was also looking to make a difference to Sigismondo's fate, it was no good to start with a man acknowledged to be a figurehead.

Figureheads are, however, necessarily at the front of affairs, and must have rituals observed in their honour. It would have been impossible for Cardinal Pantera to neglect this courtesy call, even if Sigismondo were at that moment being fastened to the rack.

In fact, he and the rack were not so many feet apart. While Cardinal Pantera mounted the long staircase in the inner courtyard of the Doge's Palace, the hem of his robes ascending two steps after him, somewhere below the great chamber where the Doge waited, in the dim-lit sewer-smelling darkness, Sigismondo received his third visitor of the day.

The eye at the grille had not been satisfied with a limited view. It belonged to the Master of Padua, and he had come, as a butcher might visit the market, to examine the carcases and assess their possibilities. At his nod, the jailer applied his jangling keys, swung back the door and stood aside to let the master craftsman enter.

Sigismondo stood up, the same height and of much the same build as the man who planted himself face to face and looked him up and down. Cosmo, nursing his hands on the bench, he ignored. There were no secrets there; *his* staying power had been exactly calculated. The man before him would be more of a problem; the shoulders and set of neck showed real strength, but that was not the basis of the Master of Padua's opinion. Shoulders could be broken. The will was another matter. By the steady gaze under the dark brows, a gaze without defiance, and by the relaxed hands, this was not one to buckle under any easy pressure. It would take hard work and a lot of intelligence.

A challenge! The Master of Padua smiled and beckoned. He had come to view; now there should be a different viewing. Cosmo sank back thankfully into the dark as the jailer picked up the lantern. Sigismondo also smiled slightly as if at what Fate had thrown at him, and at the possible fragility of Rinaldo Ermolin's promise, and followed the Master. The cell door jarred shut and was locked. The passage, lit by the swinging lantern, gleamed with what a fanciful man might have thought were the tears of prisoners as the stones sweated moisture drawn up from the lagoon. From somewhere, as they trod the flags, came a long scream like that of a fox, followed by sobs that died away in echoes.

Chapter 44

His Fate Will Be Sealed

Two storeys up, Cardinal Pantera heard only the civilised tones of the maestro da camina announcing him to Doge Scolar. He had not met the Doge before in private, but as the gold-robed figure advanced to take his hand and kiss the ring, Cardinal Pantera had a sudden compassionate sense that here was a man at the end of himself. The back was still held straight, a smile had been imposed by resolution on the lined old face, but the eyes looked out of Hell.

The Cardinal blessed him, with sincerity.

Proper greetings were exchanged. Cardinals, although they often have numerous kin and in this Cardinal Pantera was no exception, acknowledge offspring only under the euphemism of 'nieces' and 'nephews', but since Cardinal Pantera lived a life of startling chastity there were no enquiries to be made on that head; and on the other side, to enquire after the Doge's son would have been cruel. Cardinal Pantera had seen all he could need to know, in the Doge's eyes. He had been informed of Pasquale's exile and he did not need telling what future a man knows is before him when he will never see his beloved only son again.

The Doge led the Cardinal across the room, away from the chairs that had been placed for them, to a window embrasure, to a seat padded with a long embroidered cushion. They sat, and the Doge gazed at the inner courtyard through the grey glass. He said abruptly, 'The Ten want me to resign.'

Cardinal Pantera lifted the plaintive eyebrows. 'Resign, your Grace? Can a Doge resign, then?'

A small bitter smile made a thin crease either side of the thin mouth. 'That is what I said to them, your Eminence. They have made me Doge. By law the Ten alone cannot unmake me. It must be by the Great Council – a majority decision supported by six members of the Signoria.'

Cardinal Pantera studied the gold thread on the back of his scarlet gloves. 'Would they get such a decision, were they to ask the Great Council?'

'That is not the point! They will not ask, because they are a law unto themselves. There are those in the Ten – I will not say their names – who would like me dead, just as they would have liked my son dead.' The Doge gripped the scarlet glove beside him. 'They want my downfall. They snatched Pasquale from me and exiled him to bring me down.' His voice broke and grew husky. 'They shall not succeed. They cannot make me go.'

There was silence for a few minutes, broken only by the throaty cooing of a dove outside on the sill. Cardinal Pantera gazed at a swirl of cherubs on the painted ceiling as if for inspiration.

'You say, your Grace, that there are those who – God forgive us – wish you dead. I take it they have another, ready to step into your place.' Cardinal Pantera had not been a diplomat all his life for nothing.

The Doge gave a harsh bark, hardly a laugh. 'Vettor Darin slavers on the steps of the throne. He and Rinaldo Ermolin poison the Ten against me.'

The Cardinal noticed that the Doge's announced intention of saying no names had not withstood his anger. He stored the two he had heard and went on considering the cherubs.

'Have you thought, your Grace, that it might be dangerous to oppose them?'

'Have you thought, your Eminence, that I might not care for danger any more? What pleasure can life bring me now?' The old voice picked up strength with its passion. 'The only pleasure I can hope for is to frustrate the desires of those who conspired to exile my son. If they arrange my death, then I shall die, but I *will not* resign.'

The Cardinal turned to look full in the old man's face. 'My son, that is no way to face death. I have been told that in the East, men who reach old age seek to retire from the world. Of their own free will they devote themselves to preparation for that other world they are soon to enter, surrendering freely all the cares and obligations of this life. These ambitious men who plot your downfall, may they not be offering you a hidden blessing?' He lifted the hand that still gripped his. 'What is required of you, my son, is resignation in its truest sense. God sends terrible trials to us but never without a purpose. Nothing He does is without meaning. We have to seek that meaning with a humble heart.'

'You mean that you think I *ought* to resign? To let Vettor Darin become Doge?'

The Cardinal gave a rueful smile. 'Have you found it so comfortable a yoke that you would deny it to him? Let those who hunger for high office bear its burdens. He does not know that he is offering to you, in their place, freedom to attend to your soul and to pray for those who need your prayers.'

In the thoughts of both was the young son on his way to Cyprus, where he was unlikely to improve his hopes of salvation. A man does not leave his nature behind when he leaves the city of his birth, nor can a change of place at one blow install common sense.

The Doge turned his head to gaze out of the window at the roof opposite and the banner of St Mark cracking like a whip in the wind off the sea. When he spoke, it was reflectively.

'I could take a boat and visit the monasteries. I've friends there I have not seen for many years.'

'You would have my prayers. God smiles when men give up their pride.'

The Doge turned sharply. 'Their pride?'

'Is it not pride that maintains you as Doge, in this desire to spite your enemies?'

219

For a moment the Doge drew himself up. His eyes flashed; then catching the deprecatory gaze of Cardinal Pantera, he unexpectedly laughed. The servants by the double doors at the end of the room exchanged glances that said they had not heard that laugh since the departure of young Pasquale.

'Of course you are right.' The Doge clasped the scarlet-clad hand in both his own. 'It is God's grace that you came! The Patriarch gave me no such advice, but then he is no friend to Vettor Darin. *There* is one whom Darin will have to win over if he is to succeed me.' He let go of the hand and rubbed his knees as if he anticipated with pleasure the trouble, the persuasion, the bribes that would have to be expended by any who would be his successor.

Then he stopped, suddenly grave. 'One thing I regret. Under Darin, the fate of one man, Sigismondo, will be sealed. I asked him to do the impossible – to clear my son's name – and I have heard today that the Ten arrested him. For all I know, he is already dead.'

Chapter 45

Dangers

It might have been a view of Hell. Fires burnt low in braziers over which grilles were laid, and on some of these lay long irons like pokers, the ends pulsing with red heat. By the light of the fires gleamed half-seen objects hanging on the walls and on the thick pillars that made a perspective into the far dark, objects of iron: brackets, chains, a mask, frames to accommodate – oh, how painfully – the human form. In the half-dark beyond the fires lurked shapes that moved, that might pass for attendant demons there to assist in all the complicated horrors that might be devised by the chief devil who stood, feet planted well apart, in the centre of the firelight, watching Sigismondo.

If the Master of Padua was surprised, nothing about him showed it when Sigismondo, having surveyed the place with a look of keen interest, walked up to an iron cage attached to one pillar, a cage for a six-foot bird, and swung open the front of it with a creak of hinges, and a disparaging hum.

'There's a fault here. See?'

The Master of Padua was beside him at once, prodding the hinge and examining the leather straps. The two heads, one shaven, the other cropped, were bent side by side and a growl brought one of the attendant demons to be shown the hinge and to have *his* head slapped.

Sigismondo stood back. His regard strayed to another cage, far smaller, with various iron pins protruding. He picked it off its hook and turned it over in his hands, slid one inside it and then waggled the pins at the Master.

'Mm-m. Old-fashioned. This isn't what you're used to, Master! Hey, it crushes the fingers almost at once and you're left with only another hand to go.' He smiled brilliantly. 'Have you seen the one devised by the Master of Bruges? With only the most gradual pressure here,' he pulled out a pin and shed a screw that fell to the ground with a rattle, 'you prolong the suffering without injury until the last moment.'

'The Master of Bruges? Yan Limburg? You know him?'

'I've worked for him. Some years ago and only for a short time, but to be apprentice to such a master for even a day will tell you . . .'

The Master of Padua was regarding him differently. This would be more of a challenge still. The man knew professional techniques, such that he himself was not reluctant to hear. Yan Limburg was one he would have liked to be apprenticed to himself. Yet there were advantages; he was showing gear to one who appreciated the subtleties of the damage that could be inflicted. If you'd seen men suffer, you knew what the slight turn of a screw could do; he kicked the one lying at their feet towards one of his aides, who scrambled to pick it up.

All the same, it was difficult to prevent a certain camaraderie about the rest of the tour. The man knew what he was looking at and what the effects were. The Master was not a butcher, although he had to be able to butcher if an execution demanded it; they might now be two craftsmen discussing their craft, except that they both knew Sigismondo was the animal concerned.

The Master, who normally did not concern himself with such things, began to wonder what subjects of interrogation were to be put to this man. And now the man was putting a question to him.

'For some, this viewing of your mystery must be enough. Do you get many such?'

The Master of Padua laughed. 'Not many get the chance to escape the question. If they confess, it's usual to confirm what they have said, to test their statements under duress. A man, too, may admit his own crime yet be slow to name his friends. With my help all can be known. However high a man rates himself up there,' and by a jerk of his head he indicated the world that walked above them, 'he's reduced down here to a proper humility at my hands.'

'Even the Doge's own son?' Sigismondo was shaking his head in wonder. 'At your hands he confessed all.'

The Master laughed again, derisively. 'He never came *into* my hands. He was one who, as you said, confessed at sight of me. I was not expected to touch him. Some respect was due to his Grace and' – he made a grimace of disparagement – 'there was no more to say.'

'But he himself had not killed Lord Ermolin. Was there no one he could name or identify as the assassin?'

'In this city? Lord Pasquale identify someone? Assassins come hooded, and in shadows, offering not their faces but their daggers, when they hear such things are wanted. Their lordships did not look to find the assassin.'

'No doubt they had enough for their needs. You did not doubt his word? He was not protecting someone else?'

The Master opened small black eyes as wide as they would go. 'One look at me and he would have sent his own father to kneel in the Piazzetta without his head, I promise you.'

Sigismondo fingered the links of a chain hanging beside a branding iron. 'Love can make cowards brave.'

The Master snorted. 'Not that one. The Doge fought against the Turks forty years ago with honour, his son wept and pissed himself for fear of this,' he jangled the chancery which Sigismondo had criticised. 'And that's nothing, as you've seen, to what I could have shown him.'

In the world above their heads, to which the Master of Padua had referred, the Doge, counselled to a humble heart by Cardinal Pantera, was not aware that in that moment Sigismondo had relinquished his second commission in that unlucky city.

Another who had received a commission and been unable to carry it out was tossing and turning, in a bed with wooden sides resembling a coffin, under the gaze of a wooden Christ

nailed to His cross on the wall, and the monitoring one of
Sister Infirmarian. She had given him agrimony and feverfew
to diminish the heat and the sweating, and yarrow root hot,
with honey, to cool the inflammation of the wound, but she
was not optimistic as to the results. The decoctions had been
hard to administer, even with the help of her nursing sisters,
so violently did he flail and struggle; and he had abused them
in astonishing terms, at one point taking them for inhabitants
of a brothel dressed up as nuns in provocation. She had been
glad that the younger sister did not understand either his
language or his illusion, though she was in danger of being
too pitiful of so handsome a man. It had been needful to
remind her that a man so near death required their prayers
for his soul more than care for his mauled body.

They had not enquired how he came by his wounds. Their
concern was to mend whom God sent to their doors, and if
He chose a shaven-headed stranger carrying a man lacerated
by a lion, that was His affair. No sense was to be got from
the man himself, lost in a world of images that distressed.
Sister Infirmarian was aware that his had not been a good
life.

As was common with those in the grip of fever, he was
obsessed with the idea of some undertaking that he must
perform, in which he was frustrated by his weakness. Several
times he had tried to rise from his bed, only to fall back in
agony from his torn thigh. One night he had got as far as the
door before the sister saying her Office at the other end of
the room came running to restrain him and help him back
to bed, while he muttered all the time of having to carry out
the task.

Sister Infirmarian was convinced that this task was no good
one. There were old scars on him, and she thought he might
be in pursuit of some revenge, some feud that festered in his
mind. 'Vengeance is mine, saith the Lord,' and it was in Hell
that these poor souls would discover the truth of that.

She pressed a damp cloth to his forehead and his lips,
and, sitting down again on the stool by his bed, got out her
breviary and set herself to read.

It would have surprised her to know that the man with the shaven head who had so genially delivered her patient at their doors was, at that moment, in as much danger as the man tossing on the bed before her.

Chapter 46

The Cardinal Hears More

Cardinal Pantera's presence in Venice had several effects. It inspired hope in Benno and resignation in the Doge. More importantly, from Sigismondo's point of view, it kept the Ten busy. Negotiations with the Pope were of vital importance if Venice were not to find herself, very soon, standing alone against the Infidel.

Unfortunately, not one of the other powers in Italy seemed to understand that Venice, when she had trafficked with the Turk in years gone by, had not been condoning his religion but merely taking advantage of a period of peace in which a more than usually benign Sultan reigned. Indeed, some of these Italian powers pointed out that the Republic had always traded with the Turk quite regardless of who was Sultan, and to start asking for the support of Christendom now the Turk had turned nasty was decidedly too late. Nevertheless Venice had high expectations of the new Pope who, at first rumoured to be a dotty invalid, now appeared to be in robust health and in full command of his marbles. The simple fact that he had sent Cardinal Pantera, rather than a vituperative letter, as the last Pope had done, argued well.

The Venetians had been too proud to ask for the interdict to be raised. They had just continued christening, marrying, burying and holding services as if it had never been issued. All the same, if Cardinal Pantera had come with permission to restore to the Serenissima the full rites of Holy Church, the Venetians would take it as an apology. Meanwhile, as was always the best move when asking for help, everything should be done to impress the papal legate with the Republic's splendour.

So Rinaldo Ermolin found the other members of the Ten preoccupied, when he brought up the subject of Sigismondo's interrogation. The celebration of Piombo's fall had been delayed, bar a few fireworks, until the arrival of its conquerors the Marsili brothers, but the receptions and banquets for the legate were taking everyone's attention and time. Some of the Ten were for keeping Sigismondo cooling his heels for a while, arguing that waiting for interrogation was in itself one of the most subtle and effective tortures. Others held out for at least a brief softening up, a taste of what was in store.

Lord Vettor coolly had the last word: 'Cardinal Pantera has spoken to me on the subject. He assures me that the man has rendered service to the Holy Father. Too summary a treatment of him might not, at this juncture, be taken well. May I suggest that we wait and see?'

Neither Lord Vettor nor Rinaldo Ermolin thought it advisable that Cardinal Pantera should speak to Sigismondo as he requested; unfortunately for their plans, the rest of the Ten thought it politic – in view of Lord Vettor's own statement – to propitiate his Eminence and permit an interview. As opposition to this might arouse suspicion that the Lords Darin and Ermolin feared for secrets of their own rather than those of the Republic, they were forced to accede, and so Sigismondo found himself escorted, with as usual no explanation, up into daylight and a room of the Doge's palace filled with the light and smell of the sea.

The Cardinal had vivid memories of Sigismondo as he had last seen him, almost a year ago in Rome, quietly impressive in black velvet during his audience with the Pope, and as a guest in both his own palazzo and at the reception of a fellow cardinal; to that dinner he had worn a chain of gold filigree and emeralds worth a villa and its lands and a stable of thoroughbreds. The man who advanced up the chamber, with its *trompe l'oeil* marble on one side and its long windows on the other, appeared very different. The pale light was merciless in revealing straw and dust on the black cloth doublet and hose, and the dark stubble that shadowed scalp and chin. He showed no outward sign of worldly importance and yet, prisoner though he was, his expression and bearing were unchanged. When the Cardinal had first set eyes on him, he had thought there were not many faces as intelligent in the Curia, nor as boldly relaxed among such condottieri as he had met.

Sigismondo smiled when he saw who was waiting to receive him. He knelt to kiss the Cardinal's ring.

'What a pleasure, your Eminence. I did not know you were in the city.'

'I have but just arrived, and I am sorry to see you a prisoner, my son. Of what are you accused?'

Sigismondo laughed. 'And I was hoping your Eminence could tell me that! All I can make out is that I am believed guilty of some treason against the Republic, whereas my conscience tells me that I am not.'

Cardinal Pantera had drawn Sigismondo upright and, still holding one manacled hand between his, bent a searching gaze on his face. The eyes under strong dark brows regarded him unmoving.

He nodded, satisfied. 'There is certainly a mystery here. His Grace Doge Scolar tells me he had asked you to establish his son's innocence if you could. Have you perhaps broken the law in trying to do this? Or,' the Cardinal paused, 'or, which is more likely, did you offend someone who might have informed against you and be ready to lie to have you condemned?'

Sigismondo shrugged. 'My stay in Venice has offended some, I know. Men don't care to be questioned.'

'Were you here for a purpose?'

He smiled. 'You know me, Eminence. I wander. I don't have to look for trouble, it *finds* me. I had hardly arrived here when Lord Vettor Darin sent for me to look into the murder of his son-in-law, Niccolo Ermolin.'

Cardinal Pantera was shaking his head. His expressive face

showed grief. 'A dreadful business. I was told of it only today. Was it you, then, who discovered that Pasquale Scolar was the murderer? I cannot understand, then, why the Doge spoke to me of asking you to establish his son's innocence. Had you not given proof of his guilt?'

It was Sigismondo's turn to shake his head, ruefully. 'This is Venice, and therefore more complicated than that. Niccolo Ermolin had many enemies and, in spite of his confession, I'm far from sure that Pasquale Scolar was responsible for his death.'

The Cardinal's eyebrows made their plaintive arch. He tapped a forefinger against his cheek thoughtfully. 'It does seem to me, my son, that you're not in a good position. You may not know why you are in prison, but I do not think that whoever put you there intends you to leave.'

'Mm – mm. In a sack, your Eminence. By the tide.'

This man must have survived so many dangerous encounters, thought the Cardinal, and now he is suggesting that he may have come to the end of them; that, in whatever city he might have been born, Venice was to be the scene of his death. Many a man would have been on his knees, pleading, begging for help, clutching at him. This man was far too intelligent not to be afraid.

'I will do all I can, my son. I will represent that not only the Holy Father himself but also several dukes and princes would be concerned for your fate. You are not a nobody they can allow to vanish.'

Sigismondo was silent for a moment. He had half-turned, to look out over the water, and his tone was sombre. 'Your Eminence, we are speaking of the Serene Republic. His Holiness's regard for me, by which I am honoured, must carry weight at this point, but when have you known Venice to pay heed to other powers and their wishes? Isn't that the very reason why she stands alone now against the Turk?'

It was the Cardinal's turn to be silent. Sigismondo was perfectly right. Only Venice's present desire for alliance with the Pope against the suddenly belligerent Sultan operated on his behalf. It was her custom to ignore any powers whose favours she despised. Even the Pope might be supposed to have too much on his mind to regret the death of one man of no standing in the world. Sigismondo, if his enemies were determined, and the fudged-up charge of treason were proved – and even the bravest of men succumb to torture – might well disappear, in the dungeons that lay beneath their feet now, and never be seen again.

'You say Ermolin had many enemies?' The forefinger was tapping on his cheek again, the lip drawn down to show the small feral teeth that surprised those who saw the Cardinal as a gentle persuadable man and who had not encountered his ferocity in a good cause. 'Perhaps those who disliked his dealing with Rome?'

Sigismondo's eyes, which seemed to have been looking inward as if contemplating the possibility of his death, came suddenly alive.

'Niccolo Ermolin dealt with Rome? When?'

'Last year before Pope Felix was elected. I heard of various dealings – in secret, of course. The Signoria would have been incensed if they had known that one of their number was negotiating with a Pope who had laid Venice under interdict.'

'Do you know, Eminence' – the Cardinal thought that one could almost feel the force of Sigismondo's attention – 'what the negotiations involved?'

The Cardinal vouchsafed another glimpse of the feral teeth. 'I was not privy to them but heard only through a friend. Cardinal Tartaruga was the intermediary; his failure to be elected Pope must have disappointed Ermolin. No, I heard because I am kin to the girl Ermolin wanted as bride for his son.' The Cardinal paused and sighed, making the sign of the Cross. 'I hear the young man is dead too . . . poisoned by his half-brother! It is a wicked world.'

Sigismondo was not prepared to reflect on the subject. He slightly shook his head, and stood before the Cardinal, regarding the floor, preoccupied. 'So Ermolin was to have reward in a rich and' – he gave a sudden, almost smiling glance – 'well-connected bride for his son. For what was this the price?'

'I heard only rumour, my son, and I was asked to say nothing. I spoke out of concern for you.'

'I am grateful, your Eminence, believe me. These rumours show that it was Lord Ermolin, not I, who was the traitor.'

'Traitor, my son? Alliances shift continually. Lord Ermolin may have been trying to bring about peace between Venice and Rome, which is after all my purpose here, and it is natural in a man to wish to marry his son well. Had he not a daughter too?'

'Beatrice, who is not yet married.' Sigismondo gazed again out of the window at a sky he had not seen for some hours, a sky someone seemed bent on depriving him of for ever. 'I did wonder if Lord Ermolin had been executed.'

'*Executed?*' Cardinal Pantera was brought to remember the revolting sight he had been afforded on his arrival: the man kneeling in the Piazzetta watched by his own head. 'I understand Ermolin was stabbed.'

'Venice doesn't always advertise her justice. Possibly the Ten might not want it known that anyone would betray the Great Council. Nor would it be beyond them to make the death look like the outcome of some private feud.' Sigismondo was speaking almost as if to himself.

He was interrupted by the opening of the great doors at the end of the chamber, and a servant slipping into the room to whisper in the ear of the Cardinal's secretary, who advanced up the room, an apologetic vulture.

'Y'Eminence: the Ten await your presence.'

Sigismondo laughed. 'While they're concerned with you, mm-m – they can't concern themselves with me.'

The jailer, an incongruous figure in his greasy leather jerkin in this room of light and air, of gilt and marble, came forward to reclaim his prisoner. Sigismondo once more knelt to kiss the Cardinal's ring.

'I shall do what I can, my son; and my prayers are with you.'

As Sigismondo rose, he said, urgently and low, 'My servant, Benno. I'd meant to speak of him. Could you arrange that some news of me reaches him, and that he's taken care of? I can't tell you where to find—'

'It was he who found me.' Cardinal Pantera gave one of his singularly sweet smiles. 'It is thanks to him that I knew what had happened to you. I believe Lord Gamboni is taking care of him, but I shall see that he hears you are well.'

Both of them knew this meant: he shall hear you have not yet undergone the Question. Sigismondo alone knew that, if Rinaldo Ermolin's promise that he should not be tortured were to be kept, the best guarantee of this would be the strangler's cord.

Chapter 47

We Are Lost

Benno found sleeping on a stone bench to be far less uncomfortable than he had expected. He had slept in all sorts of places though never in a grand bed – and when he was a groom, had slept in straw with perfect cosiness. Pico Gamboni had offered him the bench in the arcade of a square with a gesture of lordly hospitality and, wrapping himself in an ancient cloak, lay down on the next bench. The cloak seemed to be in the custody of a food shop – the proprietor had fished it out from a corner and handed it over as soon as Pico appeared. He had also handed over a cold pancake stuffed with vegetables and cheese, which Pico scrupulously shared with Benno; both of them contributed to Biondello's supper.

Benno had not expected to fall asleep as promptly as he usually did, but on the whole the news from Cardinal Pantera was good. They had waited at the Patriarch's palace while he went to see the Doge, and on his return he could tell them that Sigismondo was very much alive and had not been tortured. The Cardinal promised to use all the influence he could to secure his release, and though the kind dark eyes said that the Cardinal doubted his success, Benno had the utmost faith in his master's ability to survive the most terrible of situations. Something would happen.

After sending a specially fervent prayer to the Virgin and pressing his holy medal to Biondello's forehead, Benno had tucked the little dog inside his jerkin, wrapped Sigismondo's good wool cloak round himself with a feeling of being protected, and in a few minutes was snoring away. A pigeon landed on the bench by his feet, regarded him with its head on one side for a bit, gave him up as a provider and flapped heavily away.

Sigismondo, that night, perhaps regretted the absence of the cloak which on his arrest he had deliberately left beside Benno, but he staved off the chill of the cell by sharing the pallet with Cosmo. *They* were regarded by rats, who were perfectly prepared to bide their time.

There were others that night who had less opportunity to sleep until much later. Cardinal Pantera was obliged to endure a banquet designed to show him the glories of Venetian hospitality, on a different scale from that offered by a stone bench or a prison pallet.

Course after course was announced by trumpets. The Cardinal, who was not a big eater, toyed politely with every dish put before him. He ate a little of the wild boar baked with nutmeg, cloves and ginger, and he enjoyed the salmon pie with prunes and dates. After Roman cooking, with its taste of the olive oil he loved, he found rice cooked in broth and wine a little strange. The famous Venetian dish of liver was served to him with braised pheasant, bacon and onions, and plenty of cinnamon – definitely as good as he had heard. By the time they reached the almond pastries flavoured with lemon and vanilla, Cardinal Pantera was resolving that as far as possible he would fast tomorrow.

The Doge, splendid in gold brocade, at whose right hand he was seated, ate nothing and drank only in sips. He answered the Cardinal's conversation almost at random and the guest saw that it would be unkind to attempt drawing him out. He looked, thought the Cardinal with compassion, like a dead man at the banquet, a *memento mori* indeed!

The Cardinal was not to know that, before the banquet, Vettor Darin had seen fit to pluck the Doge's sleeve, draw him aside and whisper to him that word had come of Pasquale's safe arrival in Cyprus. Such news might have soothed a father's troubled heart, were it not for the coda which Vettor now added: Pasquale had no sooner arrived than he began negotiations for leaving.

That would have been forgivable had the negotiations been with the Republic, begging for further mercies, but Pasquale had probably believed his luck was out, there. Instead, according to the informers who, he should have known, watched his every move, he had written, and tried to have sent, a letter asking for a ship to take him away from Cyprus, and this letter was to the Sultan of Turkey himself.

It was a death sentence and the Doge knew it.

Tomorrow he would resign. He would not be Doge when his wretched, incorrigibly foolish son was brought home in chains to take the place of Andrea Barolo between the columns on the Piazzetta. Meanwhile he sat, with straight back and impassive air, through the long banquet.

He sat through the display of fireworks later, on the Piazzetta and on rafts on the water. The citizens of Venice amiably gathered to cheer the Cardinal – by orders from above, no emphasis had been laid on last year's interdict. Priests had absolved, said Mass, married, christened and buried the citizens with no reference to the fact that the Holy Father had forbidden anything of the kind; and consequently no grievance against his Holiness's representative was felt. As the rockets soared into the night sky, reflected in the lagoon, waking Benno on his bench and heard even by Sigismondo in the palace prison, the Venetians gasped, cheered and clapped, confident that further celebrations were to come. They looked forward to the impending arrival of Ottavio and Nono Marsili and the fêting of Piombo's capture.

In fact, the brothers were nearer to Venice than anyone thought. As the Ten had instructed, they had the honour of an armed escort in every city on the way, which they had accepted as their due so that the additional instructions – to be implemented should they have objected – were not required. The day after the splendid reception for Cardinal Pantera, the two condottieri arrived. They made their way to the palace through the excited shouts of the crowds following them. Ottavio took the cap of scarlet velvet from his iron-grey hair and waved it; Nono, grinning, looked more like a gargoyle than ever. Venice was not short of dwarves, but this one was the favourite of the minute.

Their reception at the palace they found polite, though not as enthusiastic as they had expected. Again they waited in the great ante-chamber at the head of the stairs. Nono, restless as always, stroked the curves of a sculptured nymph, under the shocked gaze of the attendants standing at the double doors; wandered to the window and back again; preened himself before the huge mirrors with their gilt frames and made faces at his brother's reflection as he stood by a statue of Hercules as if inviting comparison.

Finally one of the Ten emerged, apologetic. The Doge was indisposed. The interview must be postponed. Lord Rinaldo Ermolin, bowing, escorted them to the stairs and even extended his courtesy by accompanying them down to the courtyard. There, the condottieri turned to take their way to the Riva and found it blocked by Ermolin, who still bowed but pointed to the door on the other side, the door that led to the palace prisons.

Nono began a protest, Ottavio put a hand to his sword. But the guards were there, and more came in past Ermolin, who backed away. The situation was hopeless. Ottavio spoke for the first time.

'We are lost,' he murmured. Overhead, the banner of St Mark cracked in the wind like a whip. The lion on it had its features stretched into a smile.

Chapter 48

Face To Face

When Il Lupo heard that the Marsili brothers had returned to Venice to be fêted on the conquest of Piombo, he grinned, and then explained to his employer that this was the opportunity for which they had been waiting. The Duke of Montano had, with a natural reluctance, parted with gold to these brothers who had taken, and pillaged, his own city. He now learned that the gold had not been wasted, for here was the first token of what he might expect. True, Venice had agreed to their temporary departure from the field, but the way was clear – the brothers had gone without pleading a postponement to finish the campaign.

It meant, Il Lupo informed the Duke, 'Piombo is ours!' and he triumphantly slapped the trestle table with his leather gauntlet, sturdily stitched, scarred, and unsavoury with the blood of those who had regretted meeting his sword. It must, the Duke thought, be a very old glove, for he could not recall any occasion for such bloodshed having occurred lately.

The Duke did not respond with enthusiasm either. He had been feeling poorly ever since the city fell, and he could not find in himself any urge to put on armour and take back a city that had already been gutted and whose citizens had been raped or massacred or both. He had no doubt that his father would have seized the chance to redeem territory, but all his own ideas of warfare had been shaken apart and he himself painfully disillusioned. He had set out to join his troops with such excitement. Glory was waiting! He was

237

young, in surprising health, and well learned in the theories of war. But it wasn't glorious. It rained. The outer canvas of his tent was sodden and soaked the fine lining where it touched. The pathways between the tents were churned filth, the men had dysentery and dismal coughs, and his condottiere was personally repulsive. The Duke had been horrified at the cynicism with which Il Lupo left Piombo to be taken, and in a culmination of dismay he discovered that the Marsili brothers, who had dealt him such humiliation, were to be bought.

He knew it would take him years to forget the face of Nono Marsili grinning at him from waist level with such an affable assumption of complicity. If Venice could not trust *her* condottiere, what hope was there in trusting his own? Il Lupo had in all likelihood arranged with these accursed brothers that Piombo should fall.

Obscurely, unfairly, the Duke blamed Master Valentino for the way he felt. If the physician had not encouraged him to think that exercise and not rest would do him good, he would never have attempted to join his army at all, and the horrible double-dealing would have gone on without his least suspicion. Even the news of Piombo's capture would have been less poignant had he not been within a few miles of the city he had come to save.

Master Valentino was as bored as his patron was disturbed. No interesting wounds! No healthy cadavers to dissect! And now the prospect of battle was receding. He rarely stayed long in one place and this place in particular was nothing short of disgusting. His patient was a spoilt young man relapsing into hypochondria. Master Valentino had begun to think seriously of taking up an invitation from a rich Venetian merchant who was worried about his wife's health. Most likely the man was more worried about his own health – he was elderly and childless – than about that of his wife who had the advantage of youth and, possibly, a lover. Master Valentino liked Venice. He had friends there. No problem would arise from his recent attendance on Montano, currently enemy of Venice. Physicians of Master Valentino's reputation were not expected to concern themselves with enmities, boundaries or sides.

To the Duke's surprise, therefore, Master Valentino – his sardonic face expressionless under the furred cap of black velvet, with lappets over the ears, that proclaimed his profession – said flatly that conditions in camp were not suited to his patient's humours. Relief should be gained from a return to familiar surroundings. There, dosed with various medicines he would prescribe, to be taken of course at propitious aspects of the moon and planets, the Duke should regain equilibrium. The war must be left to professionals. The Duke should even indulge himself a little with rest, strengthening food and judicious amounts of good wine.

This welcome advice caused the Duke yet more pleasure as he realised that his physician did not intend to return with him. A patient in Venice needed him urgently.

Before he met Il Lupo, the Duke would never have wondered, as he did now, if the physician were a spy as well as a doctor. However, as he handed out more gold still, and uttered counterfeit regrets, he reflected that nothing observed in his camp could do Venice the slightest good, especially since Montano had bought her generals. He could afford to go home to his palace and his books. Il Lupo would retake Piombo and *he* would not mind having to ride over charred ruins or view corpses. Peace would eventually be made, all the faster for having the Marsili brothers on his side.

Besides, once home, his comfortable old physicians would be by his side, would exclaim over his appearance – he was really looking very pale and his stomach had never accommodated itself to the ghastly way food was cooked in camp, and the men's coughing kept him awake. They would prescribe rest. He would lie on his brocaded bed, marble, not mud, all around. He would sip scented wine, listen to his viol-player and perhaps read a French romance. Somehow or other, he felt no interest at all in Caesar's *Commentaries*, or Livy on the conduct of war.

Though Fate disposed so quietly with one of the Republic's enemies, there remained another, ferocious and far harder to deter. The Captain-General of the Fleet, sailing with his well-equipped galleys down the Adriatic, had for the first time caught sight of the Turkish fleet. This moment had been eagerly sought both by Attilio and by Mehmet Bey, a Turk of menacing bulk and resourceful brain. Battle would be joined. The outcome would decide whether Venice could rejoice, or once more punish for failure.

The Venetian galleys were slightly outnumbered but splendidly manned – the rowers were not slaves, like the Turks' rowers – and the Arsenal with its unwavering efficiency had fitted them with the latest, most modern gear. Against them, the Turks had a hideous turn of speed and a commander of great experience, a mind as subtle as any Venetian's, and all the confidence of a man who had beaten one Captain-General already.

From his flagship, Attilio let his eye range over the prospect: the silken sails, the flash in the sun of scimitars and jewelled turbans, the crescent of Islam floating over all. He did not miss the figure of Mehmet Bey, shadowing his eyes to view the scene from where he stood. When either of them gave the word, hundreds – perhaps thousands – would die on that day, and blood pour into the sea from those immaculate decks.

As they gazed, a gull flew low and spattered Attilio's shoulder with white. He smiled; a cheer rose from those around him. Luck, above all, was what he needed this day. Across the water floated the sound of drums giving the beat to galleys still coming up to join the formation, a heavy pulsing like the straining of many hearts.

It was time to still a few of them.

Chapter 49

Not A Hope

Sigismondo and Cosmo were aware of sudden activity in the prison, a distant clanging of doors, a clashing of keys, a muttering of jailers. No eye bothered to study them through the grille. The Master of Padua had other fish in his net.

They sat together in the semi-dark in silence, each with his own thoughts. The dry bread provided had been almost palatable with some herbs from Sigismondo's scrip, and they drank the vinegary wine gratefully. Cosmo's hands were much less swollen; Sigismondo had examined them and renewed the cold compresses.

Sigismondo leant his shoulders back against the wall and folded his arms. He revived a conversation they had been having, about Cosmo's life as a gondolier, about his childhood and his father.

'Did he treat you and Marco alike, once?'

'He spoilt us both. Marco was the favourite, of course, but I was his firstborn and he loved my mother more than Marco's.'

'Mm . . . mm. That must have made trouble.'

'Lady Emilia – my father's first wife – didn't mind my mother; indeed, my mother thinks she was glad to have Father's attentions distracted from her. Spending money was *her* passion. You may imagine how *that* pleased my father.'

'So Marco inherited that at least. You always got on with him?'

Cosmo's teeth gleamed in the cell's dimness. 'We were

brothers in mischief then. We pestered the servants for cakes and treats of food. We used to ride the hounds round the hall and take them on hunts round all the rooms, hallooing and yelling. My father would come from his study or Lord Rinaldo would have us whipped. We hid things, we stole things . . . we stole my mother's keys once. Not the ones at her girdle, of course, but the ones hanging in the store cupboard. She'd left it unlocked as she hardly ever did. We thought we'd try them all round the house and see what we could find. There were hideous old clothes in chests in the lofts . . . we went all over, creeping about, trying to stop the keys making a noise, not letting anyone see us. We gave ourselves a great fright over our father's study.' Cosmo laughed, remembering. 'Marco dared me to try the keys there. By then we knew roughly the keys that hadn't fitted anywhere yet, and you can bet we only tried when we'd seen him lock it and go off to see Lady Emilia.'

'So the coast was clear. Did you get wrecked all the same?'

Cosmo grinned widely. 'We found the key all right. We'd that moment got the door open when we heard him coming back, shouting at the hounds. For some reason Lady Emilia couldn't receive him, I suppose. Marco's hand shook so much I had to grab hold and turn the key and snatch it out. We were only just in time.'

'You were both afraid of your father though he spoilt you?'

'Everyone was afraid of him. He tried to teach Marco business, but Marco used to come away miserable because he was too nervous to take anything in. And he was only a child.'

'What future did your father have planned for you?'

'He never said. When Lord Vettor and Lord Rinaldo came down on him to get rid of me, he sent me with money and letters to a monastery across the lagoon. They took me in. I was only seven. Father Prior said,' and Cosmo grimaced, 'all men were equal before God. They tried to treat all us boys alike – educated and fed and beat us. I was never going to become a monk, and when I was fifteen I ran away.'

'When did you come to see your mother again?'

'This spring. I'd trained for a gondolier, been accepted into the Guild . . . then I heard of my father's marrying again. I thought my mother might suffer if the new wife was jealous.'

Cosmo watched Sigismondo easing his shoulders and exercising his arms to keep them in working order in the cell's damp and chill.

'But Lady Isabella has no wish to concern herself with the household and she found my mother too useful. The lady's another who likes to spend, but she's not like Lady Emilia; she can stand up for herself.'

'There were quarrels? Hey, a man wants to please a young lovely wife. You don't tell me they quarrelled already.'

'My mother said. My father kept Lady Isabella's jewelry locked up with his treasures in his study, except when she had to appear at some grand dinner or celebration, and she hated that. They quarrelled about it the very morning he was murdered.'

Sigismondo stopped swinging his arms. 'You imply she might have killed him?'

Cosmo put his bandaged hands together as if in prayer and regarded Sigismondo over them. 'Don't you think it's possible? If children could steal those keys and find the one that fitted? She's not a woman that bears being slighted. My mother told me Father had been stabbed in the back of the neck as well as the eye. He might not have had time to turn round when she came in. He might not have heard her.'

Sigismondo came to stand over Cosmo. His voice was thoughtful. 'It was Lord Vettor who came to see him and, knocking, got no answer.'

'If she was in there, she would have heard his gondola arrive, the servants opening the doors below. She would have warning enough to get out and lock the door.'

Sigismondo hummed, and then asked abruptly, 'You don't suspect your mother?'

'My mother! She *loved* him! I told you. He was a handsome man when she was sold to him at fourteen. She always loved him, although he never confided in her – never talked to her. He was a man of secrets, always.' Cosmo had risen and, as if to escape Sigismondo's close attention, began to walk to and fro in the narrow confines of the cell, seeming to pass from one shadow to another, only the long legs in their scarlet and white stripes, and his bandaged hands, showing where he was. 'People came to see him, at night. A short while ago I was visiting my mother – at night so the servants would not see me – and we were talking in her room. You know it, with the water door on to the side canal. Well, we heard a whistle, a few notes, twice, and my father came down. When we heard him leave his study overhead, we hid in the cupboard where my mother keeps a pallet and sleeps sometimes – not that we expected him to come into her room, but my mother was frightened I should be discovered somehow. He did come in, though – I suppose he never thought of her sleeping there – and he unbarred the water door and let someone in, a foreigner with some Lombardy accent. They went upstairs and I took care to leave before he came back. He had all sorts of secrets.'

A sudden terrible cry froze them both. It did not come from very far away in the confines of the prison. Cosmo had flinched. Sigismondo went to the door. The cry came again, a cry forced from someone against their will. Cosmo shuddered involuntarily, feeling the pain in his hands again.

Sigismondo was, inexplicably, unlacing his black doublet. He undid his shirt and felt at the neck, and pulled out a thick gold chain. Selecting a link, he put it to his mouth, bit on it, and twisted with teeth and hands. A moment later he stowed the chain in his belt-purse, took the gleaming c-shaped link from his mouth and, going to the door, rattled the grille so that the whole door shook, and shouted.

Bewildered, Cosmo heard a jailer come, shouting in his turn, and saw torchlight shine in on Sigismondo's face. It was smiling.

'What's going on out there?' the deep voice asked.

'What's it to you?'

Sigismondo held up the gold in the torchlight, a seductive crooked fragment, and twitched it this way and that. A hand appeared at the grille.

'Mm . . . hm . . . tell me. What's going on?'

'You'll hear soon enough about it, fine sir. That's Ottavio Marsili singing, and when they've finished with him it'll be your turn to sing how you sold us to the Montano scum.'

He reached for the gold link and Sigismondo twitched it away. 'Hey, there's enough here to buy this door open and a boat laid on for free. I want more for my gold.'

The jailer scowled. 'Save it for your burial. It's not worth my life.'

He stumped off, the rhythmic clash of the keys drowned by another appalling scream, prolonged to a point where it snapped off in a gasp more vivid still.

Cosmo had his head between his bandaged hands when Sigismondo returned to him, and his voice was muffled.

'Do we have to die, then? Is there no way out? I'd sooner kill myself than go through this again.' He held out his hands.

'If it comes to that,' Sigismondo's voice was matter-of-fact and cheerful, 'I can kill you myself so you'd hardly feel a thing. But escape? No, I've tested the door and there's no other way unless our friends above manage to change the minds of the Ten for them.' He squatted in front of Cosmo and reached out a hand to clap his cheek affectionately. 'Life's a gamble, my friend, but it's not over till the last throw of the dice.'

Chapter 50

Benno Holds A Pose

Benno was finding the responsibility of making decisions for himself dismaying. One advantage of being a servant was not having to work out the options. Your master does that. You do what he says and take the consequences, whether it's a beating or a feast. Sigismondo's decisions up to now had resulted in quite a few feasts.

One decision Benno could not understand was Sigismondo's not resisting arrest a few days ago. Benno had seen him fighting and knew that even a party of guards such as the Ten had sent would provide no real obstacle to a getaway if Sigismondo had determined on it. What had stopped him? Had he thought Benno couldn't cope – joining the fight or making the getaway too? Had he feared bystanders getting hurt? In Benno's experience bystanders didn't stand by for long when fighting started.

No. The reason Sigismondo had gone with those sinister men could only be what had in the past impelled him, with Benno trotting after, into so much trouble: curiosity. Sigismondo had to find out what they wanted him for. Benno just hoped it was worth it.

Pico, so kindly taking Benno under his tattered wing and sharing hand-outs with him, said that he personally had never heard of anyone escaping from the palace prisons; and that Venice itself, surrounded by water, was its own sort of prison from which no captive could hope to break free. To console Benno he added that Sigismondo was unlikely to be displayed between the columns of the Piazzetta, where Andrea Barolo had by now lost the crowd's interest and could draw the attention only of dogs and flies; such treatment was reserved for the more important, the next candidates being probably the Marsili brothers. News of that arrest had flown around Venice and the outcome was obvious. Something, despite the victory at Piombo, was seriously wrong.

Benno, mulling this over, crouched in a doorway with Biondello sitting between his ankles, suddenly saw the light. Sigismondo had warned him that wherever you went in Venice you were watched and reported on. As the Marsili brothers were in trouble now, then all their past contacts had come under suspicion, and there was the liver and onions they had shared with the Marsili brothers. Someone might have heard Ottavio offering Sigismondo work, but perhaps just being seen on friendly terms was enough . . .

His brooding was interrupted; a coin span out of the air and landed in front of the little dog, making him jump and crowd back under Benno's haunches.

'Come and earn a living instead of begging.'

It was Brunelli, thumbs in belt, face smeared with charcoal, looking down at him. Brunelli too had seen the light. The drawing he had done of Gamboni as Lazarus was utterly wrong. There was an unmistakable aristocracy about the features, however tangled the hair or ragged the clothes. They belonged to the rich man Gamboni had once been. Brunelli now had a far better idea: the wild hair could writhe round that face in the flames of Hell – Pico Gamboni should be his Dives, the rich man who paid so terribly for despising the beggar at his gate. And for the beggar Lazarus, his sores licked by dogs, who better than the dismal bearded halfwit crouched before him?

Benno had no objection. He was at home with being ordered about, and Brunelli's was a face he knew among so many strangers in this unlucky city. Pico had been called to a meeting of the Great Council to debate about the war with Montano, as Venice had now no condottiere to conduct it. Benno felt more than ever alone. It had occurred to him, as

Sigismondo had hoped it would, that Miriam da Silva might be compromised if he went to her for help. Benno could not go to the bolt-hole by himself because Sigismondo had the keys. Miriam would know something was wrong, because the servants who brought food and wine, and hot water, would have reported their continued absence. She might have heard of Sigismondo's arrest. She might try to help. A great many people were likely to owe her money, so that a little pressure here and there . . . for hadn't she said she owed her life to Sigismondo's advice?

Now the Marsili were arrested, he thought that Sigismondo might be supposed to be with these brothers so deeply in the shit that they could be rescued only by the axe . . . It didn't bear thinking about.

'Where we going?' he asked Brunelli, as he watched the peeling plaster over the brick walls drift by as in a dream. Their gondolier happened to be in good spirits and was treating the world to a sad little song about a lover who left a talking bird with his mistress to remind her of his name while he was overseas. The warbling refrain, as the bird jogged the girl's memory at times when she was tempted to be unfaithful or was actually *being* it, bounced back off the walls, an effect Brunelli liked so much that he joined in, so Benno got no answer until they emerged from the side canal, swung round the corner and drew up to the landing stage of the Palazzo Ermolin.

Benno hopped out after Brunelli, clutching Biondello and with the seed of an idea in his mind.

The big entrance hall was empty save for the door servant and the major-domo who appeared for a moment, staff of office in hand, at the far end of the hall in readiness to receive any important guest. He saw Brunelli stumping over the marble towards the staircase, the scrubby nonentity at his heels, and withdrew at once. Any man who had once tangled with Brunelli was strongly averse to trying it again; whatever Brunelli was about to do, the major-domo would be powerless to prevent, and it was prudent not to show at a disadvantage before even the doorman.

Brunelli's intention, however, was harmless. He wanted to pose Benno on the mezzanine of the magnificent staircase, whose sweep and carved banisters he had designed, and there to make charcoal sketches for the mural that was to dominate the hall, and to make notes of shadow and light, for the mural was to have a *trompe l'oeil* effect. He was pleased to have found this creature who, unlike, Gamboni, was born to be a beggar.

'The difficulty,' he said to Benno, 'is in making you look like a beggar whose sores the dogs would lick. You are an innately squalid object and the dogs are more likely to turn away in disgust; except of course for that object living in your jerkin. A beggar's dog if ever I saw one. He can go in the mural as well.'

Benno, pushed down into an abject huddle at the foot of the wall and told not to stir a finger, had time to consider his plan of action. Yes, Sigismondo was in prison, but he had escaped from one prison that Benno knew of, and no doubt from others in the past that he hadn't told Benno about. Then, Cardinal Pantera had promised to do what he could, and Lord Gamboni thought that Venice was anxious to have the Pope on her side, what with the Turks and Montano being against her so hard. You'd be bound to have good luck, thought Benno, maintaining his cramped pose devoutly, if you could just get the Church on your side.

So Benno must do what he could on his own for the moment. The Doge, poor old gentleman, had asked Sigismondo to clear his son of the murder of Lord Ermolin. Mind you, that didn't seem possible, given the nasty incriminating letter about wanting him dead, but Sigismondo had taken on the commission. The snag was that Sigismondo, having been given the push from the case by Lord Vettor, could hardly walk into the Palazzo Ermolin – supposing he were free – and start questioning the Lady Isabella.

Yet Benno was here, in a perfectly legitimate way and unlikely to be recognised anywhere except in the kitchens. Certainly he hadn't a hope of questioning Lady Isabella – he wouldn't even know her if he saw her, and trying to speak to her would be a passport to the nearest canal – but he had a wilier plan.

He wouldn't be able to put this into action until Brunelli was satisfied with his work, and this involved Benno being hauled about into various eleemosynary positions, having his jaw seized and pointed at different angles and, finally, having to stand with hands uplifted and as near to an expression of saintly simper as he could manage – Brunelli closed his mouth for him until his teeth clashed – for his translation to Heaven as a reward for his suffering on earth. Benno thought hard about his favourite food, onions in cheese sauce, and turned his eyes up obediently.

Suddenly this dutiful devotion, and Brunelli's absorption, were interrupted. A door on the upper landing was flung open and someone, obscured by the sweep of the stairs, came out fast and noisily sobbing. Some object flew after her, crashed on the opposite wall and fell in flitters, many of them down the stairs. The door slammed shut but the sobbing continued, its tone choked by what seemed like efforts to pick up the pieces. Brunelli gave a loud snort and shook his head angrily as if pestered by a fly. A girl's face, alarmed, streaked by tears, looked down at them over the balustrade.

Chapter 51

I Can't Work Miracles

Benno, who knew a chidden servant when he saw one, did not dare even to make a sympathetic grimace at her for fear of Brunelli's punishing fist, so he remained, hands and eyes turned up, while she stared and Brunelli, who had broken his charcoal, cursed and fumbled for another in his scrip. Therefore it fell to Biondello to do the honours and he scampered up the stairs to fuss at the girl's feet. Biondello had, Benno knew, inverse snobbery. He ran to servants but tended to leave dukes and their like alone.

After caressing Biondello's grubby wool, the girl, her apron full of shards, came timidly down several steps to collect the fragments that had gone further. For Brunelli, this was too far. It intruded yet again on his concentration. A second piece of charcoal snapped and he swore. Turning, he ran at the girl and gave her a push that scattered every particle and sliver in a cascade down the stairs. He would have done the same if she had been a princess. Indeed, this lack of discrimination was the reason why so many of his commissions remained unfinished.

The girl's bawl settled the matter for him. Dashing the charcoal to the floor, he stamped upon it and ran down the stairs in a crunch of china. A cowering servant opened the wicket in the great doors as Brunelli approached; head down like a bull at a gate and without altering his speed the architect was out of the palace and, almost at once, could be heard yelling abuse at the workmen on the roof, who

251

were now to profit from his frustrated energies.

Benno, left alone with the girl who was using her apron to mop her tears, began to pick up the bits of china at his feet, Biondello bustling down to nose at them. When she lowered the apron, Benno mutely offered his hands full and she extended it for him to drop the pieces in. This co-operation made a good beginning.

She had eyes that could be pretty if they were not pink and swollen with crying. She sniffed, examining Benno.

'Shouldn't you of gone along with him?'

Benno played his usual best card. Rounding his eyes and dropping his jaw, he shrugged – an innocent; like her, a victim. 'Nowhere to go. My own master's left me.'

Since she did not know that this was a euphemism for being arrested on the orders of the Ten, she looked at him, scrabbling up more china, with great pity. 'Signor Brunelli's not your master? You could still run after him.' The frantic diligence of the hammering on the roof could be faintly heard, and testified to Brunelli's being still on the premises. Benno drooped, despondent.

'He just told me to come here and be drawn. He's not even paid me. I did hope to get something – for me and the dog.'

'Poor soul.' The maid, her apron full now, took Benno by the sleeve. Luckily he had on his better jerkin, stained though it was, or she might have hesitated. She drew him away down the stairs, nodding at the upper landing and whispering, 'Don't let my lady hear you. She's in a temper today.'

Benno remembered Sigismondo's opinion: it had always looked like an inside job and Lord Ermolin's wife might well have lost her temper that morning and employed the stiletto. With a nervous glance up the stairs, he hurried along, and Biondello scuttered after.

Their destination was the kitchen, where she displayed the contents of her apron to a shocked cook and a couple of kitchenmaids before emptying it into the refuse tub. Benno was greeted lovingly by the cook, who took up Biondello and crammed him to her bosom. He devotedly licked her greasy hands and she cooed at him.

'Ah, the honey! He's not forgotten me . . . Lord Rinaldo's not at home, so who's your master come to see?'

'His master's left him – cast him off.' The maid Chiara, who had not seen Benno when he was last there as she had been in attendance on her mistress, was indignant. 'Cruel, I call it.'

The cook's consolation for cruelty took the form of a wheat roll stuffed with mushrooms, while Biondello was treated to a veal bone with plenty of meat still on it, and tussled with it on the flagstones to the prim distaste of a tabby cat sitting high on a stool. Chiara made room for Benno on a bench alongside the huge table at which the maids were preparing food. Last time he was here they had just been deprived of a master, now they were bereaved of his son and, with more material consequences, of the housekeeper. Marco, whom they had been admiring for his dexterity in climbing across to the window of his father's room on the morning of the murder, was not being talked of now, although his funeral was only yesterday. Zenobia, so inconveniently fled away, was their subject. She had been resented, if respected, for her strict discipline and the scrupulousness with which she dealt out the stores while she was there, but her absence had brought chaos – they had had to force her cupboard doors to get at the linen and supplies – and Lord Rinaldo was blaming them for any difficulties.

'Mark my words, it was she who gave the poison to her son that did away with the poor young master. They'll find her, soon or late. Then she'll pay for it just like her son will. Strangling's too good for them. Flaying alive is what *I*'d do.'

This clever way of getting rid of a coloured skin without any obvious prejudice as the reason appealed to the other servants, and they began to recall, in gruesome detail and in low voices – since the cook disapproved – their visits to the spectacle provided by Andrea Barolo's remains strung between the columns of the Piazzetta.

Benno's memories of this were connected with the assassin smiling at Sigismondo and pouring the wine significantly on the ground. It still pleased him that eventually it was Dion's blood and not Sigismondo's that got spilt in a pool outside Lord Vettor's garden.

With un-Christian fervour, Benno wished again that Dion was dead. How unfair that Sigismondo should be in prison when he'd done nothing wrong, while Dion, a professional murderer, was being cared for by nurses, free to go if he got better. Free, in fact, to kill Sigismondo when he got out of prison. Benno resolutely stuck to 'when' about Sigismondo and 'if' about Dion because he had to make the future bearable.

His own immediate future was being prepared for him. The cook and Chiara were in earnest colloquy which he pretended not to hear as he ate the handful of raisins generously doled out from Zenobia's store.

'You can lodge here for the night, in Zenobia's workroom. There's a bed she sometimes used, going spare there.'

Going spare . . . Benno had a vision of a furious little bed resenting the beautiful Zenobia's absence . . . he also felt a surge of hope. The longer he stayed in the Palazzo Ermolin, the more likely he was to come across some useful knowledge. Servants knew everything that went on.

He allowed tears of gratitude to brim over, and got another mushroom roll. Chiara sat down again beside him and watched him benevolently.

'I'll show you where it is, later on. You'll have to keep out of Luigi's way, that's the major-domo, he pokes his nose into everything. Well, that's his job of course but he's mean as they come. He isn't in the kitchen much, Cook rules here. I can smuggle you into that room when it gets dark, and after my mistress finishes with me. I never know when that'll be.' Chiara grimaced. 'She's always got something to be done – sew this, wash that.'

The cook turned, scarlet from bending over a pot on the fire. 'My word, how she beat you when you couldn't get the blood out of that sleeve when the poor master was murdered.'

'*Blood?*' Benno left a mouthful of mushroom roll on view as he turned to Chiara.

'The sleeve was soaked in it. She gave it to me far too late to get it out. I told her, I can't work miracles.'

Benno was excited. If the lady stuck the stiletto in her husband she could well have been in a bit of a mess afterwards. Chewing, he asked, 'How'd she get it like that?'

'When she was holding him in her arms when he was dead, she said. Be one of the first times she'd ever embraced him of her own free will, if she did. Master was ever so taken with his new bride but she wasn't one bit impressed by him.'

What would Sigismondo say to this? Of course, the lady could have got blood on her sleeve the way she said, and it wasn't much in the way of proof that she'd killed Lord Ermolin. No one was going to come forward and say they'd happened to be looking in at the window and saw . . .

For a moment Benno had a picture of the workman Sigismondo had questioned, swinging about in his basket outside the window, peering in, cheerfully interested . . .

He would certainly have told Sigismondo. And if Isabella had seen him gawping he'd have been dead by now. Benno envisaged the lady leaning from the window and cutting the rope. He had formed a decided respect for this lady he had never seen, so much that he felt frightened by proxy when Chiara left the kitchen in a hurry, afraid she had left her mistress unattended for too long.

The day passed uneventfully and even cosily for Benno, and for Biondello although, in a tiff with the tabby cat, had he not ducked back in the nick of time he could have lost an eye to follow the ear. At the time of the main meal, activity round Benno was frantic, so he held Biondello on his lap and watched, buffeted now and then by passing elbows or dishes and once having the best part of a jug of rich sauce spilt down his neck, rather too warm for comfort. He sent Biondello in under his shirt to retrieve what he could. Luckily, the major-domo contented himself with inspecting the dishes as they left the kitchen; perhaps a few spills on his handsome clothes had taught him the wisdom of this.

Later, devouring the left-overs with the others at the table, Benno wondered what Sigismondo was having to eat.

255

Though his master had a good appetite, he seemed equally able to fast, without complaining or even seeming to notice, so Benno consoled himself by planning a splendid meal when he should get out. This helped him to shut his ears to the speculation round the table, which was about the Marsili brothers, now widely known to be traitors, awaiting their doom in the palace prisons.

'They'll have to clear away what's left of the Captain-General,' offered one of the maids, filling her mouth with a gobbet of roast goose and holding her fingers ready to be licked, 'and high time too. I had to go past there today, eugh! And there's two of the Marsili. How do they manage when there's two?'

The problem was being solved at that very moment.

Chapter 52

Discoveries

The Master of Padua, as Sigismondo had noted already, did not own his rank of master for nothing. Anybody can inflict pain but it takes an intelligent man to inflict it to some purpose. Given two such distinguished subjects as Ottavio and Nono Marsili on whom to practise his art, the master demonstrated his superiority by concentrating on one brother alone and leaving the other to sweat it out, within earshot, waiting. More people have confessed for fear of what might happen, than those to whom the worst really has – often leaving them in no state to be usefully coherent.

The Master of Padua was working for very exacting employers and he intended to give them what they required. The Ten wished to know the details of their condottieri's treachery; the Master would provide the details with the condottieri's appalled cooperation.

Nono Marsili, thus left in his cell to listen to his brother's dreadful cries, had quite different ideas. Someone who pretended to be a political prisoner had been locked in with him, to disturb his mind with hideous tales of what was in store and to report anything unguarded Nono himself let slip.

Nono dealt with this problem rapidly. He and his brother had been arrested in all their finery, put on for the interview with the Doge that never came off. What did come off now was a gold brooch of splendid workmanship – Florentine – with which Nono had decorated the collar of his sage-green velvet. He had seen his jailer's lustful regard of it when he brought them food. When he and his companion, who called himself Matteo Masso but might well not have been, were alone that first night, Nono waited until Matteo breathed like one asleep and then drove the long pin of the brooch in, deep behind the man's ear, changing his state from unconsciousness to death with fatal simplicity. Nono, nothing if not pious, said a prayer over him as he removed the brooch.

This brooch was now to serve another useful purpose. Nono went to rattle the grille on the cell door, a manoeuvre with its difficulty for him as it involved standing on tiptoe to grasp the lowest bar. He also beat on the bar with his ring. The jailer, dozing not far away over an empty jar of wine, was moved to investigate.

Nono had been counting on two facts: that jailers are in general chosen for qualities other than intelligence, and that in most circles it is the dumber who get loaded with night duty. There was also a factor unknown to him, that this one in particular had long been addicted to brawling and, not outstanding even in that, had taken many a battering of the brains. All these things did not lead to steady reasoning at this moment.

Paradoxically, it was Nono who offered freedom to the jailer, freedom from a stifling existence in the gloom of the prisons, from far too much monotony and far too little wine and no women at all. The heavy gold brooch signalled a glorious future provided that he, like Nono, could disappear.

It was Nono who first disappeared. The precedent of the siege of Piombo was repeated: the jailer, his face obscured as he bowed under the weight of the sack on his back, used his keys to pass out of the prison that night, saying at the main gates, that he had a load of stale food for his cousin's pigs. He set off, the darkness illuminated for him by the glow of what he could buy with that magnificent brooch. Nono, inert in the sack, had his own plans.

Next day was one of discoveries. To begin with there were two bodies, the first being Matteo Masso looking peaceful on his palliasse in an otherwise empty locked cell, and the second being the jailer, looking surprised and less peaceful, in a side alley outside the prison. It took people some time to find out what had killed them, but it was the same method for both.

The sack had vanished into the canal and so, at one point in the search that began at once, did Nono, under a fall of creeper against a crumbling house wall. Many of the canals were shallow, their beds regularly scoured of mud and rubbish to prevent silting up, and this one presented no problem to a dwarf clinging to strands of creeper as the palace guards went by. Nono knew very well that Venice had almost as many dwarves as it had foreigners, but that not many of them had the chance to dress in velvet and wear gold brooches. Relying on the fact that he was most recognisable in tandem with his brother, he thrust the sopping doublet up behind the creeper, pinned the brooch – now acquiring the character of a talisman – inside his shirt and went boldly in the wake of the palace guards, hose and shirt drying as he went, and enquired of Venice's citizens if any of them had seen a dwarf 'much like me only prettier' whom the guards were anxious to trace. Those who thought they recognised him told themselves they must be wrong. He strayed by design to a place where he hired a boat – he had some coins though all weapons had been taken from him on his arrest – and so he passed from the environs of Venice, judging rightly that he would be expected to escape by sea to another country rather than to the Venetian mainland. There he disappeared. You can best serve a brother by living to avenge him.

Another discovery was made by Rinaldo Ermolin. All the household was aware that its new master spent much of his time shut in his late brother's study. It was supposed that he was counting up the wealth that he alone now controlled. Only his sister-in-law, who had witnessed his quarrel with Marco while she caressed her cat, might have guessed what occupied his time. She was, however, indifferent to all that did not concern her personally.

Every time that he locked himself into the room where his brother had died, Rinaldo sat down at the desk before the window, a desk still dark with a stain he had not allowed any servant in to try to remove; and he opened the *libro segreto*, the record of Niccolo's transactions which no one had been intended to see.

No doubt Niccolo had anticipated that, at the end of a long and prosperous life, with many more children by his second wife, and having trained Marco finally in the ways of trade, he would take his son into his confidence and would hand over not only the secret book but the thing that doubled its secrecy, the code in which it was written.

On the other hand, Niccolo might have decided to erase some of the things recorded in it, things that even a much more mature and wiser Marco would not have understood; things of whose existence his brother Rinaldo was firmly convinced.

He had pressed Niccolo for details of transactions in the past, and had been blandly put off, put off even though as a partner in the Ermolin fortunes he had a right to know, in particular as he had sacrificed a normal life to the guarding and increase of those fortunes. There had been times when he felt that his brother envied that freedom from family burdens, and wanted to show that he was more in control of events than was Rinaldo. If he had known he was leaving this conundrum to be solved, he would have smiled in that bitter, superior way of his. Rinaldo, remembering it, himself smiled.

He had set about solving the code with the logic and efficiency he always showed. He had burnt effort after effort at substitutions and alphabetical changes. It baffled him that his brother had written so much so smoothly, though of course one becomes accustomed to a code until one writes in it easily. Rinaldo had found no basis, no original, from which Niccolo had first worked it out.

He had, after a search of the desk and the room, bethought himself that some paper might be in one of his brother's books. Some of these were their father's; Rinaldo did not suppose Niccolo had bought the Aristotle or others of such a kind, but they might well hide a paper. He took each one down and leafed through. It was, to his surprise, *De Rerum Natura* that fell open as if from custom on one page. Their father, perhaps, had studied these observations. Yet one passage had signs of fingering, even of a pinprick here and there.

Rinaldo walked slowly to the desk, laid the book down and reached for the *libro segreto*. He took up a scrap of paper and began to write out a substitute alphabet, taking the first letter of the passage to represent 'A', the second to be 'B'; the fifth letter was the same as the first, so he left it out and called the next letter 'E' instead. When he had finished, he began to transcribe a line of the *libro*. It was slow, with continual reference to his 'alphabet', but as he wrote, he smiled.

After a while, he frowned.

Chapter 53

The Angel Of Death Gets Busy

Discoveries weren't yet over.

The Master of Padua had spent yesterday persuading, though not convincing, Ottavio Marsili that confession of his treachery and details of his contacts was preferable to further ingenious methods of making him regret that he'd been born with a body. This morning the condottiere was discovered dead.

He had been given no companion in his cell, in order to permit him to concentrate on his misery. When the jailer failed to arouse his prisoner he sent for the Master of Padua at once. Perhaps his skilled attentions of the day before had caused death. Ottavio lay on his palliasse, his grey hair in its soldier's cut falling back on the straw, eyes staring at the brick vault above as though he saw there the Judgement to which he had been called. The Master felt at his neck for a pulse and then beckoned the lantern closer.

'Strangled.'

The Master showed the mark of a cord on the strong neck. No cord was there. The jailer knew of nothing, there had been no visitors, but he referred enquiry to the night officers.

One of these was missing. At least, he had just been found.

The Ten were not amused, but there was conspicuously little discussion. Having a recalcitrant prisoner strangled was after all among their habits, and they may have suspected that the Capi, the three who took such decisions, had reasons not to be enquired into.

The opportunity of making the usual admonitory spectacle of Venice's justice must be taken, although it was subtly altered. As the kitchenmaids at the Palazzo Ermolin had predicted, the remains of Andrea Barolo were tidied away, and the citizens of the Serenissima were supplied with a fresher sight. Ottavio Marsili, conqueror of Piombo, traitor, knelt supported by the chains that held his outspread arms, in terminal apology between the pillars. Few of those who came to gaze were sufficient as connoisseurs to know that the head in front of his knees had been removed after death rather than at the same time. Some of the sightseers regretted that tableau which Nono's presence as well would have provided – that touch of the grotesque which lingers in the memory like spice on the tongue.

The night, fatal to Ottavio, had not been uneventful for Benno. Chiara had, as she promised, come to him as he sat by the dying embers of the kitchen fire, Biondello in his lap and the tabby cat, having permitted a truce, curled up by his feet, and she had hustled him through the semi-darkness of the hall – his own face, caught by moonlight, looking upwards in Brunelli's sketch on the stair wall. Zenobia's room he remembered well, smelling of cloves and cinnamon and the other spices she had kept locked away. The linen cupboard stood open, sheets and towels no longer in perfect order but rumpled and askew, rifled by impatient hands. Chiara's lamp sent huge shadows looming on the plaster walls, and she saw Benno into another cupboard, with a pallet in it, before taking its comforting gleam away.

He felt a little lonely at first, in the silence broken only by the soft slopping of the canal waters against the outer walls. All the servants slept either in the lofts or on the kitchen side, and the rooms of Lord Rinaldo and Lady Isabella would be away from the early-morning noise of the canal traffic. The only part of the palace geography Benno was sure of was that the study also faced this side canal and must be overhead, because Sigismondo had pointed to the window when he questioned the workmen.

Benno as usual said his prayers and begged that his master

be released soon. Had he known that Ottavio's death was about to free the attention of the Master of Padua, his prayers would have been even more urgent.

It was a little before dawn that he heard the whistle, and Biondello heard it before he did. Benno sat up in his cupboard, confused, wondering if the sound had been in his dreams, wondering where he was. Biondello, standing on Benno's thighs and not in the least confused, stuck a quivering nose in the crack of the cupboard door.

The whistle sounded again, low, outside the house. The slop of water against the wall came irregularly and with more force, as if somebody steadied a boat at the little landing stage. Biondello's nose widened the crack and Benno saw a light. He smelt hot metal and hot oil, and saw the shift of shadows.

Had Chiara come to tell him he must go – had her master heard there was a stranger here? Benno held Biondello firmly to stop him following his nose beyond the cupboard door, and peered through the crack, half-afraid of what he might see. Wasn't this a house in which people died suddenly and for unknown reasons?

But he could see next to nothing. The light, probably from a lantern, was being carried on the far side of a silk gown that susurrated over the floor with ghostly speed, towards the door in the corner that led to the little landing stage. It was impossible to see who wore the gown, and Benno had no time to observe because the door was now unlocked and the person went through. From then on, Benno's ears had to tell him anything there was.

What they told him confused him more. He thought he heard low voices just outside, then came a soft thud and a heavy slop of water against the wooden platform and the wall. While Benno puzzled over this, he caught the sound of gasping breath. Was Lady Isabella keeping an assignation? Could it be a lover, more successful than Pasquale, who was embracing her out there? It might be a good deal safer to grapple with him in the boat rather than in the house, where servants or, worse, her brother-in-law might hear. Benno devoutly prayed that nothing might give away his presence to a lady who could have taken a stiletto to her husband.

The gasps were followed by a sudden quite loud *klop*! and a splash, and far more violent slaps of water on the wall and the landing stage. Had they fallen out of the boat? Had it overturned? Had she pushed him in? But there were no voices, no call for help. Could she even have stabbed him?

The door opened again. Benno held Biondello close to his chest and shrank back against the wall, terrified that she would sense someone there, come over, pull open the cupboard and plunge the stiletto in his eye.

The landing-stage door was being locked. The silk gown hissed across the floor. The light vanished as the inner door shut. She'd gone.

It had all taken so little time. Benno, driven by curiosity, risked stretching his cramped limbs, put Biondello down and crept from his closet to the side window. He craned to see out. Would there be a body on the small landing stage? Everything out there was in confused shadow. And she wasn't likely to have left a body lying about conspicuously. She would certainly have put it in the canal. There was no sign of a boat. Perhaps it had simply gone away. But he thought he could make out something, too small for a body, a smallish bulky thing, on the wooden stage.

Part of this was explained a few hours later, when the servants were round the table again, breaking their fast after their early work. The cook, who had gone out herself to bargain with a vendor selling limes and lemons from a boat, came back indignant, carrying a leather sack as well as the net of fruit. She dumped the sack with a crash on the table, making the platters rattle and completely spoiling one maid's account of an erotic dream.

'There. Look at that. I caught my foot on that and near as nothing fell in the canal. These workmen leave their rubbish all over.'

'Better be sure they're not making off with something – like tiles they can sell . . .' The porter untied the string round the sack's neck and pulled it open. 'No. Just rubble.'

'Their idea of tidying up, I dare say. That Brunelli was after them . . .'

Benno, eating bread dipped in wine, was still baffled. What *had* gone on in the night? Could the Lady Isabella have hoisted what the cook found heavy to carry, and then biffed her lover into the canal? Had he tripped on the sack, like the cook, gone into the water and drowned? She could hardly have dashed to fetch help, considering.

Benno decided to suspend all theorising about the lady until he could report to Sigismondo. Yes, Sigismondo would certainly know how to interpret it all.

Sigismondo's chances of hearing Benno's tale seemed at that moment slight. He seemed as likely to become the subject of one of the Master of Padua's experiments with nerves and sinews. Cardinal Pantera had had food sent in, covered dishes of quails in saffron rice, of veal seethed in wine, a deep basket of plums and apricots, and Sigismondo had shared it all with Cosmo in what he managed to make an atmosphere of festivity, their cell filled with a mouthwatering aroma of meat and wine and fruit. The jailer gulped in envy as he stared through the grille at them. He had not forgotten the gold link with which Sigismondo had tantalised him, and here was fresh proof that one prisoner at least had powerful friends; perhaps the gold link would come his way at least if only as a parting tip.

To earn a tip, one offers services. Prisoners always desire news of what is going on in the world.

'Want to know about the Marsili, sirs? They're gone. This morning before dawn.'

'Gone?' Sigismondo looked up from the quail, dark eyes intent in the lantern's light.

The jailer showed a number of discoloured teeth in what he supposed was a smile. 'Can't say where the little 'un is gone. Done a bunk. Left a couple of corpses – I'm not such a fool as my mate on his cell, found in an alley dead as a drowned rat.'

Sigismondo stood up and came to the door, smiling. 'So Nono Marsili has put off dying to another day. And his brother?' He offered a nice piece of quail through the grille, and the jailer took it. He ate, and said through it, 'Oh, the big one's on show in the Piazzetta.'

Sigismondo stopped eating. 'He confessed?'

If Sigismondo was supposed to be involved in the treason of which Ottavio stood accused, the torture might have got confirmation of the falsehood. This was dangerous indeed.

The jailer was really enjoying himself now.

'Not so much as a squeak, so I hear. The Master was to go on working on him today, and there he is, found strangled. And that's not a thing you can do to yourself.'

Sigismondo stood without moving. 'Do they know who strangled him?'

The jailer shrugged. '*I'm* not asking any questions. The fact is, someone wanted him dead, and quickly.'

Cosmo, putting down the plum he was holding, could not prevent a shudder. How soon might that same thing be said of either of them?

Chapter 54

Into Harbour

There was news that even the jailer had not yet heard. That
morning Doge Scolar announced to the Great Council
specially summoned to hear him, that he now resigned. They
had been urging it on him and he, with stubborn pride, had
refused. Perhaps he had hoped that his son's name could be
cleared and that staying in power could help bring this about.
Now his son had hopelessly lost his own case by writing to
the Sultan for rescue. There was no point in remaining any
longer even as a figurehead. All that was left to him was
humiliation and despair when Pasquale would be brought
back for execution.

Not one of the Great Council urged him to stay. Vettor
Darin and his following, and Rinaldo Ermolin, seconding
the speeches of praise for his past actions, for his wisdom,
for all those empty useless qualities he doubted that he
possessed, were delighted to see the last of him. The
incredibly complicated machinery for electing a new Doge
could now be started up, and Vettor Darin was all but certain
to succeed him in office.

Doge Scolar, looking round at the faces turned toward
him in the great Council Chamber, caught several warm
and regretful glances but only one who returned his gaze
with true sympathy: Pico Gamboni knew what it was to lose
a son, to lose everything – wife, house and fortune. Only
those who suffer as you suffer can understand. Why had he
never extended the hand of friendship to Gamboni, instead

of dismissing him, as all did, for a madman? Too late for regrets, he thought, as he rose from the great chair for the last time. All he could hope for was to die before he saw Pasquale again. These days, his mind kept going back to that happy Easter, seventeen, eighteen years ago, when he had been still in his vigorous sixties, and he smiled over the baby son for whom he had had so many hopes.

A certain urgency now prevailed. With Cardinal Pantera waiting to negotiate the terms of a new and important treaty with the Pope, and with the need to find and commission a reliable condottiere to replace the Marsili brothers and continue the war with the Duke of Montano, the necessity of a Doge to ratify these procedures was strongly felt. The Great Council had to get a move on.

Directly Scolar, no longer Doge, had left the chamber, voting began. Thirty of the Great Council had to be chosen, then the taking of lots would reduce these to nine, who in turn would vote for forty who would then be reduced to twelve again this time by lot. These would vote for twenty-five, lots got them down to nine who voted for forty-five, of whom eleven voted for forty-one. These forty-one at last had the privilege of electing a Doge.

This system had been employed since 1268 and was admirably suited to the intricacies of the Venetian mind.

However, it was not fast, and while the process was going through its various stages as speedily as could be managed, fresh need for a Doge was to be demonstrated.

Not long before noon, two disparate things occurred. The Master of Padua, with no one important to occupy his time, and while waiting for instructions from above, put his eye to the grille of the cell where Sigismondo and Cosmo sat, to examine the general demeanour of his next clients. Out in the Piazzetta at the same moment in the brilliant sunshine of late summer, people were shading *their* eyes and staring at the horizon.

Ships came and went all the time, but this one, hard to see against the sky and amid all the dazzle, had a pennant on which straining eyes could just make out . . . a lion? Was it a lion? St Mark's lion? Was this the Captain-General in advance of his Fleet?

After everyone in the rapidly increasing crowd agreed that it was, a far more vital question remained. Was he, like Andrea Barolo, returning to report a failure, or the longed-for victory over the Turks? The citizens had become rather disillusioned of late, with both their commanders by sea and land making a farewell appearance between the columns of the Piazzetta where, even now, Ottavio Marsili mutely begged their forgiveness in the blaze of sun.

Other ships in the harbour were setting out to greet the returning galley, with cheering crews, and the Captain-General's ship was now seen to be heading others as it advanced to the pulsing drumbeats and the squeal of fifes. Men swarming up the masts of ships at the quay had a better view than those on the ground, and could see what the flagship was trailing behind it in the water; what looked like strands of some extraordinary seaweed, so monstrously thick and long that nobody could recognise it. Sudden yells and cheers showed that some had.

Attilio da Castagna, Captain-General of the Venetian Fleet, was coming back from his battle with the Turks, dragging their captured banners in the sea – undulant in his wake – symbol of their defeat at the hands of Venice which, having married the sea with a ring, reserved the right to patrol its waters without interference from the Infidel. Here was a Captain-General confident of a hero's welcome.

The noise and excitement of such a welcome penetrated all parts of the city. With that extraordinary power of news to reach through walls and run from street to street faster than human agency, it arrived at the kitchens of the Palazzo Ermolin and Benno's ears at much the same time that it pervaded the prisons of the Doge's palace. At the Palazzo Ermolin, the authority of the major-domo was as nothing before the desire to celebrate so, while the kitchenmaids banged pans and whooped, the cook poured out wine all round to toast the victory.

Benno drank his, and before his mind's eye came the

picture of Attilio's fierce and humorous face, with its close silvery beard and the eyepatch that gave him such a brigand-like look. He had been a friend of Sigismondo's, fought beside him, told him to call on him if he wanted anything . . . Could a man want anything more than not to be tortured, not to die at the hands of an executioner?

Benno set his cup down and, unnoticed in the hubbub, slipped from the house. The workmen had left the roof after shying some perfectly good tiles into the canal in sheer elation and, reckless of the return of Brunelli, were on their way to join the crowd in the Piazzetta. Benno followed them, collecting shoves and cuffs from anyone whose way he blocked and, once, a kiss from a large matron who could not contain her civic joy and was saluting people at random.

In the gloom and echoing silence of the prison, Cosmo and Sigismondo looked at each other as distant doors clanged, voices called and yells that sprang from exuberance and not pain resounded from the sweating walls. Their jailer appeared at the grille and hailed them in great good humour.

'We've won! The Turks is beat and their commander dead. The Fleet's come home!'

Sigismondo was at the grille in two strides, the gold link magicked from his doublet to glitter in the lanternlight again.

'Your ship's come home too, man, if you do what I say.'

Chapter 55

Hot Water

So while Benno bobbed ineffectually on the outskirts of the mass of cheering people as Attilio's ship came alongside the quay, and important members of the Signoria, hastily assembled from those not engaged already in voting, greeted him without benefit of Doge, the power of gold was radiating outwards from that single link of Sigismondo's chain, through a network of the jailer's acquaintances and those who owed him favours for one reason or another, until someone useful was reached.

This someone turned out to be a servant assigned to help Attilio bathe and change his clothes. He had worn fine clothes to make a show on his return, but then he had worn the same clothes into battle too, as a matter of honour. So indeed had his opponents, but whereas Attilio's crimson doublet had merely darker crimson stains on it and slashes across the gold-embroidered sleeve and hem, Mehmet Bey had lost both his jewelled turban and the head that had worn it.

The servant regarded Attilio's side. 'Nasty cut there, sir. Lucky it wasn't a span to the right.'

Attilio briefly glanced down. 'If it had been, you could have got the Turk sailing in instead of me. You can bleed to death in battle before you've seen what's hit you. I need a bath.'

It was waiting: a wide vat, the hot water poured in over the linen sheets that softened the wooden sides, lavender and camomile strewn on the surface, and pages attending to help the hero in and wash him. The servant, however, had something else to say. It was only a whisper in Attilio's ear as he peeled off his hose, but it produced an explosion.

'God's death! Are you sure? In prison at this moment?'

The bath was left to cool. The pages eyed one another over the steaming water while Attilio plunged his arms into a gown and furling it round him strode out into the corridors of the palace where he had been lodged. It had been considered impolitic, or even unkind, to place the Captain-General in the Doge's palace where Lord Scolar, after his resignation, had at last given way to shock and grief and lay ill. Instead, Lord Vettor had claimed the honour of being host and it was he whom Attilio interrupted now, talking to Donna Claudia. She got only the briefest of bows and a more secure furling of his gown before he turned to her husband.

'What's this I hear of Sigismondo being in prison? Of what is he accused?'

Lord Vettor looked more than ever like a gnome, with his bald head and round gooseberry eyes, but he was not to be easily put out. He smiled, if without conviction.

'It's nothing, my lord, to concern yourself about. The man is a mercenary, a renegade. We have information that he is spying here for our enemies in Montano's camp. A serious matter, you understand. We have yet to find out the details.'

'You mean, he's not been tortured yet.'

Lord Vettor rolled his eyes and opened his hands as if to deplore such bluntness, and Attilio took a step that brought him chest to face with the little man.

'I want him freed. Now.'

Donna Claudia had brought her hands up to her mouth; almost beseechingly, her dark eyes turned towards her husband. His expression now struggled between anger and the need to ingratiate.

'But my Lord – I have not the authority – the Doge . . .'

Attilio showed his teeth. 'I know there is no Doge. It was explained to me. But there will be a Doge, I fancy? Cannot authority be used in advance?'

It was flattery hard to resist. Obviously Attilio had not only been told there was no Doge, but also who was the favourite in the field for the next one. Besides, Attilio might be counted on for his influence in return for his favour. Thirdly, the danger Sigismondo represented had now receded; he had experienced the Republican's prisons and had, Vettor knew, been shown the instruments of suffering. A pleasant threat should now be enough to keep the mercenary silent.

Meanwhile the hero was impatient. 'I'll take responsibility before the Signoria. I want Sigismondo delivered to my room at once.'

It was a bluntness tolerable only in the victor of the Turks. Attilio bowed briefly to Donna Claudia and strode from the room. Vettor shot an eloquent glance at his wife and followed, calling for a servant to speed with a message.

The message, and the seal which validated it, reached Sigismondo's jailers in under a quarter of an hour, and the thick link of gold which had set all in motion was placed in a calloused palm at last, though not until a final concession had been exacted. Cosmo had sat back in anguished despair as Sigismondo was told of his release. Now he had his wrist gripped as Sigismondo drew him up again.

'He comes with me.'

The jailer was appalled. 'I've orders to let only you go. It's as much as my life's worth . . .'

Sigismondo closed the man's hand over precisely what it was worth, and smiled. 'I'll take full responsibility,' he said, echoing Attilio's words to Lord Vettor with the same effect. The jailer, locking the cell door behind them, grumbled because it was traditional, but the warmth of the gold in his hand had reached his heart – there was no conviction in his complainings. This Sigismondo had food sent in by a cardinal, gold enough round his neck to buy a palace, and his release ordered by the Lord Darin himself. No point in quibbling over letting the gondolier go too if he wanted it. The jailer was a Venetian; he reckoned that if this Cosmo was in for having poisoned Lord Darin's grandson and if

Sigismondo wanted him out, there was a hidden aspect to the whole business which had better not be questioned.

Attilio was still in his bath and more hot water was just being poured in when Sigismondo was announced, and he raised a hand in salute out of the clouds of steam.

'Don't ask any questions, brother. You're here by virtue of a big Turk who dropped his head in the sea when I happened to be handy. Thank him, not me. Who's your friend?'

'Next to me on the list to be strangled.'

'Innocent like you, I suppose.' Attilio waved cordially at Cosmo. 'The story, later. What you need even more than I did, is a bath. And fresh clothes. This tub is big enough for all of us. Be my guest.'

They needed no second invitation. Sigismondo was stripped before Cosmo who, with his injured hands, needed the help of a page to take off the bandages and the clothes that stank of prison. The pages, who knew nothing of Archimedes but knew well enough what would happen as two more big men got into the tub, stood well back as the water surged over the brim and slapped the tiles.

The chill, the fear, floated away as the freed men sat propped against linen cushions, their shoulders scrubbed and massaged with scented oils that Lord Vettor's ships had brought from the East. There was even a page to strum on a lute.

Attilio had removed his eyepatch; the eye, sealed shut in the scarred socket, gave his regard a certain grimness.

'You need a shave as well as a bath, I see. And I can't make my mind up if you look more the savage with hair or without. Do you scrape it off so that no man may grab you by it? Or are you tired of being begged for love tokens to remember you by?'

'Mm . . . m.' Sigismondo, veiled by the curling steam, had his own eyes shut. 'I forget which. A barber will rid me of any prison reminders after this.' Opening his eyes, he saw Cosmo's experimental efforts to clean his own hands now the bandages were off, and sat up with a surge of water, took a sponge and delicately washed them. He remarked, 'This innocent, brother, was less lucky than I.' He dropped his voice to a murmur intended to reach Attilio and Cosmo but not the pages, who stood at a distance now, hands behind their backs, ready to serve. 'And this innocent had better stay out of sight of our host, I think, until we can persuade him that his grandson was poisoned by someone else.'

It was likely that Vettor had already been informed of the supernumerary guest, and they might have to deal with an angry interruption at any moment.

But no one came to disturb the prolonged luxury of the bath until finally, by mutual consent, the three men roused themselves from the cooling water and rose up, brushing off the sprigs of rosemary and lavender that had floated round them. The pages came swiftly to wrap them in linen and rub them dry, but not before Sigismondo's sharp eye had caught sight of something. He pointed.

'That needs seeing to. How did you come by it?'

Attilio twisted to look at his hip, where an angry gash flamed in a half-arc over the bone. He snorted. 'Some Turk nearly got lucky and took off my leg. I had the edge on him, though. It was his arm that went.'

Sigismondo, head bent, was fingering the half-healed scar, softened by the water. 'Mmm . . . he could get lucky yet. You've had this poulticed?'

'Am I a herbwife? All physicians want you to go to bed and be bled. If I want to go to bed I take a woman, and if I want to be bled, a Turk will do it. This'll mend.'

'Hey, if you want to lose a leg as well as an eye . . .' Sigismondo raised his dark gaze to Attilio's face, 'or your life. I've seen wounds like this, and buried friends because of them. It takes time, but if you're unlucky, that Turk could yet be laughing in Hell.'

Attilio, catching the note in Sigismondo's voice, looked thoughtful. 'What do you recommend? Have you herbs for it?'

Sigismondo stood back to let the page towel his shoulders. 'It's beyond my art. You need some physician with medicines

I don't carry, and with skill in wounds. If I could choose – a skilful, learned but unusual man – but I last heard of him in Rome; one Master Valentino.'

Chapter 56

The Lady's Dying!

'By your leave, sir,' a page broke in, 'Master Valentino's in Venice. My cousin's apprentice to Signor Loredan, and Master Valentino has lately come to treat his wife.'

'Signor Loredan will be honoured,' said Sigismondo, 'to lend Master Valentino to the hero of Venice. Pray ask Lord Darin if he will send an urgent message for him.'

As the page ran out, Attilio said, 'I am a child in your hands,' and his smile was a little forced, but it broadened when Sigismondo, tilting his head, replied, 'Better in mine than the priest's. But don't blame me if Master Valentino forbids the feast tonight. He is not a man you argue with.'

Attilio, grinning, said, 'I never argue,' yet as if anticipating a stricter regime he seized a goblet from the table by the couch and drank it off defiantly.

Sigismondo, already dried and swathed in cloths, was being attended to by the barber, who was a little disconcerted at his instructions to shave Sigismondo's head as well as his face but rose to the challenge with a flash of his long razor. As the blade finished its careful work, and more scented oil was smoothed on, Sigismondo spoke, half to himself.

'Benno. Where is Benno? He can't be far away.' This sensing of Benno's proximity had been noticed by Benno himself before now, and was accurate as usual.

Benno had been on his way to the Ca' Darin. He had naturally failed to get anywhere near Attilio in the Piazzetta, but heard in the crowd that the Captain-General was to be lodged at Lord Vettor's palace; he had been hurrying there as fast as he could, getting lost in byways, when past the end of his street went a gondola, in the Darin livery, and carrying two men. One of them Benno knew was Cosmo; the other made him gape in doubt. The build, the bearing were Sigismondo's, but the man had hair! Dark fur over the head and round the jaw so transfixed Benno that, stunned, he saw the gondola swing out of sight before he could stir himself to shout and run.

That livery – and they weren't in chains . . . Were they being taken to see Attilio at the Ca' Darin already? Benno's heart was bursting with hope as he pounded along the narrow alleys with Biondello all but airborne at his heels. There was his master, out of prison and seemingly unharmed. The world was a better place! He could even like Venice.

Arriving at the Ca' Darin and getting into it were not at all the same thing. Those at the back door, where Benno first humbly tried, had no patience with importunate halfwits. All their faculties were taken up with the glorious fact that the Victor of the Turks was here in their house and would shortly need to be fed. Benno, who had been sleeping rough and without a master to keep an eye on his appearance, looked even more than usually squalid. The kitchen boy deputed to get rid of Benno did it with a bowl of greasy water, which drenched his legs, and with a clout to his ear.

Benno went, forlorn but desperate, to the great front doors. Biondello shook himself and followed, and lurked at Benno's heels as he enquired of the porter if he could be admitted to serve his master.

The porter had been dealing with people of all ranks who wanted to see the Captain-General. From his surly face, even if he remembered Benno in connection with Sigismondo, he was not going to pollute his doorway with one whom the maestro di casa would only order him to throw out at once. If Benno's master, unimaginably, wanted him, he could send for him. Meanwhile, the proper place for such an object was outside.

So it was that Master Valentino, carried to the fine landing stage in a Darin gondola, saw a disconsolate huddle at the foot of the marble steps rouse itself and rush forward. The physician had eyes to observe. The combination of vacant joy in the dishevelled object trying to help him on to the landing stage, and the little one-eared dog dancing to and fro, made sense to him. 'Master Sigismondo sent you to meet me? Take me to him.'

It was Biondello who reached Sigismondo first, a blur of twisting body and flailing tail, greeting him with ecstatic whimpers. After him, the cynical dark face of Master Valentino, smiling a little; Sigismondo acknowledged his kindness in coming so swiftly, and presented him to his new patient, the Captain-General. While Attilio rolled over on the day bed and bared his hip for inspection, Sigismondo put out a hand to grip Benno by the shoulder, hard enough to excuse the tears already starting in Benno's eyes. Neither of them spoke, though the silent message might have been mutual: *you survived.*

Master Valentino held his long, capable hand above the wound. 'You are right to call me in, sir. The wound is hot. Mars is not working to your benefit in its present House. Poison has grown in this, which we must arrest before it is too late.' A dourness in Master Valentino's look hinted at coffins in attendance on such delays. He clicked his fingers for his assistant to lay his medical case open before him, and examined the vials, each secured in its wooden compartment. '*Pimpinella saxifragis,* I think, drunk in a cold infusion, both as cordial and to induce a purging sweat. Then a vulnerary, sir, and an unguent which I shall have made up immediately, now that the moon is in Virgo, moist and barren, so as to reduce the wound's heat and nullify the harm from it. We may,' said Master Valentino drily, 'save the leg, but there is to be no violent exercise during the next hours, and no more fighting for a while; for which I understand that the Turks will be grateful.'

Attilio's grin was splendid in the beard of black and silver; then a sudden commotion in the anteroom made them all turn their heads. The door was flung open and a servant, eyes staring, face scarlet, rushed in to seize Master Valentino by the sleeve, almost causing him to drop the glass vial he was holding.

'Thank heaven, sir, you're in the house! Oh sir, come quickly! The lady's dying!'

Chapter 57

Poison Again

A raised, admonitory forefinger from Master Valentino made Attilio stay on his daybed, but no one prevented Sigismondo, with Benno close behind him, from following the physician as he strode after the servant, skirts of cinnamon velvet flowing. Benno, determined not to let his master out of his sight again, was wondering: the lady? Surely not Donna Claudia. It would be a shame if she was dying, for she was a really nice lady, not the sort you'd associate with that sly Lord Vettor. He also hoped it wasn't that pretty Lady Beatrice he'd caught a glimpse of once, going into the Ca' Darin with her grandmother. What in the world had happened?

Donna Claudia and Lady Beatrice were certainly there in the room. Donna Claudia was kneeling by a girl stretched senseless on the floor, while Lady Beatrice mopped the girl's face from a bowl of water held by a maid. As Master Valentino arrived, Lady Beatrice looked up, saw the furred velvet close cap denoting his calling, and sprang up at once to make way for him.

Benno had never seen the girl on the floor in his life, and did not know he was looking at Isabella Ermolin, of whom he had heard so much; rather more, he thought, when he slept in Zenobia's room, than he had wanted.

'What happened?' Master Valentino was instantly kneeling opposite Donna Claudia and putting his fingers to Isabella's pulse at the neck. Then he gently lifted her head. Benno, craning past Sigismondo's arm, saw blood dabbling the black hair on the pale brow, and on the terrazzo floor. Donna Claudia was wringing her hands, dignity overcome by distress.

'She fell. I was clumsy, I admit . . .' She looked away, not meeting the doctor's swift glance. 'I tripped as I went to take a cup from her hand. I must have pushed her as I stumbled.'

'She struck her head here.' Sigismondo, crouching, touched the edge of a painted coffer, smeared now on its carved garland of cherubs. Master Valentino had his head on Isabella's chest, furred cap under her chin, in odd parody of a lover. Beatrice watched, her hands clasping her own throat as if she choked back what she would have said. Benno, effacing himself behind the maid with the basin, thought this young lady was even prettier than he had supposed, while at the same time he wondered why he thought Donna Claudia was lying.

'Carry her to the bed.' Master Valentino put a hand under the young woman's head to steady it and Sigismondo, with help from Donna Claudia, bundled up Isabella's skirts and swung her from the floor. The bed had a canopy of sea-green silk held up on slender gilded poles, and silk curtains looped back with gold cords. Maids pulled back the sea-green bedspread, and Sigismondo laid Isabella down. Donna Claudia came to stand by the embroidered pillows, still clasping her hands together till the knuckles showed white.

'Will she die? Have I killed her?'

That's taking responsibility for a fall a bit far, thought Benno; as if she'd pushed her a-purpose. Behind him a maid was wiping the floor. Another maid had come quickly into the room and was now helping Donna Claudia to undress the girl on the bed to her shift. Benno, recognising this maid as Chiara, knew for the first time who the young lady on the bed was. Evidently Lady Isabella had been visiting her step-daughter.

So everything became clear. Benno well remembered his last visit here, the night Sigismondo had fought Dion and the lions. Donna Claudia had been full of her suspicions of Lady Isabella, of her conviction that she had poisoned Marco and only waited the chance to kill Beatrice the same way and make herself sole heir to the Ermolin fortunes.

Wasn't she with child, too?

The sea-green curtains had been drawn round the bed now, and Sigismondo withdrew while Master Valentino conducted further examinations. His voice murmured with Donna Claudia's. Benno was now quite sure what had happened.

Donna Claudia had previously told Sigismondo that she meant to confide her fears to her granddaughter, swearing her to secrecy, so as to prevent her going innocently to the Palazzo Ermolin and perhaps suffering her brother's fate; it only needed someone else handy at the time, to be a scapegoat, as poor Cosmo had been for Marco's death. Donna Claudia had not, evidently, been able to stop Lady Isabella's coming here. So Donna Claudia had come in, perhaps from some crisis in the kitchen where a feast for the Captain-General was being prepared in a hurry, to find Lady Isabella handing a cup to Beatrice, a cup in which she might have dropped something deadly.

The accuracy of Benno's imaginings was borne out by what happened next.

'Do you wish to examine this too?'

Sigismondo held up a gold object like a pomander. It was on a chain attached to a belt of plaited silk cord, that Chiara had put, together with Isabella's head-dress of pearls and gold gauze, on the painted chest. Sigismondo opened the pomander or locket and sniffed the contents, dipped a finger and touched it to his tongue, swiftly strode to the window and spat out of it and, taking fresh water the maid had just brought in, filled his mouth, rinsed it and spat again.

Benno knew it was not this display of strange manners that made Donna Claudia stare and hurry over to seize the pomander from Sigismondo's hand.

'Don't spill it, my lady.'

'It's true, then. This is poison!'

Chapter 58

Take Me Home!

Master Valentino had straightened up from ministering to Isabella, who was beginning to stir, moan and make small movements. He came across the room, intense curiosity on his face. This was a rewarding case for a man interested in the unusual. He joined them at the window, took the pomander from Donna Claudia and imitated Sigismondo's actions exactly, down to the two expectorations from the window – the water this time immediately offered by Chiara, fascinated by the discovery that her mistress had been carrying poison.

What poison it was occasioned no dispute.

'Wolfsbane, without doubt.' And, as Sigismondo nodded, Master Valentino turned to the maid as if he had noticed her for the first time. 'Are you her maid?' He nodded towards the bed. 'Does your mistress have aches in the joints? Does she make an ointment of this powder for you to rub her with?'

Chiara's eyes opened wide. 'Oh no, sir. My lady is as active as can be. You see for yourself how young she is. It was her parents who suffered from damp in the bones. Venice makes for aches when you get on in years, sir, it's the water creeps up into you. My lady used to rub a salve on my old mistress, I know, though what it was I can't say. I remember well how my old mistress made her do it.'

'Were you there when her parents died?' Sigismondo's deep voice rode in. 'Shell-fish poisoning, I heard.'

'Oh yes, sir. Terrible pains they had, a mercy my lady ate none that day. Her nurse died too.'

'And the symptoms of anyone poisoned by this,' Sigismondo turned to the physician and tapped the pomander, 'what would they be?'

'A burning, a tingling – a deadness,' Master Valentino touched his lips as if the poison had left a trace still, 'then violent vomiting. The limbs refuse to move and then the heart also. The mind, alas, is clear to the end. I have seen these effects. One of the most deadly of all herbs. What does the young lady need with this at her side?'

The question was not to be answered. Donna Claudia moved and opened her lips to speak; Isabella put up a hand to explore the swelling bruise on her brow; the door of the room was pushed wide by a curtseying maid and Lord Vettor entered, with Rinaldo Ermolin behind him.

'What's this I hear?' Vettor's gooseberry eyes scanned the room rapidly: the physician in his robes and cap, by his face and bearing a man of experience and authority, deserving a nod of acknowledgement; his wife by the window; the man he would have preferred never to see again, looking refreshed by his stay in prison; his granddaughter; some maids he no more noticed than the furniture; and the one he was looking for, all but hidden from him by the bedcurtains, Isabella Ermolin.

Rinaldo was already at her side, holding her hand, bending over her. 'Are you all right? You have not lost the child?'

'The lady suffers merely from a slight concussion and some bruised ribs. I have conducted no more intimate an examination, but I would infer the child is safe.' Master Valentino had taken position opposite Rinaldo and possessed himself of Isabella's other hand, his fingers on the pulse. 'I would suggest, however, that she receive the rest she requires. Absolute quiet is necessary if no harm is to follow her fall.'

Master Valentino's suggestions had, customarily, the force of law, but there was one to oppose them now.

'Take me home.'

It was Isabella, more feeble than her brother-in-law had ever heard her, appealing to him.

'My dear, you heard the physician. Is it wise—'

'Take me home!' Isabella struggled to sit up, her black hair streaming over her shift, huge hazel eyes fixing on Sigismondo with the deadly pomander in his hand. 'I can't stay here! Get my clothes, take me home! I shall die if I stay.'

This might be taken as hysteria, as fever or delusion, but the patient had pulled her hand from Master Valentino's grasp, trying to swing her feet from the high bed to the platform beneath, dragging herself upright on Rinaldo's arms. Benno, pressed into a wall-hanging as far from anyone's glance as he could get, thought that if she'd had a stiletto as handy as she'd had the poison, his master ought to look out. She could always claim she'd just had a bop on the head and was totally unaware of what she was doing.

No doubt could be entertained over what she was doing now – she was going. Rinaldo, with Isabella clinging to him, asked Master Valentino's opinion.

'The lady should disturb herself no further. I shall administer a sedative and all will be well.'

Perhaps this meant she would be too doped to mind what occurred but, as Master Valentino summoned the lad with his case of medicines – who had only just managed to find where his master had got to – Rinaldo, supporting Isabella, suddenly caught sight of Sigismondo; and *he* certainly minded.

'What is that villain doing here? Why is he not in prison?' It's hard to look properly menacing when encumbered by a clinging girl in her shift, but Rinaldo achieved it.

And that's another one who'd get a knife into my master, Benno thought. Sigismondo, infuriatingly, bowed and smiled. Vettor came to Rinaldo's side and spoke rapidly in his ear, and everyone could see his expression change from fury to frustrated fury. People who want to become Doge, and their relatives who want to benefit from this, cannot cross the whim of a triumphant Captain-General who is not only fiercely popular, not only has a vote, but has also untold influence on the votes of others.

'*Take me home!*' Isabella struck the potion from Master Valentino's hand. More work for the maids, thought Benno. Donna Claudia had already sent all but Chiara out of the room.

Vettor's eyes consulted Rinaldo and turned towards Master Valentino. 'I really think Lady Isabella should be conveyed to her own home. While she distresses herself so, her condition cannot improve. In her own house she can rest completely and her own physician can attend her.'

'I have no doubt that you are right, my lord. It will be best for both the lady and the child she carries.'

As if reminded of the importance of the heir to the Ermolin name and fortune – at the moment pressed to his side by the importunacy of his sister-in-law – Rinaldo took command. A sharp word to Chiara and she hurried forward with Isabella's dress, which was got on to her piecemeal with Rinaldo's inexpert help, the other ladies standing by because Isabella could hardly be made to release her grasp of Rinaldo for more than a second.

'My belt. *My belt.*'

Chiara came to the chest by the window for the belt and head-dress, and held out her hand to Sigismondo for the pomander, the only proof they had that Isabella and not Cosmo was the one who had probably killed Marco.

'I will take that.' Donna Claudia snatched – there was no polite word for it – the pomander from Sigismondo's palm.

Isabella gave a faint scream and Vettor, astonished, broke in. 'My dear, if it is hers she must have it.'

Now we're for it, thought Benno, wishing he could get right through the wall and hide. Donna Claudia'll accuse the young lady of poisoning her grandson, the nasty old lord won't believe her, the nasty young lord'll think my master's at the bottom of all this, and the skies'll fall and we'll be underneath again.

'Your pardon, my lady, but it has served its purpose and may return to its owner.'

Sigismondo, with a brief bow, deftly abstracted the pomander from Donna Claudia's fingers as she held it out to her husband to examine, and then gave it to Chiara. Donna Claudia turned on him, eyes flashing.

'How dare you! The decision is not yours! As long as that she-devil has the poison, Beatrice is not safe!'

Here we go, thought Benno, the fat's in the fire and we'll have to fry in it.

Chapter 59

I Know He Will Forgive You

Vettor Darin might not yet be Doge, but he showed himself now to be a diplomat. A small, commanding figure, he approached his tall wife and laid a hand on her arm.

'My dear, my dear! This is not like you! These suspicions are the outcome of grief and you must not give way to them.'

He turned to Rinaldo, still in the frantic grip of Isabella who watched them with wide, staring eyes and certainly looked mad enough to have done anything at all. Rinaldo, strangely enough, showed surprise. Donna Claudia's apprehensions were evidently news to him.

Vettor spoke soothingly, rationally. 'You must see Isabella gets to her bed quickly. The servants shall put a mattress in my own gondola; Lelo shall row, he has the smoothest stroke. And you, my dear' – did he grip his wife's arm a little tightly? – 'you too must rest. All this has not been good for you. This physician will make up a sedative for you, I'm sure, so that you will be able to entertain our noble guest at supper tonight. I have invited some members of the Signoria to join us . . .'

That's put enough on her plate to keep her quiet, Benno thought, and indeed Donna Claudia did shut her mouth, fairly clamped it shut, although her manner showed that there was plenty to be said to her husband in private when she got the chance. She shook her head at Master Valentino, thus refusing in advance any potion he might offer, and swept from the room, beckoning Beatrice to come with her. Chiara opened the door for them only just in time.

Vettor followed them, saying that he would give instructions about the gondola. Rinaldo, with Chiara's help, gathered up Isabella to carry her away. As he passed Sigismondo, he had no need to speak but let his eyes do the threatening; this man knew too many family secrets even before he had witnessed this scene here. He might have escaped torture and strangulation in the Palace prisons, he might be in favour with Venice's hero of the moment, but fortune was changeful – and a time would come . . . Rinaldo's gaze promised it.

Master Valentino, not at all offended at having his potions twice rejected, was calmly restoring the vials to their compartments in the box he had laid on the bed, while a maid mopped from the floor the dose Isabella had refused, and the lad picked up the small silver cup it had been offered in. Master Valentino came to the window and methodically rinsed the cup with the wine on the chest there, and spoke to Sigismondo.

'At some time soon we must talk together.' The sardonic face showed his relish of the scene; he was well paid for this visit before he received any fee. 'But now I must return to the patient you called me for. He will do very well, if he follows my advice. And you? Where do you go? I perceive that you are not welcome here.'

Sigismondo had brought Benno to his side with a glance. 'We shall return to our lodging, together with the young man you saw with the Captain-General. Would you be so good as to look at his hands? I hope to have prevented the worst effects of the torturer's work, but I would be glad of your opinion.'

Master Valentino's professional curiosity was kindled. When they interrupted Attilio and Cosmo in deep discussion of the sea and how to remove the Turks from it, he carefully examined Cosmo's hands and pronounced them on the way to recovery; no bones were broken and the swelling was likely to reduce rapidly now. Informed that Cosmo was a gondolier, he mixed him an ointment and gave it to him with the advice,

'No rowing until your hands are supple again; no fighting, no making love, even,' and he refused Sigismondo's offered gold. 'No, no, this has all been a pleasure. After the boredom of camp life I am glad of city diversions and of patients who have something more than their idleness wrong with them. If I have a misfortune, gentlemen, it is that those who can best afford me often least need me. You can pay me by recounting, some night soon, what lies behind the poison carried by the young lady at her belt.'

'And you, Master Valentino,' said Sigismondo, gripping Cosmo's shoulder as he spoke to the physician, 'would earn any favour we can possibly do for you in the future, by bearing witness to that poison if we ever call on you to do so.'

Master Valentino bowed. His lively curiosity, he indicated with a gesture, would be ruled by patience and discretion, and would wait.

They left him applying poultices to a grimacing Attilio, who called as they went, 'When I sent for you, Sigismondo, I didn't expect to be bandaged and leeched. *You* owe me still, remember, and I want you by my side when Venice gets a Doge to do me the honours. Remember.'

'Is it possible to refuse a hero?' Sigismondo called back, and propelling Cosmo before him, descended the great staircase of the Ca' Darin, Benno a shabby shadow. All was confusion in the hall below, servants returning, the great doors open still on a view of figures in the bright sunlight on the landing stage, seeing off the gondola in which Isabella was being conveyed on a silken mattress under the tasselled canopy. Lord Vettor came up the steps and into the hall as Sigismondo and Cosmo were crossing it and stood transfixed, staring at the gondolier as if he had no wish to believe his eyes.

'My lord, you will forgive us if we take our leave with haste. I know you wish to apologise to this young man for doubting his innocence, but he is modest,' Sigismondo gave his most brilliant smile, 'he understands; and in Christian charity I know he will forgive you too.'

Lord Vettor's mouth had opened but he said nothing, only

turning like an automaton to watch them as they passed. Benno, scuttling by him, thought that their being not immediately bound for prison spoke clearly for Lord Vettor's appreciation of events in Beatrice's room just now. He might have stopped his wife from saying more, but that didn't mean he wasn't doing any thinking on his own account. Perhaps he now saw Cosmo as the scapegoat for his grandson's death rather than its cause. Benno fancied the old gentleman wasn't that fond of Lady Isabella either – he'd been ready to produce Pasquale's letter that Sigismondo stole for him although it might have scuppered her reputation. Only Sigismondo's idea, of pretending she'd brought it to Lord Rinaldo of her own accord, had saved her.

They came out into the sunlight and took a boat.

Now, with no need to hide and no lurking assassin, they could call on Miriam da Silva openly. Yet, Benno, hearing church bells chiming at the end of a canal they passed, saw in his mind's eye the convent to which they had taken Dion, and had the uneasy feeling that it was not the last they had seen of *him*.

Chapter 60

Benno Helps Out

Miriam da Silva wept and embraced Sigismondo.

'I did what I could, dear Cristobal. I threatened to call in debts all over the city, if your freedom could not be got. But I found the Darins and the Ermolins are against you – and they have no need of borrowing from me.' She wiped tears from her plump cheeks and looked up at him with sparkling little black eyes. 'I never thought to see you alive. I have prayed for you, Cristobal, and that you are here is proof that we share a God, whatever your Church may say to the contrary.' She laid her head briefly on his chest – below the breastbone, which was the nearest she could get to his shoulder and then, stepping back, she looked Cosmo up and down. 'Has your friend been in trouble too? His clothes look like yours, and yours smell of prison.'

'He's been in greater trouble than I – mmm . . . I'm not sure he's out of it yet. Still, I believe at the moment we have no need of refuge and it may be that leaving Venice will be our best remedy in the end. What is your news?'

Miriam sat down and gestured to the cushion-strewn benches in the window alcove. She beckoned to her maid to bring forward the painted tray with its glittering crystal and silver, and they surveyed the square, set with trees under which children played. She looked at Sigismondo with affection.

'No news, Cristobal, save what you've heard already. Doge Scolar has resigned, poor soul. That foolish son of his is to be summoned back here to be punished for asking the Sultan to rescue him, and the Signoria's busy voting in the new Doge – though all the city knows who *he*'s likely to be. Money is pumping through every vein to bring in Lord Darin – and here I was, prepared to be difficult as to supplying my part of it until I could see *you* again!' She leant forward to pat his knee. 'Now give me the news from prison. You were never anywhere but you managed to find something out.'

Sigismondo raised his cup to her, smiling.

'Hey, finding things out was why I was in prison in the first place. Thanks to Cosmo here, though, I did discover something that may somewhat console Lord Scolar, if anything can, now. It's possible that Pasquale, though foolish, fatally foolish as we see, was as his father hoped, innocent of Niccolo Ermolin's murder if not of the wish to bring it about.'

The little black eyes opened wide. 'Do you know who *did* kill him?'

'Mmm . . . I'm dealing only with possibilities here, Miriam. Niccolo Ermolin was found dead in a locked room to which his wife might well have had the key.'

'My mother had a bunch of old keys hanging in the housekeeper's room,' Cosmo put in, 'and Marco and I stole it when we were children and tried every lock in the house. What we did, anyone could.'

'So, anyone in the Palazzo Ermolin could have killed the master of it.' Miriam rolled her eyes. 'Are you any nearer to the truth?'

'My mother says that Lady Isabella quarrelled with my father that morning—'

'And her maid says Lady Isabella told her to wash one of her sleeves that had a lot of blood on she said she got from holding her husband after he was murdered but she could've got it from sticking a knife in him, couldn't she?' Benno, clogged by a sweetmeat Sigismondo had handed up to him as he stood beside his master's seat, was proud of his contribution, especially as Sigismondo swung round to look at him with approval.

Miriam seemed dubious. 'You're not thinking of accusing that lady. Lord Rinaldo would have you hired dead in a moment, and you know as well as I do there are assassins enough in this city to choose from.'

Benno thought instantly of Dion and hoped that by now the nuns had given him a nice burial. Sigismondo was wagging his head in agreement with Miriam.

'Lord Rinaldo already thinks I'd look better as a corpse, but you're right. He didn't get me strangled in prison, which was his best bet if he could have fixed it, but if I accuse the woman who's carrying the Ermolin heir to the Ermolin fortune, which he's given his life to protecting, I'll vanish before anyone can ask me for evidence.'

Miriam considered, following the damask pattern on her skirt with one forefinger. 'Couldn't you write down the accusation and put it in the lion's mouth?'

Benno knew about this. When first they came to this city, Sigismondo had pointed out to him one of the lions carved everywhere; this one was of a height to have its worn stone head patted supposing you'd care to take the liberty, and it had its mouth open. Even while they watched, someone slid a bit of paper into this mouth, and Sigismondo said you could accuse people to the Ten that way. The drawback was you had to sign it, or it was thrown away, and if you couldn't prove your accusation there was a swingeing fine. The Venetians were fair.

'It's no good, Miriam. That would go straight before Rinaldo's eyes and, if Vettor becomes Doge, I'd be a dead man. Not even the Captain-General *and* Cardinal Pantera could get me out of that. There are risks it's no sense to take. If Isabella Ermolin did kill her husband, I'll not be the one to say it in public – though I think Vettor suspects her, now, of poisoning his grandson.'

'It was she who accused me,' Cosmo said.

'She, poison that poor young man? What had he done?'

'Nothing but to be who he was. When Rinaldo dies, Marco would have inherited the Ermolin wealth, even if the child she's carrying turned out to be a boy. As it is, the child will have to share only with Beatrice, provided she too survives long enough.'

'You think that young woman capable of anything!'

'What's more, she's got a lover and she may have killed *him*.'

Benno was once more the focus of all attention.

Chapter 61

Noises In The Night

'A lover?' Miriam was shocked. 'What, a lover too? What makes you say that?'

Benno was pulled forward by his sleeve to stand in front of them, Biondello peeking intelligently from his jerkin as if to add his corroboration.

'I got taken to the Palazzo Ermolin by that Signor Brunelli to draw me for a painting on the wall, and we got interrupted and he went off in a huff' – Sigismondo's mouth twitched at this familiar picture – 'and he left me talking to Lady Isabella's maid, the one that was with her just now when she fell, and *she* said I could stay the night in the housekeeper's workroom' – he turned to Cosmo – 'your mother's room, in a bed in a cupboard she used now and then, and I heard a whistle out on the canal that woke me and someone came down in a silk gown with a lantern—'

'Did you see all this?' asked Sigismondo, still and intent.

'I just looked through the crack,' Benno mimed, making a crack between his two hands, Biondello lifting his muzzle to see what he was doing. 'She had the lantern on her far side so it was mostly dark. She unlocked the door to the landing stage and went out to the fellow who'd whistled—'

'The lover!' Miriam was enjoying this. 'You saw him?'

'No, oh no, I was in the cupboard all along and I wasn't going to come out and get stabbed through the eye, m'lady. I couldn't see but a piece of the room,' his hands made a quadrant, 'and then there was a splash as if something had gone in the water and then a lot of gasping and grunting . . .' he paused, conscious of the erotic interpretation he had put on this at the time, and conscious of Miriam's eager listening, 'and then a different great splash, and then she came in and locked the door and went back out of the room.' He heaved a great sigh of relief at the memory. 'Must've got tired of him and pushed him in the canal, I should think.'

'Two splashes,' Sigismondo mused. 'How was this a different splash?'

'A sort of hollow sound, like it smacked on the water.'

'The gasping sounds like effort. The boat the man came in could have been turned over to look like a capsize. It would have floated away in a little, with the tide.'

'But if she stabbed him anyway?'

Sigismondo hummed. 'You heard what Signora da Silva said: there's plenty of assassins in this city, no one's going to think Lady Isabella did it.' Sigismondo was silent a moment and then turned to Cosmo. 'You and your mother heard a whistle once, and it was your father who came down and let in a man from the landing stage. No talk of lovers then.'

'But,' Cosmo was puzzled, 'do you think this was different? Was she meeting this man for another reason? We never found out who it was my father saw. I told you he had secrets no one knew, not even his brother.'

'Perhaps his brother knows them now,' said Sigismondo enigmatically. 'He knows, too, that his sister-in-law carries poison at her belt. In the family a secret can't be kept for ever – though the Ermolins didn't know anyone ever slept in the housekeeper's room.'

The explanation of all this could not be kept from Miriam, and while the tale was told Benno stepped back into his preferred obscurity. He was worrying again, with this talk of assassins, about Dion. The Ermolin family could be avoided; Brunelli would have to get someone else for his fresco; but suppose Dion should miraculously get better of a sudden? Sigismondo could be attacked at any time, and just because he'd been lucky so far didn't mean his luck would last for ever . . .

Speculation about Dion must have been in Sigismondo's mind as well, because he soon excused himself to Miriam and, leaving Cosmo telling tales of his life as a gondolier, which she evidently found fascinating, they took their leave. After a visit to the bolt-hole for a change of clothes, they set out again. Benno as usual did not ask where they were going but he became nervous when, once back over the Grand Canal, they seemed to be heading for the Ca' Darin. Benno had no wish to go anywhere near that dodgy old gentleman again even if they went there under the wing of the Captain-General.

He relaxed when they passed the turning to the Ca' Darin but then he saw they were going the way they had gone by moonlight, a little time ago, when Sigismondo had carried the wounded Dion. Benno almost expected to see marks of blood on the ground, but if any had been there they were scuffed out by now. Sigismondo was going to the convent of the nursing sisters.

Was Dion still there? Benno dreaded to hear that he was not; but they were assured he was, although Sister Infirmarian was reported to be not happy about his condition, both physical and spiritual. Sigismondo said he was sorry to hear it and he sounded sincere.

'May we see him, sister? Perhaps we may bring him some comfort. He has no family left.'

Which is, thought Benno, thanks to *you* for ridding the world of his brother Pyrrho. Sister Portress, however, was suitably touched and said she would make enquiries. These resulted in Sister Infirmarian herself greeting them and leading them to where Dion lay. His delirium, she explained, kept other patients awake and alarmed them, so he had been moved to a small room where he could be more easily watched.

'His fever drives him to try and rise. We've had at times to bind him so that he does not wander and do himself harm.' Her pale face, framed by the wimple, was anxious. 'He believes he has some task to perform, and chides us for hindering him.'

Chides, thought Benno. A man like Dion isn't going to be as ladylike as to chide; poor nuns. And that task he was so set on performing could only be to kill Sigismondo.

'It distressed him so much when we took away his clothes that we have put them where he can see them – cleaned and mended, of course.'

'And his wounds?'

Sister Infirmarian paused as they came to a door and touched the crucifix on her breast. 'We pray, sir, but I fear there is infection or he would not wander in his mind as he tries to do in the body. Indeed, we judged the wounds were healing a few days ago but he pulled off the dressings in his sleep and the fever has returned. I doubt if he will know you, sir.'

Thank God for that, reflected Benno. It's a wonder my master doesn't suggest calling in Master Valentino; anyone else would have left Dion to die of lions and serve him right.

He kept well behind Sigismondo as Sister Infirmarian opened the door on Dion lying there; the nun reading her breviary by his bed stood up and exchanged bows with the sister.

Benno, very much to his surprise, felt a twinge of pity at the haggard white face with a bright flush over the cheekbones. He certainly looked too ill to be dangerous, and it sounded as if the nuns expected him to die.

Dion's eyelids flickered as he looked at them under his lashes. He'd been a handsome man, like his brother, and lots of girls must have fancied him. Somehow, Benno doubted if there was one in Venice to weep for him now. Men like Dion never settled long enough. Cutting throats was a restless occupation.

'I know something of wounds. May I see?'

The Infirmarian probably had no doubt that a man of Sigismondo's build and bearing had an acquaintance with battle and its consequences. She nodded to the nun by the bed, who turned back the coverlet and the dressing to reveal several jagged and inflamed gashes down hip and thigh. Benno knew very little about wounds but these had a nasty

301

puffy look to them. Sigismondo was holding the back of his hand to them and then to Dion's brow.

'We have been treating the fever but it returns.'

'Mmm.' Sigismondo's hum was profound, funereal. He brushed the dank hair back from Dion's forehead and the eyes beneath flashed suddenly open, Dion started up on one elbow, fixed his wide glare on Sigismondo and said: 'I'll do what I undertook. I'll keep my word before I die.'

As he lay back, and the nun replaced the dressing and fastened it, Sister Infirmarian turned to Sigismondo. 'You don't know sir, what it is that so troubles him? Is there something you could do for him to set his mind at rest?'

Sigismondo gravely shook his head. 'He shall have my prayers, sister, but I can do no more.'

And that's fair enough, thought Benno, following them out. My master can't really be asked to commit suicide.

When they had left, a weak but frantic cry from the ward beyond fetched the nun from Dion's side to help the sister in charge there, very busy just now because several men had been brought in after a fall from a roof. Had Benno known, he would certainly have thought they might be from the Palazzo Ermolin, victims of Brunelli's rage.

Left alone, Dion ceased tossing and lay still, eyes open. Then he flung off the covers and got his legs over the side of the bed, choking back a groan. Slowly, pale now rather than flushed, his teeth clamped shut, one hand on the wall of the narrow cell, Dion practised walking.

Chapter 62

The Wolf's Head

The city was in a state of happy ferment. Foreigners, of whom there was always a plentiful supply, trading on the Rialto, bringing their ships into harbour, living in their own busy communities, had all been witness to the triumph. The Turkish banners, dried now, tattered and creased and white with salt, were to be hung in St Mark's; daily the Signoria expected the Sultan, robbed of his Mediterranean fleet, to sue for peace. The laborious process of voting for a Doge was being rushed along as fast as decency allowed, indeed far faster than those who disliked or distrusted the Darins and the Ermolins at all cared for. There were those too who deplored the resignation of Doge Scolar, while admitting he had been left with little choice. They felt that Vettor Darin was not the man to succeed him; yet the result was inevitable. Vettor was of ancient family, his name had not been sullied by scandal, he was immensely rich and of a respectable age, though younger than many past Doges who had been elected in their seventies and eighties – Doge Dandolo, nearly blind, nearer ninety than eighty, had been first up a scaling ladder at the Siege of Constantinople; and for certain, if Doge Scolar had not had a foolish son, he would never have relinquished office when only in his seventies.

Vettor Darin, in his late sixties, would have many useful years in which to serve the Republic.

So, as the announcement came that Darin was Doge, the city rejoiced. At last the disgrace Pasquale Scolar had brought

303

could be put away: murder and, a crime against which the Republic was implacable, treason. Now the Sultan hardly had a ship to send Pasquale and, thanks to alert spies, would not even find him in Cyprus to be rescued if he did. There was argument only about the business of banquets. Should there be one for the Doge and one for the hero, on successive days, or a single stupendous celebration? Handouts were confidently expected by the poor. Cutpurses and cooks sharpened their knives.

In this heightened atmosphere, things that might have aroused more curiosity went all but unnoticed, such as the discovery that an upturned boat drifting on the lagoon had a dead man floating beneath it. He was not recognisable but his clothes had been taken for examination. In many cities his death would not have interested the authorities, but this was Venice.

Sigismondo, having crossed from the Giudecca, and looking for the ferry or another boat to take him on to the Piazzetta, was offered a place in a gondola by a large, soft-spoken man – the Master of Padua.

'Your man can come by the ferry.' The Master, nodding at the approaching boat, tacitly showed that he did not intend taking Benno on board; and Benno promptly sat down on a bollard, ready to wait, while Sigismondo joined this stranger whom he seemed to know.

Out on the water, shaded by the canopy, the two men surveyed the distant rosy palace and the tall houses to their left. Sigismondo remarked, 'A beautiful prospect.'

'For a free man.' The Master of Padua smiled, his pockmarked face looking pleasant. 'All my subjects have been snatched from me and left me at leisure.'

'It surprised me to hear of the Marsili brothers.'

'It was a surprise to me . . . When I showed you my workplace – according to instructions – I was at first of the opinion that your comments were mere bravado. I've seen every approach there is: defiant, cool, abject. There's no one who isn't afraid. You, however, knew what you were talking about, at least. You'd have been an interesting subject.'

Sigismondo tilted his head and looked sideways at him. 'May my patron saint and guardian angel prevent it, Master.'

'It seems they do. Venetian politics . . . Oh, an admirable people, generous, just and clever . . . their politics are inexplicable to a stranger like myself. Ottavio Marsili, now. I am told he was a friend of yours.'

'We had fought on opposite sides a few years ago. We met again by chance here and ate a meal together.'

'Indeed.' The Master's tone was not ringing with sincerity. 'It was my impression that he had been silenced before he could implicate his associates. You must have powerful friends in the Signoria.'

Sigismondo silently blew between his lips. After a moment he said, 'Master, I'm sure he would have implicated St Mark himself if he'd remained in your hands. Were the interrogators suggesting my name?'

'How easy it is to see you're not a Venetian,' said the Master of Padua, gazing at the long line of the Riva ahead. 'So direct an enquiry. The actual propositions put to my subjects are not my concern. However, I expected that the ban on putting you to the question would be lifted in a day or so.'

Sigismondo gave a prolonged and thoughtful hum. Then he said, as if pursuing a matter they had been discussing, 'Padua, now, is a splendid city. I went there some years ago to hear a dissertation at the university.'

'Were you there long?' The Master accepted the change of subject with perfect amiability.

Benno was not at all put out by the unknown man's refusal to include him in the gondola. He was used to being found unsuitable or even obnoxious, for although he periodically made efforts to clean up his clothes, and now possessed two shirts, a spare – best – jerkin and far fewer fleas, he was intractably unkempt and his clothes had a natural affinity for grease. Biondello roamed the landing place for the few minutes it took for the ferry to come up, but he ran at once to his master's whistle and was lodged in his accustomed hammock. Benno waited while people got off, and then trod warily on to the boat, very aware of the dark wet gap between the wooden stage and the wooden deck. As he looked up, a much-worn red silk gown was in his way, and he found the cheerful, resigned face of Pico Gamboni, while he heard the ferryman's voice in a propitiatory whine, 'It's more than my job's worth, my lord. I'm sorry, really I am, but—'

Pico nodded to Benno. 'I haven't the fare to go any further. I must get off here.'

Benno was, thanks to his master, well in pocket, and he took the liberty of turning Gamboni round and offering the ferryman money for two. Pico had not, for years, resisted any kind of charity, and he thanked Benno and sat down on the deck in the corner where a fragment of perished red silk proclaimed he had just been sitting. Benno hunkered down beside him, and turned to face the breeze.

'My master's free,' he told Gamboni, in explanation of the inane grin he was aware he had worn ever since seeing Sigismondo being rowed to the Ca' Darin with no chains and no guards.

'Bravo! I heard that the Captain-General had demanded his release.' Pico slapped Benno on the back in congratulation, and Biondello shot to the deck. Picking him up and restoring him to Benno's arms, Pico went on, 'I missed you last night; I hope you had a good haven.'

Benno did not wish to explain where he had been. He had no fear that Gamboni's knowing would get Chiara into trouble for harbouring him, but he was still afraid because he had seen Isabella at her dreadful tryst.

Pico hadn't waited for an answer. He was chuckling. 'Do you know, I was sent on a civic errand today. They're all so busy with their voting and, as I was one of the first not chosen to vote, I'd to go and inspect a fellow who'd got himself killed, a foreigner by his clothes so they thought he might be a spy. He was supposed to have drowned at first until they found the wound in his throat. A stiletto. So they sent to the Signoria, a matter of routine. His scrip had been emptied, of course, and the crayfish had been at his face and hands. Whoever killed him had overturned his boat on him to make it look like an accident on the water.'

Benno turned a vacant face to Gamboni, the smile wiped off it. He gulped, remembering the splashes he had heard. 'Why'd they think he was a spy? I mean, I should think lots of people get killed here for lots of reasons, don't they?'

'Venice is not short of corpses,' Pico assented, with a touch of civic pride. 'Nor of foreigners, either. This one had something suspicious about him, though: a wolf's head in bronze on his belt buckle.' Pico nodded significantly.

'What's wrong with a wolf's head?'

Pico's grey hair was blown back by the breeze. 'You can't expect to keep up with our wars, but you can't have forgotten that though we beat the Turks at sea we've still got Montano to deal with, and Montano means Il Lupo. Il Lupo is said to be fond of seeing his badge on his men, a wolf's head. Naturally we think he's an agent of some sort, but what was he up to?'

Benno stared at the rough dirty boards of the deck. A spy would hardly be making love to Isabella. Pico stood up as the ferry came alongside the quay and said, 'Can't have been on account of the Marsili brothers, although it turns out they were hand in glove with Il Lupo – word must've got back by now as to what happened to *them*.'

'There's Nono.'

'If this fellow had come to help Nono's escape, would Nono have stabbed him in the throat? That's taking ingratitude a bit far.'

Benno, shuffling off after him, had to agree. Of course, the man Pico had gone to inspect might not be the man he'd heard go into the canal, in spite of that sound he was now sure had been that of a little boat being overturned, but if he *was* that man, the sooner Sigismondo heard about it the better. There was something fishy going on connected with the Ermolins, and Benno's brain didn't feel up to working out what it was.

Chapter 63

Long Live The Doge!

The day had arrived for Doge Darin to be installed, and the excitement of it pervaded the city, penetrating even obscure and normally calm regions such as the convent where Dion lay. The words 'the Doge's procession' were spoken in his hearing and he opened his eyes. The nuns attending him had noticed his general improvement and that he seemed to have more strength, although he was still visited by fever and delusions. They were not aware how much mobility he had managed to regain by his secret walking.

Now that his condition was no longer critical, he was not supervised all the time, and Sister Infirmarian considered moving him to the public ward despite his occasional ravings.

No matter what festivities took place outside, convent life had to continue as usual. Beggars were waiting at the gate to be admitted to the courtyard where they were fed. The cauldron of soup was hooked on its pole, the bread was piled on the wicker trays, and the gate was opened. The beggars knew the routine and got themselves into an orderly-enough line along the arcade, taking their pottery bowls from the pile. The soup and the bread had been carried out and put down, and the beggars were arranging rags and crutches to best advantage to attract pity and, depending on which nun served them, perhaps a larger helping, when suddenly, news came that a wooden bridge across a side canal by San Zaccaria had collapsed under the press of people crowding to get good places for the show. The wounded and the half-drowned were already being brought in at the Infirmary door, on stretchers, shutters and over friends' backs, and a sister came hurrying from the hospital side to call everyone to help.

Unwisely, both sisters in charge of the distribution of bounty rallied to the emergency. Accustomed to the strictest of discipline themselves, and to the usual obedience of the hungry crew, they could not, as they told the beggars to be patient, envisage what would occur.

Beggars who had been at the extremity of frailty, beggars faintly supporting themselves along the wall, erupted towards the food; anarchy prevailed. They fought, grabbing the bread, spilling the soup on themselves and on the paving as they plunged the bowls in to get all they could. A bowl smashed. A cripple genuinely unable to use his legs was pushed over by one swinging on crutches to give the illusion that his own legs were useless. The strange thing about all the fighting and pillaging was the near silence in which the whole horde colluded, so that no nun should be alerted to what was going on and come back. All this was watched by a tall man in the arcade, leaning on one of the columns. He was not a beggar, but as he was clearly not a nun, he was ignored.

Soon all that could be taken was taken and the beggars scurried to leave. One, more pious than the rest, pursued another, forcibly removed the wicker trays from under his arms and returned to prop them against the cauldron. All the same, his piety ended there. He made no attempt to get the capsized cripple back on his unreliable feet, but ran off, leaving him inching painfully towards the crutches that had been knocked away from him and lay near the arcade. The onlooker came forward now and picked them up.

Words of thanks and blessing died on the cripple's lips as the man tucked the crutches under his own armpits and swung out of the gate after the rest, without a parting glance. The cripple beat his fists on the ground and blasphemed.

The man on crutches found the going hard. The cross-pieces soon irked his armpits, the crowd pressed onward with no concession to the disabled, and he was forced to stop and rest from time to time. The noise and movement tried his senses. A kind woman attempted to give him money, but the look in the handsome cripple's eyes as he brushed her aside made her reconsider her charity. Beggars can, it seems, be choosers, and he chose to reject alms from her. No doubt he had better things in mind, gold in the Piazza where the Doge and his family would scatter largesse to celebrate his installation. Every soul in Venice hoped to catch the Doge's eye this day!

Here she was wrong. Dion most particularly did not wish to catch the Doge's eye, although he was intent on getting a good view of him. Luckily, just as he arrived on the outskirts of the Piazza, which had been cleared to allow the procession to circle it, a matron unwise enough to risk her advanced pregnancy in the front ranks of the crowd was overcome by excitement and labour pains just as Dion struggled forward, and he managed to make his way to the place she had left as she was borne off. Few men now would see the procession better than he.

It was hot. The sun beat down on the men filing into the Piazza, at least on those unprotected by the canopies of white and scarlet silk, gold-fringed, embroidered, carried over the heads of the most important – the Patriarch of Venice, Cardinal Pantera, the Captain-General of the Fleet and, of course, the Doge himself.

Here came the attendants, men-at-arms, pages, priests with banners and incense. Now the hero of the city, the Captain-General, with his silvered beard and his eyepatch, greeted by a clamorous outburst of cheers, raised his gilded baton in salute. Before him went the evidence of his victory, the tatteredTurkish banners, some with the crescent of Islam, going to their resting-place before the body of St Mark under the high altar of the Basilica, to signify the power of Venice over her enemies and the power of Christ over the Infidel. Infidels in the crowd, silent in their turbans, were less pleased, but they stood unmolested and perhaps comforted themselves with the thought that Venice, the most tolerant city in the world, had last year traded amicably with the Turk and probably would do so again next year. Fortune's wheel turns.

It had turned for one man in the procession, walking behind the Captain-General although not actually among his captains. Last time Attilio had circled the Piazza in procession for his own installation as Captain-General, his old comrade-in-arms had watched from the crowd. Now, at Attilio's special request, Sigismondo, splendid in black velvet with a chain of emerald leaves and pearl flowers around his shoulders, came gravely after him, provoking some speculation as to whether he might be a Turkish pasha, a prisoner of war.

As Sigismondo's eyes roved the crowd, Dion dropped his crutch and went down awkwardly to retrieve it, shielded by the voluminous skirts of the woman in front of him. When Sigismondo had paced on and there was no risk of recognition, Dion came upright again with something concealed in his hand. He was flushed and breathing in gasps, dizzy with having bent down and with a sudden pang from his wound. Collapse was not far away; the crowds, the sky, the procession swam before him in the dazzle of sun and the mirage of his fever, and only the strength of his will supported him.

Had he been a less experienced professional, he might yet have failed in this task, but he steadied himself, waited, and took aim.

The Doge, gold-fringed glove obscuring his face as he acknowledged the roar of the crowd, riding high, in gold brocade, was approaching, under the white cap and _cornu_ that covered his baldness, his chair of state borne on poles by men in the Darin colours. Over him swayed the canopy, held aloft on tall poles to clear the _cornu_, throwing a deep shadow on the man beneath. Pieces of gold were fountaining out from the procession behind him, while all along the route the crowd flung up their caps and cheered.

At first he stayed upright, the force of the blow driving him against the back of the chair, gloved hands at his throat. The flash of the knife had been no brighter than the glitter of sun on armour and on gold chains, and the movement of Dion's arm as he threw, no more violent than that of his neighbours brandishing their caps. It lost him his balance but his fall sideways was cushioned by a stout matron, not at all displeased at so handsome a man suddenly reclining on her bosom.

The men carrying the Doge's chair were the first to know something was wrong, as the weight on their shoulders shifted abruptly forwards. A gasp rose from the crowd as Doge Darin slowly toppled from his chair to sprawl across one of the poles and from thence to the ground.

As happens with such events, no one at first realised what had occurred. The leaders of the procession had already reached St Mark's and been solemnly received into its glittering dark. Out in the Piazza all was confusion. The most dramatic change was the sound of cheering transformed to universal question, the crowd straining to know and see, while the bearers of the Doge's chair dumped it unceremoniously in the path of those following and struggled to raise him. Voices said the heat had overcome him in the heavy brocade of his robes, that the swaying motion had made him lose his balance. Once they had turned him over, however, there was no mistaking the reason for Doge Darin's plunge from the heights.

The small, horn hilt of a knife protruded at the base of his throat, from which the gloved hands had fallen away, their silken palms dark with blood. Doge Darin lay, round accusing eyes on the heavens that had ruled he was not to have his triumph, *cornu* tipped over one ear, the white cap beneath making him look like an aged baby. A dead baby.

'Let me see.'

The men clustered round the figure on the ground did not argue with this deep voice of authority and drew aside thankfully. Someone from further forward in the procession had swiftly turned back at the first gasp of the crowd and now knelt by the Doge's side, feeling under the ear for the pulse, bending to lay a shaven head on the heart. He prevented one of the priests from trying to pull out the dagger.

'There will be much blood if you do that. What Lord Darin

needs now is your prayers. Where is the guard?'

The guard, to give them credit, once they took in that someone had thrown a knife at the Doge, had scattered into the crowd, pushing spectators back, asking questions and threatening people, to assuage a sense of guilt that the man they had been protecting – symbolically only, they had thought – was now beyond protection. Their captain returned from this foray to find the formidable Captain-General himself standing over the dead Doge, supervising the lifting of the body, while a stranger in black discussed with him the angle of the knife and the area of the crowd from which it might have come.

'Hey, no hope of finding him now. All a man has to do if he's being looked for in a crowd is to stand with the rest. Anyone running away will get grabbed for sure.'

The crowd's voice had turned to wailing and screaming. The Signoria had gathered in an anxious cluster of red robes, possibly wondering if the Doge was to be the only target. The Patriarch had been summoned out of St Mark's, crossing the still empty centre of the square, the guards were still combing the crowds in vain and priests had begun a frantic rattle of prayer. A group of women on a balcony supported the dazed Donna Claudia while Beatrice, given the task of throwing gold into the crowd, had dropped the bag and collapsed in shock, not surprising in one from whom Fate had removed by violent means father, brother and now grandfather, all in the space of a few weeks. At the procession's head the Turkish banners caught a sudden gust of wind from the sea and cracked, as if reminding everyone that Fate could take its revenge on even the most glorious day.

'The Turks are the best bet for this.' Attilio not unnaturally was inclined to blame the enemy he knew.

'Mmm . . . keep your voice down. Do you want a riot against those that are here? Why kill a man who does not fight, and leave the man they really have to fear? If the Turks wanted revenge, Attilio, this knife would have been in *your* throat.'

They watched the men get the Doge's body on to a

makeshift bier, covered by the white silk of the canopy lifted off its poles.

'I'm not going to complain that their aim is so bad that they can't have meant to get me. If not the Turks, say an agent of Montano's. I was told by one of the Ten that a dead man with the insignia of Il Lupo was found drifting under a boat beached on a mudflat. He too had a knife in the throat, it seems.'

The procession and the crowd were intermingled now, the dispersed guards making a poor job of stopping those who wanted a closer look at the scene of the tragedy. The bier had been borne across to the Doge's palace, for all that could be done for him there – the extraction of the terrible knife, the washing, the laying out. Physicians who could contribute nothing but grave faces and Latin would be there, along with the priests who could at least offer prayers for a man who had died without confession or the last rites and, very likely, in a state of sinful pride. The ceremony Doge Darin would attend in St Mark's was not the one he had looked for.

Benno had seen everything except the assassin. He had managed to get quite a good place and had been thoroughly enjoying the spectacle and cheering vociferously with everyone else, shouting himself hoarse when the Captain-General came near, yelling cheers as his own master paced by, while Biondello, succumbing to a rare excitement, barked joyfully and quite unheard from his jerkin. When the Doge approached, Benno had actually seen the flash of the knife in the air, but the dread that suddenly silenced him had been for Sigismondo, so vulnerable and on view. Tears of relief flooded his eyes when he saw the chair lurch and the Doge precipitately leave it. He had moved with the surge of the crowd and, after being hustled roughly by two guards who saw him as a criminal but at once decided he had not the brains for an assassin, he eeled his way to Sigismondo's side and, overhearing Attilio, tugged at his master's sleeve.

'Lord Gamboni told me – the boat was upside down. What about it being—'

Sigismondo cut short the suggestion with a light cuff to Benno's head, and turned to Attilio. 'There are deep waters here, I think. We must take care or we'll drown.'

Chapter 64

Remember Me In Your Prayers

'But why would he kill the Doge? It's *you* he wants to kill.'

Benno looked anxiously up into Sigismondo's face as they traversed an alley, deserted except for two cats, one white and one black like its shadow, dozing on a doorstep. He was not happy to be retracing their route to the convent. He was not happy to think that the Dion they had seen incapacitated, with a fever Sigismondo had confirmed by sight and touch, could have come gruesomely to life and been able to get to the Piazza in murdering trim. Sigismondo's reply was brief

'He's a professional.'

Benno whistled to Biondello who had stopped to investigate the cats, one of whom reared up like a snake and struck at his nose. Biondello leapt back in time and dashed to join Benno. He had not yet succeeded in taking a Venetian cat by surprise.

'But why would anyone hire him to kill the Doge? And I mean, who'd hire him in that state?'

'Who says he wasn't hired before he got into that state? Think where we met him that night. He may not have been following me; he may have been there on his own business. Sigismondo was on the convent steps, pulling the great twisted iron bell-pull.

Before the guichet in the door slid open, Benno blurted out, 'But that was at the Ca' Darin! Lord Vettor wouldn't've hired him to kill himself—'

The guichet clacked open. A sharp black eye regarded

them and unexpectedly narrowed with the crease of a smile. Sister Portress opened the wicket part of the big door and they stepped into the tiny courtyard with its trees in tubs and its spotless flooring of inlaid pebbles.

'You've come with news of your friend! We were worried about him.'

Benno thought: not half as worried as we are. Sigismondo asked questions. Yes, the patient was missing, must have left in the confusion when everyone was attending to the injured from the bridge collapse. And he was in no state to be wandering on his own. He must have strayed out in one of his fever fits – men can have great strength at such times, no doubt God gives it for His own purposes . . . Nobody thought him capable of walking, but a beggar they were feeding lost his crutches that morning and it must be supposed he had taken them. Perhaps the poor man wanted to see the procession. He always had something on his mind, something he had to do. It might be that God had sent him the strength to pay some debt or duty.

'It may be, sister. Strength may come from the Devil too, I've heard.' With this enigmatic comment Sigismondo left, Benno, baffled, following.

'If he did it, who hired him? Of course, lots of people might not have liked Lord Vettor. Or was it a grudge?'

Sigismondo hummed cynically. 'You don't get paid for grudges. If he wanted to kill for pleasure I'd be the target, not Vettor Darin. If he killed the Doge, it was because Lord Vettor hired him to.'

Sigismondo had stopped at a stall with a brazier, by a little church, to buy chestnuts. The stall-holder twisted yesterday's proclamation of Doge Darin into a cone and filled it, talking. 'Terrible, terrible thing! It was because of the lion. Everyone said it was a bad omen when that lion was killed. When I heard of it I said to my wife, "Mark my words, Lord Darin will come to a bad end too." You keep lions for luck, so Fate sent him a pretty clear message.'

Benno, juggling with hot chestnuts as they walked on, thought busily: if Sigismondo was right as he usually was, and Dion *had* killed Lord Vettor, he'd also been the one to kill the lion, so Fate wasn't fooling.

'But why – hoh!' Benno spat a too-hot chestnut into his hand. '*Why* did Lord Vettor hire Dion to kill him? No one gets someone to kill them, particularly when they're looking forward to a lovely time being Doge.'

Sigismondo ate chestnuts, Benno saw, as if he didn't notice how hot they were. He split one up, blew on it for a moment, and tossed it to Biondello before he replied. 'And if he hired him to kill the Doge? Have you forgotten who the Doge *was*?'

Benno stopped dead, and dropped a chestnut. Biondello snapped it up, dropped it, nosed it about, and ate it again. 'You mean Doge Scolar? But he'd resigned.'

'He hadn't resigned the night the lion was killed. He resigned only after news came of his son's letter to the Sultan. Until then he'd resisted every effort to shift him, even the revelation – through the letter I stole for Darin from Lady Isabella – that Pasquale wanted Niccolo Ermolin dead.'

'Then why didn't Lord Darin cancel the commission when *he* was going to be Doge? Oh yes, of course, he wouldn't know where Dion was, would he? He must've been getting pretty furious when the old Doge went on not getting killed when he'd hired it done.'

'Remember Dion left a sword in among the lions and a trail of his blood – a pool of it outside the house. Lord Darin may have concluded, if he recognised the sword, that his hired assassin might not be able to earn the fee.'

Benno was wiping greasy fingers down the sides of his jerkin; before he met Sigismondo he would automatically have wiped them down the front but he was acquiring a kind of manners. He shook his head, and stared into the cloudy green waters of a canal they were crossing.

'It's a joke, isn't it? Hire a man to kill a person who's standing in your way and it turns out to be you. Why didn't Dion see it wasn't the right Doge?'

'He certainly can't have heard the Doge had changed . . . I don't suppose the nuns thought it a priority to keep their patients up to date with the latest events. And if you have a fever, you're standing on crutches in the hot sun, waiting for a chance to throw your knife, and there's the Doge in shadow under a canopy . . . The sisters were right. Dion had something on his mind. Professionals keep bargains.'

Benno was silent. If Dion had kept his word to Lord Darin – and did he know yet he'd killed his employer? – he'd be free to spare attention for his promise to Sigismondo. He had told Sigismondo he would kill him, and he would try. 'I hope murdering the Doge was all he could manage. P'raps his fever'll get worse and kill him. After all, he can't go back to the nuns and say, "Sorry, I just wanted to go for a stroll," – can he? And if he isn't being nursed . . .'

Sigismondo took hold of the back of Benno's head and wagged it to and fro.

All the same, when they came to a crowded square, Benno felt cold and flinched at a man on crutches, and glanced nervously at the blank wall of unshuttered windows. He was about to ask where they were going when Sigismondo unexpectedly turned in at the door of a church, pushed through the curtain and bent his knee towards the altar. He sat on the broad stone base of a pillar, apparently contemplating the statue of the Virgin, her blue cloak scattered with stars, in a side chapel nearby.

'What do we do now?' whispered Benno, cradling Biondello.

'Wait. Mmm . . . if Dion can find me, let him. He's not so wild for revenge, I would judge, that he'll risk being taken in the act of killing me. Nor will he in his present state want to get too close.' Sigismondo smiled, his dark face calm in the dim light. 'I need help and so does he. God will decide which of us gets it.'

The summons which was to decide the matter came quite soon. Doge Darin, whose enjoyment of office had hardly been long enough for him to taste it, nevertheless qualified for a full Ducal funeral with all the trimmings: the lying-in-state in the Signoria di Notte, the lower arcade of the palace, in full regalia, sword, spurs, *cornu*, and gold brocade covering the ghastly hole in his throat. Then the body had been carried under a golden umbrella through Merceria, over the Rialto Bridge to the Fratri, Rinaldo Ermolin one of the twenty pallbearers. Donna Claudia, shrouded in black veils as was her grand-daughter, followed with dignity, much admired by the crowd. The widowed Lady Ermolin, expecting a child and, it was said, in fragile health, did not attend the funeral Mass. Attilio da Castagna was present, magnificent in black velvet scrolled with gold arabesques, his one eye raking the congregation for the man he wanted to see.

There was someone else who also desired a glimpse of Sigismondo. Benno had vainly hoped that his master would not go to the Doge's funeral, but he did not dare to say so. Sigismondo had been in a sombre mood since they had talked in the church, and Benno wondered what it was like to live a life in which there was always a valid possibility of death round any corner. Dion had shortened the odds in this city.

Sigismondo, probably pursuant of his policy of luring Dion into the open, was among those at the funeral Mass, his bearing, as well as the quality of the chain round his neck, earning him a place denied to many in the crowded church. As luck would have it, his position behind a pillar kept Attilio from seeing him but, as the congregation broke up at the end and began to spill into the street, it was evident that someone else had.

'I must speak with you in private. Come to the Palazzo Ermolin in half an hour. I have fresh evidence about my brother's death and it may be that I was too hasty in thinking you could not assist me.'

A generous admission, and the lean clever face looked haughty at having to make it. Sigismondo merely bent his head in acquiescence as people pushed by, talking in murmurs, the heavy sharp smell of incense clogging the air. Rinaldo was at once lost in the crowd, all now draining from the church as though a tide swept them out towards the bright sun that still beat on the living. A heavy hand descended on Sigismondo's shoulder.

'You're too large for a moth, man, but you flit about like one. I've been trying to get hold of you for days, to tell you that damn physician of yours has frightened Death from my door yet again. I can walk as if no Turk ever tried to kiss me goodbye.' He shook the shoulder he had gripped, which was relaxed enough to move under his hand. 'Come to drink my health. I'm to hang around here until we have a new Doge to celebrate the victory, but you and I don't have to wait for that.'

'If I live, I'll drink with you tonight, that I promise. First I must go to visit Lord Ermolin.'

'Thought I saw him at your ear a moment ago. What does he want with you – to hunt down Darin's murderer for him? To do what the Doge's ornamental guard failed to do?'

Sigismondo smiled. 'Mmm . . . I rather think he has another murder in mind. Lord Scolar may not be the only one to think his son guiltless of Niccolo Ermolin's death; that's what his brother says he wants to discuss.'

Attilio nodded. They had reached the open doors, the sun beat down on them and he screwed up his eye against the dazzle, surveying the dispersing crowd. 'They threw you in prison, as a traitor against a city you don't even belong to. It's my thought that they should look closer to home. They're saying an agent of Montano's killed Darin. Who knows but such a one killed Niccolo Ermolin, supposing he got to know what they were up to, by some chance? Wasn't he Darin's son-in-law?'

'I'll remember what you said.' Sigismondo had hailed a gondola and now raised a hand in farewell as he got aboard. He gave the direction to the Palazzo Ermolin.

Benno, hunkering down and releasing Biondello to roam the boat, was silent, but felt a certain comfort that Attilio at least knew where they were going to. No Ermolin, as far as Benno was concerned, could be trusted for a single moment, whatever they said, and he couldn't help thinking this boat was taking them back into danger. Something about his master, too, made him feel that Sigismondo expected trouble to be waiting.

In one sense, it certainly was. On the Ermolin landing stage, Brunelli was pummelling a protesting workman with his fist till the dust exploded from his shoulders, watched by a cowering couple over the roof parapet, but he broke off when the gondola came alongside. Sigismondo was paying the fare when Brunelli rushed forward and seized Benno, painfully, by the ear.

'Where have you been, rascal? I've not finished with you yet!' He dragged Benno, yelling, up the steps to where the Ermolin porter, resigned, had the wicket already open. He had evidently been warned of Sigismondo's coming, too, and kept it open for him respectfully.

'My lord wishes you to go up to his study. He says you know where it is.'

Sigismondo, on his way up the great marble stairs, passed Benno standing under the fresco on the half-landing, hands raised in saintly pose as Brunelli drew on the plaster and, catching Benno's anguished roll of the eyes, smilingly shook his head.

'Mmm . . . You've reached Heaven before me. Remember me in your prayers today.'

Chapter 65

Secrets

This was not the best way to calm Benno. Not daring to move, with Brunelli's eyes flicking from him to the wall and back again as he shadowed in his Lazarus, Benno tried to console himself with the knowledge that he wouldn't anyway have been let into the room after Sigismondo. He listened to the soft tread of leather boots going up the second turn of the stairs, across the landing; the soft tap on the door, the click of a lock turning, a murmur, the click of a lock turning again. His master had been shut in with Lord Ermolin and his secrets.

Sigismondo stood once more just inside the study where he had first been summoned to examine Niccolo Ermolin's body. Some things, he observed, were different. The desk-table still stood under the open window through which came the soft warm air, the cry of a gondolier rounding the house corner below, and indignant thudding down of tools and shouting from the roof. The inkstand in beaten silver, and the violet-glazed jar of quills, were set facing Sigismondo at the door, though Rinaldo had taken the high-backed carved chair round to the left of the desk. The dark stain was still on the polished wood where Niccolo had bled; either it had not yielded to any efforts to remove it, or no one had been allowed in here to try.

The tall cupboards were of course the same, making almost an entrance passage between them either side of the door, though a pile of books stood in a corner to the right on top of a chest that had not been there before. The day-bed which had stood there was missing, perhaps because it had held Niccolo's body. Other chests, their padlocks gleaming, stood on shelves ranged round the walls, almost close enough in that secretive small room to be touched by an extended hand. The room itself was like a locked box, crammed with power testified by those ledgers, account books, cloth-swathed dishes, cups and flagons of gold and silver, chests of rich clothes, coffers of coin and jewels hidden from sight. In this room the fortunes of the Ermolins resided – and lived and breathed at that moment in Rinaldo Ermolin, tapping a ringed hand on the table and regarding Sigismondo out of narrow, almond-shaped eyes.

'You don't think, do you, that Pasquale Scolar was responsible for the death of my brother? In spite of the letter he wrote to my sister-in-law and his own confession!'

Sigismondo smiled. 'It's true I think the letter could be an empty flourish and the confession because of a very natural dislike of being tortured. But the world is convinced, my lord. Why ask me?'

Rinaldo reached beneath the desk to a shelf out of sight and brought up a leather-bound book with brass clasps and lock. Like the table it bore the dark stain, and Sigismondo recognised the *libro segreto* over which Marco and his uncle had quarrelled.

'It took me some time to decipher the code in which this is written but, when I did, several things became clear. My brother, who had the welfare of the city at heart as deeply as he had that of his family, had been making his own overtures of peace towards those with whom we are at war.'

'The Turks, my lord?' Sigismondo added a hum, prolonged and cynical. 'Or the Duke of Montano? Dangerous correspondents at this time, surely.'

Rinaldo frowned at this criticism of his brother; and yet he did not make it clear why Sigismondo, whose head already carried more Ermolin secrets than Rinaldo had been happy that it should, had been summoned here to listen to more of them.

In the next few minutes it became clear.

'See.' Rinaldo had opened the book and laid it, open, towards Sigismondo, pointing to one of the pages. 'I have put the translation opposite.' He sat down in the tall chair. The heavy book lay on the table, held open by Rinaldo's hand. Sigismondo, thus prevented from picking the book up to read, placed his hands either side and leant to look.

What happened next came very fast indeed. A slight noise near the locked door behind Sigismondo was followed in a second by a violent blow between his shoulders, driving him forward on to the book and the inkstand much as Niccolo Ermolin had been driven. Rinaldo had snatched his hand away and now drew back, gripping the arms of his chair, staring avidly.

He saw Sigismondo – struck down, but not dead nor pouring blood – twist swiftly under the raised arm of his attacker and rise to grip his wrist and hurl him away. Since he hurled him at Rinaldo, the spectator lost sight of events and almost lost his breath, pinned under the awkward weight of Dion sprawled across him. In Dion's left hand, still in Sigismondo's grasp, glinted the stiletto he had just used, its snapped blade witness to the excellence of the *cuir bouillé* under Sigismondo's doublet. As Rinaldo struggled to push Dion away, he caught sight of Sigismondo's face, the eyes intent on Dion, lips parted and a thick seep of blood coming from one corner of his mouth. Rinaldo had no time to hope this came from a punctured lung, that the stiletto had snapped on Sigismondo's spine, not on armour; Dion tried with the jagged stump of the stiletto at Sigismondo's eye. Sigismondo swung his head in that second to spit out the clogging blood, and the stiletto raked the air where his face had been.

Dion was doing his best to rise, and Rinaldo abetted him with his own not inconsiderable strength. Sigismondo went with this movement, stepping back and wheeling to swing Dion against the shelves, which he struck with his wounded side. He snarled, face convulsing. Sigismondo's back was to Rinaldo, who surged from his chair, drawing his own dagger; but Dion was swung round once more, his lighter weight a disadvantage, and Sigismondo slammed the back of the stiletto-wielding hand down on the edge of the desk. The broken weapon skidded across the *libro segreto* and dropped from sight.

The right hand might not be Dion's hand of choice, but his left was still implacably in chancery; so the right snatched a knife from his boot-top. It was a heavier blade, and caught Sigismondo's arm in an upward blow that would have ended under the jaw but went wide as Sigismondo, pivoting, whirled him into the pile of books on the chest. He made an animal sound and, using Sigismondo's grip on his wrist, pulled himself forward to strike again.

Rinaldo had come a step closer. He had no wish to do the work for which he had hired Dion, but Sigismondo's failure to be killed first thing, as planned, alarmed him and he was ready to damage him if he could. At the moment Dion was between them, breathing visibly hard but fighting, his dagger clashing on Sigismondo's as the hilts locked for a moment. They turned again. Rinaldo this time caught sight of Dion's face, the eyes glittering, pale but flushed on the cheekbone, mouth shut hard in a thin line. He wondered for a second if the eyes were focused, then Dion raised his knife to disable Sigismondo's arm.

A sudden move, and in the confined space Dion fetched up against both men. Both were moving as he struck and his blow came up below Rinaldo's breastbone. Sigismondo's dagger would at that moment have invaded Dion's heart had Rinaldo not come down, a dead weight on his arm. As Rinaldo crumpled to the floor Sigismondo's blade in Dion's body went from midriff to hip.

Sigismondo pulled his knife clear, and watched as Dion, both hands pressed to the wound, subsided among the books, taking shallow breaths to minimise the pain. Experienced in the ways of assassins, Sigismondo even now searched him briefly for weapons before he crouched and supported him with an arm across his back. Dion's eyes looked at some inner landscape although he seemed to be regarding Rinaldo's empty face.

'Tell me.' Sigismondo put his free hand on Dion's over the wound and said, 'You can't live. So tell me.'

Benno had, with hands and eyes uplifted as Brunelli arranged him, strained to hear how the interview in the study went, but he was thwarted by the thickness of the study door and by the amazing noise Brunelli was putting up. When the artist was satisfied with the work's progress – and the Lazarus on the wall was assuming an almost epic mawkishness in his hard-earned Heaven – he would underscore his success with a tuneless humming which occasionally burst out into full-throated but no more tuneful song. Benno at one moment wondered if he could hear thuds from the room up there. Was Lord Ermolin getting angry and beating his fist on something? But Brunelli had taken up the chorus to the song he was trying to remember:
'Do you remember once we swore . . .'
in an enthusiastic bellow, and was repeated as he forgot the next lines, until he came out with:
'Whose arms are round you?'
As a result, when the door of the study was unlocked and then locked again, no one heard and the first Benno knew of anything having happened was the sight of Sigismondo at the head of the stairs.

That was frightening. Sigismondo was unusually pale, in contrast with the streak of blood running from the corner of his mouth, which looked swollen. His right hand gripped his left shoulder, and below it a rent showed in the black sleeve and the white cambric inside, from which came a crimson ooze down his arm.

To Brunelli's amazed annoyance as he drew, his Lazarus dashed past him, snapping his stick of charcoal on the wall. He wheeled. His astonishment increased. Even he, architect and painter to a number of patrons who had abruptly signalled their withdrawal of patronage by some act of physical violence, had never actually been stabbed by an employer. His respect for Sigismondo burgeoned.

'What happened? What did he *do*?' Benno had visions of

327

Rinaldo erupting from that door to cause further damage. If he could have seen Rinaldo sprawled on his side staring at a pile of ledgers he would never consult again, he would have been saved the worry.

'No questions now. We must hurry.'

'Not so fast!' Brunelli caught Benno by the collar as he came down the stair again. 'I've not finished with you yet.'

Sigismondo stopped in his swift tread down and whispered in Brunelli's ear, making him drop his jaw to rival Benno's.

'The devil he is! God's teeth, you're in trouble! What will you do now?'

For answer, Sigismondo pulled off a piece of ripped shirt, spat on it and wiped the blood from his face. Then, turning Brunelli round and putting his left hand on his shoulder so that the painter obscured both rent and wound in the arm, he propelled him down the stairs. 'I'll find you another commission. You won't get paid for this one now.'

The porter opened the door for them, a little surprised to see anyone on such familiar terms with Brunelli, who so often inspired a desire to avoid him if you couldn't strangle him. It was nice to be relieved of that horrible noise he'd been making on the stairs. He only wondered Lord Rinaldo hadn't come out and ordered him to stop it.

The gentleman with the shaven head was generous with his tip, though. Pity there weren't more like him.

It was Brunelli's stentorian shout that hailed a gondola from across the canal, and Brunelli who pulled off the hat that hung by its cord from his shoulders and, putting it on Sigismondo, arranged the dagged liripipe to conceal his wound. The prospect of outwitting the whole ungrateful class on whom he wasted his genius appealed to him as nothing else could. How often had he longed to leave one of them dead as Sigismondo had done! As for his interrupted work on refurbishment and fresco, well, he had received a retainer and he was used to being sacked before he could finish his masterpieces. His immense confidence in his own genius led him to believe the crowning work of his career was still to come, and he could afford to dismiss what he had been doing.

He got into the gondola after Sigismondo and Benno with every intention of hearing Sigismondo's story, and he wanted also to make a quick sketch of him to be used one day in a picture of Samson pulling down the temple – that look of concentration hardly touched by pain.

'Where to?'

It was the gondolier who asked. Benno wished he could yell, 'Rocca!' and find himself transported to his native city, so gloriously remote from Venice and based so reassuringly on dry land.

'The Ca' Darin,' was the direction given, however, and Benno almost protested until he recollected that it was no longer home to the man who had been buried that morning, and that Attilio might still be there. If anyone could help them now, it was Venice's hero, though if Sigismondo had really killed Rinaldo Ermolin, one of the dreaded Ten, Benno could not imagine that anything short of an angel straight from the Lord could save them, and *he*'d have to come equipped with a fiery sword.

As they went, Biondello's ear and nose drew Benno's attention to a slight movement Sigismondo made; he seemed to let some small object fall from his hand into the water. Benno, scooping the dog up before more attention could be drawn, saw the object shine brassily in the sunlight before it was obscured by the waves.

Attilio was at the Ca' Darin. He was in the fine room the late owner had placed at his disposal, and Master Valentino was making the final examination of the healthy cicatrice on Attilio's hip. When they saw Sigismondo they both exclaimed, Benno believed, not so much at the look on his face but because they caught the whiff of danger.

Brunelli, who had stumped along after them, whipped away the hat he had placed on Sigismondo to conceal the wound, with the air of a conjurer asking for a trick to be applauded.

'Look at that! And Ermolin dead in his own palace!'

Master Valentino stepped instantly to inspect the wound, while Attilio's one eye opened wide. 'By the Nails and Blood!

You make yourself welcome in this city. How did it come about? Were you hired to do it?'

Benno, indignant, only just suppressed: '*My master's not an assassin!*' Sigismondo, submitting to having his sleeve removed and the shirt cut away and the wound bathed, probed and bandaged, replied, 'On the contrary. He'd hired a man to kill *me*. The same man who killed the Doge.'

Attilio brought his hands together in a resounding clap. 'Just as I was about to say: "I can't protect you now." Have you proof of this?'

'Hey, he died after telling me. Unless Master Valentino has the art of revivifying corpses, we won't get a second confession. But we don't need one.'

At this even Master Valentino, busy on the wound, paused to gaze at Sigismondo. Attilio exploded. 'Man, you come here hacked like a hunted boar and tell us that you left Ermolin dead, that he tried to have you killed by the man who murdered Doge Darin – and you say you don't need a confession to clear you? The only confession I foresee the Ten getting is from *you*, courtesy of the Master of Padua.'

Sigismondo had a genial smile that quite transformed his face. 'Oh . . . ho, no need to put him to any trouble. When the household get around to breaking down the door of Ermolin's study they will find two bodies there: that of Ermolin himself and of the assassin who killed him. It's true the key is missing – perhaps it was thrown from the window! But who is to say anyone else is involved? Brunelli and I left together, to which the porter will testify. In my guess, the man Dion was let in by Ermolin at the side door in the housekeeper's room (at a time which will be thought to follow my departure), so that they might be ready for my coming. I saw a pile of books on a chest, which argued that a cupboard had been emptied to make room – for what?' Sigismondo smiled. 'For someone to hide.'

'If this Dion jumped on you, out of a cupboard, how is it you only have a gash in the arm and not in the heart? Even though you may be expecting attack it's hard to watch all four corners at once.'

Sigismondo pulled open a lace of his doublet and parted his shirt with his free hand. Attilio peered.

'Aha! Armour! Forewarned is forearmed. But what made you think Ermolin wanted you dead?'

'For the same reason he had me denounced as a spy and would have had me strangled in prison. The only thing he was not anxious to happen to me was torture, for fear I'd spill the very family secrets he was trying so hard to protect.'

Attilio picked up a carved and gilded stool with a gryphon embroidered on the seat, put it down facing Sigismondo and sat, planting his feet apart and placing his hands on his knees. He fixed Sigismondo with the fierce eagle eye.

'Are you going to tell us those same secrets?'

Sigismondo's hum was prolonged and tantalising. He glanced round, from Master Valentino's lean satirical face intent on bandaging, to Brunelli, half-absorbed in tapping at a fresco of Bacchus to discover if it had been properly keyed, and back to Attilio keenly watching him. His eyes passed over Benno, which Benno took as a compliment: he was too much an extension of his master to count. He was still stunned at the revelation of Dion's presence in the study and Dion's death.

'Mmm . . . To tell may be safe now Ermolin's dead, though there's always Lady Isabella.'

'And what can *she* do – a girl, a widow?'

'A viper,' remarked Master Valentino conversationally, stepping back to admire his bandage. 'She would make arrangements to poison you. Her parents, they say, died suddenly, and I understand that she and not the gondolier poisoned Marco Ermolin.'

Sigismondo nodded. 'And she's now sole heiress, apart from what will have been left as dowry to Niccolo's daughter. I hope that Donna Claudia need not fear for Beatrice any more. The viper should have enough for her and her heir-to-be.'

Sigismondo leant to pick up something from inside the crumple of his doublet on the floor: a leather-bound book with brass clasps unlatched, a dark stain on its cover. 'The secret records of Niccolo Ermolin, kindly unlocked for me by his brother with, as you can see,' he turned the pages with slips of paper interleaved, 'his translation of the code Niccolo wrote in.'

'He showed you *that*?'

'Mm. It was bait. I wasn't meant to read it. As I read, Dion was to stab me.'

Benno, visualising it, felt queasy although the danger was done with. He had not even known that Sigismondo had been wearing the boiled-leather jacket, part of their usual baggage. He ought to have noticed – Sigismondo must have been looking bulkier than he normally did. He'd been too busy thinking of the trouble Sigismondo was walking into. His master must have stood there with his back to a cupboard he'd guessed was inhabited, and waited to be attacked . . .

'What secrets do you think are in it?' Attilio tapped a finger on the book and at once withdrew it almost as if the thing might bite him.

Sigismondo, provokingly, closed the book and stowed it away. He looked at them again and the deep voice was serious.

'Enough to destroy the Ermolins in Venice.'

Attilio pressed a hand on Sigismondo's right shoulder as he began to rise. 'You're not leaving here before you've said more. God's teeth, man, you tease worse than any courtesan I've ever met. *What* secrets can destroy the Ermolins? Come on now. No one here has a loose tongue.'

Sigismondo's dark glance surveyed them. Master Valentino had secrets about distinguished patients that no gold could buy; his discretion was complete. Brunelli had given up listening for the time being, absorbed in a sketch of Attilio's profile, and even if he took in anything that was said, there was but a minimal chance of any future patrons indulging in chit chat. Moreover, he was likely to be leaving Venice after the Ermolin commission had so spectacularly fallen through.

Attilio himself was a Venetian but a Venetian who had spent most of his life out of the city and, by virtue of his post as Captain-General, might need a few secrets to bargain with if victory did not always attend him. Sigismondo smiled.

Attilio sat back. 'Begin.'

'Where do I begin?'

'What's in the book? What power could it have to ruin the Ermolins? Two of them are dead and past ruin anyway.'

'Mm . . . mm. I could say, this book killed them both.'

Chapter 66

Brotherly Love

'This is a book in code, such as many merchants keep, secret records of inventories, transactions. With whom had Niccolo Ermolin been transacting business, if his record of it could destroy him?' Sigismondo put a broad hand on the book. 'What if I said, the late Pope? And the Duke of Montano?'

Brunelli snorted and checked the swift glide of charcoal over paper as Attilio hit his forehead with the palm of his hand and cried, 'By Our Lady! The man sailed close to the rocks! If the Ten had suspected that . . . or did they? Was it a stiletto in the eye rather than the strangler's cord? On the sly instead of stringing him up in the Piazzetta?'

'So I thought when I first saw him dead, long before I knew what I know now. But no.' Sigismondo shook his head, and accepted the cup of medicine Master Valentino had been mixing while he listened. He drank it off, and tightened his lips at the bitterness no honey had alleviated. 'No. The State had not a hand in Niccolo's death. It was to *prevent* a State death that he was killed.'

'To prevent – no! That's enough riddles. Who'd want to protect a traitor from a full and public punishment?'

'You're shrewd enough at sea, Attilio. You're a Venetian, too. You can't be ignorant of politics and motives on land. Who would protect a traitor from death?'

'Those who stand to lose by it?'

'And who would lose the goods and estates of a convicted traitor? Another Ermolin. And whose daughter had been married to Niccolo and still had the closest ties with him – a man who wanted above all to be Doge and could not afford to be linked with a traitor?'

'Vettor Darin?' Attilio's changes of expression were annoying Brunelli, who kept throwing bits of paper down or turning his book to get at a free corner of the page. 'That is fantasy, man. Do you tell me the old fox stabbed Niccolo to keep his name clear? How had he come to know, then, what the fellow was getting into?'

Sigismondo began to shrug, made a face and put a hand to his bandaged shoulder. Master Valentino wagged a finger. Sigismondo turned his head and said to Benno, 'Before we leave, we must without fail buy some *teriaca*; Venice treacle for wounds and ailments.'

'Shall we be going soon?' Benno asked with sudden joy. Attilio stood up, dangerously flushing, and Sigismondo grinned.

'Yes, I will go on . . . No one is as private as he thinks he is. An old fox may work by instinct, by the smell of the ground. He had spies everywhere. Cardinal Pantera told me of Niccolo's negotiations with the late Pope, and although he knew of them because he is a Papal adviser, I don't doubt that Vettor had informants in Rome as well. They may have picked up rumours – or have found that the Holy Father was peculiarly well-informed of the Signoria's private sessions.'

'What was Niccolo to get, by passing on such information to the enemies of Venice? If I were doing anything half as dangerous I'd need to have promise of a big reward.'

'A reward the Pope's death cheated him of.' Sigismondo's broad hand patted the book. 'A splendid marriage for Marco, to a Roman heiress, no less than an illegitimate daughter of his Holiness.'

Attilio, deaf to a protest from Brunelli, paced across the room. He swung round, to stare at Sigismondo. 'The Serenissima would never have countenanced such a marriage. You must be mistaken.'

'Ask his Eminence. The purpose of Niccolo's dealings with

the Holy See was to hurry on a peace by giving the Pope an advantage in his dealings with the Republic. And once peace was made, such a marriage would be possible.'

Attilio, tugged by Brunelli, sat down again. 'You haven't said how Vettor killed him; why no one thought Vettor had killed him.'

'Vettor didn't do it.' Sigismondo flung up a hand as Attilio opened his mouth. 'I told you that Rinaldo hired an assassin to kill me today: you hire such men, often, on word-of-mouth recommendation. Dion told me before he died that Vettor had hired him originally to kill Niccolo but that someone had done the job before he could.'

'WHO?'

At the demand, flung at Sigismondo in a roar of Attilio's impatience, Master Valentino paused in the locking of his box of medicines, and even Brunelli, who had scarcely heard what was going on, stopped drawing to look at Sigismondo.

'Hey, I've already told you: the other one who would suffer most from the family's name being tumbled in the muck and all its riches sequestrated. His brother Rinaldo.'

Chapter 67

Secrets To Burn

'I call this a really nice view.'

Benno looked round him with enormous satisfaction. Distant hills were hazy in the noon sun. Trees overhead moving in the slight wind dappled the cloth spread before them with shifting shadows. Sigismondo sat on a mossy boulder, Benno and Biondello on the grass, and a stream lipped and gurgled over stones not far away, winding into a little wood. Scattered at their ease, on the grass all round, were men eating and drinking, waited on by servants in the Pantera livery. The Cardinal sat under a painted cloth skilfully rigged over branches to provide the maximum shade, listening to his chaplain reading to him from a devotional book, eating cold chicken and hot venison and permitting himself to be sketched by Brunelli who sat on the grass at his side.

Sigismondo spat out an olive stone and laughed.

'By nice view, you mean -- no canals.'

Benno, chewing vigorously, nodded and slapped the ground beside him. 'That place'll sink one day and good riddance.' It was wonderful to be on the road to Rome in the Cardinal's train, away from that unchancy city Venice with its sinister glitter and its horrible people. 'Those Ermolins deserved to live there.' He scrambled forward on hands and knees to fish up a flagon of wine cooling in the stream. Biondello went with him to lap a drink and then was off to forage what he could.

Returning, Benno refilled Sigismondo's cup and his own.
'D'you reckon they'll have worked out what happened yet?
Why they couldn't find the key to the locked room, and why
Dion did it and all?'

Sigismondo smiled and tilted his head back to look up
through the branches. 'Who's to know what Venetians think?
They like to be mysterious. I presented them with a mystery.'

Benno lay back to look at the branches too. Sparkles of
sun moved on his face. The leaves were turning gold and he
reflected that, back in Venice, he'd never even noticed
summer was spilling into autumn. Biondello bustled over
from exploiting the Cardinal's secretary who had a weakness
for small animals missing an ear and had fed him bits of
meat; investigated Benno's beard and licked his face to assure
him that he had not been forgotten. 'I s'pose they had to
believe what you told them – about Lord Rinaldo sending
for you to hire protection because he thought he was being
followed. After all, the Cardinal could tell them you'd helped
all sorts of grand people in the past – a lot grander than
Lord Rinaldo.'

'His Eminence is a diplomat. He wouldn't point out that
there are grander people than a Venetian nobleman. And
they must have thought I'd fallen down on the job straight
away when Rinaldo's murdered as soon as I leave the house.'

Benno sat up, indignant, bowling Biondello over. 'You
couldn't be expected to know an assassin was going to climb
through the window when you'd left.' To Benno, the story
was almost as true as the facts, especially as his master had
told it. 'After all, that's what everyone thought had happened
to his brother Niccolo. And all the workmen had downed
tools and gone off because Brunelli beat the foreman and so
there was that rope waiting to be climbed up and nobody to
see it. Bet those nuns in the convent opposite the Palazzo
Ermolin aren't allowed to look out of windows, and anyway
if they had seen anyone – and they hadn't,' Benno added,
recollecting, 'because it hadn't happened – they'd think it
was a workman. Nobody could blame *you*.'

'Luckily, they didn't. They preferred the idea I'd put into

their heads about someone with a grudge against the Ermolins.'

'Somebody bent on wiping out the lot of them *and* Doge Darin for being connected with them.'

'I wondered if that would be too far-fetched for them. Pico Gamboni was ready to believe it, however.'

'Was he in that lot of the Signoria that were asking you questions?'

'He was, and he gave them his opinion: that the Evil Eye is a curse that can rebound on the owner of it.'

'Sort of like seeing yourself in a mirror, right?' Benno had seen himself in a mirror for the first time only a few years ago, and the oddness of it had impressed him enormously, looking into his own eyes.

Sigismondo laughed, and tossed a piece of roast pigeon towards Biondello, who rose into the air to receive it. 'Something of that nature. But the Signoria still tend to believe that the Doge was killed by an agent of Il Lupo's. It took all Cardinal Pantera's diplomacy to engineer the peace when Montano's envoys came to ask for it.'

Benno was busy wiping the worst of the grease from his fingers on the grass; now that was a luxury you didn't find in Venice. He wondered if he could get second helpings for his master, and of course himself, from the servants basting what was left of the deer still turning on a spit not far away. 'Reckon that poor Duke was sick of fighting Venice and not getting anywhere much.'

'He'd got back Piombo, or what was left of it which certainly wouldn't be much – but it seems that was all a deal between Il Lupo and Ottavio Marsili.'

Benno was silent, remembering the bad sights between the columns of the Piazzetta: first the unlucky ex-Captain-General and then Ottavio Marsili, who, if he really had made a deal with Il Lupo, better deserved his fate.

'That Niccolo Ermolin,' he pursued the matter of treason, 'he was running a fearful risk, right? Suppose he thought he was safe, writing everything in code and locking it away in that book. How could his brother've found out?'

Sigismondo looked up at the sky, blue between the shifting golden leaves, and blew softly between parted lips. 'Most likely some messenger from Il Lupo not well enough briefed, bringing a letter and asking simply for Lord Ermolin. If Rinaldo got the letter and read it, found that Niccolo was dealing with the enemy . . . or he could have heard the whistle outside the water-door that you heard, and spied on Niccolo's meetings with Il Lupo's agent. He may have known of Niccolo's negotiations with the late Pope to marry off Marco to the Roman heiress.'

'What I *don't* understand,' said Benno earnestly, selecting one thing out of many and leaning forward to emphasise his point, 'is why would Lord Rinaldo *kill* his brother for messing about with Il Lupo and the rest. I mean, it's his *brother*. Why didn't he just ask him to stop?'

Sigismondo smiled and reached over to pinch Benno's jaw. 'How do we know he didn't? Then, you know, Rinaldo had given up his life to the family the way many Venetians do, sacrificed his own chance of marriage and children to concentrate on the Ermolin fortunes; and what did he get in return?'

Benno considered. 'Well, Marco was a dead loss from the start, if the fortune was to go to him. I sh'd think he'd have spent it all pretty quick.'

'Unless Rinaldo thought that with Niccolo dead, he could train Marco rather better than Niccolo had managed to do. Fathers can spoil sons. What Rinaldo stood to gain by Niccolo's death was security for the family.'

'But his brother *was* family!'

'Mm . . . m. Everything Rinaldo had worked for, all that wonderful Ermolin gold, would have been confiscated by the State if Niccolo had been found out as a traitor: the end of the Ermolins, including Rinaldo.'

Benno watched the stream without seeing it, as if the moving water reflected the events he thought of. 'He must've got the key to the study somehow and gone in and stabbed his own brother in the neck. Why'd he go for the eye too?'

'Perhaps to point suspicion at Pico Gamboni, who was

getting rowed past every day shouting predictions of death and raving about the Evil Eye. He'd be first choice, with possibly Cosmo the next, with a grudge against his father for sending him away.'

Benno scratched his beard thoughtfully, getting his fingers greasy again. 'Cosmo turned out to be a godsend to Lady Isabella, didn't he, when she wanted to be rid of Marco and blame someone . . . What a lovely lot! I mean what a *family*. I'm glad he and Zenobia went to work for Signora da Silva, she'll look after them. Thank goodness the Council believed Lady Isabella was mistaken – about Cosmo, I mean, poisoning Marco. After all, Lord Gamboni said he'd eaten the same stuff and Marco'd bought it himself anyway. But listen, if that was a messenger from Il Lupo who Lady Isabella stabbed that night, was she in on the secret?'

'Hey, did you *see* the lady that night? You heard a silk gown, you saw a lantern. Don't you think Rinaldo would know, once he'd broken the code – or if he heard the whistle at night – what to expect? Was he going to let someone – a messenger from the enemy – survive, who could still give him away?'

'Then he ought to've got Il Lupo killed as well, seeing he knew about it. That'd have been a bit difficult, right? And another thing . . .' Benno glanced at Sigismondo, who normally discouraged questions severely. He met an amused look and an inviting wave of the hand. 'I mean that bag of rubble the cook found on the landing stage. What was that for?'

'Rubble weighs heavy. It could be taken for gold, payment to Il Lupo perhaps. Rinaldo needed to deceive the messenger for only a minute.' He gestured across his throat. 'Not much time to wonder if you're getting what you came for, when you find yourself reporting to St Peter.'

Benno spluttered. 'But what'd Lord Niccolo want with Montano's condottiere, Il Lupo, anyway? What could the Duke of Montano do for him?'

Sigismondo held out his cup, and drank before he replied. 'That's in the secret book. Niccolo had *two* children to marry advantageously. He wanted the best for both. If Il Lupo had fixed the war in the right way and Montano had Piombo back – which he had – the town would be something to offer Venice if he wanted peace. The Marsili brothers had reduced the place to a shell stuffed with corpses but Venice would have built it up and used it—'

'Put up a lion, I shouldn't wonder, all triumphant. Holding a book with that message you told me, about going in peace.' Benno sniffed. The only lion he approved of was the one that had savaged Dion so conveniently.

'Certainly they would. And Venice likes to bind an ex-enemy to her with ties that are hard to break. The Signoria would look around, to close the deal, for a Venetian girl of good family and a generous dowry. Niccolo was ready to hint at his daughter Beatrice for the sacrifice.'

'Sacrifice? Not much! I mean, she'd be a Duchess. But, didn't the Cardinal say . . . ?'

'That if Donna Claudia consented, when the treaty was signed between Venice and Montano, her granddaughter was to become the Duke's wife.' Sigismondo turned his head to glance affectionately at the man in scarlet listening with attention to his chaplain's reading. 'Niccolo might be consoled, if they can receive any consolation where he probably is, that his plans went right in that respect at least. No one could produce any other girl of marriageable age but not betrothed, so pretty and so likely to please, with a splendid dowry secured to her in her father's will, and of such aristocratic connections. It was felt, I understand, that the State also owed it to the Ermolins for all the tragedy they had suffered.'

The State hadn't recompensed poor old Doge Scolar for *his* tragedy: though perhaps it was a blessing that Pasquale, lucky at the last, had died in a shipwreck on the way from Cyprus before he could get home to be executed. Sigismondo had gone to see the old man before they left Venice, and relieved his mind by telling part of the truth – that his son had not actually caused Niccolo's death.

It wouldn't have consoled Lord Scolar at all if Sigismondo

had told him that Vettor had bought his own death by ordering his. It still amazed Benno, looking back, that Lord Vettor had the nerve to call in Sigismondo to find who killed Niccolo when he himself had hired Dion to kill him. He couldn't be expected to guess that Rinaldo had beaten him to it.

Sigismondo said that Lord Vettor was most likely providing cover for his guilt by doing what a murderer wouldn't ever be thought to do – asking to be found out. The fact is, Lord Vettor had simply underestimated his master.

Benno scrambled to his feet and held out a hand for his master's plate. Having his curiosity satisfied made him feel hungry again. 'I'll get you some more, shall I? Just think, if you'd showed that book with all its translations of what Lord Niccolo had been up to, his daughter never would've got to be Duchess, eh?' It crossed Benno's mind suddenly that Sigismondo had kept so quiet about the book just because it might involve the innocent in trouble. Beatrice Ermolin, though she mourned a murdered father and an inexplicably poisoned brother, was herself tainted with no hint of ill-doing in the family. She could leave Venice to make a new and, it was to be hoped, a happy life. She might even take her widowed grandmother to Montano – and she wouldn't have to see her stepmother Isabella ever again.

Sigismondo gave Benno the plate and got to his feet. 'I'll come with you. I've something still to do.'

Well, thought Benno, at least it isn't getting rid of Dion. What awful luck that man had! Doing in two of his employers by mistake, annoying a lion, and above all the bad luck of coming up against Sigismondo. Pico Gamboni would have said someone had given Dion the Evil Eye.

When Sigismondo locked the door of that study in the Palazzo Ermolin on the two dead bodies lying there, he had left a conundrum as complicated as any Venetian could wish, and one it was to be hoped they'd never solve. Benno grinned happily as he followed Sigismondo strolling towards the fire-pit where the men were almost ready to take down the remains of the deer from the spit. Sweat dripped from their faces and hissed on the blazing embers beneath.

Benno waited for Sigismondo to point to some part he fancied, and a servant advanced, knife ready to carve for him, but was startled at what happened.

Sigismondo slipped a hand inside his doublet and, bringing out the *libro segreto*, cast it into the shimmering bed of the fire. The servants exclaimed; one of them offered, with the fire-rake, to try to recover the book. Sigismondo shook his head.

'Let it burn. There are things that deserve to be destroyed.'

Benno, fascinated by the swift writhe of the leather cover, like some tortured thing as it blackened in the palpitating glow, thought of the Master of Padua and sent up a prayer that never again would they come across him.

Sigismondo was already making for where Cardinal Pantera, smiling, beckoned him. Benno got the plate filled and followed. He didn't think his master meant to accompany his Eminence as far as Rome but, wherever they went, it would be blessedly on dry firm land and free, God willing, from all lions stone or alive.